Presc[illegible] Pregnancy!

Doctor Dads…and Mums

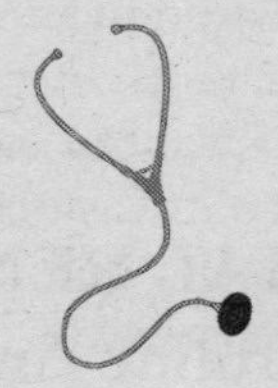

Prescription: Pregnancy!

ONCE MORE, WITH FEELING

by

CAROLINE ANDERSON

STORM HAVEN

by

MARION LENNOX

FOR NOW, FOR ALWAYS

by

JOSIE METCALFE

MILLS & BOON®

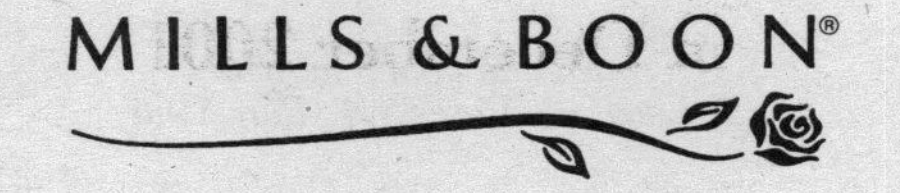

Harlequin Mills & Boon Limited,
Eton House, 18-24 Paradise Road, Richmond, Surrey, TW9 1SR

Once More, with Feeling, *Storm Haven* and *For Now, For Always* were first published in Great Britain by Harlequin Mills & Boon Limited in separate, single volumes.

ISBN 0 263 82776 3

05-0801

Printed and bound in Spain
by Litografia Rosés S.A., Barcelona

For Mary, who made it, and for Rhea,
with many thanks for all the help.

Caroline Anderson has the mind of a butterfly. She's been a nurse, a secretary, a teacher, run her own soft-furnishing business and now she's settled on writing. She says, 'I was looking for that elusive something. I finally realised it was variety, and now I have it in abundance. Every book brings new horizons and new friends, and in between books I have learned to be a juggler. My teacher husband John and I have two beautiful and talented daughters, Sarah and Hannah, umpteen pets and several acres of Suffolk that nature tries to reclaim every time we turn our backs!'

Caroline also writes for the Mills & Boon Tender Romance® series. In October, Caroline teams up with **Betty Neels** to bring us two wonderful short stories in THE ENGAGEMENT EFFECT.

ONCE MORE, WITH FEELING

by

Caroline Anderson

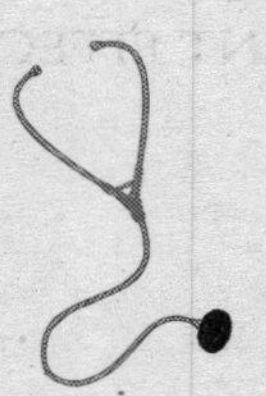

CHAPTER ONE

'AT LAST!'

Emily turned into the health centre car park and killed the engine, glancing at her watch with a sigh of relief. She still had three minutes to spare, but only by the grace of God.

With a wry grin she recalled the advert for the job.

'Four-partner practice in rural North Devon urgently needs full-time replacement partner because of unforeseen retirement due to ill health. Must be on obstetric list and do minor surgery, CHS and IUCD. Most important qualification an ability to map-read. . .'

They weren't kidding! She had meandered back and forth across Exmoor, which would have been lovely if she'd had time to appreciate the scenery, but she was determined not to be late.

The trouble was, the roads were all so tiny it was hard to tell which were major and which were minor. Assumptions, she had fast discovered, were a foolish luxury. Still, she was wise to their tricks now and read every single sign—hence her arrival with three—no, two now—minutes to go before her interview.

She had spoken on the phone to the senior partner, Dr Allen, who had sounded very welcoming and encouraging—or was that just wishful thinking on Emily's part? Whatever, she would still have to run the gauntlet of the other two partners.

And she wouldn't do it sitting in the car.

She glanced at her reflection in the mirror, dragging a comb through her thick dark hair. It swung neatly back into the bob, the ends curling obediently under, just grazing her shoulders. Her smoky green eyes, wide and incapable of deceit, stared unblinking back at her.

Just for courage, she winked at herself and her reflection winked cheekily back.

Here goes.

She got out of the car, locked it and strode confidently to the door.

The waiting-room was deserted, and the receptionist looked up with a smile. 'Can I help you?'

'Yes, I'm Emily Thompson. I'm here for an interview.'

The smile widened. 'Oh, hello, Dr Thompson. Dr Allen wasn't expecting you just yet—you can't have got lost.'

Emily laughed softly. 'Only a little. The directions were excellent.'

'I'm glad you thought so. I'm Sue Hooper, by the way—receptionist and general dogsbody. I'll tell Laurence you're here. Would you like to take a seat?'

'Thanks.'

She settled herself in one of the hard, upright chairs and looked around. Tiled floor—practical, but not very welcoming. Neat pile of magazines, but none of your glossies. *Farmer's Weekly*, *Woman's Weekly*, *My Weekly*, the odd *Reader's Digest*—a far cry from her last practice in Surrey.

There were pictures on the wall, faded and fly-blown, and the paint had seen better days, but the health-promotion posters and clinic details were fresh and up to date.

She glanced towards the door that must lead to the consulting-rooms, and saw an indicator board, with names and coloured lights, clearly used to call the next patient.

She scanned the names, and her heart came to an abrupt and grinding halt.

Dr D Trevellyan.

David.

Her mouth felt suddenly dry, and she flicked out her tongue and ran it over her lips. It couldn't be. Surely not? Trevellyan was a common enough Cornish name, and here, only forty miles or so from the Cornish border, it wouldn't be so very unusual.

And besides, the last she had heard of David he was working in London—probably destined for stardom as a Harley Street surgeon. God knows he had been a brilliant doctor even then, eight years ago. By now, with experience under his belt, he must be superb.

She glanced around the shabby, simple waiting-room. There was no way he would have to settle for this.

No, it couldn't be him. She hoped it wasn't, with all her heart, because quite apart from the fact that she wanted this job desperately for Jamie's sake she wasn't sure she could bear to see him again.

Sue came back, followed by a tall, stooping man with twinkling blue eyes and a welcoming smile.

'Dr Thompson—I'm sorry to keep you. You made very good time. I'm Laurence Allen.'

She rose to her feet, praying for calm, and returned his smile and handshake. 'You did specify an ability to map-read,' she reminded him.

He laughed. 'Yes—Robin's idea. The roads are a bit

like that, and the practice is very widespread. Come on through and meet him. I'm afraid David's not here at the moment, but he shouldn't be long. He had to go out on a call, but there'll be plenty of time to meet him.'

David. Oh, God, no, it couldn't be. . .

'Right, you'll do, Joe. Take it steady, give yourself time to get over this before you get back out there.'

The old man's wife gave a wheezy laugh. 'Might as well save your breath, Doctor—you know well as I do soon's your back's turned he'll be out there on the hills again.'

'Just give him the antibiotics and make sure he takes them regularly, Mrs Hardwill. Nothing you can do to help those that won't help themselves, eh, Joe?' David fixed the old man with his best steely glare. 'You help me, and I'll help you. I can't fix you without co-operation.'

Joe's racking cough filled the dingy, smoky room. He reached for a cigarette and David calmly removed them from him and put them on the mantelpiece.

'No—absolutely not.'

'Evil bugger, you are.'

'And I love you, too,' David said affectionately. 'Just be sensible, eh? Give your lungs a day or two to shake off this latest bout of bronchitis before you start poisoning them again.'

'Cough worse without,' he grumbled.

'Yes—because all the little hairs inside your tubes come back to life and start trying to sweep the rubbish out of your lungs——'

'Little hairs—load of old——'

David tutted and shook his head. 'Some people just don't want to be helped.' He snapped his bag shut and straightened up. 'Right, I have to get back; we're interviewing for the new partner.'

'Woman again?'

He nodded. 'Hope so.'

'Why any sane woman'd want to live in this God-forsaken part of the world beats me,' Mrs Hardwill said. 'Bain't nothin' here—no shoppin', no dancin'—or is she old, this one?'

'My age.'

'Spring chicken, then—bit of love interest, eh?' Joe ribbed wheezily.

David smiled dutifully. 'I doubt it, Joe. Don't hold your breath. Anyway, she's only recently widowed—and that's if we even appoint her. She's one of several we've seen. Now, remember, no smoking for a couple of days at least.'

He left the house to the sound of Joe's hacking cough, followed by his voice, wheezy and cracked, demanding his cigarettes.

'Damn quack—give me them down, woman.'

'No, I shan't, Joe Hardwill. You heard the doctor. . .'

He smiled and pulled the door to, and climbed back into his car.

Love interest, he thought as he headed back to the health centre. That was a joke. Since the disastrous demise of his marriage there had been no 'love interest'. One or two abortive attempts at rebuilding his life, but no relationship that offered any permanence or hope for the future.

No, there was only one woman—had only ever been one—and like a bloody fool he'd sent her away.

As he turned into the car park he noticed a strange car, and the number-plate had the name of a Surrey dealership on it.

So, the interviewee had made it. Their merry widow, as Laurence called her. Dr Emily Thompson. Even the name hurt him, he thought. Emily. Not his Emily, of course, but the name dragged up so many thoughts and feelings. Night after night he woke reaching for her, only to find his arms empty—as empty as his heart. Emily. . .

He squared his shoulders, threw a slightly off-centre smile at Sue and headed for the common-room. The sound of masculine laughter drifted to him down the corridor.

The interview was obviously going well. Thank God for that, because the other candidates had been decidedly weak. He could always call her Dr Thompson if he found the name too much.

He pushed the door open, and froze on the threshold. His heart crashed against his ribs, his mouth felt filled with cotton wool. From somewhere far away, he dredged up his voice.

'Emily. . .'

Like an old movie, frame by frame, heartbeat by heartbeat, she lifted her head and met his eyes.

'David. . .'

His name was a prayer on parched lips, and her eyes drank in her first sight of him in eight long, lonely years.

He hadn't changed at all—not in ways that mattered.

His hair, thick and dark, like polished mahogany, tousled by his impatient fingers, as always threatening to fall across those same incredible, clear grey eyes, the colour of morning mist; that full, sensuous mouth that had known her so intimately; the broad, square set of his shoulders set off by the soft lovat-green of his sports coat; the deep bottle-green polo neck that hugged his solid chest and smoothed over the flat, taut abdomen above lean, narrow hips and long, straight legs in well-cut cavalry twill; feet planted squarely on the floor, the tan brogues well-polished but worn and comfortable.

Only the smile was missing, and she found her own had gone the same way, together with her voice.

In silence she stared at him, absorbing the wonder of seeing him again at the same time as she registered regret, because now this job couldn't be hers, working with these wonderful, warm, friendly people in this beautiful part of the world.

'You two know each other, I take it?' Laurence said into the stretching silence.

Emily opened her mouth, but no sound emerged. She looked pleadingly at David.

'You could say that,' he murmured. 'We were married for five years.'

'Ah. . .'

Robin rose to his feet first. 'Um, Laurence, why don't we give these two a few minutes together?'

'Good idea.' Laurence scraped back his chair and stood up. 'We'll be in my office, David.'

David nodded. 'Fine. Thanks.'

The door closed softly behind them, but the two

hardly noticed. Their eyes were locked, trapped like flies in amber, unable to escape.

Then finally David dragged his eyes away and moved across the room, freeing her.

'Is the coffee still hot?'

His voice sounded strained—as well it might. Eight years was a long time.

'I think so,' she replied, and was amazed at the normality of her voice. Her greedy eyes sought out every tiny detail of his movements as he reached for the coffee-pot. Were his shoulders just a touch broader? Maybe. 'You're looking well,' she added.

He turned towards her, pot in hand. 'So are you—as lovely as ever.' His eyes flicked away. 'You got married again, I gather. I'm sorry to hear you lost your husband.'

Emily thought of Philip, one of the kindest, most generous men she had ever known, and felt a wash of sadness. 'Thank you,' she said quietly.

'You've got a son.' His voice sounded harsh, accusing almost. She ignored it.

'Yes—James. He's six now.'

'Rather young for you to have a full-time job.'

'I have to live,' she said, still quiet but defensive now.

'Yes—I'm sorry, your child-care arrangements are nothing to do with me.' He sat down in one of the easy-chairs, big hand wrapped round the mug of coffee, and eyed her over the top. 'So, what do you think of the practice?'

She shrugged. 'Wonderful. I would have loved working here, I'm sure.'

'Would have?'

She lifted her shoulders again. 'Of course. This changes things, don't you think?'

David was silent, regarding her through veiled eyes. She wished she could read his expression, but, like his looks, that aspect hadn't changed. She could never read his eyes if he didn't want her to.

The silence stretched on endlessly, and then finally he spoke. 'It needn't change things—not necessarily. We need a woman partner, and you were definitely the favoured candidate. We're very pushed, and we have been for some time. We need to make an appointment as soon as possible, really. Locums are difficult to come by. In this part of the world they want to work in Exeter or Barnstaple, not sleepy little Biddlecombe.'

His eyes traced her features one by one, then flicked back to lock with hers, their expression still unreadable. 'As for us—well, after all, it's been eight years. We should be able to be civilised about it.'

She thought of all the rows, and then of the making up, the desperate depths of passion he had aroused in her. Civilised? Somehow, knowing him, she doubted it.

She glanced around at the tired decorations. 'I wouldn't have thought this was your thing. I had you pegged for Harley Street.'

He gave a rude snort. 'Me? With my rural background and Cornish accent? I wouldn't smell right—that faint tang of manure that's so difficult to shift. Besides, I like it here.'

Her shoulders twitched. 'I just thought—you were such a brilliant doctor. I never expected you to bury yourself in obscurity.'

'Too good for general practice?' He snorted again.

'Was that why you went in for it? Because you weren't good enough for hospital medicine?'

Her head came up. 'How dare you? I am a good doctor——'

'So why bury yourself in obscurity?'

Their eyes clashed for a long while, and then a slow, lazy smile curved his lips. 'My round, I think,' he murmured, and his voice curled round her senses and sent a dart of something forgotten stabbing through her body.

She scraped up her ragged defences. 'I don't think this will work,' she said stiffly. 'We're fighting already.'

'Hardly fighting,' he countered, and she could see from his eyes that he was remembering—remembering the fights, and then the long, slow hours of making up. Sometimes she had wondered if they hadn't provoked half the fights just for the making up.

The pause stretched on. 'Give it a try, Emily,' he coaxed at last. 'If the others agree, give us six months—a probationary period. We would have had one anyway, whoever the candidate. See how it goes. If it really doesn't work, then fair enough, but give us a chance.'

Us? she thought. Which us? Us, the practice—or us, you and me, David and Emily, one-time lovers and best friends, with the stormiest marriage on record behind us? And a chance for what? To prove we can work together—or a chance to try again, to breathe life into the corpse of our long-buried love?

'I don't know,' she said quietly. 'I'm not sure I'm strong enough to handle it.'

'There's nothing to handle, Emily. Eight years is a

long time. We've changed, grown up, matured. We can deal with this.'

She looked at him, but he was staring out of the window and wouldn't meet her eyes.

Did he still feel anything for her? Possibly. Nostalgia? Fondness? Unlikely, considering the vitriolic row they had had before she walked out.

She could hide behind her widowhood, and Jamie—dear, sweet Jamie, so battered already by his short life. Nothing must hurt him now.

'I won't have an affair with you,' she said, hating to bring it up but needing to make the ground rules clear before they went any further.

He turned towards her then and met her eyes with a level stare. 'Did I suggest it?'

'No—but if you intended to the answer's no.'

His smile was slow and did terrifying things to her heart.

'I'll bear that in mind,' he said softly, and opened the door. 'Shall we go and have a word with the others?'

'They haven't said they want me yet,' she cautioned him.

He grinned, catching her off guard again with the boyish quirk of his lips.

'They want you—and so do I.'

The smoky glitter in his eyes made her heart race. 'David——'

'As a partner,' he added softly.

'No affair,' she reminded him, conscious of the ambiguity of his last remark.

'You've already mentioned that,' he said.

It was only later she realised he hadn't agreed to co-operate—and by then it was too late, because she'd agreed to take the job.

David spent the rest of that day wondering if he needed to have his bumps felt. He must have been nuts to suggest she take the job—just when the nights had begun to seem less long, when his career was on track and his life was ordered and tolerable.

He gave a bitter grunt of laughter. Tolerable? Who was he trying to kid? Emotionally it was a wasteland, a desert crying out for the sweet rain of her love, but would letting her back into his life be anything other than a mirage on the horizon, taunting him with the promise of long, cosy winter evenings by the fireside, followed by slow, lazy nights filled with passion and tenderness?

He dragged his thoughts to a halt, cursing softly as his body throbbed readily to life. Damn her. Damn her for coming back into his life. Damn the coincidence that had brought her back—and damn her for being so shatteringly, sweetly beautiful. All age had added was a soft, womanly maturity. There was no sign of the ravages of childbirth—at least none he could detect, and despite his better intentions he had looked hard enough.

No, she was still his Emily, the woman who had haunted his days and nights for the past eight years, the woman who had taken away his future and left him with nothing but bittersweet memories of a less than perfect past.

He stared out of his surgery window at the hillside opposite, the rolling folds of the valley that fell steadily to the sea two miles away.

It was a beautiful place to live, a place to find peace and tranquillity, if not happiness—until Emily.

Except, if he had to be honest, he had come here initially because of her, or at least because of those accursed memories.

They had spent two blissful, glorious weeks here on their honeymoon, courtesy of Emily's old schoolfriend Sarah, whose parents had owned a cottage not five miles away—a cottage where they had both given up their virginity in a fumbling, earth-shattering explosion of tension—at least his tension had exploded then. Emily's explosion had been a little later, when he had blundered his way towards a better understanding of her body and its responses, but when he had. . .

Remembering those responses drew a deep, agonised groan from him now, and he dropped his head into his hands, knuckling his eyes and forcing his breath through a chest that felt as if a steel band was coiled tightly round it.

Need—years of aching, unsatisfied need—rose up to swamp him. The dull, heavy throb of his body taunted him, and every time his eyes flickered shut she danced naked against his lids as she had in the cottage that bleak December of their honeymoon, her smooth skin lit only by the dancing flames of the fire.

He groaned again and stood up, only to sit down again and force his attention to the demands of paperwork until the embarrassing and unmistakable hunger in his body subsided.

Damn her.

And damn him for stopping her when she had wanted to go away earlier today and forget all about this job.

He should have let her go while the going was good.

Idiot.

It was no good, he was never going to get this paperwork done today. What he needed was some fresh air. There was a patient he needed to visit, too—he'd go and do it and take his mind off his folly, at least for a little while.

The door creaked open, cobwebs clinging to the frame, and Emily stepped cautiously over the threshold. It smelt musty, but it seemed dry enough. She walked hestitantly into the sitting-room and faltered to a standstill.

It hadn't changed—not since—oh, lord.

Memories came back to swamp her—David, lying naked on the hearthrug, watching her hungrily as she danced in front of the flames, his eyes warming her pale skin as effectively as the fire. He had reached for her, drawing her down beside him, then his body had claimed hers again——

She became conscious of a dull, heavy ache of need, buried long ago deep down inside her, and the slow, insistent beat of her heart beneath her breasts.

She must be mad, she thought with a moan as she pressed cool palms against her flaming cheeks. Mad to think she could come back here to live, in this cottage which held so many memories. And madder still to think she could work side by side with the man who had helped to make those memories.

Her eyes strayed back to the fire, and, sinking down on to the hearthrug, she let her fingers stray over the soft woollen pile.

He had been so tender with her, so nervous himself and yet so thoughtful of her. . .

'Isn't it lovely?'

David glanced round, then back to his bride, her cheeks glowing with health and something else.

'Absolutely,' he said huskily, but she knew he wasn't talking about the cottage and her throat went dry.

Her whole body tingled with anticipation, with the tension that had built between them until now.

But it would end here, tonight, their wedding night.

'It's cold,' he murmured. 'I'll light the fire.'

It was reluctant, and she laughed at him and pushed him out of the way, interfering.

In the end, amid much teasing and hilarity, they got it going, and David went out to the car and brought in the luggage and a bottle of champagne.

The fridge, they found, was full of goodies courtesy of Sarah's parents—the lady who looked after the cottage had been in and cleaned it, made up the beds and stocked up with groceries at their instruction.

'How kind,' Emily said to David, and he agreed and turned to her.

'What about supper?'

'I'm not really hungry,' she confessed, her eyes tangling with his.

'No, nor am I. Shall we sit by the fire and open the champagne?'

They found glasses and settled down on the hearth-rug. Although the heating was on it was a cold, cheerless day and darkness had fallen some time before. There, though, in the flickering firelight, the outside world was forgotten.

'To us,' he said softly, touching his glass to hers, and, their eyes locked, they entwined their arms and sipped deeply.

She wrinkled her nose. 'Bubbles,' she said, a little breathless, and he leaned back against a chair and pulled her between his legs, her back against his chest, one arm resting comfortably across her waist.

Her head was tipped back against his throat, and she could feel the beat of his heart against her shoulders.

'It was a lovely day, wasn't it?' she said softly.

'I thought it would never end,' he murmured.

She turned her head a little and stared up at him. The flames were reflected in his eyes, but then he moved his head and she saw a fire in them that was all his own. She swallowed, her heart suddenly pounding, and he took her glass away and set it down with his.

Then he reached for her, a little clumsily, and she turned in his arms to meet his kiss. Their passion caught and blazed, yet he seemed reluctant somehow, as if he was holding back.

She lifted her head and looked at him. 'What's wrong?'

He shook his head slightly. 'I so badly want this to be special for you, but I expect it's going to be a disaster,' he confessed, his voice trembling a little. 'I've never done it before, so don't expect miracles.'

She reached up and cupped his cheek. 'Nor have I, so don't worry. I don't know what to expect—except that it might hurt.'

His eyes clouded. 'I don't want to hurt you, Emily.'

'Well, we can't wait forever,' she told him with typical candour. 'I suppose it will only be the once.'

'I'll be as gentle as I can.'

'I know.'

He reached out his arms again and kissed her once more, slowly, softly, with all his love—or so it seemed, because suddenly Emily found she didn't care how much it hurt, she just needed to hold him and be held by him, to feel his body on hers, to know him in the oldest sense.

She reached for his shirt buttons, freeing two and sliding her fingers inside against the warm, smooth skin. A light scatter of hair grazed her knuckles, sending shivers down her spine.

'Cold?' he asked, but she shook her head.

'No—no, not cold.'

He moved away a little from her, and stripped off his jacket and tie, then his shirt.

Her heart thudded and crashed against her ribs. He was so—male? She felt liquid heat pooling low down, just where her body ached for him. She couldn't drag her eyes from him, and as he slid his trousers down the taut, well-muscled thighs she thought she would die of wanting him.

He turned back to her, his scanty briefs doing little to hide his need for her, and she flicked her tongue out and moistened her dry lips.

'Your turn,' he said gruffly, and helped her to her feet.

'You do it,' she whispered.

'I don't know where to start——'

'Zip at the back,' she told him, and, turning round, she lifted her hair and bent her head forward.

She felt the slide of the zip, then the warmth of his lips pressed against her spine.

'You smell wonderful,' he breathed against her skin, and a shiver ran over her.

Turning in his arms, she slipped the dress down over her shoulders and stepped out of it.

The breath left him as if he'd been punched. He lifted trembling hands and curved them lightly over her barely covered breasts.

'Emily,' he whispered raggedly, and she arched into his hands, pressing her aching breasts against his palms. His fingers tightened convulsively as her hands locked behind him and drew them together, then as their hips brushed against each other they both gasped.

'I need you,' he said, the words shattering against her cheek.

'I'm yours,' she said simply, her shyness forgotten.

He drew her down on the rug and slowly, his hands shaking, he stripped away the scraps of silk and lace that hid her from his eyes.

'Emily,' he breathed.

She'd thought she would feel shy, but the awestruck reverence of his expression dispelled her last fears. Slipping her fingers in the waistband of his briefs, she eased them down and abandoned them, turning back to study his now totally naked form.

He took her breath away.

'Let me touch you,' he murmured, and she lay down again beside him, her hands reaching for his shoulders, smoothing the hot satin of his skin.

Tremblingly, his hands traced her body, cupping her breasts, gliding over the sleek skin of her flank, his knuckles grazing her inner thighs. Her legs fell open for him, her hips arching up against his hand as he straightened his fingers and laid his palm against the damp nest of curls.

Her own caresses grew braver, her hands sliding down his sides, her fingers curling round him, hot satin over steel.

His breath caught and he dropped his head against her shoulder.

'Steady,' he muttered.

She could feel the moisture pooling as he stroked her, feel the tension rising even higher. She didn't want to be steady. She wanted to be his.

'Oh, David, now,' she moaned.

Her breath was choking her, her heart thrashing against her ribs as he moved awkwardly over her.

'Help me,' he pleaded, and just as awkwardly she did as he asked, guiding him towards the heavy ache inside her.

'I love you,' he said against her mouth, and there was a brief flash of pain and then fullness—fullness that she had never even dreamt of. . .

'Are you OK?' he asked, his voice taut.

'Oh, yes—oh, David. . .'

Her hands gripped his shoulders and she strained up against him, unable to bear the tension. 'Oh, David, please, do something. . .'

'Oh, Emily—oh, God, I. . .'

His body started to move, winding the tension higher, and then suddenly he stiffened, dropping his head into the curve of her shoulder, his harsh cry muffled against her skin.

Then he collapsed, his body trembling under her hands, his chest heaving.

She lay there, her hands smoothing him, and slow tears slipped from her eyes.

She needed more—her body screamed for more, for some elusive release that only David had found.

He lifted his head. 'I'm sorry—oh, Emily, you're crying. I did hurt you.'

'No—no, you didn't. It's just. . .' She hesitated, unable to voice her need, but it was unnecessary.

Shifting slightly, he slid his hand between them and touched her. 'Is that right?' he asked softly. 'Tell me.'

She was beyond speech, beyond anything but the feel of his hand touching, soothing, yet winding the tension even higher until——

'David!' she sobbed, and, burying her face against his shoulder, she felt the ripples spreading, lifting her higher, higher, until suddenly she was over the crest and there before her was paradise. . .

They came slowly back to earth, their arms wrapped tightly round each other, their legs still tangled, and David rained tiny, butterfly-kisses over her face.

'Are you OK?' he murmured softly.

'Mmm. You?'

Shyly, she met his eyes, and nearly melted at the love in them.

He was speechless, just hugging her closer. 'You were wonderful,' he said eventually. 'I had no idea it would feel so—oh, Em. . .'

'Nor did I,' she whispered, thinking of that unbelievable fullness, the rightness of his body joined with hers.

'Next time I'll wait for you,' he vowed.

They grew cold, and while David explored the fridge she unpacked her dressing-gown and had a shower.

By the time she went back down he was dressed

again in jeans and a sweatshirt, and had put some salad out on plates.

'We've got champagne to finish,' he told her, and they sat together on the hearthrug and fed each other nibbles of salad and toasted their toes in front of the blazing logs until the champagne was finished.

David had put on some music, and, emboldened by the champagne and the look in his eyes, she stood up, swaying softly to the music.

'Dance with me,' she said.

He shook his head. 'Dance for me,' he murmured.

So she did, slipping the dressing-gown over her shoulders to puddle on the floor, teasing and taunting until with a ragged groan he drew her down before the fire and made love to her again. . .

'Emily?'

She turned, startled, to find David framed in the doorway.

Her first thought was that he wasn't naked. Her second was that her memories must be written all across her face in letters ten feet high.

She felt colour rush to her cheeks and was grateful for the gloomy light in the room.

'Why are you here?' she asked breathlessly.

'I was just passing and I saw your car,' he told her. His eyes were on the fireplace, then flicked back to her kneeling on the hearthrug where they had made love that very first time. Something flickered in his eyes, and she could tell he was remembering, too.

She struggled to her feet.

'I was just having a look.'

He glanced round. 'For old times' sake? It hasn't changed,' he said softly.

Their eyes met, clashed, locked. Her breath clogged her throat, her heart beating a wild tattoo against her ribs.

'No,' she murmured.

'No, what?' he asked, his voice husky.

'No, not for old times' sake,' she said, firming her voice. 'I'm going to be living here.'

'Oh.' His eyes travelled slowly over her, so that she was conscious of her nipples straining against the fine fabric of her blouse. His eyes strayed lower, then jerked back to her face with an almost physical effort. 'Good idea,' he said, his voice still touched with that smoky gruffness she remembered so well from the intimate moments of their marriage. 'It's very handy for the practice—is Sarah renting it to you?' he asked.

She dropped her eyes. 'No—she's—Sarah died two years ago. She left me the cottage.'

'Oh, Emily—I'm sorry. What happened?'

His voice had changed instantly, softening with compassion, and she swallowed the lump in her throat as she thought back to the awful night when Sarah had died.

'A car accident,' she told him hollowly. 'It was foggy. A drunk driver——'

David groaned. 'What a waste. Oh, my love, I'm sorry.'

So was Emily, because she hadn't wanted Sarah to drive in the fog. 'Stay,' she had begged her, but she should have been more insistent, hidden her keys or something. Sarah had been upset, too, too upset to drive really, because that was the day she had found out that Philip was dying of cancer—Philip, her beloved husband, Jamie's father—and the man Emily had then married so that her godson's future would be secure.

CHAPTER TWO

EMILY arrived to take up her post two weeks later, having sent the housekeeper on ahead to clean up the cottage and prepare it for her arrival with Jamie.

He was thoughtful about leaving the big house in Surrey where he had lived with his parents, but she explained that they wouldn't be selling it yet and could always come back for visits. Anyway, she remembered how much Jamie had wanted to move to Devon, how he had begged her. That was one reason, probably the most significant, why she had taken the job. She just hoped for all their sakes that it didn't prove a huge mistake.

'Are we going to live in Mummy's cottage, Emmy?' he asked for the hundredth time on the drive down. He was so insecure now, and she hastened to reassure him.

'Yes, darling. We'll be there tonight.'

'Will I have my own room?'

'Yes, of course.'

There was the question of where she would sleep, but as the cottage had four bedrooms there was no need for her to use the room that Sarah and Philip had used—and that she had slept in with David on their honeymoon.

Mrs Bradley, the housekeeper who had been with Philip's family for years and who was to stay on to help care for Jamie at Philip's behest, would have the large room next to Jamie as her bed-sitting room. Emily would have the fourth bedroom.

It was small, but she was on her own, so it didn't matter. Anyway, it had a distant view of the sea down the valley and across the rooftops of Biddlecombe, and the sun would wake her every morning.

They arrived at the cottage to a warm welcome from Mrs Bradley, and within a very short time Jamie was settled in his bed, his teddy under his arm, his thumb tucked in his mouth, and Emily was sitting down with Mrs Bradley going over the arrangements for the beginning of the next week when Emily started work and Jamie would join the village school. She had managed to get a place for him, and the headmaster was looking forward to meeting the boy on Monday.

The only thing left to concern her was David, and the prospect of working with him made the ergonomics of her accommodation and Jamie's schooling pale into insignificance.

In fact her first morning at the surgery was much easier than she had expected, because he greeted her with a friendly smile, gave her a cup of coffee and took himself off, leaving it to Laurence to make her feel at home and show her where everything was kept.

Her first patients were genuinely in need, but she had no doubt that after a few days word would get round and she would be inundated with people giving their noses a treat.

Her clinics, she noticed, were already booked some way ahead, especially the family planning and antenatal.

'They like a woman for a woman's domain,' Sue said with a smile. 'I have to agree—but if you feel you've got too many I can shift some back to David, although he won't like it. Some of them flirt with him, but you can't blame them. He's just such a sexy beast——Oh, lord, I'm sorry!' Her hand flew over her mouth, and Emily smiled at her discomfort.

'Sue, forget it. It was ages ago, and I'm over him,' she lied. 'Don't feel you have to walk on eggshells, please. One thing, though—I'd rather the patients didn't know we'd been married.'

'Oh, of course not,' Sue agreed. 'It's nobody's business but your own, and I'm sorry I said what I did.'

Emily smiled again. 'You're right, though—he is a sexy beast.'

'You couldn't be talking about me, could you?'

David's voice behind made her jump, and she turned towards him with a cool smile. 'Your ego's still intact, I see. No, we were talking about Robert de Niro, actually. Excuse me.'

She slipped past him and retreated to her office, closing the door behind her.

It opened almost immediately.

'Can I have a word?'

She shrugged. She couldn't shut him out of her life completely; they had to work together.

'Of course.'

She waved to a seat and positioned herself safely behind her desk. 'What can I do for you?'

He sighed thoughtfully. 'Oh, Emily, there's a question and a half.'

'David. . .' Her voice contained a warning, and he grinned, melting her insides.

She almost groaned aloud. Sue was right—he was a sexy beast.

'This afternoon,' he said, the grin replaced by a businesslike expression that wasn't nearly so heart-melting—thank God, she thought. He went on, 'Mr and Mrs Blake are coming to see you. They're my patients, and I don't know what they want—perhaps it's family planning or something. Anyway, they specifically requested an appointment with the new lady doctor when she arrived, and the appointment's been booked for over a week.'

'I'll tell you what it's about,' she promised.

He nodded. 'OK. I'll be around if you want to refer to me—perhaps sneak out to get a form from reception or some such excuse.'

She eyed him curiously. 'Do you really think that'll be necessary?'

He shrugged. 'Probably not. I just get a feeling about them. I don't think they're all that happy together, and a joint appointment with a stranger——' He shrugged again. 'Could be nothing, of course, but I just thought I'd prime you. Right.'

He unfolded his legs and stretched his hands over his head, yawning widely. 'Oh, God, I hate weekends on duty. I'm going home to walk the dogs—I'll be back before two for my clinic. What are you doing about lunch?'

She opened her drawer and pulled out some sandwiches.

'You don't want to come with me and grab a snack at home and a quick stroll over the hill?'

It sounded lovely, just the way they had spent their honeymoon, but she forced herself to shake her head. This was hardly the way to start, and working with him would be hard enough without encouraging little intimate walks over the hills.

'I think not,' she said as firmly as she could manage, and with a rueful grin he left her alone, wondering if she'd lost her marbles completely or if it just seemed that way.

She should have known to trust his instincts, she thought as she studied the couple opposite her.

They were in their thirties, a very average professional couple, but the way the consultation was going was far from average.

'Of course,' Mr Blake was saying, 'we'd probably stand more chance of having another child if the first one wasn't always in our bed.'

Mrs Blake's eyes slid away, and Emily's own instincts prickled. Her attention switched to the woman.

'How old is your child?'

'Four—and she has terrible nightmares. If we don't have her in bed with us, she wakes screaming and it takes ages to settle her down again.'

'Not that long,' her husband argued.

'No, well, it isn't you that ends up doing it,' she returned bitterly. 'You just lie there on your back snoring your head off and complain that I've woken you with the creaky boards—though if you'd ever put them down again properly after you fixed that pipe they wouldn't creak——'

'I think we're rather getting off the point,' Emily interjected gently but firmly. 'I have a son of six, and when his father died recently he was very upset. He started getting into bed with me at night, and I could see this becoming a pattern, so what I did was when he woke I got into his bed for a little while and gave him a cuddle, then slipped out again when he'd gone off. If he came to me, I'd carry him back once he'd settled.'

She regarded the couple in front of her. 'It worked for us—it might work for you. I certainly don't think you can leave a child upset in the middle of the night, but to allow her presence to affect your relationship to this extent I think is probably not healthy either for the child or for you——'

'Not healthy?' Mr Blake bristled. 'Are you accusing us of abusing her or something?'

'No, of course not,' Emily soothed. 'I'm simply suggesting that a better sleep-pattern, undisturbed by a frightened child, or more opportunities to concentrate on the physical aspect of your relationship might be emotionally and physically healthier for all of you.'

'Well, it wasn't my idea to have her in bed with us in the first place, and she's much worse now than she used to be.'

'And I suppose that's my fault!' Mrs Blake said defensively—too defensively.

Clearly, Emily thought, she wasn't going to get anywhere until she split these two up—and perhaps a word with the intuitive Dr Trevellyan might be in order.

'I don't seem to have all your notes here,' she said blandly to them. 'If you'll excuse me a moment, I'll just go and see what I can find in the office.'

She nipped out of the door and down the corridor. Sue was on the reception desk, and Emily asked if she knew where David was.

'In his office—he's alone, so if you want to go in you can. I think he's half expecting you.'

She knocked on the door and went in. 'You were right,' she said directly.

'The Blakes? What's the problem?'

'He's complaining that they can't have another child because the first is still coming into their bed at night and so they don't have the opportunity. Reading between the lines, I would say Mrs Blake isn't keen anyway. Apparently they've been trying for over a year.'

David's eyebrows shot up. 'Have they, indeed? So why did she come and see me six months ago for another diaphragm?'

Emily's jaw dropped, and then she nodded. 'Oh, that figures. The child's a smokescreen—she's using her so she doesn't have to sleep with her husband—or, at least, can only sleep.'

'Hmm.'

'Hmm?'

'I heard a rumour—it might be nothing, but she could be having an affair.'

Emily's mouth formed a round O. 'Tricky.'

'Very. I'll give you the details later. Split them up, send him in to me for a physical, and get her to spill the beans.'

'OK. Now?'

'Yeah, send him straight in. I'll return him to the waiting-room.'

She went back and sent Mr Blake to David, then confronted Mrs Blake.

'OK. On your notes it says you have a diaphragm. I've spoken to Dr Trevellyan; he confirmed it.'

Panic flared in the woman's eyes. 'He won't tell Neil, will he? I mean, it is confidential?'

'Of course he won't tell him. And clearly you haven't, or else you wouldn't be here today talking about infertility.'

She let the silence stretch, then Mrs Blake gave a shaky sigh and reluctantly met Emily's eyes. 'I don't want another baby,' she said slowly. 'At least, not Neil's.'

'Things don't seem all sweetness and light between you,' Emily acknowledged.

The woman gave a short, bitter laugh. 'You could say that. It was OK for a while, we struggled along making the best of it, but then—there's someone else, someone I love——' She pressed her fingers to her mouth, clearly upset, and Emily settled back in the chair.

'Take your time,' she said reassuringly.

'He's wonderful—warm, tender, understanding.' She paused. 'He's also married.'

'Ah.'

'His wife's disabled. He loves her, but like a sister, you know? Not that there could be anything else between them. She's got multiple sclerosis, and she's—well, she's bad.'

'Oh, dear.' Emily's soft heart went out to the unknown woman whose husband apparently loved her, but not enough to stay at home.

'She's permanently bedridden now—she's incontinent and her limbs are very spastic. She finds swallowing difficult, and she's very depressed.' Ann Blake looked at Emily. 'I'd hate her to find out about us, but Richard's coping all alone and someone has to help him through it. He gives her so much, not just his time but friendship, support—he gets really depressed. That was how it started, really—he was sitting in the park, and I was out with Jane and the dog. He looked so bleak, so alone. We started to talk, and. . .'

Ann paused, her face softening. 'He laughed, for the first time in months, he said. I saw him again by accident, and then we began arranging to meet, always quite innocently. We never meant this to happen.'

'But it did.'

'Yes. And all I want is to be with him, but I can't.'

'And meanwhile you're living with a man you no longer love, who wants to have another child.'

She nodded, and her eyes filled. 'What can I do? Richard can't leave Jenny, and I can't afford to leave Neil and live on my own with Jane. Anyway, he'd probably want custody and she loves him.'

'Is it fair to her to use her as a smokescreen?'

There was silence for a long while, then Mrs Blake shook her head. 'No—no, of course not. I didn't even realise I was doing it until just now. It was only when you suggested that if we put her back in her own bed it would give our physical relationship a chance that I realised how badly I didn't want that to happen.'

Emily eyed her thoughtfully. 'Mrs Blake, when did you and your husband last make love?'

She snorted. 'We don't make love, Dr Thompson. We had sex back in—June? July? And that was the first time since Easter.'

'And it's now September. How long can you fool him?'

She shrugged helplessly. 'I don't know.'

'Nor do I,' Emily told her, 'but one thing I do know—it isn't fair to Jane to use her like this. She must start sleeping in her own bed again, and I don't mean with you. How you persuade your husband that you aren't going to have intercourse is your problem, but if you want any help or counselling advice you can always go to Relate, the marriage guidance people. They're very good. Perhaps you ought to try it.'

'And what can they do?' Ann asked heavily. 'Make me fall back in love with Neil again? I doubt it.'

So did Emily, but there was nothing more she could do. There was clearly no fertility problem that exposure to the appropriate opportunity wouldn't solve, and there was obviously no need for any further medical involvement. How Mrs Blake dealt with it from here was her own problem, and it was one Emily didn't envy her one bit.

As she was leaving, she turned back to Emily. 'Dr Thompson, this is confidential, isn't it? I mean, whatever we've told each other in here won't get back to Neil?'

'No, of course not. Not without your permission.'

'So he won't ever know what went on in here today?'

As Emily confirmed that, it occurred to her that it was a strange way to phrase the question. After her surgery was over she went and sought David out.

'Tricky one,' he said. 'I expect she intends to lie through her teeth to him.'

'Oh, dear. Do you think he'll come back for some answers?'

David shrugged. 'Depends how convincing she is. Some women aren't very convincing liars.'

He was looking at her oddly, as if he was referring to her, and she felt her heart thud uncomfortably. Not that she had lied—except by omission, to allow him to think that Jamie was hers.

Still, his eyes searched hers as he stood up and came slowly round the end of the desk.

'I ought to tell you all about the man she's having the affair with. Why don't we do it over a drink on the way home?'

She had to physically stop herself from backing up against the wall to get away from him.

'No! I mean—I'm tired, and it was Jamie's first day at school. I ought to get back and see him and ask Mrs Bradley how he was when she picked him up.'

'Mrs Bradley?'

'Our housekeeper.'

David's brows quirked slightly. 'Housekeeper, eh? I thought you'd have an au pair.'

Emily shook her head. 'No—it was a provision of Philip's will that she have a home with us for life, and a living allowance. He left us all very well provided for, and Mrs Bradley's just another example of his thoughtfulness. She's been with his family for years, and Jamie knows her. It seemed very sensible, and to be honest I'm very grateful to her for all she does. I couldn't do my job properly without her.'

'No, I can see that,' he said. He paused, those soft grey eyes searching her face until the need to run was paramount. And yet he wasn't threatening—rather the reverse. His hand came up and brushed a stray lock of hair away from her face, and she quivered at his touch. 'Poor Emily,' he said softly. 'It must be very hard for you. How does Jamie cope with his mother working when his father's died so recently?'

She should have corrected him then, but she didn't—another lost opportunity. Tonight, though, didn't seem to be the time. Instead she focused on his words. 'I haven't worked since Philip became very ill near the end.'

'Was it cancer?'

She nodded. 'Yes—stomach cancer. For ages he thought he had an ulcer. By the time they realised it wasn't, it was too late.'

'But you didn't pick it up?'

She shook her head. How could she have done? She wasn't there; but David didn't know that. She must find a time to tell him all that had happened, before he thought she was deceiving him. After all they had been through, she owed him honesty, even though Jamie made a useful smokescreen.

To think she had just finished telling Ann Blake that she couldn't use her daughter to hide behind!

And Jamie, her son or not, needed her now. She might not be his mother, but she was the closest the poor child would ever get, and she fully intended to do her job well. 'I must get home,' she said now. 'Jamie will be fretting.'

'Of course.'

He seemed suddenly distant, and for a moment Emily felt a shocking sense of loss sweep through her.

Absurd.

Without giving herself time to think, she bade him goodnight and made her way out.

He was the last person she would want to see, David told himself disgustedly, but it didn't stop him pulling up outside her cottage with a pot plant from the local garage and a bottle of plonk.

It was only a welcome to the area, after all, a simple gesture from an old friend.

And he might get to meet this child of hers, the child she had conceived not two years after their separation—before their divorce was final, even.

He fought down the bitter jealousy that surged in his veins, and concentrated instead on juggling the plant and bottle while he locked his car. Perhaps he should just go, he thought, take the stuff to the surgery in the morning and forget about invading her privacy——

'Can I help you?'

A matronly woman stood in the open doorway, lit from behind by the welcoming glow that spilt from the cottage across the path to his feet. It didn't quite reach him, and somehow stepping into the light suddenly assumed an almost mystical significance.

'Is Emily at home?' he asked, remaining where he was.

'Who should I say it is?' she responded, without inviting him in.

'David—David Trevellyan.'

The door was immediately held wider, and a smile broke out on the woman's face. 'Come in, Dr Trevellyan. I'll fetch her—she's putting Jamie to bed.'

He stepped into the light, his heart easing even as he did so. 'Could you find a home for these? Just a sort of housewarming present.'

'How kind.' The warm hazel eyes twinkled like currants above plump cheeks that rose with her smile and squashed her eyes into merry slits. David found himself returning the smile and feeling grateful that Emily and her son had such a kindly soul caring for them.

'Make yourself at home, Dr Trevellyan—I'll just pop these in the kitchen and go and find Emily.'

He stood in the hallway while she bustled into the kitchen and then out again, hurrying up the stairs.

He heard a mumbled conversation overhead, then Emily appeared at the top of the stairs.

'David?'

Was it his imagination, or did she sound breathless?

He tipped his head back and shielded his eyes from the overhead light. 'Hi. I just wondered if you wanted to go out for that drink now—if Jamie's settled.'

'Oh.' She looked flustered, her hands fluttering over her clothes. 'I'm not really dressed for going out.'

'That's OK. The local isn't smart; your jeans are fine.'

More than fine, if the tightening in his body was anything to go by.

'Um—let me brush my hair and I'll be down.'

He watched as she turned, the faded denim taut over the smooth curve of her bottom, and cursed softly under his breath.

He must be mad.

Emily felt sick with fright—or was it anticipation? Ridiculous. She brushed her hair until the roots protested, then dragged a scrape of colour over her lips and smudged them hastily together. That would do. It would have to.

Abandoning her brush, she ran down the stairs like an eager teenager.

'Ready?' he asked.

She nodded. 'I just need my coat.'

He held it for her, his fingers brushing her neck as he lifted her hair away from the collar in a gesture she remembered so well. A little shiver ran over her skin and, forcing a smile, she turned to him.

'Shall we?'

He opened the door for her, closed it behind them and then settled her into the car before going round and sliding behind the wheel.

The inside of the car seemed suddenly terribly small and intimate, and her breathing seemed unnaturally loud.

'Where are we going?' she asked to fill the emptiness.

'The Bull—remember it?'

She did—vividly. They had spent many a happy lunchtime there, sandwiched between long, lazy mornings in bed and long, equally lazy evenings in front of the fire at the cottage.

'Has it changed?'

'Not much. Nothing round here changes much. It gets a bit hectic in the summer, but at this time of year it's mainly locals.'

They pulled up in the nearly deserted car park, and she followed him through the low doorway into the heavily beamed lounge that was empty except for a grizzled, thick-set man wiping down the bar.

'Evening, George.'

'Evening, Doctor. What'll it be?'

'I'll have the usual—Emily?'

'Dry white wine, please.'

George set the drinks on the bar and eyed her curiously.

'This is Dr Thompson—she's just joined the practice,' David told him.

'Pleased to meet you—you'll cheer that place up no

end,' he said gruffly, and pushed a glass of wine towards her. 'Here—have them on the house.'

She smiled, his welcome warming her. 'Thank you. Cheers—your very good health.'

His rusty laugh crackled in the empty room. 'Of course, you've got a vested interest in that, haven't you? Keep the surgery empty.'

She smiled again. 'I don't think there's much chance of that. Still, at least you won't have to pretend to be ill to satisfy your curiosity.'

He laughed again as he headed for the other bar, and David steered her over to a table in the corner, tucked in behind the deep chimney breast where they had often sat during their honeymoon. It was too intimate, and she was very conscious of his nearness.

He lifted his glass, condensation beaded on the outside, fogging the pale beer. 'Here's to a long and happy partnership,' he murmured.

His eyes were in shadow, but she sensed the intensity of his gaze. Was he talking about the practice? Or them? She didn't dare ask.

She lifted her glass, dropping her eyes to the contents. Silently she drank, the chilled wine soothing her tight throat.

'So,' she said eventually, 'tell me about Ann Blake and this affair.'

'Ah.' He set his glass down precisely in the centre of a beermat and squared it up with the edge of the table. The task seemed to require an inordinate amount of attention.

'Richard Wellcome is a local farmer. He and his wife are patients of mine. His wife, Jenny, has MS and is in a pretty sorry way. She hasn't had much in the way of remission, and I don't think she will. She's getting increasingly spastic—she's on Baclofen to combat it, but it's a bit of a juggling act because it makes her very sleepy, and she keeps dropping things. Last week it was a cup of tea. Luckily it wasn't too hot or she could have had a nasty scald.'

'Poor woman.'

'Mmm. And Richard, of course, is having a hard time. The farm's not doing too well, and he's hiding the real situation from Jenny because he doesn't want to worry her. What with one thing and another, I'm not surprised he's having an affair.'

'Do you condone it?' Emily asked sharply.

He sighed. 'Don't be judgemental, Emily. Life's hard. We take what ease we can. If Ann helps him to cope, then so be it.'

'But her own marriage is in ruins as a result.'

'Her marriage has been in ruins for years. Women don't have affairs with other women's husbands if everything's rosy at home. She was ripe for the picking.'

'And that justifies it?'

He shrugged. 'Maybe.'

She felt anger stir her, an old, familiar anger remembered from their earlier fights. It shocked her, but she couldn't help responding to it.

'David, you can't just accept it like that. You should encourage her to seek help, to go to Relate and find a solution——'

'Why? I'm their doctor, not their priest.'

'But you should treat the whole person.'

'You're assuming that infidelity is an illness. You

can't interfere in people's lives, Emily. That's not what you're there for.'

'But what about the child?' she argued.

'What about her? They'll sort themselves out, one way or another.'

She let out her breath on a whoosh. 'I can't believe you're that callous.'

'I'm not callous,' he reasoned. 'I just know my limitations. Medically speaking, Richard Wellcome is the one with the need. He's a depressive—and if Ann Blake acts as an antidepressant that helps him through his life, then who am I to take her away from him? Besides, if he can cope, then Jenny can stay at home, which is what she wants. She was born there; technically it's her farm. Richard was employed by her father to work the farm once he became too ill to manage it any more. I think he feels that quite keenly.'

'And if it's going badly, that's quite a responsibility.'

'Exactly. It's a hell of a coil, Emily. You're better off having as little to do with it as possible.' He tipped back his head and drained his glass, his throat bobbing as he swallowed.

Emily watched, transfixed. He set the glass down. 'Another one?'

She shook her head. 'No, I don't think so. I ought to be getting back; I'm quite tired.'

'You've had a busy day,' he said softly, and, helping her into her coat again, he ushered her out of the door.

They were silent on the journey back, and when he pulled up outside her cottage she reached immediately for the handle.

Her mouth, however, was on his side.

'Coffee?' she found herself asking.

'In a minute.'

His hand on her shoulder turned her back towards him, and in the light from the porch she could see need glittering in his eyes.

She knew he was going to kiss her before he reached for her—before the warmth of his arms enfolded her against his chest, before the softness of his lips brushed against hers once, twice, before settling firmly against her mouth. One of them sighed, a ragged, broken sigh of remembrance, and then thoughts fled, lost in the heat that flared between them as their mouths met and melded, locked in a passion as old as time.

After an age he lifted his head and stared down at her, his eyes dark. 'You taste the same,' he whispered wonderingly.

'So do you.'

Her voice was fractured, scrapy. She eased away from him, needed room to order her thoughts.

'Coffee, I think,' he said, and his voice was ragged too.

She had forgotten her offer of coffee, but it was too late now to take it back.

They got out of the car and went in.

CHAPTER THREE

EMILY led him into the sitting-room, gleaming with polish and warmed by the flickering flames of the fire.

'It's a little early in the year, but I always think a fire's so cheerful, don't you?'

David's mind was hardly paying attention. The flickering firelight brought back so many memories. Fighting back the lump in his throat, he dredged up a smile. 'Absolutely,' he said. Damn, she looked so lovely, her lips lush and full, just kissed.

He shouldn't have done that, yet for the life of him he couldn't have stopped himself. In fact, if she didn't move away from him soon, he was going to do it again——

'I'll go up and check on Jamie,' she said, and backed away, her eyes wide.

She almost ran through the door, and his eyes tracked her departure, lingering on the smooth curve of her bottom, tightly clad in the jeans. His hands itched to cup the sleek swell, to grasp her hips and pull her hard against him, as if that would somehow ease the gnawing ache he felt for her.

Alone, he wandered round the room fingering her possessions. Some, like the little jade buddha, he remembered. Others were new, like the table smothered in photographs in old silver frames. There was one of her with Sarah taken in their teens, and another, also with Sarah and obviously at her wedding.

He studied them, needing the distraction, and found a photo of Sarah and her husband staring into each other's eyes, their love clearly visible. He felt a pang of sadness for her young life snuffed out in its prime. He had always liked Emily's old schoolfriend.

Another photo, this one of a christening, with Emily holding a baby and Sarah and her husband flanking them on the steps of a church.

Another of Sarah and her husband, presumably taken a couple of years later because the baby had become a toddler, his wild tangle of curls framing a cherubic little face. They looked radiantly happy.

David smiled, fingering the photo, and then stilled.

Another photo caught his eye, this time of Emily, but again Sarah's husband was in the picture, and so was the little boy.

It was another wedding photo—a much simpler affair, the man looking drawn and weary, Emily smiling bravely, the little boy looking lost and rather sad.

The truth registered slowly. Anger flooded him as he stared down at the image, hot, blinding anger—and under it, connected somehow to his jealousy and pride, was relief. The child wasn't hers. Whatever had happened, it hadn't happened while their marriage bed was still warm.

Even so, she had deceived him now, lied, if only by omission.

He heard a footfall behind him and turned, photo in hand.

'When were you going to tell me?' he asked coldly. 'Or weren't you?'

* * *

Emily closed her eyes and sighed. She should have told him right at the beginning, but if she had she would have had no defence against him, nothing to protect her from the full force of his magnetism.

'I was going to tell you, of course I was. I had no reason not to,' she lied, and instantly remembered his remark about some women not being able to lie. Guilt must have written itself on her face ten feet high, because he snorted softly and put the photo down.

'So why not straight away?'

'Because it was irrelevant——'

'Irrelevant? You let me think you had conceived a child before our divorce was even final, and you think that's irrelevant?'

Jealousy, fierce and bitter, flooded Emily and drowned out all reason.

'You can talk,' she bit back. 'Within six months you were living with that damn blonde!'

He jerked as if she'd struck him, angry colour flooding his face. 'So what?' he said softly. 'At least I didn't do it for money.'

Emily's eyes widened in shock, and before she could turn away she felt the first tears well up and spill over.

'Bastard—get out!' she whispered.

'With pleasure,' he said coldly, and, brushing past her, he let himself out of the door.

'Emily, would you and Dr Trevellyan like——? Oh, he's gone! Emily?'

She stood frozen, her arms wrapped round her waist, hugging herself.

'Emily?' Mrs Bradley repeated softly, and, coming round in front of her, she tutted and folded her against her ample bosom. 'Oh, dear. I wondered if it was such a good idea you going out, but when he came with the plant and the bottle of wine—'

Emily sniffed and lifted her head. 'When?'

'Tonight—housewarming present, he said. It's in the kitchen.'

She went out to the kitchen and saw a lovely miniature rose smothered in blossom. Was it just coincidence that it was a deep, glorious red?

The blooms blurred, and she blinked hard to clear her vision.

'We always fight,' she said brokenly. 'Why do we always fight?'

She gave up with the blinking and turned her head into Mrs Bradley's comfortingly available shoulder.

'There, there, my treasure. You get it out of your system,' she crooned, and Emily allowed herself to indulge in a few seconds of luxury before straightening up and sniffing.

'Sorry,' she mumbled, and, fishing for a tissue in her pocket, she scrubbed at her cheeks and blew her nose.

'I ought to talk to him,' she said.

'He's still outside,' Mrs Bradley told her quietly.

'He is?' She peered through the window and saw his car still sitting by the kerb. She could just make out his figure at the wheel, but it was too dark to read his expression.

Was he still angry?

He probably had a right to be, she acknowledged. And anyway, it was hardly the first time he'd been angry with her. She could deal with it. Straightening her shoulders, she went to the door and opened it, to find David on the step.

'I was coming to apologise,' he said gruffly. 'That was a cheap shot. I'm sorry.'

She managed a wobbly smile. 'I was coming to apologise to you. It was none of my business who you were living with.'

'That's debatable,' he said, and his mouth quirked into a tentative grin that tugged at her heart. 'Can we call a truce?'

'We ought to talk. There's a lot to tell you, and I owe you that at least.'

'Do you mind if we talk inside?' he asked softly, and she blinked and stepped back.

'Of course—I'm sorry. Come in.'

She closed the door behind him and led him through to the sitting-room.

Mrs Bradley popped her head round the door. 'I've put the kettle on, or there's the wine in the fridge for you, and there's some cheese and biscuits on the side. I'm off to bed now.'

'Thank you, Mrs Bradley. Goodnight.'

'Goodnight, dear; goodnight, Dr Trevellyan.'

'Goodnight.'

They listened in silence to the soft tread on the stairs, and the slight creaking of the boards overhead. Then David sat at one end of the settee and turned to her.

'Sit down,' he told her.

She sat, twisting her wedding-ring on her finger, unable to look at him. She needed to explain everything to him, but it was where to start that was so difficult.

'Why don't you start at the beginning?' he said quietly.

So she did.

'Sarah and Philip were married the year we split up. He was very wealthy, ten years older than her, and his first wife had left him and taken him to the cleaners. He'd rebuilt his empire, straightened out his life and then when he met Sarah he fell for her like a ton of bricks.

'It was mutual, and within weeks they were married. A year later Jamie was born, and they asked me to be his godmother. I agreed.'

'Never imagining what it would lead to.'

'Oh, no, I never even dreamed I would end up fulfilling my obligation to James in that way. Don't get me wrong, I'm only too happy to do it, but at the time there was nothing to indicate that things would go so disastrously wrong.'

'It's a good job we don't know what's going to happen. Life would be intolerable if we were constantly counting down to tragedy.'

'Sometimes I think it's a relief,' she said quietly. 'If things are intolerable anyway, it must be a blessing to know it can't go on forever.'

David watched her silently, his eyes searching. 'Are you talking about Philip?'

She nodded. 'After Sarah died his life was hell. His life revolved around her and Jamie, and all he could think about was that he would die and Jamie would be alone.'

'Hence his proposal.'

'Yes.' She sighed softly. 'I was happy to accept it. At least that way I could make some reparation to Jamie for the loss of his mother.'

David regarded her oddly. 'Reparation?' he murmured. 'That's a strange word to use.'

She laughed, a hollow, empty sound in the quiet room. 'Not really. Sarah died because of me.'

'What?' David shifted round so that he was facing her, his eyes trained on her face, missing nothing. Emily looked away.

'She came to see me. She had just found out that Philip had cancer of the stomach and that it was inoperable. She was devastated. Jamie was four, she was thirty, and her whole life lay in ruins at her feet.'

'It must have been dreadful for her.'

Emily sighed. 'It was. Unbelievably awful. I've never seen such desolation in anyone's eyes—until I saw Philip after she'd died.'

David's hand curled round hers and squeezed comfortingly. 'So what happened?'

'It was foggy—great banks of impenetrable fog rolling up the valleys. I begged her not to go, to ring Philip and stay the night with me, but she refused. She said even one night away from him now was one night too many when every one of them was numbered.'

'So you let her go.'

'I should have made her stay,' Emily whispered. 'I should have phoned Philip myself and made him talk to her, but the fog wasn't so bad near me and I knew she'd be careful.'

'And?' he prompted after a moment.

'It was the other driver's fault—he'd been drinking,' she told him in a quiet monotone. 'The post-mortem revealed his blood alcohol was way over the limit. He crossed the central reservation and smashed into her car. She didn't stand a chance.'

His hand tightened on hers, and with a muffled sound she turned her face into his shoulder, burrowing her fingers into his jumper and hanging on, as if she could ride out the pain better in his arms.

He held her gently, rocking her against his chest, his hand smoothing her hair while he murmured softly against her ear.

Eventually she relaxed against him and he eased her closer so that her side was firmly against his and his arm lay loosely round her shoulders.

'Poor Em,' he murmured. 'You do know it wasn't your fault, don't you? She was an adult, fully capable of making her own decisions.'

'But she wasn't!' Emily lifted her head and met his eyes. 'She was so upset she was hardly in any state to drive. She wasn't crying—it was deeper than that. I think she was still in shock. As a doctor I should have recognised that.'

'Don't flagellate yourself with if onlys. It wasn't your fault she died. It was the other driver. It could have happened just as easily on a clear night, or in broad daylight.'

'That's what Philip said, but I still feel guilty. If I'd made her stay, she'd still be alive today.'

'That's what I meant about not knowing. I could be killed on the way home tonight, or shot in the surgery tomorrow by an aggrieved patient—anything could happen.'

'Don't!' she cried softly, and his eyes narrowed and searched her face.

'Don't tell me you still care, Em,' he said softly.

'Of course I care! I wouldn't want you to die, however bad our marriage was.'

'Was it so bad?'

His voice was hushed, wistful, almost yearning. How

she wished they could turn back the clock and try again.

'No,' she said softly. 'No, it wasn't so bad—at least, not for a long while. It only really fell apart at the end.'

His knuckles traced the line of her jaw, sending fire racing along her veins.

'I still loved you, even then,' he confessed.

'So why send me away?' she asked, her voice raw.

'God knows,' he said heavily. 'We were both on overload—working a hundred and twenty hours a week, hardly ever at home at the same time, too exhausted to speak to each other—we didn't stand a chance.'

There was a pause—a heavy, breathless pause, then he spoke again.

'We would now, though. We're older, wiser—we could try again.'

She eased out of his arms. Even though what he was suggesting was straight out of her own thoughts, still she knew it was impossible.

'It wouldn't work,' she told him. 'I have Jamie to think about. He must come first. I couldn't expose him to the possibility of any more heartache.'

'Why do you assume that if we got back together it would mean heartache for him?'

She stared at him in surprise. 'Well, of course it would. When you decide it's all too much effort and chuck us out——'

His eyes flickered shut, but not before she saw the pain in them.

'I'd never do that again. Anyway, I'm not suggesting we move in together yet or anything like that—just that we give ourselves time to find out if we still have something there worth working on.'

'Did we ever?' she asked bleakly.

'Oh, Emily—did it mean so little?'

Tears filled her eyes. 'Not to me. It wasn't me that moved in with someone else almost immediately.'

'Josie,' he said flatly.

'Was that her name?'

He nodded. 'Yes—that was her name. She was an SHO too—attached to the other surgical firm. She was attracted to me, and told me so. I was lonely—I took her out several times, and then she got fed up with pussyfooting around and took me back to the flat and tried to seduce me.'

'Tried?'

He laughed, a forced, painful little sound. 'Tried. She failed—or rather I did. I ended up lying in her arms crying my eyes out. Very romantic.'

'Oh, David. . .'

'She mopped me up and made me coffee and let me pour my heart out for hours, and then she told me she didn't think I ought to be living alone—I think she imagined I might do something stupid. Anyway, the upshot of it was that she moved into the spare bedroom and mothered me for the next two years.'

Emily was amazed. It was too fantastic not to be true, but why would any woman want to do that?

'Why?' she asked now.

'Why? Search me. All I know is I probably wouldn't have survived without her. I don't say I'd have tried to top myself, but I might well have starved to death or succumbed to food poisoning.'

They shared a smile of remembrance. David's housekeeping skills were strictly limited to boiling the kettle. In fact, Emily thought, looking at him, she wondered how he looked so well now unless he ate out all the time.

'I've improved,' he told her, as if he'd read her mind. 'I can't cook anything fancy, but the odd bit of steak or a grilled trout isn't beyond me any more, and even I can manage a salad and oven chips.'

Their eyes met, the rueful humour in them fading to a gentle regret.

'What happened to us, Em?' he asked gruffly. 'We were so happy at first. Was it just pressure?'

His hand came up and smoothed her cheek, and she turned her face into his palm, pressing her lips to the warm, dry skin. 'I don't know,' she mumbled. 'Maybe our love was never destined to last.'

'So why do I still love you now?' he asked softly.

Her eyes widened and she straightened up, searching his face.

'You don't,' she assured him.

'Oh, but I do.'

'No,' she protested gently. 'You might think you do, but it's just nostalgia. Once we see more of each other we'll be fighting again in no time flat. You'll see. We're incompatible, David. You know that.'

'Do I?'

'Don't you?'

'No. I love you. I've missed you. The last eight years have been a living hell.'

The gruff sincerity of his voice made her eyes fill. 'Oh, David,' she whispered. 'Don't say that. I've missed you so much.'

'Oh, Em——' He pulled her back into his arms, rocking her firmly against the hard expanse of his chest.

'You've ruined me for anyone else, you realise that, don't you?'

She twisted round and met his eyes, unable to believe what he was saying. 'What?'

'There's been no one else. After the fiasco with Josie my ego was too battered to try again for years, and then when I felt confident enough to try again I found I didn't want any other woman. None of them matched up to you.'

'But—it's been eight years. . .'

'I know.'

She was stunned. That David, of all people, could have abstained for eight years was beyond her comprehension. He had always been eager for their love-making when they were married—but then, so had she, and there had been no one for her since, either; even with Philip, whom she had married, there had been no intimacy, certainly not at first, and later, when their affection had grown, he had been too ill.

No wonder, then, that the kiss in the car had inflamed them both so rapidly and to such an extent.

'I want to kiss you again,' he said softly now.

'No,' she moaned, but he tilted her head gently and brought his lips down against hers, brushing them lightly until she yielded to his demands and opened her mouth.

With a ragged sigh he settled his mouth more firmly against hers and gave in to his instincts. His tongue sought hers and found it, suckling it, teasing it, playing tag until he grew bored and eased away, drawing her bottom lip into his mouth and suckling on it, biting it gently and then soothing it with his tongue.

By the time he lifted his head she was almost sobbing with need.

'I have to go,' he said almost roughly.

'No,' she pleaded.

'Emily, for God's sake,' he groaned, and then his hands were in her hair, his mouth clamped on hers again, their tongues embroiled in a mad dance that led to damnation.

Her body ached for him, her hands sliding feverishly under his jumper to seek the warm, firm planes of his chest.

As her fingers threaded through the soft hair he shuddered, his body trembling under her hands, and his own hands cupped her bottom and pulled her hard against him.

'Feel what you do to me,' he muttered harshly. 'Damn it, Emily, let me go before we do something we'll both regret.'

She pulled her hands away reluctantly, and as he sat up she let her eyes drift shut. Anything rather than look at him, see the flush lying on his cheekbones, the wild light in his eyes, the soft fullness of his mouth reddened from their kisses——

'Stay there. I'll see myself out.'

She listened as the door closed softly behind him, then toppled over on to the settee, still warm from his body. Hugging a cushion against her chest, she let the tears of frustration and anguish fall unheeded.

He wanted to try again. Dear God, so did she, but could she risk her heart? If it had hurt the first time, how much more could it hurt her now?

She buried her face in the cushion to muffle the sobs. Her body throbbed and ached, her heart felt as if it would burst—and upstairs, sleeping peacefully, was the reason she dared not try again.

CHAPTER FOUR

THE following morning Laurence Allen took her up to the cottage hospital to show her round. The practice took it in turns with another group in the little town to man the small casualty clinic, and each practice was responsible for its own patients in the hospital. Every day one member of the practice would visit the wards and check on the in-patients in their care, and the casualty rota was worked out on an alternating basis.

It was a pleasant little hospital, Emily thought, overlooking the wide stretch of the Bristol Channel. There was a glassed-in balcony attached to each of the wards where patients could have their meals if they were able to get up and about, and where they could sit during the day and look out over the changing sea.

On a clear day, Laurence told her, it was possible to see Wales. Today, however, there was a slight mist rolling across the water—a mist the colour of David's eyes, she thought absently, and had to drag her thoughts back in line for the umpteenth time that day.

There were eighteen beds in each of the four wards, two male and two female, and most of the beds were taken up by the elderly.

'It's halfway between a cottage hospital and a convalescent home,' Laurence told her. 'We use it for respite care, for those needing a bit more medical attention than it's possible to give them at home and for those who've been in Barnstaple at the North

Devon General and are making progress but still need hospitalisation.'

'It's a long way to travel to visit them in Barnstaple,' Emily said thoughtfully.

'It is, and people whose relatives are finding the travelling a bit much are very grateful to have this facility. We also have the odd maternity case. I don't know how long we can keep it going, though, but now we hold our own funds we can juggle where we spend the money and it stands more chance now, I suppose, provided we all agree it should remain.'

'And don't you?'

'Mostly,' he said, but didn't elaborate. She had already heard David and Robin Black talking warmly about the hospital, so assumed it must be someone from the other practice who was against the facility. Strange, she thought, because without it the demands on the medical and community staff would be much more intensive, let alone the inconvenience to relatives and the burden on the North Devon General.

'We're in the process of setting up a new scheme of emergency cover, based at the hospital, where one doctor runs an emergency clinic from after surgery till midnight every night at the hospital.'

'What about access to notes?' Emily asked, seeing pitfalls.

'No problem,' Laurence told her. 'Because the notes are all computerised, we can access them through a modem and there isn't the problem of having to cart notes around and then update the computer in the morning after home visits, and most of the patients seem quite happy with the scheme. It's cut down the number of house calls at night dramatically during our trial run, but we still run the normal service at the weekend except for a surgery Saturday and Sunday mornings. Still,' he said with a laugh, 'we're getting our patients trained. They don't call us out if they can come to us, and they get better treatment in the hospital because we've got the facilities there on the spot.'

'Makes sense.'

Laurence beamed at her. 'So glad you agree. Actually it was Maureen who thought of it—she's a real stalwart. You'll meet her in a minute. Let's go and do the clinic—want to give me a hand?'

'Sure,' she agreed.

They made their way down to the small casualty area, where the few patients had already been screened by a nurse and some had been treated without the need for medical assistance.

There was one query fractured toe, a dislocated shoulder and a splinter in an eye that needed their attention.

While the lady with the injured toe was being X-rayed, Laurence talked to the man with the dislocated shoulder.

'So, how did you do it?' he asked.

'Damn bull—I should've known better'n to try and hold the gate when he charged it. Stupid great brute. Just caught me at a funny angle.'

'Mmm.' Laurence prodded gently and the man winced.

'Sore?'

He nodded.

'Has it happened before?'

'Oh, ar—often. Like I said, should've known better.

Just give it a wrench, Doc. That's all it needs. Slips back a treat.'

Emily was sceptical, but Laurence shrugged. 'On your own head be it. Are you sure you don't want an anaesthetic?'

The man laughed. 'What? Jostle me all the way to Barnstaple just for that? Give over.'

'We could give you a muscle relaxant.'

'No—don't worry, Doc. Just a quick jerk is all it takes. The wife's done it before now.'

'OK. Are you ready?'

He nodded.

'Dr Thompson, could you grip him round the chest and steady him for me?'

Laurence took the man's arm in a firm grip, placed his foot against the man's armpit and on the count of three he applied a steady, even pull and twisted, and the head of the humerous slipped neatly back into place.

The man swore softly under his breath, sweat beading his brow, and then a nurse appeared in the doorway of the cubicle.

'Oh, Harry, not you again!'

'Hello, Maureen! Come back to see you, my love, didn't I?'

'Oh, Harry. How did you do it this time?'

'Rufus charged the gate.'

Maureen sighed. 'Playing King Canute again, were you? That bull of yours needs seeing to if you ask me—and so do you.'

Harry chuckled. 'Going to strap me up again?'

Laurence Allen nodded. 'Put it in a sling, could you,

Maureen? Thanks. Oh, by the way, this is Dr Thompson. Emily, Sister Maureen Whitaker.'

'Pleased to meet you—I gather you're a font of great knowledge and even better ideas.'

Maureen chuckled. 'Did he say that? What's the matter, Dr Allen? Trying to get me to work at the practice again?'

'Maureen, would I?' Laurence's eyes twinkled. 'Anyway, you're much too valuable here.'

'And I wouldn't dream of giving up real nursing to do smears and pre-school boosters. OK, Harry, let's have you in the treatment-room. Oh, by the way, I've put fluorescein in the eye, and the toe is fractured. The plates are on the lightbox.'

'OK. I think I'll take a look at the eye first—unless you'd like to do that?'

'I'll do whatever you want me to,' Emily told him.

'OK. Do the eye, could you? I forgot to bring my glasses, and you need clear vision and steady hands for eyes.'

Emily introduced herself to the man with the damaged eye, who was sitting with it covered by a large white handkerchief. He was in late middle age, and said his name was Frank Dooley.

She led him into a treatment-room, and a staff nurse came with her and produced a trolley already laid up for eye examination.

She laid the man down and he removed the handkerchief, revealing a streaming, firmly shut eye.

The foreign body had induced a condition known as blepharospasm, a big word, Emily always thought, for an eye that insisted on staying very sensibly and firmly shut while watering like mad to wash out the foreign body—and who could blame it? However, her first task was to persuade the man to allow her to open the eye, a mildly unpleasant procedure, so that she could examine it and anaesthetise it before removing the splinter, if indeed there was one.

Once she coaxed him into co-operation, she could see the splinter quite clearly, but under ultraviolet light the stain of the fluorescein showed no further corneal damage, thankfully.

'How did you manage it?' she asked conversationally as she carefully scanned the cornea.

'Chopping logs—my wife thought it might be nice to have a fire.'

'So when did you do it?'

'Last night. Thought it would pass, but it's been like this all night, so I thought it was time to come.'

'Past time,' Emily told him, but there was no damage done by waiting, luckily, as there might have been if the foreign body had been contaminated.

She flooded his eye with anaesthetic, waited a few moments until she could see that the eye was relaxing, then, using a sharp spatula called an eye spud, she carefully scraped the splinter out and then lifted it clear of the eye.

'Got it,' she announced, and the man sighed with relief and closed his eye.

'We'll cover it and keep it under wraps for a few days, and you'd better have some antibiotic drops with hydrocortisone in—it's called Neo-Cortef, and it'll reduce the inflammation and combat any possible infection. Whose patient are you?'

'Dr Allen's practice.'

'Oh. Right, well come in—where are we now?

Tuesday. Come in on Friday and let one of us have a look, and we'll go from there. OK?'

'Thank you, Doctor.'

She left the nurse dressing the eye and went out to find Laurence.

He was lounging in the office with Maureen, chatting over a cup of coffee.

'Perfect timing,' Maureen said to her, and pushed a full cup towards her.

'Oh, thanks. Life-saver.'

'How's the eye?'

'OK. I got the splinter out, no further damage, he's coming in on Friday for a check.'

'Good girl,' Laurence said approvingly. 'Right, finish your coffee and we'll get round the wards and see the old dears while we're here. Oh, has Amy Richardson had her baby yet?'

'No. I think she's hanging on for Christmas,' Maureen said with a twinkle.

'But it's September!' Emily said with astonishment.

'Only joking. She goes over every time. She's only got two more days before she has to go to Barnstaple to be induced, so I'm fully expecting her to walk twenty miles or something to get it going.' Maureen laughed. 'She'll try everything. One time it was Chinese take-aways, another lots of nookie—mind, that one worked.'

Laurence chuckled. 'And it's more fun than a twenty-mile walk.'

Smiling, Emily followed him along the corridor to the wards, where she was introduced to many of the patients.

'Don't try and remember them all,' Laurence advised.

Good job, Emily thought later when she was back at the surgery, because she could remember hardly any of them at all.

She did find she had one patient that day she remembered, however—Neil Blake. She couldn't imagine what he wanted, but he didn't make her wait.

'How long is this condition of my wife's going to last?' he asked her directly.

Condition? Emily thought. What condition?

'What has she told you?' Emily asked, playing for time.

'Just that until it's cleared up it's better to avoid sex, but once it's sorted we should be able to have a baby without any problem. Trouble is, when I asked her how long it would take, she got very vague. I wondered if you could help.'

Emily let out a mental sigh. Clearly the woman had told her husband a tissue of lies to hide behind, which would have been fine if he weren't here now asking her to explain. And Mrs Blake must have known he would come in—hence her question about confidentiality and him never knowing what had taken place.

Well, whatever the woman's motives, Emily was bound by the rules of confidentiality, so her secret was safe.

'I'm sorry,' she said to the man. 'I'm afraid I can't discuss your wife's condition with you without her consent——'

'She hasn't got anything wrong with her, has she? She's lying to me.'

'Mr Blake, I'm sorry, I really can't discuss it with you——'

'Damn the woman! I knew it!' He stood up and paced across the room, then whirled to face Emily. 'It's true, isn't it? She's having an affair.'

Emily sighed. 'Mr Blake, what goes on between you and your wife is nothing to do with me. I would say, though, that you didn't seem to be communicating very well yesterday when you came to see me.'

He snorted rudely. 'Dr Thompson, we don't communicate.'

'Then don't you think it would be wise to learn how to before you consider the idea of another child?'

He was silent for a moment, then he met her eyes with a level look. 'There isn't anything wrong with her, is there? Don't bother to answer; I know you can't say anything. And don't worry, I won't tell her I've been here. I won't trouble you any more. Thank you, Dr Thompson, you've been very patient.'

He left, and Emily sighed and pushed back her chair. He had been the last patient in a long and trying day, made more so by the almost total lack of sleep the night before.

The few hours of sleep that hadn't eluded her had been filled, like her waking hours, with David—only while she slept there was no rein on her emotions or her imagination.

How she was going to cope with working alongside him every day was difficult enough to fathom. If he decided to launch a sensory offensive, bombarding her with romantic gestures and tender little moments, coping would be wellnigh impossible.

And if he persisted in telling her that he loved her. . .

A tap on the door jerked her back to reality.

'Come in,' she called, and her heart thumped when she realised it was David.

'Hi.'

'Hi,' she managed.

'How are you?'

She looked away from him. His eyes were too searching, too all-seeing for her comfort.

'OK.'

He made himself at home on the edge of her desk, his lean thigh inches from her hand. She shifted it slightly before it disobeyed her and reached across to stroke the fine wool of his trousers stretched over taut, hard muscle.

'What did Neil Blake want?'

She blinked, trying desperately to concentrate. 'Neil Blake?'

'Yes—he just came to see you.'

'Um—he wanted to know how long his wife's condition was going to last.'

'Oh, hell.'

'Precisely. I told him I wasn't at liberty to divulge that information, and he had a fit. Said it was true, she was having an affair, and then told me he didn't expect me to say anything and he wouldn't tell her he'd been to see me.' She looked up at David. 'Actually, he sounded very sad.'

David nodded. 'I think he probably is. He's a faithful sort of type—not the last of the great romantics, but a good husband for all that. He doesn't really deserve this—as far as one can tell. It's difficult to judge from outside a relationship, of course—God knows it's difficult enough to judge from inside!'

She glanced down at her hands, twisting her wedding-ring again. 'Yes,' she murmured. 'It is—very difficult.'

His hand picked hers from her lap, his finger rubbing gently over the ring. 'Is this Philip's?'

She shook her head. 'No. No, it's yours.'

'Emily?' His fingers tipped her chin, bringing her eyes up to meet his. 'Indulging in sentiment?'

'I never took it off. Philip gave me another ring. I wore them together.'

Something strange happened in his eyes, something that could have been to do with pride and yet was strangely humble.

'Come for a walk with me this weekend—you and Jamie. We'll take the dogs down to Hunter's Inn and give them a run beside the river.'

'No.'

'Why? He ought to see the area. Can you remember the way?'

'I'll find it—I can map-read.'

He grinned, a little off-centre. 'So you can. I just thought it might be nice for him to have the company of the dogs.'

Wonderful for her, too, to have David's company—and with Jamie there she would be safe from the sensuous assault. She felt her defences crumbling.

'Don't try and work your way into his affections,' she warned.

'Is that a yes?'

His grin broadened, and something bright and beautiful lit his eyes. 'Thank you,' he whispered, and, bending foward he captured her lips in a fleeting kiss.

Seconds later, the door closed softly behind him.

* * *

She was on duty the following night, the Wednesday, and went up to the hospital for the emergency clinic. It was fairly quiet, but there was a steady stream of patients and she realised it would have been quite a hectic night had they all been house calls.

The odd one or two, of course, had used her as a convenient after-hours surgery, but it didn't really matter. She was there anyway, and if it meant they didn't have to take precious hours off work it couldn't really be a bad thing.

She was just packing up at midnight ready to go home when a car pulled up outside and a heavily pregnant woman was helped out and led into the reception area.

'Don't tell me—you're Amy Richardson.'

'Oh—you've heard about me.'

Emily smiled. 'Twenty-mile walk today?'

'No—five. I did fifteen yesterday.'

She paused, leaning against her husband and breathing lightly and quickly for a minute.

'It's obviously worked,' Emily said with a grin. 'Shall we take you through to the maternity-room?'

'I think that might be a good idea,' her husband said. 'She always hangs on, but once she starts there's usually no holding her.'

'How many have you got?' she asked as she led them through the quiet hospital.

'Four—this is five.'

'And definitely the last,' her husband added firmly.

'Spoilsport.'

'Amy, we're broke!'

Emily allowed herself a secret smile. There was broke, she mused, and broke. The BMW they had pulled up in was no more than a year old, the clothes they were wearing were far from chainstore seconds, and she'd lay odds that the children would have a private education.

The staff nurse on duty called the community midwife while Emily called up the notes on the computer and decided there was no need for her to panic.

Not that she was about to. The woman was clearly as strong as an ox, very used to childbirth and extremely sensible. And anyway, obstetrics was Emily's favourite speciality.

The midwife arrived just as Amy was settled into bed, and she examined her and told Emily that she expected no complications.

'You can go, if you like.'

Emily smiled. 'Do you want me to? I'm on call anyway, so I might have to leave, but I'd be happy to stay if you don't mind. I love babies.'

'Please yourself. You're very welcome. She'll do it without either of us.'

They shared a smile, and the staff nurse brought them all a cup of tea while they settled down to wait.

Amy didn't keep them long. By twelve-thirty she was getting to the end of the first stage, and at a quarter to one, with very little fuss and bother, the baby arrived, a lovely healthy boy.

'Oh, look at him, Jeremy! He's wonderful.'

'Another mouth to feed,' he grumbled, but his eyes were misted and he hugged his wife hard. 'Well done, darling.'

They turned their attention to the new arrival, and after the placenta was delivered they watched as the baby was cleaned up and checked.

'Super—they don't come better than that,' Emily said with a misty smile, and handed him back to his proud parents. 'Have you got a name for him?'

'David—what do you think?'

She swallowed the lump. 'I think that's a very good name.'

They celebrated his arrival with another cup of tea, and then Emily went home.

Even though she knew she ought to make the most of her few hours, she found it difficult to sleep. Her arms felt empty, her breasts ached, and low down there was an almost physical yearning in her womb.

Slipping out of bed, she went into Jamie's room and smoothed his hair back from his little face. She loved him dearly, but her body cried out for more.

Swallowing the tears that made her throat ache, she made her way back to bed, lay down and curled on her side, arms wrapped round her waist.

She wanted a baby, and not just any baby.

David's.

Need ripped through her, and with it anguish.

It wasn't fair! It was hard enough to resist him without her body joining forces with him and turning on her. Her biological clock, a gentle tick in the background until now, had suddenly begun to clamour.

It was a relief when the phone rang.

Saturday dawned clear, bright and with only a light breeze. It was a beautiful mid-September day, and she dressed Jamie in a thick tracksuit with a polo neck underneath. It was when she found herself vacillating over her own clothes that she pulled herself up short.

Jeans and a lambswool sweater would do fine, she told herself, and pulled them on just as the doorbell rang.

She tugged the sweater straight, flicked a brush through her hair and ran down to the hall to open the door.

He looked wonderful—tall, wind-swept, rugged—her heart crashed against her ribs until she was sure he'd see it through the fine wool of her sweater. 'Come on in—we're almost ready.'

He followed her into the kitchen where Jamie was sitting at the table with Mrs Bradley, eating cornflakes.

'Jamie, this is Dr Trevellyan. David, my son James.'

The introduction was deliberate, and David acknowledged her choice of words with a wry smile before turning his attention to the boy.

'Hello, James.'

'Hello,' Jamie mumbled round a mouthful of cereal.

'Don't talk with your mouth full,' Mrs Bradley said instantly, and softened the reprimand with a smile. 'Eat up, love, you'll keep the dogs waiting.'

He shovelled the food in quicker, clearly enthusiastic. David greeted Mrs Bradley, refused a cup of coffee and watched Emily as she slid her feet into trainers.

'I think you'll need wellies—it can get a bit muddy down by Heddon's Mouth, although it's usually OK on the path. Jamie might want to cross the river, though, and in shoes you'd have a problem.'

'OK. We'd better take something else in case of accidents.'

David chuckled. 'Very wise. Small boys and water make a fairly lively combination.'

With a smile, she put the trainers into a bag and

tugged off Jamie's shoes, putting them in there too while he gulped down the last of his milk and dragged his hand over the back of his mouth.

'Can we go, Emmy?' he said, and the enthusiasm in his voice brought a lump to her throat. It was the first time he had been keen about anything since before Philip had died, and she had despaired of ever seeing him smile again.

Not that he was smiling now, but his face was certainly more animated than of late, and the way he was fidgeting from foot to foot was a clear indicator of his excitement.

She passed him his wellies and tugged her own on, straightening up to find David watching Jamie with a strange expression on his face.

She tilted her head enquiringly, but he shook his head and picked up the bag with their shoes in.

'Right, are we done? Don't expect them back for lunch, Mrs Bradley. I'll treat them.'

'All right, Dr Trevellyan. I'll see you later, then.'

They went out to his car, a Volvo estate, to find the two dogs sitting up in the back, their faces expectant.

'OK, chaps, let's go,' David said, and after strapping Jamie in the back he slid behind the wheel and they set off.

The drive took about twenty minutes, and they parked by the river at Hunter's Inn and took the track beside the old pub down towards the sea.

Jamie ran on with the dogs, completely fearless, and Emily watched him anxiously.

'He'll be fine, Emily. Don't worry.'

'He's been so withdrawn.'

'That's only to be expected. He's had a lot to cope with. He's a lot like Sarah.'

'Isn't he? He's got Philip's curly hair, but otherwise he's the image of his mother.' She sighed. 'Sometimes I don't know if coming here was the right thing. Perhaps we should have stayed in Surrey, but he seemed to want to come to the cottage. They came here on holiday quite often before Sarah was killed, and I think his memories of it are all happy.'

'I'm sure that's very important, for him to remember the good times. We all need to do that.'

Emily swallowed. Just recently she'd been remembering the good times all too often, and her sleep had suffered as a result. She decided to change the subject.

'How are your parents?'

'Oh, OK. They've sold the farm. They're living in Putsborough now, near Croyde. They've got a little bungalow near the beach and they do B and B in the summer.'

'I can't imagine them without the farm,' Emily said thoughtfully. 'Do they miss it?'

'Dad does. Mum's relieved, I think. Of course they couldn't keep all the dogs, hence these two. Do you remember Bridie, the setter?' David asked. 'She would have been a puppy.'

Emily looked at the lovely red setter and nodded. 'Yes—your mother's dog.'

'Uh-huh. And Ruffian is Scoundrel's son.'

She remembered Scoundrel, too, a lovely Irish wolfhound with a wiry grey coat. Ruffian had the same coat, but a different, much more solid build.

'His mum was a Labrador—you never knew her. They've still got her, and Scoundrel, but when they sold the farm they had to cut back drastically. Three of the cats were found local homes, but they've still got two and the two dogs. Oh, and the donkey. We ought to take Jamie over and let him ride it.'

'He'd like that,' Emily said pensively.

'They'd love to see you again.'

The air was suddenly thick with tension. She stopped and turned to him, desperation showing in her eyes.

'David, please. Don't pressure me. I have to put Jamie first—even you can see that. Just now there isn't time in my life for trying to salvage a relationship that doesn't include him.'

'Of course it would include him,' David argued, but she shook her head.

'No. No, it wouldn't. I can't trust either of us, David, and there's no way I'd let him be hurt by our making a stupid mistake. I don't mind the odd walk like this, and I agree it's good for him to have the dogs to play with, but I won't have him hurt. Just remember that.'

His jaw worked, as if he was on the point of saying something, but then he turned on his heel, whistled the dogs and strode off towards the beach, leaving her trailing behind.

She caught up with them at the beach, to find Jamie playing inside the old lime kiln.

'Is it safe?' she asked worriedly.

'Of course. Jamie, come out now; let's go and have a look at the rock pools. There might be some sea anemones that can suck your finger. Have you ever touched one before?'

Wide-eyed, Jamie shook his head.

'Come on, then.'

David held out his hand, and after a second's hesitation Jamie slipped his smaller hand into it trustingly. Emily followed them over the rocks to the tideline, and watched as they crouched down, their two heads bent together, peering into rock pools.

'Here's one—give me your finger. It doesn't hurt; it's just like being kissed. Feel.'

'Oh!'

A delighted giggle broke loose from the child, and he turned a radiant face up to Emily.

'Emmy, come and try! It's really funny!'

A lump forming in her throat, she approached the boy and the man she loved. Crouching beside them, she let Jamie guide her finger into the open mouth of a sea anemone.

'It tickles,' she said, and her voice must have sounded odd because David shot her a strange look and then straightened up, leaving Jamie to his exploration.

'He's a lovely boy. You've taken on a hell of a lot.'

She took a steadying breath. 'I know. Still, I love him.'

David nodded. 'I can see that. You'll be good for him. I admire you.'

She almost wept.

CHAPTER FIVE

DESPITE Jamie's obvious enjoyment, Emily was glad when their outing came to an end. Watching him with David was too bittersweet to bear, and his thirst for masculine company brought back sad memories of Philip and Sarah.

All in all it was a melancholy mood she found herself in the rest of the weekend, and although she did her best to keep cheerful for Jamie she was glad when Monday came round again and she could get back to the busy routine of work.

And they were busy. After her first whole week, she was the subject of much curiosity and the influx of patients she had been expecting materialised as if by magic.

'You must be the most popular person in Biddlecombe today,' Sue told her cheerfully at their mid-morning break, and Laurence laughed.

'She's welcome to my patients, too. Just transfer them all to her—she's all they want to talk about—that and their piles.'

Chuckling, he put down his coffee-cup and left to go on his rounds. After seeing the last few patients in the emergency overspill clinic, her task today, Emily went on her own visits.

One was to a family in the area on holiday, and the man was complaining of pain in his shoulder. As he was the only driver and his wife felt he was unable to drive, Emily went to see him.

The pain turned out to be in the upper right side of his chest, had started quite suddenly and was worse when he breathed in, he said.

'Where were you when it started?' she asked him.

'We were going out—the car wouldn't start, and I had to push it while my wife sat inside to bump-start it.'

Emily examined him thoroughly, checking his pulse for irregularities, listening to his chest and sounding it for any unusual resonance, and came to the conclusion that he had probably strained his pectoral muscles. However, because of the danger of myocardial infection, she decided he ought to go to the hospital and have an ECG. 'I'll get the ambulance to pick you up,' she told him, and, having prescribed paracetamol for the pain, she left.

On returning to the surgery she went and found Robin Black, who was just on his way out for lunch.

'What should I do about this man?' she asked him. 'He's a temporary resident, but I don't want him dying of cardiac problems because I've just assumed he's strained his chest.'

'No, quite right,' Robin agreed. 'What about pneumothorax?'

She shook her head. 'No, I don't think so. It could be, but there was no reduction in breath sounds or hyper-resonance.'

'There might not be if it was small,' Robin said thoughtfully. 'I reckon you're probably right, but he ought to come in for an ECG. Have you asked transport to pick him up?'

She nodded. 'Sue's organised it.'

'Good. He'll need the temporary residence form filled in—it's probably got a number but I'm damned if I can remember it.'

'All done.'

'Good girl.' He grinned. 'Maureen will do the ECG and you can go up and check it out later. She'll see to all the details if you ring her.'

'Sue's done that, too.'

'Marvellous woman. I don't know what we'd do without her.'

'Maureen or Sue?'

He laughed. 'Either, but I meant Sue. Right, I'm off. Jill's expecting me for lunch.'

Emily, who didn't have time for lunch, felt her stomach growl in protest at the thought. She ought to grab a sandwich, but there never seemed to be time.

She finished her visits and made her way up to the hospital where she found Mr Warren in the waiting area with his wife and children.

'How is it now?' she asked him.

'Oh, pretty grim. It's getting worse if anything.'

He looked as if he was in pain, and Emily went into the office with Maureen and studied the ECG.

'It looks quite normal,' she said, puzzled but relieved. 'So not his heart, then.'

'No. How about a pneumothorax?'

Emily shrugged. 'I checked him for symptoms, but he seemed OK. I think I'll have another look, see if anything's got more obvious. Perhaps he's dislocated a rib or got intercostal neuralgia from a thoracic subluxation.'

'Pulled a muscle, even.'

'That's what I thought at first, but it shouldn't deteriorate.'

'No. Do you want me to get a bed ready?'

Emily glanced through the door at the man, now hunched over, his arms round his chest.

'It might be a good idea. That pneumothorax is looking more and more likely. Have we got a radiographer in?'

'Yes—do you want some pictures?'

'Yes, please. I'll write up the forms if you could contact her.'

'Sure.'

A few minutes later the diagnosis was confirmed on X-ray. A small, dark patch over the top of his right lung clearly indicated that air had leaked into the pleural space and was compressing his lung, causing the pain and the breathlessness he was now experiencing. It wasn't a large enough leak to justify putting in a chest drain, but Emily thought she could aspirate it with a needle.

Once he was transferred to a treatment-room, she infiltrated the site of the puncture with local anaesthetic and, using a large syringe and needle, she was able to remove most of the air, relieving his symptoms. The rest would absorb given time.

'I'm afraid you should probably spend the night in here just to be on the safe side, and the rest of the week very quietly. Have you got holiday insurance?' she asked.

He shook his head. 'No. Didn't think we'd need it.'

Emily found his wife discussing bus services to and from the area of their holiday cottage, which fortunately was in the town and so not too difficult for her to cope with the children and visiting. They might even manage to have a bit of a holiday, especially if he made a good recovery, but she was concerned about him driving them all back to London at the end of the week.

'We'll have to see how he is by then,' she told the woman, and then, having filled in the necessary papers for his admission, she made her way back to the surgery.

Once there she told Robin the outcome, and congratulated him on his diagnosis. 'How is it that everybody but me was looking for it?' she asked wryly.

'Because you were looking for something much more sinister,' he said with a laugh. 'Oh, well, it's sinister enough to wreck their holiday.'

'It must happen a lot,' she mused.

'Oh, yes. All the time, especially in the height of the summer. Tourism is our main product round here—that and clotted cream, and that's mainly for the tourists!'

'Oh, that reminds me, there's some clotted cream in the fridge for you and Laurence, Emily,' Sue told her. 'Courtesy of Harry Orr and his dislocated shoulder.'

'Oh, how kind. Jamie will love it.'

Jamie did—and so did Emily and Mrs Bradley. They abandoned sensible eating that night and feasted on scones and rich yellow clotted cream, and if Emily felt a touch queasy that evening she thought with satisfaction that she had only herself to blame.

Roy Warren and his pneumothorax made excellent progress over the next few days, and by the end of the week she felt confident letting him drive them all home.

She felt less confident, however, about David and

her relationship with him, particularly when he asked her again if they could go to his parents on Saturday afternoon so that Jamie could ride the donkey.

'They'd love to see you again, Emily. They're lonely now—it would make them so happy to see you and to have young Jamie to spoil for a couple of hours.'

'I'm not sure,' she told him, and promised to think about it, but despite her misgivings they did end up going to see the Trevellyans in Putsborough, and Jamie spent ages patting the donkey and sitting on its back while David's father patiently walked him up and down.

Emily would have hovered anxiously but Mrs T collared her and removed her to the kitchen.

'Help me with the scones,' she instructed, and although Emily knew full well that the woman needed no help at all she allowed herself to be engineered.

Anyway, it would be lovely to spend time with her in the kitchen again. They had done it so many times in the past, and if it brought a lump to Emily's throat, well, so what? So did everything else she seemed to do these days.

'You're looking well,' Mrs T said, eyeing her with undisguised curiosity. 'I was sorry to hear about Sarah—and her husband. It was very brave of you to take the child on, knowing you'd be alone.'

'I'm not really,' she protested. 'Mrs Bradley's there all the time—actually, she could probably cope perfectly well without me.'

Mrs T made a non-committal noise and plopped the bag of flour on the worktop. 'He seems a nice child.'

'He is.'

'David would have made a good father, you know.'

Emily's eyes found him through the window, hands thrust deep into the pockets of his old waxed jacket, the dogs sitting at his side.

'Yes, I know,' she said quietly. The biological ache started again, low down, and she almost groaned aloud.

'You should have had children. Maybe then you wouldn't have given up so easily.'

'Mrs T, please,' Emily pleaded, close to tears, and the woman sighed and backed off.

'Sorry. I didn't realise it still hurt you, too.'

She chewed her lip. 'David said there'd been no one else.'

'Not as far as I know, and I'm sure he would have said. Not since Josie, anyway. He hasn't seemed to want to bother.' She spooned flour into a bowl, cut a big chunk of butter off the block and dropped it in, then plunged her plump hands into the mixture. 'Of course, you know he wants to marry you again.'

Emily's heart thumped.

'Has he said so?'

Mrs T's hands stopped and she turned slightly, regarding Emily thoughtfully over her shoulder. 'Does he need to?'

She sighed. 'Probably not. Mrs T, I can't. I have to care for Jamie now, and I can't let my personal life influence my decisions about what's best for him.'

She snorted. 'Isn't it best for Jamie that his mother should be happy?'

'Exactly. David didn't always make me happy, Mrs T—nor I him. There were often times when we were both miserable.'

'Lack of communication.'

'Quite. What makes you think we'd be any better now?'

She snorted again. 'Seems to me a great waste of being alive if you don't bother to learn from your mistakes.'

'Meaning?'

She gave up any pretence of making the scones. 'Meaning that you'd try harder this time, make more effort to communicate your thoughts and feelings. Last time you made too many assumptions.'

'Perhaps you are now,' Emily said quietly. 'Perhaps it isn't what I want.'

'Still lying to yourself? Oh, well, you'll come round. He's got a persuasive tongue.'

Emily thought of his kisses, and flushed. Mrs T, however, had turned back to her scones and missed the tell-tale colouring, to Emily's enormous relief.

She set the table while Mrs T cut out the scones and popped them in the oven, then ladled out great dollops of clotted cream and home-made strawberry jam.

'They'll be ready in a minute,' she said, putting the kettle on. 'Better get the menfolk in. They'll all need to wash their hands.'

A tap on the window brought a nod of acknowledgment from the men in the garden, and David lifted Jamie down while his father led the donkey back to her stable and fed her.

They came in, Jamie beaming, and after a great production of hand-washing they settled down to have tea together. It was a cheerful, friendly meal, and Jamie ate hugely, to Emily's relief. He had been picky of late, but today he tucked into the ham sandwiches and scones and cream.

'He's eaten well,' Mrs T said as they were leaving.

'All that fresh air,' Mr T said with a wink, and Emily smiled at him.

'Thank you for letting him ride Topsy. I'm sure he's had a lovely time.'

'I have—thank you ever so much,' Jamie said, his eager face tipped up to David's father. 'Can we do it again?'

Mr T bent over and knuckled the boy's hair gently. 'Of course you can, son. Any time you like.'

'We'll see, Jamie. We don't want to be a nuisance.'

'He's not a nuisance—he's a delight, and more than welcome—and so are you,' Mr T added.

Emily looked helplessly at David, but he smiled innocently and let her struggle.

'You're very kind,' she managed, her voice choked.

'Come on, Jamie, let's strap you in,' David said finally, and opened the car door.

'Seems to me if you want the child to be happy you're worrying about all the wrong things,' Mrs T said. 'Give him a chance, Emily. He's a good man. He's older now, and wiser. And he does love you.'

She saw tears glitter in the older woman's eyes, and turned away. 'Thank you for a lovely tea,' she said as she climbed into the car. 'We'll be in touch, I expect.'

She shut the door, staring stonily ahead, and David climbed in beside her and started the engine, pulling away with a wave.

'She been giving you a hard time?' he said softly.

'What do you think?'

His hand came out and found hers, clenched tightly on her lap. 'I'm sorry. I should have warned her to leave you alone.'

'She means well.' The feel of David's hand on hers was warm and comforting, and she was almost sorry when they reached a junction and he removed it so that he could drive.

She didn't ask him in when they got back, and he didn't press it, just dropping them off and driving away.

Jamie watched them go, then turned to the house with a sigh. 'I wish we could have a dog like Ruffian or Bridie.'

'Maybe we can, one day,' she said. She'd been thinking about it for some time, and his whole-hearted response to David's dogs had made her more sure that it was the right thing to do. They were just so devoted and uncritical, she thought, loving you regardless of your mistakes and failings. Perhaps she ought to have one!

During the course of the following week she met Jenny Wellcome, the wife of the man who was having an affair with Ann Blake.

Her MS had flared up again, leaving her even weaker, and the spasticity in her limbs had increased despite the Baclofen.

As Emily drove up to the farm, she found herself curious to meet the man Ann Blake would sacrifice her marriage for, and the woman he was too devoted to to leave.

She was met at the gate by a man who introduced himself as Richard Wellcome. He was of medium height, balding, older than she had expected—not in any way the sort of person she would have anticipated would appeal to Ann Blake. And yet his eyes were filled with a wealth of kindliness, tinged with despair. There was a dog beside him, leaning against his leg, clearly his shadow.

'How is your wife?' Emily asked him.

He sighed, his shoulders lifting in a helpless shrug. His hand automatically found the dog's head and rested there, as if for comfort. 'She seems to be going downhill fast. I don't know—I just get the feeling she won't be here much longer.'

'I'm sorry,' Emily said quietly, and he met her eyes, his own full of sorrow.

'So am I. Whatever you might have heard, I do love her.'

'I know.'

They exchanged a smile of understanding, and she followed him into the little farmhouse.

Jenny was in a makeshift bed by the fire, a hoist near by for lifting her in and out, and as they went in she turned her head and gave a slightly lop-sided smile.

'You must be Dr Thompson. I'm Jenny Wellcome.'

'Hello, Mrs Wellcome.'

She crossed the room and took the frail hand in her own much stronger grip. 'It's nice to meet you. What can I do for you this morning?'

'I wanted to talk to you about something. I would have preferred to see David, but he wasn't on duty and I didn't feel it should wait. Richard, you couldn't make us a cup of coffee and then leave us for a while, could you, love?'

'Of course.'

He went quietly out, and they could hear him pottering in the kitchen, muttering gently at the dog who was obviously underfoot.

'Shall I check you over while I'm here? David tells me your Baclofen wasn't working and he'd increased the dose. Does the stiffness seem any better?'

'Oh, that Baclofen's hopeless. I drop things all the time now.'

'That may not be the muscle relaxant, of course.'

'You mean it could be another area of attack?'

'It's possible.'

'I don't think so. It doesn't feel the same. My legs have gone now, this time. I can't feel them at all, and I don't even know when I've wet myself any more.'

Her voice was flat, accepting, and Emily found her courage rather humbling.

Richard came back in then, set down the coffee and hovered anxiously.

'Can you manage it?'

'I'll help her,' Emily said with a reassuring smile. 'Don't worry. I'll come and find you before I leave.'

He nodded, kissed his wife with every appearance of devotion and left them alone.

'Have you been here long enough to garner the gossip?' Jenny asked after a moment.

'Gossip?' Emily said, dreading what was coming next.

'About Richard and Ann Blake?'

'I don't listen to gossip.'

'You should. They've been having an affair for months. She's a nice woman. Pity about the little girl, though.'

Emily didn't know what to say, but it seemed Jenny was quite happy with her silence.

'I understand, you know,' she told Emily. 'He's a very passionate man, and I'm no good to him any more—not like that. He's worried, too, about the farm. Things aren't good. He doesn't realise that I know, but he ought to sell up and cut his losses. He won't talk to me about it, though, because it's my farm and he doesn't want to worry me or let me down.' She gave a small, wry laugh.

'He's always unhappy after he's been with her. Guilty, I suppose. I know about guilt. I have to live with it every day. I'm ruining his life. If it weren't for me he would have been able to concentrate on the farm, maybe turn it around. This hoist was expensive, too, but it means I can get myself in and out of bed. Well, I could. I can't now, and most of the time it just stands there mocking me.'

She gave a shaky sigh. 'You can't imagine what it's like to lose your independence.'

'Oh, I can,' Emily assured her. 'My husband was very ill with cancer for nearly a year before he died, and he became very dependent by the end. I think I was closer to him then than I've ever been to anyone. We talked all the time. It was very important to us both, and I think he helped me to understand a great deal.'

'Richard and I used to talk,' she said softly. 'We used to discuss everything, but since I've been ill he carries everything alone. That's why I don't mind about Ann—he needs someone to lean on, and if it can't be me it might as well be her.'

Emily found her philosophical attitude and selflessness very humbling. To lie there and know you had lost your husband to another woman, without any weapons to fight for him, must be savagely painful.

She helped her drink her coffee, and when she set

the cup down and blotted Jenny's lips the woman smiled.

'Thank you. That was lovely.' Her eyes flicked across to the bureau beside the television. 'Could you do something for me? In that bureau, at the back, behind all the papers is a document. I want you to see it, and attach it to my notes.'

Emily got up and opened the bureau, pulling forward the clutter of old letters, bills and other paraphernalia until she found a sealed envelope.

'Is this it?'

Jenny nodded. 'Yes, that's the one. Open it.'

She sat down again on the edge of the bed and carefully slit the envelope, pulling out the single sheet of paper.

'It's a living will,' Jenny said quietly. 'I don't want any further treatment. I don't mind alleviation of my symptoms, I'm not heroic enough to want to suffer, but I don't want any treatment that will extend my life. No antibiotics, no other fancy drugs—enough's enough. We've all reached the end of our rope. When I come to the point where I'm no longer mentally competent, I want that document to stand as an advance directive of my wishes—and I don't want Richard overruling it.'

She had clearly done her homework, Emily thought as she scanned the document. 'Have you discussed this with your husband?' she asked.

'No. He wouldn't agree.'

'Maybe you should talk it over.'

'No.' The woman was adamant. 'He feels bad enough. I don't want him finding out—I want him to think it was inevitable. Anyway, nothing's going to happen for ages. It's just insurance.'

Emily was concerned. 'Please talk it over with him. It's your life, and if it's intolerable, then I believe you have the right to make a decision about prolonging it artifically, but I don't think it's a decision you should make alone.'

Jenny shook her head. 'You don't understand. Richard gets depressed. He's been ill. He can't cope with this sort of thing; he finds it too distressing. I wouldn't want him to have to carry the burden of being part of the decision.'

Emily nodded. 'OK. I'll talk to Dr Trevellyan. I imagine he'll want to discuss it with you himself, but I'll take it now and attach it to your notes.'

She put it in her bag.

'Richard'll want to know what we were talking about,' Jenny told her. 'Could you lie to him? Tell him I wanted to ask you about my periods and thought it might embarrass him?'

'Would it?'

She smiled. 'Possibly. You can just be evasive, if you'd rather, let me do the lying.'

Emily stood up and snapped her bag shut. 'I wish you'd tell him the truth.'

'No. Don't worry, I'll deal with him. Thank you for coming.'

'My pleasure. I'll see you again.'

She let herself out, and the dog gave a sharp woof and trotted over to her, followed more slowly by Richard.

'Everything all right?' he asked.

She nodded. 'Jenny just wanted to chat about something.'

'There's nothing new? Nothing I should know about?'

She decided to answer the first part of the question only. 'No, nothing new. She's unhappy with the Baclofen. It's a difficult compromise.'

'The whole damn thing's a difficult compromise,' Richard said heavily, and then forced a smile. 'Well, thank you for coming, Dr Thompson. And thank you for being so good with Ann the other day.'

She gave him a smile as forced as his own had been, but didn't answer. What could she say? Unhappy with the whole situation, she began to believe David was right when he said she should have as little to do with it as possible.

Climbing back into her car, she set off down the hill towards the surgery, and on the way passed David's cottage. His car was outside, and on imuplse she pulled up and went to the door.

He opened it almost immediately. 'Emily! Come on in.' He held the door for her, his face registering surprise. 'What brings you here?'

'This.' She pulled the document out of her bag, watched him scan it and then shrugged when he raised an enquiring eyebrow.

'She wanted to see you, really, but she didn't want to wait. I checked her over—there was no sign of an infection that I could see, but I wondered if she was feeling off colour and thought she'd get that in quick before she went down with flu or something.'

'She shouldn't—she's had a jab already. I know it's early, but she can't cope with that sort of infection.

Perhaps she's worried she'll get brainstem involvement and lose her ability to communicate. Had lunch?'

'No—no, I haven't.'

'I was just about to heat up some soup. Want to join me?'

'I ought to let the surgery know where I am.'

'Phone's there. Cream of chicken OK?'

'Fine.'

She rang the surgery and then followed him into the kitchen. Bridie lifted her head and wagged her tail, Ruffian opened one eye, yawned and carried on sleeping. She sat down at the table and watched David struggle as he sliced bread and laid it in a wire frame, then clamped it under the lid of the Aga. Perversely, he was heating the soup in the microwave.

As if he saw the irony, he grinned. 'Old meets new. The toast tastes better this way,' he explained.

He dished up, joined her at the table and then dipped a piece of toast into the soup. 'So, what did you make of the situation?'

'Awful.' She told him about her conversation with Jenny, and how she knew about the affair, and David sighed.

'Oh, dear.'

'She seemed very accepting.'

'Difficult to see how she could be anything else.'

'Mmm. Anyway, I said I'd talk to you about it.'

'Thanks. I'll go and see her. Have you forgiven my mother yet, by the way?'

She blinked. 'Your mother?'

'For the third degree.'

'Oh, that.' She laughed. 'It was nothing. She just

loves you, and she loves happy endings. It would be nice and tidy, I suppose.'

He made a non-committal noise and wiped his bowl with the last scrap of toast.

'That was delicious,' she said, to change the subject. 'Don't tell me you made it.'

'No, Mum did. She does batches for me for the freezer. Want some more?'

She shook her head. 'I ought to be getting back.'

'Why? They can call you. Have a cup of coffee and a bit of Mum's fruit cake.'

She gave a low laugh. 'You know just how to push my buttons, don't you? I love her fruit cake.'

'I know. Do you blame me for using underhand tricks?'

Suddenly the tension crackled between them. Their eyes were locked, their breath halted.

'I'm going to kiss you,' he warned, and, pulling her gently to her feet, he drew her into his arms and locked his hands together behind her back, easing her against him.

Desire, hot and sweet, sprang to life inside her. Mesmerised, unable to turn away even though she knew she should, she watched as his mouth came slowly down. As it closed over hers, her lids fluttered shut and a tiny sigh escaped her.

She gave up all attempts at reason, ignoring her conscience, her common sense, everything—nothing mattered any more, only the feel of his mouth, the warm, velvet sweep of his tongue, the hard jut of his body locked against hers.

The phone ringing in the background was shattering.

They broke apart, their breath dragged in in painful

gasps, eyes locked. Finally he turned and lifted the receiver.

'Trevellyan—yes, she's here.'

He held the receiver out to her, and pushed a pad and pencil towards her. Shaking, her hand refusing to co-operate, she jotted down the address of the patient and rough directions.

'I have to go,' she told him. 'A farming accident—Joe Hardwill?'

'Joe? I'll come. We'll take my car; it's a bit tricky to find.'

She went without question, and as they wiggled across Exmoor she was glad she didn't have to find the way herself. As they turned into the farmyard several dogs bounded to greet them, followed by a panic-stricken woman in her late fifties.

'Oh, Dr Trevellyan, thank God you're here. It's Joe—he's turned the tractor over in the top field. I think he's dead!'

CHAPTER SIX

JOE was still alive when they reached him, but he was in a serious condition and David was worried.

'When did it happen?' he asked the man's desperate wife.

'I don't know—I expected him in for his dinner at twelve. Well, he's never late, Doctor—not for his dinner. By twelve-thirty I was really getting worried, because his chest has been getting to him again.'

David frowned. The man's colour was poor, his lips slightly blue. He was lying under the huge mudguard of the tractor, but by a miracle he had been thrown into a hollow. Although he was trapped by the legs, his chest wasn't compressed unduly, and that gave him more chance. How long he'd been there, though, was anybody's guess. Something between one and three hours, Mrs Hardwill thought, since he had been in for breakfast at nine-thirty and had come out again at ten. It was now a little after one.

'The ambulance is on its way from Barnstaple,' Mrs Hardwill told them, 'and Sam next door is getting his tractor to lift the Fordson off, but—oh, Dr Trevellyan, tell me he's going to be all right.'

David straightened and squeezed her shoulder reassuringly. 'We'll do all we can. Why don't you go back and wait for the ambulance? They might be able to drive fairly close.'

With a brisk nod she turned away, her panic eased by the performance of a necessary task.

Keep everyone busy, give people a job to do to occupy their minds. It was the old training ethic of emergency procedure, and Emily was pleased to see it work on Joe's wife.

'What can I do?' she asked David.

'We need to get a line in and get some plasma expander into him. I think he's got multiple leg fractures, almost certainly—he'll need an op, and a good anaesthetic risk he ain't. We'd better do all we can for him, though.'

They worked in silence, except for the odd necessary comment, and by the time the intravenous line was in and fluid was running into him they could hear the ambulance approaching up the valley, its siren going.

'Good. Now all we need is to get him out and off to hospital. The orthopods can glue him together. Ah, here's the tractor.'

David stood up and waved to Sam, who manoeuvred his tractor so that it was on the other side, facing away, and then jumped down and ran round.

'How is he?'

'Rough. The ambulance is here. I think the best thing is to wait till they've got a stretcher, then lift the tractor a little and I'll crawl under and check him before we pull him out. I don't want you lifting it too far and doing any more harm if his leg is stuck in the wheel or anything.'

Emily's heart nearly stopped at his words. Crawl under? It could slip, lose traction in the mud and crash back down on him, killing him.

She bit her lip. There was no point in arguing. It was

her or him, and the men would all shoot themselves before they'd allow a woman to perform such a dangerous act. So she swallowed her fear, and when the time came she held the bag of plasma expander and her breath, and watched him as he wriggled face down in the mud to a point where he could see the legs.

'OK, lift a bit more—that's fine! Chock it at that point!'

They quickly pushed broad timbers under the tractor, wedging it up, and then David and the paramedic carefully eased Joe on to the stretcher and slid it out from under the tractor. He moaned slightly and then was silent again, and David's face was grave.

'Right, I think he needs to go in fast,' he said. 'Right tib and fib have gone, and the left femur, I should say. Maybe pelvis, too. He's a chronic bronchitic, recent bout of bronchitis that didn't respond terribly well to antibiotics. Probably pseudomonas. Oh, and he's a heavy smoker.'

'Aren't they all,' the paramedic grunted as he splinted the legs. 'Right, let's get him away before he comes round and starts to hurt.'

They loaded him into the ambulance, and Mrs Hardwill climbed in after them, a small, weary suitcase clutched in her hand.

'Poor old boy. Do you think he'll make it?' Emily asked as they followed the ambulance slowly back along the track to the farm.

'God knows. Probably not. He's a disagreeable old blighter, but he's got a certain amount of charm nevertheless.'

They reached the car, and David gave his clothes a cursory glance before getting into the car.

'You'll ruin the upholstery.'

'It's only mud. It'll brush off. The red earth round Wiveliscombe is much worse.'

She admired his philosophical attitude—and his courage. Suddenly, the danger passed, she began to shake almost uncontrollably.

'Are you OK?' he asked, turning his head to glance at her.

'Just reaction.'

'It was fairly gruesome. Sorry.'

'Not the accident,' she said, her voice unsteady. 'You crawling under that thing like that.'

He shot her another look, this one compounded of disbelief and curiosity. 'Worrying about me, Emily? Such progress.'

'Don't be stupid,' she muttered. 'I'd worry about anyone.'

His smile was wry. 'And there I was hoping it was because of your undying love for me.'

Little did he know. . .

Joe Hardwill survived the operation to pin his femur and plate his lower leg, but only just. He was in Intensive Care on a ventilator for over a week, and it was some time before the danger of pneumonia was past.

David went to see him in Barnstaple, and reported his disgust at having been unconscious and missing Emily.

'I think he's looking forward to meeting you,' David said with a teasing laugh. 'You'll have plenty of chance—once he's a bit better he'll be discharged to the cottage hospital under our tender ministrations.

You can go and make friends with him and try and persuade him to stop smoking.'

'He's not still smoking now!'

'He's trying—the sister caught one of his visitors giving him a crafty drag the day before yesterday. I think she nearly flayed him alive!'

'I should hope so! What an idiot!'

David sighed. 'Ah, Emily, he's just an old man. You'll like him. He says he hears you're the prettiest thing to happen to Biddlecombe since he brought his wife home forty years ago.'

She blushed and laughed. 'I hope you set him straight.'

'Oh, yes—I told him that, delightful though his wife was, you had her beaten into a cocked hat.'

'David! You didn't!'

He laughed. 'No, of course I didn't, but I could have done.' His face changed, the laughter giving way to something softer and infinitely more tender. 'Oh, Emily. I've missed you.'

'David, please. . . Not here.'

'Where, then?'

Her heart thumped. 'Nowhere. I've told you, it won't work.'

'Not if you won't give it a chance,' he agreed. 'Oh, well, you're right. This isn't the time or the place. I've got an antenatal clinic, and you've got a family planning clinic. We'd better get to it.'

The family planning clinic was interesting, a mixed bag of different ages and requirements.

She fitted an IUCD with the help of Eve Jenkins, the practice nurse, and then measured for, fitted and checked the insertion of a diaphragm, advised one woman of thirty-five who was an ex-smoker to come off the Pill and consider some other form of contraception, and then fitted another IUCD in a twenty-year old who was unable to take the Pill because of family history.

A busy afternoon, and by the time her surgery came round she was tired and hungry.

The last patient was a surprise. She was young, still fifteen, and came on her own without her mother. It was a general surgery, and Emily wondered what had brought her.

However, as soon as she came in, alarm bells rang. The girl looked so uncomfortable, almost as if coming had been a mistake. Emily tried to set her at her ease.

'Hello, Clare—can I call you Clare?' she asked.

She nodded, giving little away.

'So, Clare, what can I do for you?'

'Um—I wondered—can you put me on the Pill?'

Emily put down her pen, leant back in her chair and studied Clare's face. She looked embarrassed and awkward, as well she might, discussing this rather difficult topic for possibly the first time.

'How old are you?' Emily asked her, although she knew full well.

'Nearly sixteen.'

'And are you already in a sexual relationship, Clare?'

She nodded, blushing.

'And what are you doing at the moment about contraception?'

She shrugged diffidently. 'He uses something—well, mostly.'

'Mostly?'

'Well, sometimes he's run out.'

'You do realise that could get you pregnant?'

The girl's eyes were scornful as only a teenager's could be. She was also highly defensive.

'Of course—why do you think I'm here? Oh, it's hopeless—I knew you'd say no!'

She stood up and was about to flounce out of the room when Emily called her back.

'Clare, sit down and discuss this with me like a mature adult. That is, after all, how you want to be treated, isn't it?'

The girl subsided. 'Sorry.'

'That's OK. I know it's difficult. Now, there is one very important point I have to make. This boy that you're having the relationship with—you do both realise that he's breaking the law, don't you?'

She nodded. 'It's so outdated, though. Everybody does it these days.'

'I'm sure not everybody does,' Emily argued gently. 'It just seems like it. Now, there are all sorts of things I have to discuss with you. Do you know that being on the Pill can have side-effects?'

'Such as?'

She outlined the problems, the need to take it regularly and without fail, the physical and psychological effects of early intercourse, and the need to involve her parents in her decision.

'No!' she said to this last point. 'I couldn't! Dad'd kill him!'

'You must face the possibility that they could find out. What if they find your pills? Wouldn't it be better to have their knowledge and consent? They might not like it, but they are your parents and they love you. Doesn't their opinion matter to you?'

'They're old and stuffy—they wouldn't understand.'

Emily smiled gently. 'I think you might be surprised. If you tackle it head-on, like an adult, they might well respond better than if you sneak round behind their backs and they find out later by accident. Most parents do find out, you know.'

She was thoughtful for a moment, but then shook her head. 'No. They'd die, and so would Gran. I couldn't handle telling them. Put it like this—either you put me on the Pill or sooner or later I'll get pregnant by accident. It's a miracle it hasn't happened already.'

'Are you sure it hasn't?'

She nodded. 'Yes. I'm all right, I've just finished a period.'

'OK. I'll examine you, make sure everything's all right and ask you a few questions about your family history, then if I think you're able to take it I'll put you on a low-dose pill, but you must take it without fail, and if you forget or you have a tummy bug or feel sick or for any reason take it late you must use condoms for the rest of the cycle. On the other hand, you could, of course, have a diaphragm.'

'A cap? Yuck, no! One of my friends had one, and she said the cream goes everywhere and it stinks, and half the time she can't get it in—anyway, she's pregnant now, so that's no good!'

Emily gave up. The girl was clearly informed, knew what she wanted and was likely to get pregnant if she resisted prescribing. She examined her thoroughly, took a complete history and then prescribed a low-dose pill.

Repeating the warnings about taking it regularly,

and still with some misgivings, she sent the girl on her way.

Moments later David came in.

'Fancy a drink?'

'No, I must get back. Sorry. Perhaps another night.'

He looked disappointed, and for a second she regretted her refusal. Why shouldn't she go out for a drink with him? It hardly counted as a reconciliation, did it? And it couldn't harm Jamie.

'What did Clare want?'

'Oh—to go on the Pill.'

'What?'

She was startled by his reaction. 'Do you know her?'

'Yes—her grandmother lives with them and I visit her regularly. I know the whole family. Clare's often there. They'll go off the deep end, you know. I hope you've covered yourself in scrupulous depth.'

'Don't tell me—they're Catholics.'

'Catholics? He's a Baptist. He makes the average Catholic look like something out of Sodom and Gomorrah.'

Emily groaned. 'Oh, no. David, she's already sleeping with the boy.'

He sighed and stabbed his fingers through his hair. 'Well, God help you when her father finds out, is all I can say. What did you advise her?'

'Anything and everything but.'

'You could have simply refused.'

'And had another teenage pregnancy on my conscience? No way. I'll brave his wrath if necessary. He can only sue me.'

David laughed. 'Oh, Em. Come on, have a drink. You look as if you could do with it.'

She shook her head. 'What I could do with is a hot bath, a warm drink and a lazy hour by the fire.'

Something flickered in his eyes.

'Sounds inviting. Want to share?'

'David. . .'

Her protest was breathy and without conviction.

'We never did finish that kiss the other day,' he said softly.

She backed away, her heart thumping. 'Please—stop it. It's unfair.'

'I quite agree. I don't know why we keep beating about the bush. Perhaps we should just get it out of our systems. Then maybe we could both get on with our lives.'

He turned on his heel and strode away, frustration in every line of his body, and Emily sagged against her desk and wondered if her foolish heart would ever stop yearning for what it couldn't have.

The autumn wore on, filling the wooded valleys with a blaze of glorious colour, the reds and golds brilliant in the late October sunshine.

Jamie was on holiday, a week for half-term, and Emily had a day off on the Tuesday and took him to Watermouth Castle just outside Ilfracombe. They listened to the old musical instruments, marvelled at the kitchen implements of yesteryear, spent a small fortune on the old slot machines and were frightened to death by the animated displays of smugglers and witches.

Out in the garden there were more animated displays, little gnomes all busy about their work, and a playground with a tube slide that Jamie decided was the most wonderful thing in the world.

After he had had a dozen goes Emily managed to drag him away, and she took him then as promised to Putsborough, to have tea with David's parents.

'Can I ride the donkey?' he pleaded, and so David's father took him out into the paddock while Emily swallowed her panic and prayed that Mrs T wouldn't give her the third degree again.

She didn't. Instead she apologised for doing so last time, and then showed Emily a tapestry she was doing to while away the evenings.

'It seems so strange not having the chickens to worry about, and the calves to feed.'

'You must miss the farm.'

'Yes and no. We're happy here, and we see more of David. It was too much for Bill to cope with any longer, anyway, so we had no choice, but we couldn't part with Topsy and when we have children staying in the summer we let them have rides. Bill loves it. He's just a natural grandfather.'

Emily's eyes misted as she watched the old man leading Topsy up the paddock, Jamie's skinny legs dangling down her round sides, a broad grin on his face.

He said something, and David's father turned and laughed, looking so like his son that a pain stabbed through her.

'Oh, Emily—you still love him, don't you?' Mrs T said softly, and she nodded.

'Yes. Yes, I do. It isn't always enough, though, is it?'

'Not when you're too pigheaded to let it be, no,' Mrs T said calmly, and picked up the kettle. 'Time for tea, I think.'

Emily said nothing. How could she make the woman understand? Her rows with David had been bitter and vitriolic, the gulf between them unbreachable. How could she expose Jamie to that, after all he'd been through?

She couldn't, was the simple answer.

With a deep sigh that expressed more than words, she turned away from the window and forced a small smile.

'I'll lay the table, shall I?'

Mrs T said nothing, merely gave a sad, understanding smile and nodded.

They didn't linger over tea, because Mrs Bradley was due to have a few days off and Jamie was going to stay with Philip's parents in Surrey until Saturday. They were leaving early the following morning, and she wanted him to have a good night's sleep.

How she would cope with the emptiness of the cottage she wasn't at all sure. She would have to find herself something to do—perhaps tapestry, like Mrs T, or hire a few hundred videos and tune out the world.

Even so, she would have to sleep, and that was always the worst part. . .

Jenny Wellcome's husband phoned the following day to say that his wife was complaining of double vision and giddiness.

'Brainstem involvement,' David said heavily. 'Oh, hell.'

'Do you think she knew it was coming?' Emily asked.

'Possibly. I don't suppose for a moment she's discussed her living will with him.'

He left to see her, and reported afterwards that she was confused and lacked co-ordination in her hands.

'She's also finding breathing a bit harder. She might have the beginnings of a chest infection. Are you on duty tonight?'

'Yes, I am. Why? Do you want me to look in on her?'

He shrugged. 'I might admit her. I'll go and see her myself again later, and if I think she should come in I'll try and talk her into it, but I imagine she'll resist.'

By five that night she had deteriorated, and David admitted her—albeit reluctantly—to the cottage hospital. Emily went and saw her later, while she was at the hospital for the emergency clinic, and found her frail but stubborn.

'I won't have any antibiotics,' she warned her. 'Don't you let Richard talk you into it. If this is it, fine. I'm ready.'

'You're sure?' Emily asked her.

There was no hesitation. 'Yes, I'm sure. I've had enough. It's time to go.'

Maureen was on duty, and Emily made sure she was aware of Jenny's wishes.

'Oh, hell,' the sister groaned. 'Wait till Richard hears. It'll really hit the fan.'

He did hear—later that evening when he came back to the hospital to say goodnight to his wife and found that she had developed a temperature and was showing signs of a chest infection.

Emily was called to the ward to talk to him, and she phoned David.

'Perhaps you'd like to come and deal with this as he's your patient. He's very upset.'

He was indeed upset, and wanted to talk to his wife about it, but by then she was too ill to concentrate and simply pleaded with him to sit with her. 'Just hold me,' she whispered, and Emily and David watched helplessly as Richard screwed his eyes shut and wrapped his arms tenderly round his wife.

'Please, Jenny, don't leave me,' he murmured brokenly, and they went into the office, leaving the couple with their privacy.

'Are we doing the right thing?' David asked softly.

'Of course. It's what she wants. We have no choice. As the doctor on duty I can't go ahead and treat her against her wishes, knowing how she felt about this at a time when she was perfectly lucid. She's still lucid enough now to change her mind if she wants to, but I don't think she does.'

'Are you absolutely sure? You'll have to live with it on your conscience, Emily.'

'And would that be any harder than living with the knowledge that I'd preserved her, like a vegetable, kept under the most appropriate storage conditions—irradiated if necessary to maintain her freshness?'

She couldn't keep the sarcasm out of her voice, and David gave a sharp sigh.

'Don't fight with me. I'm not arguing against you, just trying to examine all the aspects while there's still time.'

'But there isn't. Time for Jenny ran out years ago. Let her go, David. Please. Give her her dignity.'

He was silent for a long time, then he sighed.

'I'll go and talk to Richard. Carry on with your clinic, I'll take over here.'

'David?'

He turned back to her, his face sober. 'Don't worry, Emily. I'll respect her wishes.'

She felt her shoulders droop with the relief of tension. She had been so afraid that he would disagree and override Jenny's wishes, not only for Jenny's sake but for her own, because that would mean he doubted her professional competence, and for some obscure reason his faith in her judgement meant a great deal to her.

She finished her clinic and went back to the ward, to find Jenny still in much the same state and Richard sitting beside her, holding her hand, his face tortured.

She didn't disturb them, there didn't seem any point, so she asked Maureen to contact her if there was any change and made her way out to her car.

The night was cold, and as she walked out of the hospital she realised that the mist which had hovered over the sea all day had rolled in up the valley, blanketing the land with thick fog.

It was a night like the night on which Sarah had died, and as she drove carefully towards her cottage she found herself panicking. What if she lost her way? Perhaps she already had?

Her headlights just seemed to make the fog worse, and she switched them off, crawling forward by the dim glow of her side-lights and the moon overhead.

The road was muddy, rutted in places where tractors had turned out of the fields, and after a while she realised she was helplessly, hopelessly lost.

Somewhere back there she had made a wrong turning, and her only hope was to turn round and head back to the town.

She stopped the car and got out, checking behind

her, and then carefully reversed off the road into a gateway.

So far so good, she thought, and then as she pulled forward there was a slither and a crash and the car slipped sideways with a sickening lurch.

Stunned, she lay against her door, her lights pointing up into the sky, and let her heart steady. She was all right. She must have misjudged the gateway and turned into a ditch. She would be all right, she would. All she had to do was climb out of the car and walk back towards town. That was all. . .

Turning off the ignition and pocketing the keys, she clambered awkwardly across the tilted seats, and paused. She couldn't hold the door open and climb out, she realised, so she wound down the window and struggled through the little gap, dragging her medical bag behind her. She would need that. She could use the light from her little torch to help see the way—if the battery lasted long enough. . .

She stuffed her fist in her mouth to stifle the sob. Where was she, for heaven's sake? She didn't even know for sure which way the town was!

Downhill, her brain told her. Trembling, her legs still weak from reaction, she turned downhill and slowly, stumbling over the verge from time to time, she began to walk.

She came to a junction and read the sign, then read it again. She was near David's house! Surely this was the lane that led past his cottage! If she could only find it, she would be safe.

Shivering, the cold air seeping through her coat, she began to walk uphill again, away from the town.

Was she right? After a while her brain began to play

tricks on her, and she paused. Downhill was the town. If she was wrong, and this wasn't the lane, she could be walking round in the fog for hours!

Just then there was a teasing breath of wind, and, like a tearing of gauze, the fog lifted for a moment and she saw a cottage, the outside light glowing like a beacon, calling her.

She started to run, her heart pounding, and as she reached the cottage she stumbled and fell against the door.

'David!' she sobbed. 'David!'

The door opened and she fell inside, into his arms.

'Emily? For God's sake, what's happened?'

'I got lost in the fog—I put my car in a ditch and I couldn't find you——'

The sobs refused to be held back, and he scooped her up in his arms and carried her into the sitting-room, flicking on the light as he went.

'Are you all right? Are you hurt?'

She shook her head. 'No—just—oh, I'm being so stupid. . .'

'Shh. You've had a fright. You're OK now, I've got you. You'll be fine. I've got you.'

He settled on to the sofa, still cradling her against his chest, and let her lie there until the sobs died away and her shivering stopped. Then he tipped up her chin, wiped her eyes and smiled.

'Better now?'

She nodded, ashamed of her silliness but unwilling to give up her seat on his lap.

He slid her off, however, and went out, returning with a bottle of brandy and two glasses. 'Here, have some of this then go and have a hot shower while I get the fire going. You'll be fine in a bit.'

She nodded, cupping the glass in her palms.

'Drink some,' he told her, and she tipped the glass and swallowed, choking.

'That's it. OK?'

She coughed again and nodded, her eyes streaming. 'Oh, gosh, that's lovely and warm.'

'How about a shower?'

'Yes—please.'

He led her upstairs to his little bathroom, gave her a fresh towel and left her alone.

The water was wonderful, piping hot, the stinging spray warming her chilled flesh and dispelling the fears. After an age she turned off the taps and stepped out, wrapping herself in the towel.

'I've put a dressing-gown out for you. Why don't you just put it on instead of getting dressed?' he said through the door.

'OK. Thanks.'

She dried herself and then opened the door, to find a thick, fluffy towelling robe folded neatly on the landing. There was also a pair of snuggly socks and an old T-shirt, and she pulled them on, turning over the sleeves of the robe so that she could see her hands.

Her hair was wet but there was nothing she could do about it. She borrowed his comb from the shelf over the basin and got rid of most of the tangles, then went back down to the sitting-room, supremely conscious of her nakedness under the robe and T-shirt.

He smiled, and her insides melted. 'OK?'

'Yes—thank you.'

'Come and sit by the fire and finish your drink.'

He drew her down to the rug, pulling her between his legs and easing her back against his chest, his arm round her waist. Then he put the glass in her hand and picked up his.

'Cheers,' he said softly, his voice oddly strained, and she tilted her head to look at him.

'Cheers,' she echoed, but her eyes were on his, her shoulders conscious of the rapid thud of his heart, its beat matching hers.

'The last time we did this it was our wedding night,' he told her softly. 'Do you remember?'

She nodded. 'Yes—yes, I remember.'

He set his glass down, then took hers from her and put it on the table too. Then he shifted slightly so that she lay against his shoulder, and slowly, infinitely carefully, he brought his mouth down against hers.

An anguished moan broke from her lips, and, curling her arms around his neck, she turned herself more fully into his arms.

The kiss was long and slow, thorough, and when he lifted his head she made a tiny sound of pain and tunnelled her hands through his hair, pulling him down to her again.

He groaned, a deep, shattered sound from low in his chest, and his hand slid down her hip and shifted her against him.

'Feel what you do to me,' he grated. 'I want you, Emily—I want you, now, here, tonight.' He drew a ragged breath. 'If that isn't what you want, then for God's sake stop me now.'

She met his eyes, those beautiful, misty grey eyes, so full of love and tenderness and need—years and years of need that found an echo in her heart.

'It's what I want,' she told him softly. 'You're what I want—now—here—tonight. . .'

His breath seemed to lodge in his throat, then with a shattered sigh he drew her down on to the rug and cradled her against his chest.

'I want you so badly—it's been so damn long. . .'

His hands were trembling, nearly as much as hers, and he parted the robe and eased it off her shoulders. The T-shirt followed, pulled slowly over her head to leave her sitting naked in front of him.

He stood and turned off the light, then came back, his hands tracing her skin with a trembling, reverent touch.

'The firelight on your body looks like gold,' he murmured. 'You haven't changed—you look just the same, just as lovely as ever.'

'Take off your clothes,' she whispered. 'Let me see you.'

Standing again, he stripped off the jumper first, then the jeans, tugging them down his long legs and kicking them away.

He straightened, and her breath caught, her heart slamming in her throat like a wild thing.

'David,' she mouthed, and then he was beside her, his arms around her, his body warm and hard against her side.

She slid her hands over the smooth skin of his shoulders, wider now, more solid, and then down, feeling the changes in his ribcage, the depth that maturity had brought. He was truly in his prime now, even more beautiful than in his youth.

His mouth found her breast, teasing the aching peak until she arched against him. She felt the soft puff of his laughter, then he relented and drew her nipple into his mouth, suckling deeply.

She cried out and he lifted his head, his eyes smoky, lazy, teasing. 'Do you like that?'

'You know I do,' she said raggedly.

'And this?'

He slid lower, his tongue trailing fire over the shallow dip of her pelvis, over her hip, down her thigh to the sensitive skin behind her knee, then up again, wreaking havoc with her control, over the soft skin of her inner thigh to her very secret depths.

She sobbed his name, her hands burrowing in his hair, the tension unbearable.

When she could stand it no more he lifted his head, his eyes glittering.

'Now?' he asked her.

'Yes—for God's sake, yes. . .'

The fullness was more than she could stand. The need had gripped her for so long, the wait had been so lonely, and now he was here, with her, inside her. . .

'Now, Emily,' he ground out, the words splintering against her lips. 'Come with me. . .'

The waiting was over.

CHAPTER SEVEN

EMILY woke some time later to the fresh smell of clean sheets, the pillow cool and welcoming beneath her cheek. She was naked, her body warmed by the soft thickness of the down-filled quilt that snuggled round her, and her body ached with the once familiar ache of loving.

In the distance she could hear David's voice as he held a one-sided conversation, and as she lay there she heard his tread on the stairs and he came back into the room.

'Emily?'

'What is it?' she asked softly.

'I have to go out—Jenny Wellcome's going downhill fast. You stay here; I'll be back as soon as I can.'

'What time is it?'

'Nearly four. Go back to sleep.'

She waited till he had left the house, then she slipped out of bed and showered, then went downstairs and made herself a cup of tea.

The fire was still just about alight, and she poked it to life and stared into the flames, thoughtful.

Their loving had been a very beautiful thing, she mused. Her body had remembered his, welcoming it like the prodigal son.

And she had certainly killed the fatted calf. No holding back, no hesitation—it had been beyond her.

Instead she had given him her all, and he had taken it in his hands as if it had been the most treasured gift.

The flames blurred, and she blinked away the tears. She loved him; there was no question of it. And he loved her. If only there was a way she could guarantee their happiness.

Her tea grew cold, and she made another cup and curled up on the rug, her fingers absently smoothing the dogs' ears. They had come in to keep her company, and now lay, one each side, their heads on her lap.

'Soppy great things,' she scolded fondly, and their tails thumped in response. She wondered how Jamie was getting on with his grandparents. After he came back she planned to get him a puppy from the RSPCA. They had a litter of Labrador crosses, too young yet to leave their mother, but she had chosen a little black bitch with a white star on her chest and the sweetest, softest nose she had ever felt.

She wondered how the dog would get on with David's two—not that it mattered, she told herself, because they wouldn't ever need to be together.

An ache started, deep in her heart, and she bit her lip and wondered how she could be so foolish.

What was she doing, sitting here in his dressing-gown with the smell of his body warm about her, waiting for him to return? She must have been mad to let him love her last night, crazy to allow her body to override her common sense.

Belatedly she thought about Jenny Wellcome and wondered if she was still alive and if she would see the dawn.

Perhaps they should take love where they found it, because there might not be a tomorrow. For Sarah and

Philip, at least, there would be no more tomorrows. She might have died herself last night if the ditch had been deeper or full of water.

She thought of Richard, worried about his wife, about the farm, about Ann. She thought of Neil Blake and the wife who no longer loved him, and their child used as a weapon in their marriage.

And she thought again of Jenny, who might not see the dawn.

It made her problems seem very trivial.

David returned shortly before seven.

She was still sitting on the floor, and as the dogs leapt up to greet him she climbed stiffly to her feet.

'Jenny?' she asked, but she could see the answer on his face.

'She died shortly after I got there. I've been with Richard.'

'How is he?'

'Wrecked. I've taken him home and made him a drink and put him to bed with a sedative, but he's very shocked. His mother was coming over, and the man who does the milking was already there. He'll keep an eye on him.'

He gave a harsh sigh and rubbed his hand over his eyes.

'I need a hug,' he told her gruffly, and she went unquestioning into his arms.

'Come back to bed,' she coaxed.

He followed her, his hand in hers, and their loving was wild and tender and touched with fear.

Afterwards he held her close, his heart beating beneath her ear.

'I couldn't bear to lose you again,' David whispered. His voice was raw, his hands trembling as they smoothed her shoulders. 'Stay with me, Emily. Marry me—let me love you.'

She turned her face into his shoulder, her heart aching.

'David, I daren't. What about Jamie? He's been through so much. What if things go wrong again? What if we start to fight?'

'We won't,' he promised, but she didn't believe him. They were too different, too opinionated, both of them, to offer such assurances.

'We will. And when we do it will tear him apart.'

He sighed. 'You won't even give us a chance.'

'We had a chance, David. We blew it.'

'We were kids. We didn't know about compromise. We just took, and if it wasn't there we sulked.'

He smoothed her hair, his hand warm and gentle against her head. 'I love you, Emily. You mean everything to me. I'd cut my tongue out before I lost you again because of anything I'd said to hurt you.'

She squeezed her eyes tight shut. 'David, please——' Her voice broke and she turned her face into his shoulder. 'It isn't possible.'

'It could be,' he told her, his voice harsher now. 'We might have a chance, only you won't even dare to try. Damn, Emily, what have we got to lose?'

'But Jamie——'

'To hell with Jamie—leave him out of this.'

'But I can't! That's just it, David—I can't leave him out!' She struggled into a sitting position and turned to face him, her eyes wide with pain. 'He's had enough,' she said with emphasis. 'He can't take any more change, any more trauma. I *can't* forget him.'

He sat up, dragging the quilt up over his chest and folding his arms over it like a shield.

'I didn't mean like that——'

She snorted. 'How else, for God's sake?'

'I just meant now, for a while, until we see——'

'You're yelling at me.'

His mouth opened, then clamped shut into a grim line. 'I'm sorry,' he muttered. 'I just meant—give us a chance, without worrying about Jamie. Give us some time alone, away from him, to see if what we have can be made to work. I don't want him hurt any more than you do, but if our marriage could be made to work, if we could only find a way to live together in harmony—wouldn't that be better for him—to live in a real family, with other children, rather than with two lonely widows?'

Her shoulders drooped. He was right, of course, but she was so afraid. What if it didn't work? Was it really Jamie she was trying to protect? Or herself?

'Emily?'

She took a steadying breath and met his eyes.

'OK. We'll give it a try—find some time on our own, see if we can make it work.'

His eyes blurred and filled. 'Thank you,' he breathed, and then he drew her into his arms. 'Thank you,' he said again, his voice gruff with emotion, and then he laid his lips against hers.

It wasn't really a kiss, she thought—more like a prayer.

A prayer for peace. . .

* * *

The surgery was subdued that day. Jenny Wellcome's death was felt keenly by all the residents of the town where she had been born and raised, and it was the first and last topic on everybody's lips.

'Poor Jenny,' they all said.

'Poor Richard,' some said.

Ann Blake came in for her share of flak. It seemed their affair was more widely known about than had been appreciated, and it certainly didn't go down well, especially with the women.

Emily kept out of it, making non-committal noises if a patient brought up the subject, and bit by bit the day was eroded.

After evening surgery David came in to tell her that her car had been pulled out of the ditch and was in the local body-repair shop where it would be fixed by tomorrow.

'I'll drive you home,' he told her. 'Your place or mine?'

Her heart thumped. 'Mine, please. I need a change of clothes and a shower, at least.'

'OK. We'll start with that. I have to go out and see Richard Wellcome later, and I have to see to the dogs, so perhaps we'll adjourn to my cottage after you've picked up some things for you, if that's all right?'

'Fine.'

His smile was warm and filled with tenderness. 'Don't worry, darling,' he said softly. 'We'll be all right. Just give it time.'

They had a lovely evening. They called in briefly to collect her things, then went back and took the dogs for a quick stroll down the lane before lighting the fire and making a cup of tea. After they had drunk it David went to see Richard and she fossicked about in the freezer for something to eat.

By the time he returned the house was redolent with the scent of herbs and wine, the chicken casserole simmering gently on the Aga.

'Oh, wow, that smells good.'

'You've got all the ingredients, but I bet you never put them together.'

He wrinkled his nose. 'I always mean to, but I somehow never get round to it.' He tugged her gently into his arms and nuzzled her nose against his. 'Mmm. You feel good.' His hips shifted against hers, and desire widened her eyes.

'David. . .' She laughed raggedly, and he smiled and shifted again.

'Oh, yes—does that feel good?'

'You know it does.'

'So tell me. Communicate. That's where we went wrong, darling. We never bothered to communicate except in bed.'

Her face lost its sparkle. 'Maybe because that's all there was to our marriage.'

'Oh, no.' He released her and stood back. 'No, Emily, you're wrong. There was much more than that. We just never bothered to look for it. That's why I want to try again, to see if we can find the good things and bring them to life, instead of just going through the motions.'

'Once more, with feeling?' she said wryly.

'Exactly.'

She held out her arms. 'Oh, David—I do so hope you're right.'

'I am. Trust me. Now, where were we?'

His hips lifted against hers and pushed her back against the worktop. She was wearing a denim skirt that fastened with press-studs down the front. With a quick tug he undid it from hem to waist, sliding his hand inside along the length of her naked thigh.

'I want you,' he said gruffly.

'Here? Now?'

'Here. Now.'

The air shivered with the rasp of his zip, and then they were joined, their bodies locked together, their mouths meshed in a desperate kiss.

Suddenly her legs gave as wave after wave of ecstasy pounded her body.

'David,' she sobbed, and she felt him stiffen and drive into her one last time.

'My God, woman—we haven't even closed the curtains,' he muttered gruffly, and, easing away from her, he reached behind her and twitched the curtains shut.

She started to laugh, bubbles of hysteria mounting up inside her like champagne, flowing over and caressing him.

'You're a crazy woman, do you know that? I love you.'

'I love you, too.'

He was absolutely still, then his eyes welled and he tugged her back into his arms. 'Thank God,' he said gruffly. 'Now let's eat; I'm starving.'

The rest of the week passed in a haze of sensuous langour. Emily's car was returned, and they made sure it was outside her cottage at night even though they spent most of the time at his.

The locals loved a scandal, and Richard Wellcome and Ann Blake were getting to be old news.

On Saturday afternoon Jamie and Mrs Bradley returned, their faces beaming, and it was clear that they'd both had a wonderful time.

Mrs Bradley's daughter had recently had another baby, and the motherly woman had obviously spent the past three days thoroughly enjoying being a grandmother.

As for Jamie, Philip's parents had probably spoiled him to death but he seemed to be thriving on it.

'We went to the cinema,' he told her, 'and Grandad took me to the airport and we watched the planes take off and land——Emmy, can I be a pilot when I grow up?'

'I expect so,' she said fondly, and hugged him. 'Would you like that?'

He nodded furiously. 'The planes are t'rrific—huge, and all shiny.' He glanced out of the window as if to assure himself that there really wasn't room to park one in the garden, and Emily had to school her expression.

'Grandad said Daddy used to have a plane, but I don't 'member it.'

'No, it was a long time ago. He used to fly a little plane.'

'Is it mine now?'

'No, darling, it was sold.'

'Oh.' He looked wistful. 'We could have kept it for me to learn on.'

She hugged him. 'You can have a new one when you're old enough, if you still want to. You might not.'

'I will,' he assured her, his eyes like saucers, and she had the distinct feeling he might. Philip had loved flying, and he had been very sad the day the plane was sold.

'There's no point in keeping it; I shan't ever fly again,' he'd said heavily, but it had hurt him none the less. As Emily looked at his son now, she could see the same wistful look in Jamie's eyes.

Yes, there was a lot of his father in him. Philip would have been very proud, and so would Sarah.

The huge weight of her responsibility seemed to settle on Emily's shoulders then. Raising someone else's child was a mammoth undertaking, there was no doubt.

Maybe she had misjudged herself. What if she failed in her task and let them all down—Sarah, Philip and little Jamie? What if she allowed her need for David to cloud her judgement over Jamie's well-being?

'Oh, God, help me to do the right thing for him,' she whispered.

'Did you say something, Emmy?'

She looked down at the trusting little face turned up to hers and smiled. 'Nothing important. How about some supper?' she suggested.

'Can I have beans on toast with cheese?'

'Yes.'

'Goodie. Now?'

'Yes, now.'

She let him tug her into the kitchen, and resolved to put David out of her mind. While she was with him, she would think of him. Now, though, she was with Jamie, and she would give him the attention he needed and deserved.

* * *

Jenny Wellcome's funeral took place on the first Wednesday in November. It was a brilliant, beautiful day, unseasonally warm, and the clear air rang loud with the tolling of the church bell.

Emily didn't go to the funeral—she didn't feel it was her place—but David went and sat at the back of the church.

'How was Richard?' she asked him when he returned to the surgery.

'Grim. I'm worried about him.'

'Do you think he needs psychiatric support?'

'Probably. At the very least he needs bereavement counselling. I imagine he's a seething mass of guilt and self-recrimination. I'll go and see him later.'

But later he was busy, called out to an elderly lady who had fallen and refused to go into Barnstaple to have her hip pinned. He phoned Emily and asked her if she could pop in on Richard on her way home, as he was going to be held up for some time, and so after she had finished her surgery she made her way up the valley to the Wellcomes' farm.

A car passed her on the way down, and she thought she recognised the driver as Ann Blake. She looked upset, and Emily wondered if she'd been to see Richard.

Not, perhaps, the most opportune timing—or maybe it was.

She found him in the farm office next to the back door, his feet on the desk, his head sunk forward on his chest.

He had been drinking, and Emily noticed a hand-written letter lying on the pile of paperwork.

She hesitated in the doorway. 'Can I come in?' she asked.

He looked up, his eyes unfocused, and his shoulder shifted slightly.

She took it for assent and tipped a ginger cat off the chair by the window, sitting down and eyeing Richard thoughtfully.

He looked grim. His eyes were red-rimmed, his face was pale, and there was a bleak set to his mouth.

'Are you all right?' she asked him gently.

He gave a short grunt of laughter. 'Oh, fine, Dr Thompson—just dandy.' He sighed and lifted a bottle off the floor beside him, tipping it back and swigging deeply. 'I buried my wife today, Doctor—how the hell do you think I feel?'

'Very sad, I would imagine. Perhaps angry with her for dying, guilty for still being alive yourself.'

He laughed again. 'Guilty?' He dropped his feet to the floor and swung round to face her. 'Did you see Ann leaving?'

'I thought it was her. She looked upset.'

'I just told her it was over.'

'Ah.'

The ginger cat rubbed against Emily's legs and she bent and stroked it absently.

'She knew.'

'Your wife?'

'Knew all about it—had from the beginning, apparently. Said she understood.' Again, the bitter laugh. 'Damned if I did. Ann just filled a need. I never loved her—not like she loved me. I knew it was wrong, but it seemed to help me cope. I still loved Jenny—still do——' His voice cracked, and he closed his eyes briefly. When he opened them, his voice sounded stronger.

'The farm will have to go, of course, to pay the debts. Funny, I would have moved heaven and earth to save it while she was alive, but it doesn't seem to matter now. They can sell it, do what they like with it. It won't matter to me.'

His gaze switched to her, focusing for the first time.

'I'll be all right, Dr Thompson. Don't you worry about me. I'll be fine.'

She stood up and shook his hand. 'Call if you need us,' she told him, and then she left.

As she walked past the window she glanced in at him and saw his eyes drop to the paper on the desk.

A note from his wife?

Quite possibly.

She left him alone with his grief.

The phone rang at six the next morning. It was David.

'Could you come up to the Wellcomes' farm, Emily?'

She was still groggy with sleep, and rubbed her eyes as she hitched up the bed and propped herself on the pillow.

'What, now?' she mumbled.

'I'm afraid so. The police would like to speak to you.'

She was wide awake now.

'Police?' she said, filled with foreboding.

'Richard Wellcome shot himself last night.'

'Oh, my God—is he dead?'

There was a slight pause. 'Yes—extremely. Could you come? They want to talk to you before they move the body.'

She woke Mrs Bradley, explained the situation and quickly pulled on some clothes. She would come back and shower later. Just now, though, she wanted to get up to the farm and find out what had happened.

The farmyard was littered with vehicles when she arrived—police cars, an ambulance, David's car and another she didn't recognise that turned out to belong to the milker, the man who had found Richard at five-thirty that morning.

She went into the office and winced.

'A shotgun in the mouth isn't a very tidy way of doing away with yourself,' the police officer said apologetically. 'I wonder, Dr Thompson, if you can confirm that he was the man you spoke to last night?'

'Yes—yes, of course he is.' She turned her head away from the grisly sight and sought David's eyes. 'What happened?'

'The milker found him this morning. It seems likely that you were the last person who saw him alive—unless Ann Blake was here after you?'

'She'd been,' Emily confirmed. 'I passed her going the other way. She looked upset—I don't know if it's relevant but they'd been having an affair.'

'So I understand,' the policeman said. 'We'll be talking to Mrs Blake later. Have you any idea of the content of their meeting?'

'He told me he'd just ended their relationship.'

'Really?' David sounded surprised.

'Really. He said he didn't love her—I think he'd just discovered that Jenny knew all about their affair, and possibly he felt guilty. There was a letter on the desk, handwritten on blue paper.'

'This one?' The policeman held up a blood-splattered piece of paper sealed in a plastic folder.

'That looks like it.'

'You'd better read it—see if it sheds any light for you on his behaviour.'

She ran her eye over it. It was tender, understanding and very much the way Jenny had spoken of Richard in their conversation back in September. It held no surprises for Emily, but for Richard it might well have done.

'He didn't realise she knew—he told me that. Otherwise I don't think there's anything there. He was worried about the farm—said he would have moved heaven and earth to save it when she was alive, but it didn't matter now. He said something odd, actually. He said they could sell it, whoever "they" are. The executors, I suppose. God, I should have realised—he told me to go. Said he'd be all right. I told him to phone if he needed us.'

She handed the note back to the policeman. 'Did he leave a note himself? Anything to indicate why he did it?'

The man shook his head. 'Not that we can find. He'd been drinking.'

'Yes, he was drinking while I was here.'

He asked her to go over the whole content of their conversation the previous evening, and she did so, twice. Finally satisfied that he had all the information he was likely to get from her, he dismissed them and she and David went out into the yard.

She took a great, steadying gulp of fresh air and closed her eyes.

'Are you all right?'

She nodded. 'Not a pretty sight.'

'No. I'm sorry they called you.'

'It's OK. David, I should have done something last night. I should have realised he was a danger to himself. He was too calm.'

'You can't be clairvoyant, Emily. Perhaps this is for the best.'

'How can you say that? The man's life has just been thrown away and you say it's for the best? Where's your compassion?'

'Where's yours? Like Jenny, he'd reached the end of his rope, but unlike Jenny he didn't have the easy way at his disposal. Whatever, it's done now and flagellating yourself won't do any good.'

'I still think you're wrong,' she said stubbornly. 'I should have done something more to help him. Maybe letting Jenny die was the wrong thing to do.'

'You had no choice over that.'

She turned to face him. 'Didn't I? I think we both did—and I think somewhere along the line we both made the wrong decision.'

CHAPTER EIGHT

EMILY'S doubts about her handling of Richard and Jenny Wellcome persisted, despite all that Laurence Allen said to her in the long case-conference she had with him after the tragic events of that week.

He supported her actions entirely, but she was still racked by guilt, and David's dismissal of her worries was hurtful.

It caused a rift between them, and even led to a bitter row one evening in the surgery.

He found her sitting at her desk long after her last patient had left, and came in.

'Come on, Emily. Buck up and come and have a drink. You need cheering up.'

She shook her head. 'No—I don't want a drink.'

'No, you want to turn the clock back and you can't. You did the right thing, Emily.'

'I don't think so.' She stood up and snapped her bag shut, lifting it on to the desk and leaning on it. 'I think I should have tried to talk Jenny out of her living will, and I think I should have insisted that she discuss it with Richard before it went on her records, and I think I should have admitted him to hospital the night he killed himself because I should have realised he was unstable.'

'He wasn't.'

'He was! And I didn't realise, because my professional judgement was at fault!'

David snorted. 'Not nearly as at fault as it was when you put Clare Remington on the Pill!'

'Oh, brilliant! What was I supposed to do, let her get pregnant? She was already sleeping with him!'

'Don't yell—there are still people in the building.'

'So what?' she snapped, but she lowered her voice none the less. 'David, I put her on the Pill because the consequences of not doing so were predictable and more potentially harmful than not doing so.'

'I agree—but the shades of grey in that are much more pronounced than in the Wellcomes' case.'

'No, they are not! There are no shades of grey where Clare is concerned, none at all. Having sex without contraception is foolish in the extreme——'

'So what have we been doing?'

She froze. 'Oh, God.'

'Quite.' He turned away. 'Just remember—what Jenny Wellcome wanted to do was within the law. What Clare Remington and her boyfriend are doing is not.'

It was a chilling thought—nearly as chilling as the one which followed.

She could be pregnant.

As the days went by, her fears turned to reality, and then a slow, warm joy that filled her as surely as David's child would do in the months to come.

She was pregnant, the baby conceived within that first hectic twenty-four hours after her crash.

At first she was horrified, but then she thought it would make no difference. She had Mrs Bradley and Jamie, anyway—another child would fit neatly into the puzzle, with or without its father.

She wouldn't deny him access, of course—she couldn't even consider anything so cruel—but whether they ended up together or not was almost immaterial. She would have her child—David's child—after all. She decided not to tell him, although it was difficult to hide her happiness.

Clare Remington came to her for a check-up and seemed well and settled nicely on the Pill. 'It's great,' she told Emily. 'There's a hole in my mattress—I hide them in there and no one knows.'

Emily, who still wished the girl would discuss it with her parents, tried once again to persuade her, but without luck. Physically, though, the girl was well and suffering from no side-effects, and so she was unable to fault her decision on medical grounds.

Ethics she tried not to think about.

They were busy in the hospital as the winter drew on, with flu epidemics and tummy bugs and the usual falls on slippery paths.

Harry Orr, the man with the recurrent dislocation of the shoulder, came in yet again to Casualty at the hospital. This time Emily was on duty on her own, and, not being strong enough to return the arm to its socket the way Laurence had, she laid him down on his front and supported his arm for him, gradually allowing it to hang until it was totally supported on the joint. Then she pulled gently and with a sloppy click it slid back into place.

'Ooo, damn,' he muttered, and lay there for a moment, the arm dangling.

'You know, Mr Orr, you really should have that seen to. You could have an operation to tighten the supporting structures so that such frequent dislocation couldn't happen. Wouldn't you like that?'

'Like the result—not so sure about the op,' he said with a laugh, and carefully, supporting his arm in his other hand, he swung himself into a sitting position. 'Damn, that's sore.'

'I'm sure it is—and just as sure that you need to get something done about it. You'll get arthritis in it if you let it go on like this, and one day you might get severe nerve damage.'

'I dare say,' he mumbled. 'Maureen on?'

'No, there's a staff nurse on. Shall I get her to put it in a sling for you?'

'If you wouldn't mind,' he said wearily. 'Suppose I ought to be thinking about this op.'

'I think you should. Come and see me if you decide you want to go ahead—we can always get you an appointment with the orthopaedic surgeon while you consider it.'

'Mmm.'

She left him sitting there, his face thoughtful, and asked the staff nurse to attend to him while she dealt with the other patients.

She was unsurprised when he came to see her the following week.

'Decided to see the surgeon,' he told her. 'Oh, and the missus sent this for you.' He set a large white pot on the table.

More clotted cream, the thought of which turned her stomach, which was just getting delicate.

'Thank you,' she said, forcing a smile. 'My son will be thrilled.'

'You mind you have some, too. Put a little meat on those bones. You lost weight?'

'Only a little—it's you. You keep me so busy rushing round putting your arm back.'

He winked. 'Not the way I hear it.'

'Pardon?'

'The way I hear it, you're giving that Dr Trevellyan the run-around, like you did before all those years ago.'

Emily was startled. 'What?' she whispered.

'Oh, don't worry, pet. We know things went wrong and you got married again. No one holds it against you. It's just that Dr Trevellyan's very popular about these parts, and we'd all like to see him marry again. His own wife'd be even better.'

Emily sat back in her chair and put her pen down. 'Is it common knowledge?' she asked quietly.

'Lord knows. I heard it from George up at the Bull. He hasn't been here long enough to remember, but there are those in there—regulars, you know—who remember you from your honeymoon. Old friend of Sarah's, weren't you? She and Philip were popular in these parts. Gather you married him and now you've got the lad. Big responsibility, that.'

Emily was amazed by the extent of his knowledge—and by the fact that she had let him discuss her in this open way without any attempt to halt him.

She opened her mouth to speak, but he held up his hand.

'I shan't spread it, my love. Only them as knows already will know. I'll see to it. Don't want lots of nasty gossip spreading, do we? Now, about this blasted arm of mine. . .'

* * *

Emily told David, but he wasn't surprised. 'Harry knows most things worth knowing. If he says it'll go no further, it won't.'

He pushed her door shut and came over to where she was sitting at her desk.

'How about a drink tonight? We haven't spent any time alone together for weeks.'

'I didn't think you wanted to,' she said bitterly. 'You don't seem to trust my judgement.'

'I trust your judgement,' he said, surprised. 'It's you that has trouble with it.' He sighed. 'Emily, forget our ethical differences. What about us?'

'Aren't they the same thing?'

'No. Surely we can agree to differ about work.'

'On something so fundamental? It's not quite like the difference between prescribing Amoxil or Ciproxen for a chest infection!'

His mouth tipped into a wry smile. 'It is—in a way. We're both qualified, we make valued judgements. Who's to say if we're right or wrong? Being right most of the time is what it's about.'

'No,' she argued. 'Being right all the time is what it's about.'

He laughed. 'Well, lady, I'm not vain enough to imagine I ever could be.'

'You've changed, then. There was a time when you would never admit you were wrong.'

Their eyes locked.

'I have changed. I keep telling you that. I just wish you'd believe me.'

'I wish I dared.'

'Come home with me tonight. I need you.'

'I can't. Mrs Bradley's got the evening off.'

'Then let me come and sit and watch television with you and have a cup of coffee by the fire.'

'You'd be content with that?'

He smiled. 'I'd have to be. Well, I might try and sneak the odd kiss.'

She laughed. 'All right, but come at eight-thirty, after Jamie's safely in bed. Oh, and there's a surprise.'

'A surprise? What sort of surprise?'

She thought of the puppy, probably curled up fast asleep beside Jamie as they spoke. 'You'll see.'

He arrived just before eight-thirty—and just as Beauty, the puppy, piddled on the sitting-room floor.

'Oh, Beauty! Oh, darling, not now!' Emily wailed, and, scooping her up, she went to the door. 'Here, hold this; she's just peed.'

'Wha——? Hello, sweetheart. Aren't you lovely?'

The puppy decided he was dirty and washed him thoroughly while Emily blotted the carpet.

'It's bound to stain,' she groaned.

'No, it won't. She's gorgeous; when did you get her?'

'Tuesday—I've been dying to show her to you.'

His look was reproachful. 'You only had to ask.'

'I didn't like to. I thought——'

'What?'

She shrugged. 'I don't know. We seemed to be fighting again.'

He shook his head and sat down, pulling her down beside him. 'No, we weren't fighting, we were disagreeing, and the only reason it seemed as if it was all we were doing is because it's been the only communication we've had. As soon as we disagree about anything, we cut off all other lines of communication. We always did.'

She slumped against his side, her finger tracing the wave in Beauty's fur. 'We did, didn't we?'

'We should stop—make ourselves talk about anything and everything, try and get to know each other instead of assuming. We've both changed. Time does that to people.'

He smoothed her hair back from her face and leant across, dropping a light kiss on her lips. 'I love you. Remember that when you get cross with me, when things go wrong and we can't seem to find a way out.'

'I love you, too,' she told him softly. 'I try and remember, but there are times when other things seem more important.'

'No. They aren't more important. They just tend to overwhelm it.'

She nodded, and scooped the puppy off his lap. 'Come on, nuisance—you need to go in the garden for a minute and then have a sleep. You're still a baby.'

He followed her out to the kitchen and watched as she put the puppy out. 'Coffee?' she asked as she washed her hands.

'Mmm, lovely—can I do it?'

She laughed. 'Probably not. You make everybody's thick and black like yours. I'll do it.'

He pulled a face and tugged her into his arms. 'Critical witch, aren't you? I want you to myself.'

'Mmm,' she murmured.

'When?'

'Tomorrow?'

He nodded. 'That'll do, I suppose.'

A sharp yap from the back door drew them apart, David to let the dog in, Emily to make the coffee.

As they went back into the sitting-room, David told

her that Joe Hardwill had been discharged from the North Devon General to the cottage hospital.

'He's still on crutches and very weak, and still coughing like crazy, but he's making progress.'

'I'm on duty there tomorrow—I'll go and introduce myself.'

'He'll be delighted. I told him you might come—he said he'd have to find his comb. I ought to warn you, I think he probably knows about us. At least a certain amount.'

'Doesn't everybody?' she said with a sigh.

'We could always satisfy their urge for romance.'

She sighed again, this time more heavily.

'Sorry, I'm pushing you.'

His face was tight, his eyes closed, and she felt guilty for what she was doing to him. Still, until she was sure—and at the moment she was far from sure—there was no point in discussing it any further.

He went at eleven, after a kiss that left them both hot and aching for more.

'Till tomorrow,' he said, and his words throbbed with promise.

'Mr Hardwill? I'm Dr Thompson.'

The old man in the chair on the balcony turned towards her, bright, curious eyes searching her face.

'Well, there's a sight for sore eyes,' he said slowly. His voice was scratchy, and he coughed at the end, pressing his hand against his ribs. 'Oh, damn cough.'

'Well, it should improve now you've given up smoking.'

The beady eyes twinkled. 'Who told you that malarky?'

She smiled. 'Well, almost. I don't imagine you get much past Maureen Whitaker.'

'That old battleaxe! Have to wait till she's off duty before they can sneak me any in. I hide them.'

'Do you?' she said, playing along with him. 'Where?'

He laughed, a rusty cackle that turned into a racking cough. 'That'd be telling,' he said finally.

'Hmm. You're a fool to yourself, you know. You nearly went—they almost lost you after your operation.'

He made a dismissive noise. 'Going to look at my leg?' he asked.

'No. I gather it's doing well, and Dr Trevellyan looked at it yesterday. I'm sure it hasn't changed.'

'Told you all about it, did he?' the old man asked, a sly note creeping into his voice. 'Over dinner, perhaps?'

She schooled her smile. 'Over coffee, actually. If you give me your cigarettes, I'll tell you all about it.'

He chuckled. 'You doctors've got more tricks than a magician's rabbit. I'll hang on to the fags, thank you, my dear.'

She smiled. 'Oh, well, it was worth a try.'

She left him chuckling, and checked the other patients on the wards before heading back to the surgery.

She had a family planning clinic that afternoon, and one of her patients was Amy Richardson.

'Hi,' Amy said, a smile across her pretty face.

'Hello. How's the baby?'

'Lovely. He's nine weeks now, and I think we ought to do something about contraception. Jeremy wants a vasectomy, but I'm not sure.'

'Isn't five enough?' Emily asked her. 'Just thinking about all that washing and cooking gives me the shivers.'

Amy smiled. 'I have help. It's just—when the baby gets to about a year, I get this ache—sort of a crazy, biological bomb—do you know what I mean?'

Emily nodded. She did, only too well.

'I just have to have another baby. Do you know what it's like to feel a baby grow inside you, to know that this week it's got fingers and toes, this week eyelashes——? You feel it move, like a butterfly, then a team of fullbacks——' She laughed. 'Then they arrive, small and defenceless, and all your energy is focused in on them, on caring for them, watching them grow. Then suddenly they can walk and talk, and bang—off goes the bomb again.'

Emily closed her eyes briefly. Oh, she knew so clearly what the woman was talking about. Under cover of her desk, her hand slid across and cradled her child, buried deep in her pelvis, still too tiny to be noticeable but there, a powerful presence for all that.

'I think I understand,' she said quietly. 'The thing is, when do you stop? Obviously economic and social decisions have to be made, but there are medical decisions too. How well is your body taking the demands of so many pregnancies?'

'Oh, fine. I'm religious about my pelvic floor exercises, and we've got a swimming-pool that I use every day. Jeremy freaks a bit about all the school fees, but we aren't exactly strapped for cash. He's a writer, a very successful one—political bestsellers. He's had one televised as a series, and they want a sequel.'

'He said you were broke,' Emily reminded her with a smile.

'Oh, he fusses. He'd just had a tax demand. The next advance paid it with tons left. Trust me, money isn't a problem, and nor is my body.'

'You could have a coil.'

'That's how we had David.'

'Ah. Well, a cap?'

'That was Julian.'

Emily rolled her eyes. 'The Pill?'

'I can't take it. I forget. It isn't medical, it's just that I'm useless. That's how we had Lucy. I don't suppose—I read about these implants. They last five years or something.'

'Norplant. Yes. They're like little rods of contraceptive inserted under the skin of your upper arm, and they prevent pregnancy just like the Pill—only more effectively, if you forget to take it.'

Amy laughed. 'What about if we decided we wanted another? I mean, I really don't think we do, when I'm being sensible, but if we did?'

'You can have it removed, and fertility is quickly restored.'

'Can you do it?'

'Yes. Well, I've done the training, but I haven't done one recently. Perhaps one of the other partners has.'

'Is it difficult?'

'Oh, no. You make a tiny incision, about two millimetres long, and push the rods in under the skin. They're very tiny. The whole thing is done under local anaesthetic and takes about twenty minutes.'

'Can I go for it?'

Emily nodded. 'I don't see why not. We may not

have any stocks here in the dispensary, but we should be able to get it fairly quickly. In the meantime, what are you using?'

'Condoms.' She wrinkled her nose, and Emily smiled.

'It's better than getting pregnant again so quickly. Can I ring you?'

'Sure. You should have my number.'

Emily checked it and then promised to get on to it straight away.

She tackled Laurence over tea.

'Norplant? Yes, we can get it. Takes about twenty-four hours to come. Who wants it?'

'Amy Richardson.'

He laughed. 'Bit long-term for her, isn't it?'

Emily grinned. 'I think she's trying to buck the habit—unlike Joe Hardwill. David, he's still smoking.'

David smiled lazily. 'What did you expect? Devious old bugger. I wonder where he hides them?'

'I tried to bribe him into telling me, but he wouldn't play.'

David chuckled. 'Surprise, surprise. Did he embarrass you?'

She shook her head. 'No, I was expecting it. He said I was a sight for sore eyes.'

'And so you are, my dear,' Laurence said, getting to his feet with a sigh. '"Once more unto the breach, dear friends"—oh, that reminds me, Mr Remington's coming to see me tonight. From what Sue said, I think you'd better stand by, Emily. Looks like he's found out about his daughter.'

* * *

Nigel Remington was a big man—tall, solid and very, very angry. He insisted on Emily's being present at the consultation, as well as Laurence, the senior partner, and Clare, the cause of all the trouble.

His wife, pale, tired and obviously upset, hovered by his side. Clare stood awkwardly in the corner, her face sulky, her eyes red-rimmed.

'I want an inquiry,' her father said furiously, 'into how a fifteen-year-old girl came to be prescribed a dangerous drug without her parents' knowledge or consent. You should be struck off! What did you think you were playing at?' he demanded, turning to Emily.

'I wasn't playing at anything, Mr Remington,' she told him as calmly as she could. 'I took a very detailed history, we spent a great deal of time discussing it and in the end I did what I considered to be the right thing for Clare, in my professional judgement.'

'Your what?' The man snorted. 'Let me tell you, Dr Thompson, there's nothing professional about your judgement, though what one can expect from a doctor with your sort of moral standards is difficult to anticipate.'

Emily drew in a sharp breath. 'I beg your pardon?'

'Don't pretend not to know what I'm talking about—unless you'd like me to elaborate in front of Clare?'

'I think,' Laruence said, his voice tight with anger, 'that we are rather getting off the point. The point is, your daughter, for whatever reason, sought contraceptive advice *after* she had embarked on a sexual relationship. In my opinion Dr Thompson did only what I or any other of my partners would have done in the same circumstances. She took steps to ensure that the girl was protected from the effects of an unwanted teenage pregnancy—a pregnancy that I'm sure you would have found a great deal more offensive than the alternative.'

The man's cheeks were mottled with rage, but he contained it. 'She should have been advised against the relationship. She should have been given moral advice to protect her from the evils of the flesh——'

'I quite agree,' Emily butted in. 'And as I see it that advice is the province of the parents. Where were you when she needed to talk to you?'

'We were there,' he said furiously.

'Yes—stuck up on your high horse, too busy stuffing the Bible down my throat to bother to listen to what I had to say!' Clare cut in. 'Well, now you know! I'm sleeping with Colin, I love him, and as soon as I'm sixteen we'll get married!'

'Over my dead body!' her father roared.

'It can be arranged,' Clare muttered under her breath, but her father heard her and raised his hand as if to strike her.

Emily stepped quickly between them.

'I shouldn't,' she said calmly.

Slowly, inch by inch, his hand fell. His eyes burned into Emily's, the hatred and fervour in them terrifying.

'You haven't heard the last of this,' he said, and the volume of anger bottled up behind his words chilled Emily to the bone.

He ushered his wife and daughter out, and Emily sank down on to a chair and looked helplessly at Laurence.

'What a monster,' she said, her voice trembling.

'Isn't he just? Don't worry, Emily, I'm behind you. He can't touch you. I've looked at the notes, and they're very thorough and comprehensive. You covered everything a judge might want to consider.'

The mention of a judge made Emily's blood run cold. She was, after all, only on probation. If things got messy, perhaps they wouldn't want her to stay on.

'You look worried.'

She met his eyes. 'Laurence, do you trust my professional judgement?'

'Of course.'

'What about the Wellcomes?'

He shrugged. 'That was tricky. David should have gone to see him that evening. He knew he was upset.'

'He asked me to go. He trusted me to make the right decisions about his state of mind and treatment.'

'And you don't think you did.' It wasn't a question.

'Do you?'

'On balance, no, but that's with the twenty-twenty vision of hindsight. However, there is a lot of evidence to suggest he would have done it some other time, if not that night. Let's face it, he had precious little left to live for. No, Emily, you did the right thing, both with Jenny and with Richard. And, I believe, with Clare.'

He rested a large, comforting hand on her shoulder. 'Don't worry. It'll all come out in the wash.'

She dredged up a smile and left, tidying up a few things on her desk before heading for home.

Jamie was tucking into chicken pie, peas and carrots when she arrived, and she smiled and kissed him on the forehead.

'Hello, darling. Good day at school?'

'Mmm. I'm a shepherd in the Nativity play. I wanted to be a king, but there weren't enough crowns and besides, I've got a sheepdog. Emmy, can I take Beauty with me to do the play?'

'Oh, darling—she might piddle on the stage.'

He giggled. 'Yes, she might. I know, you can video it and we can show her.'

'I'll do that,' she promised, and then straightened up. 'I must go and get changed; David's taking me out for supper tonight.'

'Can I come?'

She looked down at the bright, eager face and her heart sank. 'Not this time, sweetheart. Maybe another day—perhaps at the weekend.'

'This weekend?'

'No, I'm on duty.'

His face fell. 'You're always on duty.'

She sighed softly. 'Oh, Jamie, I'm sorry. I'll have to make sure I can come to your Nativity play.'

'You must,' he said determinedly.

'I will.' It was a promise, and one she vowed would not be broken.

Running upstairs, she showered quickly, blow-dried her hair and pulled on a sweater-dress in soft lovat-green. She took more than usual care with her make-up as well, and then stood back to examine her handiwork.

She'd do. She didn't have time to worry, because she wanted to read Jamie a story before she went out.

Running downstairs, she found him playing with Beauty on the rug.

'Story?' she said to him, but he shook his head.

'I'm playing with Beauty,' he told her.

There was something, a catch in his voice, that worried her. Was it David?

The doorbell rang, and Jamie jumped to his feet and ran through into the hall. Emily smiled, thinking he was running to answer the door, but then she heard his feet on the stairs and realised he'd run up to his room.

Why?

She opened the door. 'Come in—I must just go and talk to Jamie; he's being funny.'

She left him there and went up to his room. He was sitting at the desk playing with a model, his back definitely towards her.

'That's David,' she told him.

'OK.'

I'll see you later. We won't be very late.'

'OK.'

She crossed over and kissed him, but he didn't react. With a sigh she went downstairs.

'OK?'

She shrugged. 'He said so—several times. It was all I could get out of him.'

'Maybe he's missing his parents.'

'Very likely. I'm ready, if you want to go.'

'Sure?'

She nodded. 'Yes. He's all right. I'll talk to him later.'

They went to a pub—not the Bull, by mutual consent, but another pub further away with a restaurant licence and an excellent reputation.

The meal was wonderful, and for once they kept their conversation strictly off medical matters. He made her laugh, and took her mind off Mr Remington and his threatening behaviour, the Wellcomes, and Jamie.

By the time they left, she had laughed herself silly

and they went out to the car with their arms round each other, still laughing.

When they pulled up outside his cottage and went inside, however, the laughter faded, replaced by need.

'Coffee?' he asked, his voice husky.

'No.'

Their eyes met and desire arced between them.

'Come on,' he murmured, holding out his hand, and he led her upstairs to his bedroom and slowly, methodically, he undressed her, kissing every single inch as it was revealed.

By the time he peeled away the last stocking, she could barely stand. Her fingers trembling, she tugged off his tie, fumbling with the top few buttons and then giving up.

'Pull it over your head,' she told him in an unsteady voice, and as he did so she pressed her lips to the smooth, sleek muscles of his chest. Soft hairs teased her lips, and she burrowed between them and caught one flat male nipple between her teeth.

He groaned and pulled her against him, pressing her against his hips.

She eased away and turned her attention to his trousers, undoing first the belt, then the trouser bar and then the zip, the slow, deliberate rasp scraping on their senses.

'Damn, woman,' he muttered, and she smiled, a secret woman's smile.

Calm now, recovering her poise and enjoying her power, she slid one finger inside the waist of his briefs and ran it round, tormentingly, against the flat wall of his abdomen. It jerked under her hand, tensing, and she turned her palm flat against the warm skin and slid it down, cupping him.

A low oath caught on his breath, and he dropped his head into her shoulder and sighed.

'That feels wonderful.'

'Mmm.'

She moved her hand, tormenting him, and his hips jerked involuntarily. He reached down and shackled her wrist, ending the torment, and met her eyes.

His were smoky with desire, lazy, predatory. Shucking off his remaining clothes, he lifted her and placed her in the centre of the bed.

'You want to play games? We'll play games.'

He nearly drove her crazy, but in the end he lost his control, too, and they tumbled over the edge together, their hearts thrashing in time, locked firmly in each other's arms.

She roused herself as soon as she could bear to.

'I have to go back to Jamie,' she told him.

'He'll be asleep.'

'I know, but if he wakes up—sometimes if he's a bit funny like this he has nightmares. I should be there.'

'OK.'

He kissed her, his lips lingering, and then reluctantly eased away.

They dressed quickly, in silence, and once back at her cottage she didn't invite him in.

'Thank you for a lovely evening,' she said softly, leaning over to kiss him. 'It's been wonderful.'

'It has, hasn't it? We must do it again—soon.'

'Yes—yes, we must.'

She watched him drive away, then went upstairs, her heart light. Maybe, just maybe, it was going to work after all. Jamie would have a father figure, and the baby——Her hand slid to her baby, and a slow smile blossomed on her lips. She would tell him tomorrow.

She went into her room to find Jamie sitting in the middle of her bed, wide-eyed and reproachful.

'I had a dream,' he told her. 'It woke me up, and you weren't here.'

His accusation cut her to the heart. 'Oh, darling, I'm sorry. What was it about?'

He slid off the bed. 'It doesn't matter. I don't like you going out with David. I want you here, with me. I don't like it when you're out.'

'We were only gone for a little while, Jamie,' she reasoned, but her heart was breaking.

'I needed you,' he told her stubbornly. 'I don't want you to go out with him.'

He walked away, his head down, leaving her in the middle of her shattered dream.

CHAPTER NINE

EMILY's first instinct was to phone David immediately and talk to him, but she had only dialled the first few digits before she thought better of it.

She would give Jamie time to settle, talk to him, see how he really felt. Then she'd talk to David.

How Jamie really felt was clear the following morning. He was subdued, and asked her several times if she was going out with David that night.

'No,' she told him each time.

'Tomorrow?' he asked.

'No. No, I won't be going out with him tomorrow either,' she assured the worried child, and was rewarded by a wobbly smile.

'I love you,' she told him, and he flung himself into her arms and hugged her desperately.

During a break in the day she nipped back and had a word with Mrs Bradley.

'He was ever so upset when you weren't here,' the older woman told her. 'I didn't think I'd be able to console him.'

She gave a wavering smile. 'So that's that, then. I rather thought it was too good to be true.'

'Perhaps he just needs more time to adjust.'

'Perhaps.'

Emily thought it was possible, and so decided still to say nothing to David, other than that Jamie had been upset and they should avoid going out in the evening for a while.

At first she thought he was going to argue, but then his mouth curved in a rueful smile. 'You're his mother. We'll play it your way.'

So easy.

Mr Remington was less so. A couple of days passed, and then the practice recevied a letter from his solicitor.

'Stupid man,' Laurence grumbled.

'He's doing what he thinks is right for his daughter,' Emily reasoned, and Laurence gave a startled snort of laughter.

'You're being very philosophical considering it's you he's trying to lampoon.'

'I just know how I would feel,' she said, but couldn't explain any further. It was just a sort of gut feeling, to do with being a parent—not that she was doing so well at that, she thought with a pang.

And she still had to tell David about the baby.

Mrs Richardson came back for her Norplant implant, and Emily did it under the watchful eye of Laurence Allen, who had performed the procedure many times in the past year since it had been available. Although she had done it herself, it had been before Philip became very ill and she had given up her job, and she just felt more confident with Laurence there, too.

Having infiltrated the skin with lignocaine, Emily made a shallow two-millimetre cut in the skin on the inside of Amy's upper arm and inserted six tiny rods impregnated with the contraceptive hormone under the skin in a fan shape. It was all over in less than quarter of an hour, and Amy was thrilled.

'That's brilliant,' she said delightedly as they finished. 'Now I can't possibly forget to take it!'

'Just think long and hard before you let the bomb go off again,' Emily told her as she left.

'I will. This time, at least, someone's going to have to pull the pin, so to speak. It makes it more conscious, and a little harder to be so indiscriminate. Children are so precious, I truly think they ought to be really wanted. Not that ours aren't, of course—even the accidents, which outnumber the planned ones now!'

Emily laughed with her, then turned, her hand automatically lowering to her baby. Wanted? Oh, yes. . .

'Are you OK?' Laurence asked.

She jumped. She had forgotten the other doctor's presence, and snatched her hand away from her abdomen as if she'd been scalded. 'Yes, I'm fine. Just a twinge. Right, I'd better clear up in here. Thank you for your support.'

'You're welcome. Do you feel happy doing it now?'

'Oh, yes.'

'Good. Look, about Clare Remington.'

Emily sighed. 'Yes?'

'I'll go and see her father again, see if we can't defuse this before it goes any further.'

'Do you want me to go?'

He shook his head. 'No. I think he finds your behaviour with David—questionable.'

Emily flushed, but Laurence was undeterred.

'Ignore him. You have a right to your private life. This town is too small for secrets, Emily, but you mustn't let that stop you in your search for happiness.'

She swallowed, and blinked away the tears that

threatened. 'I'll bear that in mind,' she said unsteadily, and busied herself with the debris of the minor operation.

Little did Laurence know that there would be nothing in the way of secrets to keep from now on, she thought sadly.

David appeared at her elbow. 'Are you finished?'

She nodded. 'Yes, why?'

'I've got an hour for lunch, so have you.'

'So?'

'So come home with me.'

'David, it's the middle of the day!' she murmured in protest.

'So? I need you, Em. I want to hold you.'

'I can't.'

'Why?'

'Because.'

'Because what?'

Her shoulders drooped in defeat, her need too great for her fragile self-control. 'I'll follow you,' she told him with a rueful smile.

He left her, and when she'd finished clearing up she drove to his cottage.

He opened the door and pulled her into his arms, his mouth coming down hard on hers. After an age he lifted his head. 'I've missed you,' he muttered.

'It's only been three days.'

'I've still missed you.'

He led her upstairs and made love to her with savage urgency, as if he knew he was losing her, and she clung to him and blinked away the tears.

'I love you,' he whispered in her ear. 'Remember that.'

She said nothing. Her heart was too full, her throat clogged with tears.

She eased away from him and slipped off the bed.

'Where are you going?'

'To shower.'

'No!'

She turned, shocked out of her own sadness by the pain in his voice. 'David? What's wrong?'

His face was tortured, showing his feelings for perhaps the very first time. 'You always do it,' he rasped. 'As soon as we make love, you rush to the shower, as if you can't bear to have any trace of me on you.'

Stunned, she walked back to him. 'That's not true——'

'Isn't it? It damn well feels like it.'

She knelt on the bed, her hand cupping his cheek. 'No—no, that isn't it at all.'

He gripped her wrist. 'What, then?'

She flushed. 'It's for you—I don't want you to feel that I'm. . .'

'What? Loved? For God's sake, Emily, can't you imagine how I feel, how I felt for years, watching you run away as soon as we've made love to scour yourself, as if you feel contaminated by me, by my touch, by my body. . .?'

She dropped her head forward. 'No! Oh, darling, no!' She reached out her other hand and caressed his face, forcing herself to hold those tortured eyes. 'I just—I don't want to offend you——'

'Offend me?' He reached for her. 'You don't offend me, you couldn't. Let me love you.'

'But I——'

'Please?'

She lowered herself to his side, feeling the warmth of his arms encompass her. She touched his shoulder, revelling in the smooth, soft skin over firm muscle.

'I'm sorry I hurt you,' she whispered.

'Forget it.' His voice was gruff, his hands warm and strong. The sweet, musky scent of their loving drifted between them, inflaming her.

'Love me,' she pleaded, her heart breaking.

'I do—until the end of time.'

This time he was slow and gentle, his body calling to hers, and when they reached that tender, glorious peak in harmony her tears refused to be held back.

'Emily?'

She turned her face into his shoulder and bit her lip to hold down the sob, but he wouldn't be shut out. Gripping her chin in tender fingers, he turned her face up to his, searching her tear-filled eyes.

'Darling, what is it? What's wrong?'

'Jamie doesn't want me to see you any more.'

His body jerked, a fine tremor like a small electric shock, but she felt it all the way to her bones.

'What did he say? I thought we were getting on well.'

'So did I. He's decided he doesn't like me going out with you. I thought he might get over it, but I asked him last night if he would mind us going out perhaps next weekend, and he stuck his chin out and his lip wobbled and I didn't have the heart——' Her tears came again in a rush, and David's hands curved protectively round her and cradled her against his chest.

'Ah, love—is this goodbye, then? Our swansong? Is that what you're telling me?'

She tipped her head back and stared into his eyes. 'It has to be,' she said brokenly.

His eyes slammed shut, a single tear squeezed out between his lids, falling on her face.

'David?'

'I'm OK. I knew it was coming. You'd better go back—I'll follow you in a bit.'

He went into the bathroom and turned on the shower, and she dressed quickly and left.

What a time to tell him, she thought, right in the middle of a busy working day, with no opportunity to discuss it.

Still, perhaps that was for the best.

The rest of the day was hectic, and when she emerged from her evening surgery she was told he had gone up to the hospital because he was on duty that evening.

Sue watched her curiously, but she refused to allow herself to be drawn into a discussion. She knew she looked terrible, and, if her last glimpse of David was anything to go by, so did he.

She went home, cuddled her son and the puppy in front of the fire and tried to hide her misery until she was alone in her bed and could let the tears fall.

The weekend was busy. She was on call, and spent the Saturday and Sunday mornings at the hospital running an emergency surgery and casualty clinic combined, followed by a quick check round the wards before going home.

On Sunday afternoon, shortly after they had finished lunch, the phone rang.

'Emily? It's Maureen Whitaker at the hospital. I

wonder if you could come back? I've got Clare Remington here—she's slashed her wrists.'

That was all Emily needed—a potential suicide to muddy the already fraught waters. She rang Laurence before she left, apologised for disturbing him on Sunday and asked if he could meet her at the hospital.

'I just get the feeling this could drive the father over the brink,' she told him.

He agreed to go straight there, and she left immediately.

When she arrived, it was to find a silent and grim-lipped father and daughter sitting in the waiting area.

They both stood up, but she wanted to deal with Clare alone.

'I wonder if you'd mind waiting out here?' she asked Mr Remington with no great hope that he would co-operate.

To her amazement he sat back down and carried on staring at the floor.

She led Clare through into a treatment-room, sat her down and held her hand.

'So what happened?'

'He said I couldn't see Colin again. I love him—you don't know what it's like!'

Emily did know. She knew exactly what it was like.

'Let me see, love,' she coaxed gently, and took the temporary dressings off the wrists. They were only slightly cut, one more than the other, and it was definitely a cry for help rather than a serious attempt to take her life, for which Emily was profoundly grateful.

Her left wrist needed a couple of stitches, but the right, presumably cut last with the weakened left hand, she just cleaned up and dressed while the local anaesthetic took effect.

'What did your father say?' she asked as she gently drew the edges of the wound together.

'Nothing. He just covered my wrists, put me in the car and drove me here. He hasn't said a word to me.'

Just then there was a kerfuffle in the waiting-room and the door was pushed open.

'Clare? What happened?'

A young man in jeans and a denim jacket crouched beside Clare, taking her hands tenderly in his and staring down at her wrists. 'Why?' he asked, his face tortured.

'He wouldn't let me see you. He said I couldn't see you again.'

The youth's face worked, and then he lowered his lips to her hand and kissed it. 'Silly girl,' he muttered. 'I'm not worth this.'

'You are to me.'

'Oh, God,' he groaned, his voice cracking, and, wrapping his arms around her, he hugged her tight.

'I don't want to interfere,' Emily said wryly, 'but do you suppose I could finish putting in this last suture before you get carried away?'

Flushing, he released her and straightened up, his hand on Clare's shoulder offering silent support while Emily knotted the silk and snipped the stitch off, then dressed it. 'There. Now I'll have a word with your father, and you can go.'

She left them alone together while she sought out Mr Remington, but Laurence had arrived by this time and had wheeled him off to Maureen's office. He beckoned to Emily through the glass, and she went through and joined them.

'How is she?' Mr Remington asked.

'She'll be fine. It was relatively superficial. A cry for help rather than a serious attempt to do away with herself, but I would take it seriously if I were you.'

He nodded. 'I will. I think it's time we sat down and had a really serious talk. Maybe she's old enough now for this relationship, maybe not. My gut reaction is still not, but perhaps I ought to start really listening to her.' He swallowed, and forced himself to meet her eyes.

'I owe you an apology. I realise now that what you did was the best option in difficult circumstances, and I know you didn't prescribe the Pill for her lightly. I just assumed you dished them out like dolly mixtures, but obviously you don't. You care—perhaps more obviously than I do. And you listened—which I didn't. Thank you.'

Emily was completely taken aback. She had expected another assault on her integrity, and instead there was a complete retraction and apology.

She made the appropriate noises and went back out to find Clare and her boyfriend. Mr Remington followed her out of the room and stood staring at the lad for some time, then extended his hand. 'Colin—perhaps you'd like to come back and have some tea with us.'

Clare's face lit up. 'Oh, Dad, thanks,' she said, and threw herself into his arms.

'I don't approve, mind,' he told her warningly. 'We are going to sit down, all of us, and have a good, long, serious talk.'

Emily and Laurence watched them leave, then turned to each other and smiled.

'Well, fancy that.'

'Fancy. End of court case.'

She laughed with relief. 'Thank God.' She glanced at her watch. 'I'd better get home.'

Laurence's hand on her arm stopped her. 'Are you OK?'

She didn't pretend not to understand. 'I'll live.'

He nodded, and without another word she turned and left.

Clare came to see her on the following Friday to have her stitches out of her wrist, and she told Emily she was coming off the Pill.

'Dad says we're both very young and we've got our whole lives ahead of us. He says we can still see each other, but only supervised and in company, and not too often. Then if we still feel the same in a year's time we can think again.'

'How do you feel about that?' Emily asked her, concerned that if it wasn't the girl's wishes she would find a way to be with Colin without supervision—and with possibly disastrous consequences.

'I think he might be right,' she said, a touch sheepishly.

Emily smiled, truly relieved. 'I'm so glad—glad you're talking to your parents, glad they're listening to you, glad you and Colin have decided to be sensible. You are still terribly young for such a serious commitment, and if it isn't that serious you really shouldn't be making love.'

Clare blushed and dropped her eyes. 'I know that now. I didn't realise before. It's very special, isn't it?'

Emily felt a lump in her throat. 'Yes, Clare, it is—or it should be. There, your arm will be fine now. Look after yourself—and if you change your mind for goodness' sake come back first!'

She smiled. 'I will. Thank you for being so kind. I'm sorry Dad got all bent out of shape.'

'I think he had a right. I think if you'd been my daughter I might have got all bent out of shape too.'

They exchanged a smile of understanding, and Emily watched her go. A success story? Hopefully.

She finished her surgery and went into the common-room to find Laurence to tell him the news. He wasn't there, but David was, and her footsteps faltered.

'Hi,' he said softly.

'Hi. I was looking for Laurence.'

'He's gone home.'

'Oh.' She twisted her wedding-ring. 'Well, I suppose I should be leaving too——'

'Emily?'

She turned back to him.

'Are you happy here?'

'Happy?' she asked numbly.

'Yes. If it weren't for me, I mean, messing things up for you. Are you happy in the practice, in Biddlecombe, at the cottage? Is Jamie happy?'

'Yes—yes to all of them. Why?'

His shoulders lifted slightly. 'I just wondered.'

'David. . .?' She hesitated.

'Yes?'

'I—nothing. I'll go home.'

She turned away, unable to stand the pain he was

trying to hide. Of course she was happy, happier than she had been for years—or would have been, had Jamie not come between them so effectively.

She would have to talk to him again, try and sound him out a little further. Once he was used to the idea of David in their lives, perhaps he would accept it more readily.

She hoped so, quite desperately, because one thing she was sure of—without David she was nothing. Far from messing it up, his presence in her life had brought back a meaning to it that had been missing for eight long, lonely years.

But enough was enough. What was it Mrs T had said? 'Seems to me a great waste of being alive if you don't bother to learn from your mistakes.'

Well, she had learnt from hers. David was more important to her than anything else, and she wasn't going to give up on him again. She would talk to Jamie, and, please God, he would learn to love David as she had.

The alternative didn't bear thinking about.

CHAPTER TEN

EMILY wanted to wait for the right moment to talk to Jamie—but, like all right moments, it came when it was least expected.

It was late on Sunday afternoon, and Beauty was playing with a ball, dashing after it and then running into the corner with it to chew it, much to Jamie's chagrin. He was trying to teach her to fetch, and she was being thoroughly difficult.

'I wonder if David could teach her?' he said thoughtfully. 'Bridie and Ruffian fetch.'

Emily's heart crashed against her ribs.

'Would you like him to try?' she asked cautiously.

'Mmm—do you think he would?'

'We can certainly ask him. Of course,' she added casually, 'if we aren't seeing him, he can't really train her.'

'But he could,' the boy said absently, wrestling the ball from Beauty and rolling it again. 'Fetch, Beauty, good girl—oh, no! She's done it again!'

He turned to Emily, laughing. 'David will *have* to do it—I'm hopeless.'

Emily patted the sofa beside her. 'Jamie, come here for a minute, sweetheart. I want to talk to you.'

He wriggled up beside her and snuggled under her arm. 'What's wrong?'

'Nothing—well, not really. I wanted to talk to you about David.'

'He hasn't been here for ages—doesn't he like me any more?'

She blinked. 'I thought you didn't want us to see so much of him.'

'What? Why do you think that?'

'You said so. You said you didn't like me going out with him——'

'I don't. I don't like it when you go out to work either, but you have to do that, so it's OK. I like David, though. He's really nice.' He paused for a moment, then added thoughtfully, 'He's a bit like Dad.'

Emily hugged him gently, hardly able to believe what he was saying. 'Yes, he is, a bit,' she agreed, trying hard to keep her voice steady. 'Jamie, how would you feel about having David as a sort of dad?'

'Like you're my mum now?'

She nodded.

'That would be really cool, Emmy! I could ride the donkey, and play with Bridie and Ruffian—do you think he'd want to?'

Emily wanted to cry. She felt the tears pricking behind her eyes and blinked rapidly. Could it really be so easy? 'Yes, Jamie, I think he might,' she told him.

'He'll have to ask you, though—girls can't ask boys that sort of thing. It isn't right.'

She bit her lip to stop the smile. 'Then I'll have to make very sure he knows to ask the question, won't I?' she said seriously.

Her first opportunity to talk to David was on Monday, but the surgery was crowded, patients were waiting and it was not a very good time. Anyway, she found she was suddenly nervous.

'Can I see you later?' she asked, surprised by the slight tremor in her voice.

He looked serious. 'I was going to ask you the same thing. How about lunchtime, at my place?'

She nodded. 'Fine—thanks. I'll see you about one.'

'Fine.' He walked away, and she noticed the tension in his shoulders. She would have to rub them later—once she'd given him the necessary lead to pop the question. . .

She went back to her consulting-room and called the first patient.

It was a girl of about twelve, who was listless and had a slight fever. She was complaining of a sore armpit, and on examination Emily found her lymph glands were swollen. She checked her throat, all other glands and her spleen, but could find nothing wrong in any other area.

Odd, she thought, and then noticed a tiny, healed scratch on the girl's hand, the same side as the swollen glands. At the end of the scratch was a small, swollen papule, like a blister.

Emily looked at it, then turned to the child.

'Have you been scratched by a cat recently?' she asked.

'A cat—no, I don't think so,' her mother replied.

'Yes, I was—at Susie's house the other day. Fluffy scratched me.'

'Oh, yes—but that was ages ago—the beginning of last week.'

Emily nodded. 'That's right. I think you've got a thing called cat scratch disease. It's caused by a bacteria—we don't know which one yet, but it makes the nearest glands swell, and sometimes there's a slight temperature and a general feeling of being unwell.'

'That's just how I feel,' the girl told her.

'There you are, then. Problem solved. Nothing nasty, nothing to worry about. I'll give you some antibiotics to clear up the infection in your lymph glands and you'll be fine. All right?'

They left, clutching their prescription and a new body of knowledge, and Emily smiled to herself. Thank goodness she had noticed the scratch!

It was obviously hand day, she thought a couple of patients later, because a lady with a sore, itchy rash on both hands came in.

'Look at me!' she exclaimed, pulling up both sleeves. 'I look as if I'm wearing gloves!'

Emily looked carefully at the skin, and saw a fine, diffuse rash over the whole area. In places it was coming up in vesicles and beginning to scale.

'It must be my new oven cleaner,' she said crossly. 'I knew they were dangerous!'

'Did you wear rubber gloves?'

'Of course! Lot of good it's done me; it's just soaked straight through!'

'No,' Emily assured her. 'It's the rubber gloves themselves. You've got allergic contact dermatitis.'

'From the rubber?'

'Yes, I think so. Were they a new brand?'

'Well—I don't normally wear them at all, so I bought them especially to do the oven.'

Emily nodded. 'Don't worry, it'll soon clear up. I'll give you some Betnovate cream to rub on the rash, and some antihistamine tablets to take to subdue the itching. Do you get drowsy if you take Piriton?'

'I don't know, I've never taken it, but it doesn't matter. I don't have to drive or operate machinery—well, only the Hoover.'

Emily smiled. 'That's OK, then. Here, take these as directed and you'll soon notice an improvement.'

'I'll tell you one good thing,' the woman said as she stood up to go. 'My husband'll have to clean the oven from now on.'

Emily chuckled. Every cloud, and all that. She glanced at her watch as the woman left.

Ten-fifteen. Two and a quarter hours to go.

Her stomach was fizzing, her heart pounding.

'Don't worry, baby,' she told her child. 'We'll soon get all this straightened out and then we can be a real family.'

She pressed the buzzer for the next patient, and carried on with her surgery.

At eleven she went out into the office to ask Sue for another packet of prescription stationery for the computer, and found she wasn't there. She checked the usual place under the counter, but there wasn't any.

'I wonder where she keeps it?' Emily muttered to herself, and she turned to the desk to leave Sue a note.

As she did so, a letter caught her eye. It was to a professional journal, and was asking for an insertion in the 'Partners Wanted' column. Attached to the letter was an advert. She read it, her lips moving as she did so.

'Partner wanted in rural North Devon practice. Must be qualified in minor surgery. . .' blah, blah '. . .ability to map read. . .' Damn! My job! They've decided to get rid of me, and they haven't even told me! I've got two more months!

Rage boiled over, fuelled by her anxiety over David and her uncertain future. She grabbed the paper and stalked down the corridor to the common-room, throwing open the door.

Laurence and Robin were in there, and she marched up to Laurence and thrust the letter under his nose.

'What the hell is this?' she demanded ungraciously. 'You might at least have had the decency to tell me you wouldn't be keeping me on at the end of my trial period before you placed the damned advert!'

Laurence came slowly to his feet, his eyes searching her face.

'It's not your job, Emily.'

'What? But of course it is. Who else's?'

He let his breath out slowly. 'David's.

She felt her blood run cold. 'David's?' she whispered.

'Hasn't he said anything?'

'No—no, not a thing. When did he. . .?'

'The weekend. I thought you knew.'

She shook her head, unable to believe it. 'I had no idea.'

'You'd better go and talk to him. He's at home now.'

'But—I've got visits to make.'

'I'll do them.'

She swallowed. 'Sue's got the list. Laurence, are you sure?'

He nodded. 'Go on. I'll see you later.'

She turned on her heel and ran back to her surgery, grabbing her bag and keys before running out through the waiting-room to the car park.

She drove to his cottage as if the hounds of hell were after her, which indeed she felt they were.

His car was outside, and she pulled up behind it and got out, running to the door.

Once there, her courage deserted her. What could she say? How could she persuade him to stay?

The door swung open before she touched the bell. He eyed her for a moment, then stood back. 'You know,' he said flatly. 'I was going to tell you at lunchtime.'

'Why?' she asked. 'You can't leave me—not now. Where are you going?'

'I don't know. Cornwall, perhaps? I just know I can't stay here being torn apart like this any longer. You're settled, Jamie's settled—it makes sense that it's me.' He paused for a moment, then his hand came out and brushed her cheek. 'I'll miss you.'

'No,' she said firmly.

'I will, Emily.'

'No, you won't, because you won't be going anywhere without me. Not if I have anything to do with it.'

He turned away. 'Don't be daft. Even without the problem of Jamie, what have I got to offer you? You've got a better house than I have, more money than I could ever dream of earning in a lifetime, and without me to mess things up you could be happy.'

She almost stamped her foot. 'Would you just listen to me for a minute? The house is neither here nor there, all Philip's money is in trust for Jamie, except Mrs Bradley's wages and a small amount for untoward necessities. I have nothing—a few hundred pounds in savings, that's all. And Jamie——'

She swallowed and touched his rigid shoulder, the temper going out of her voice. 'Jamie would like you to train the puppy to fetch.'

He turned slowly towards her. 'What?'

She smiled tentatively. 'Jamie told me last night that he likes you. He thinks you're a lot like his father, and he'd like you to be a sort of father to him, the way I'm a sort of mother. He didn't like you taking me out because he doesn't like it when I go out, not because he doesn't like you. He doesn't like me going out to work either, but that isn't going to be a problem soon because I'm going to have to give up, because of the baby—if you'll agree to support me, that is.'

David stared at her, his face uncomprehending.

'Baby?' he croaked. 'What baby?'

'Our baby—the baby we started the night I crashed the car.'

A puzzled frown crossed his face, then a smile started deep in his eyes, in among the tears. 'A baby? We're going to have a baby?'

'Yes—and in this town that could be a problem, so unless you want me to be the object of considerable gossip you'd better ask me the question Jamie says I'm not allowed to ask you, and we'd better get on with it.'

'Are you all right?'

'That's not the question,' she told him softly, moved by the wonder on his face.

He laughed, a tiny, incredulous chuckle, followed by a full, deep belly laugh. It was cut off abruptly as he tugged her into his arms and crushed her against his chest.

'Oh, Emily—marry me, for God's sake—now, today.'

'I can't. It's too soon.'

'It can't be too soon for me.'

'No, but there's the small matter of the law.'

He laughed again and leant back to look down into her eyes.

'Who cares about the law?'

'I do. I want this marriage to be a proper one.'

He was suddenly sober. 'So do I,' he said, with deep sincerity. 'It's going to work, Emily. Trust me. We'll make it work—for everybody's sake.'

He lowered his lips to hers, and as the passion rocked them he lifted her carefully and carried her to his room. There he made love to her, with infinite care and tenderness, and when it was over he cradled her against his side.

'Now, about this wedding,' he murmured against her hair.

'Mmm?'

'How about Friday?' he suggested.

'No. It's Jamie's Nativity play. He's a shepherd and I promised I'd be there.'

'Monday, then.'

'That's our wedding anniversary.'

He looked down at her. 'Is that a good omen or a bad one?'

She smiled. 'I don't know. Are you superstitious? It would have been our thirteenth.'

'Perhaps it would bring us luck this time. It would keep it tidy,' he said with a smile. 'Only one date to remember—you might get a bunch of flowers on the right day if I had two reasons to remember it.'

She laughed softly. 'That would be a first.'

'There'll be lots of firsts, I promise. Trust me, Emily. This time we'll make it work.'

David went to the hospital the following morning to see Joe Hardwill among others.

He sounded his chest and found it clearer, at last, and then checked his lower leg for tenderness and mobility of the ankle.

'How's the physio going?'

'All right. I can get about now without crutches. Time to be going home soon, I fancy.'

'Yes, I think so.' He pulled the pyjama leg down and stood up slowly. 'Joe, do you remember when we were talking about the new doctor, back in September, and you said there might be a bit of love interest?' he said as he straightened.

Joe's twinkling eyes searched David's face. 'Popped the question, boy?'

David grinned. 'Yes, I have.'

'So when's the big day?'

'Monday—if the vicar can fit us in.'

He nodded. 'Bit of a hurry, eh?'

David's grin became sheepish. 'Well, there are two reasons for the hurry. One of them is that it's our original wedding anniversary.'

Joe nodded. 'I'd heard about that. The Miles girl left her the cottage, didn't she?'

'Yes.'

'The other reason I can guess,' Joe said with a wheezy chuckle. 'Still, after so many years I reckon it's about time.'

David patted him on the shoulder. 'I think you're right, Joe—I think you're right.'

They saw the vicar together at lunchtime, and although he was a little surprised he nevertheless agreed to marry them in the church in Biddlecombe on Monday, at the exact time of their first wedding.

'It's a sort of action replay,' David told the vicar, 'only this time we're going to do it right.'

The vicar nodded, and then went through the details of the special licence with them.

There was no question of doing it quietly, of course. Everyone who came into the surgery had an opinion, and expressed it freely.

All were pleased, but a great many thought it was desperately romantic and a few were bold enough to say it was about time, the way they'd been carrying on.

Emily, who thought they'd been very discreet, hid her blushes and did her best to ignore them all. David, who was far better known and definitely much loved by his patients, was teased mercilessly. He took it in good part, however, and just hoped none of them would find out about the baby.

They went together to Jamie's Nativity play on Friday, and then Emily went home to her parents in Oxford for the weekend and dug out her old wedding-dress from the back of the wardrobe. It still fitted as it had when she had first worn it—slightly better, perhaps, with the fullness of maturity—and they took it to a dry-cleaners and collected it two hours later, good as new.

'Are you sure, darling?' her mother asked her over and over again. 'He hurt you so badly before.'

'I hurt him, too,' Emily assured her. 'We were too young. We're older now, and wiser. Anyway, there's another reason.'

Her mother's eyes widened. 'Emily! You're a doctor—how could you be so silly?'

She laughed. 'Silly? I thought you wanted to be a grandmother.'

'Well, I do, but—you aren't marrying him just for the baby, are you?'

'No,' she assured her emphatically. 'Definitely not.'

Two hundred miles away, David was having the same conversation with his parents.

'Should have thought you'd know better,' Bill said crisply. 'Well, you'll have to take it seriously this time—no mucking about, not with children involved.'

'I'll take it seriously, Dad. I love her, I always did. And this time I'll make sure we both remember it.'

Monday dawned cold, wet and windy. By eleven o'clock, however, the wind had blown away most of the cloud and the sun was out, gleaming on the wet rooftops and bringing colour to the winter landscape.

Emily's mother helped her to dress, and Mrs Bradley sorted Jamie out. He was a page boy—not in all that 'cissy stuff', as he put it, but in a new suit, with a proper tie, and a carnation in his buttonhole.

David had sent the buttonhole together with a bouquet of red roses for Emily—thirteen, one for every year since their marriage.

They drove down to the church in her parents' car, Emily perched in the back trying not to crumple her wedding-dress, and Mrs Bradley and Jamie each side of her holding up her veil.

As the clock on the town hall struck twelve, Emily

stepped out of the car, straightened her veil and smiled at her mother and Mrs Bradley.

'You'd better go in,' she told them.

Her father tucked her hand in his arm and smiled down at her. 'All set?'

She nodded. 'Jamie, are you all right, darling?'

'Yes.'

He looked nervous, and she felt a moment of panic. What if he changed his mind?

She heard the organist strike up the first notes of 'Here Comes the Bride', and, tightening her grip on her father's arm, she walked calmly through the door and down the aisle.

David was standing there, his broad back towards her, his hair gleaming mahogany in a stray beam of sunlight. His brother was beside him, identical save for the darker hair, and he turned and winked.

She walked past old friends and loved ones: Philip's parents, beaming delightedly and winking at Jamie, Mrs Bradley at their side; Emily's mother, a handkerchief at the ready; the Trevellyans, behind David.

And then she was there, standing by his side, and he turned to look at her. She felt his strength pouring into her, his love, his steadfastness, and a smile touched her lips.

Suddenly his jacket was tugged from behind and he turned, puzzled.

'You will bring Ruffian and Bridie to live with us, won't you?' Jamie stage-whispered.

David nodded.

'And train Beauty?'

He nodded again. 'Yes—I promise.'

'OK.' He grinned, and his face screwed up in a wink.

David returned the wink and knuckled his hair, then turned back to the vicar, a broad smile on his face.

'I think we're ready now,' he said softly.

The vicar cleared his throat and raised his hands to the congregation.

'Dearly beloved, we are gathered here together. . .'

As Emily listened to the familiar words, she thought back over the past thirteen years. So many mistakes, so many things they had left undone, so many times they had turned away from a difficult problem. Instead of talking it through, they had rowed, stalked away from each other and then made up later without exchanging a word to resolve the initial conflict.

Never again. They would row, she knew that. But they would talk about what worried them, sort out their differences, respect each other's opinions.

As David made his vows, his voice clear and steady, his eyes locked with hers, she felt a deep and enduring peace steal over her heart.

And as he took his ring from her finger and handed it to the vicar for the blessing, then returned it to her she felt a sense of rightness in her world that had been missing for eight long years.

'I now pronounce you man and wife,' the vicar said. 'Those whom God has joined together let no man put asunder.'

'They won't,' David vowed softly, and lifting her veil, he bent his head and brushed her lips.

'Is that all I get?' she whispered.

'Hussy,' he mumbled, and, dragging her into his arms, he kissed her soundly.

She heard a sniff—her mother, or David's?

Or both?

And behind them Jamie, quite distinctly, said, 'Yuck!'

David threw another log on the fire. 'Hungry?' he asked.

'No—how about some champagne?'

His eyes gleamed in the firelight. 'Just what I was thinking.'

He disappeared to the kitchen, returning moments later with two glasses and an open bottle.

'It was good of your parents to do this for us twice,' he said with a smile, handing her a glass.

'I think they were glad to—anything rather than have an illegitimate grandchild.'

He chuckled, and, sitting on the rug by the fire, he propped his back against the chair and patted the rug between his legs. She bunched up her wedding-dress and sat down, leaning back against his chest.

'Mmm. This brings back memories.'

'It's meant to. How are you feeling?'

'Oh, I feel wonderful.'

He slid his hand over her still flat tummy and sighed. 'You do, don't you?' He nuzzled her neck, the slight scrape of his beard doing amazing things to her nerve-endings.

'Sexy beast—you'll slop my champagne.'

'Mmm—you don't need it anyway, not when you're pregnant. Give it to me.'

He put it down, then turned her in his arms.

'Do you know what I'm going to do?'

She shook her head, laughter brimming in her eyes. 'I can't imagine.'

A sly smile crept on to his face, and his hand found

the tiny buttons at the back of her dress and slowly, one by one, he unfastened them.

'Oh, you cheeky thing.'

'Mmm. I don't suppose you'd like to strip for me?'

'There was a time,' she told him, 'when you weren't too lazy to undress me yourself.'

He rose to his feet, grasped her hand and drew her up beside him.

'Turn round.'

One by one, slowly, he unfastened the rest of the buttons, laying a trail of fire down her spine with his lips. Her dress slithered down, pooling at her feet, and he held her hand as she stepped out of it.

He threw it on to the sofa and she chided him.

'Careful!'

'Why? You won't need it again.'

A smile bloomed on her face. 'I know.'

Her fingers rose to his tie, tugging it off, then quickly worked the buttons down the front of his shirt, exposing the broad expanse of his chest. Mischievously, she tweaked a hair and he swore softly and grabbed her hand.

'You're in one of those moods, are you?'

She giggled.

'I'm going to have to do something about you. Sit down—just there—and don't move.'

He undressed as she watched, kicking off his shoes, throwing his trousers and shirt after her wedding-dress. Then he knelt in front of her and unclipped her bra, catching the burgeoning fullness of her breasts in his hands.

'Maternity is going to suit you,' he murmured,

lowering his head to the smooth curves, and slowly, lavishly, he paid them homage.

'You were in too much of a hurry thirteen years ago,' she said softly.

'You want to hurry?'

She shook her head. 'No—we don't need to. We've got all the time in the world.'

He lay down and drew her into his arms, cradling her head against his chest.

'I love you, Emily Trevellyan.'

Emily Trevellyan. Funny how absolutely right it sounded.

She lifted her face to his.

'I love you, too—so very much.'

His eyes darkened, the flames burning hotter, and lowered his mouth to hers.

Their prayer for peace had been answered.

EPILOGUE

EMILY heard his key in the door, then the soft slam and his brisk stride on the stairs.

'Hi. All done?'

'God, I should hope so. What a weekend! Have I got time to get back into bed for a cuddle?'

She shook her head. 'No—David, how long does it take to get to Barnstaple?'

His eyes cut into hers. 'About twenty-five minutes. Why?'

'Because I don't think I'm going to make it.'

His eyes widened. 'Have your waters broken?'

She nodded. 'A few minutes ago. And I have this very definite urge to push.'

'Oh, my God.' The blood literally seemed to drain from his face. 'Emily, I'll call the ambulance——'

'What for? I'm fit and healthy, you're a doctor——'

'But it's twins! For God's sake, darling!'

'So? You just have to do it twice.'

'Not at home. Please, Emily. . .'

She shrugged. 'The cottage hospital, then, but we'll have to move very fast.'

'I'd better look at you.'

'No,' she said firmly. 'Just put me in the car and get me there.'

So he did, carrying her carefully down the stairs, fastening her seatbelt awkwardly round her swollen abdomen and then driving like a bat out of hell for the hospital, the green light on his car flashing all the way.

'That's pulling rank,' she told him as he switched the siren on to cut through the early morning traffic in town.

'Damn job has to have some privileges,' he grunted, and swung into the ambulance bay of the hospital, siren still blaring.

Maureen rushed out, took one look at Emily and went back for a trolley.

Minutes later, without bothering to wait for the midwife, their first daughter made her appearance.

David sighed, wiped his brow with the back of his arm and grinned at her weakly. 'One down, one to go.'

She cradled her first-born child against her breast, her eyes filling.

'She's beautiful.'

'She's noisy,' he said, but she noticed his eyes were suspiciously bright.

The midwife arrived at the same time as the second baby, another girl.

'Identical,' she said in satisfaction. 'That'll keep the teachers on their toes in a few years' time.'

David grinned. 'Runs in the family, like wooden legs.'

'Are you a twin?'

He nodded. 'Yes.'

'Oh, well, get's it over with in one fell swoop, I suppose—unless you're going to do an Amy Richardson on us?'

Emily, totally fascinated by her two beautiful daughters, looked up at David and smiled mistily.

'They are so lovely.'

'Are you all right?'

'Never better. Are you?'

He sat down suddenly. 'It's a bit much, all at once.' He dredged up a shaky smile. 'I love you, clever girl.'

She grinned, very pleased with herself. 'I could have had them at home.'

'You damn nearly did. Why didn't you ring me?'

She smiled. 'What, and have you take me all the way to Barnstaple?'

His eyes narrowed. 'You planned this.'

She blinked innocently. 'Me?'

He scowled, then his face softened and he reached out to touch his tiny daughters, still resting against her breasts.

'What are we going to call them?'

'I thought—Sarah,' she said quietly. 'And maybe—Jenny?'

He nodded. 'Yes. Yes, I think so.'

He stood up and bent over her, placing a tender kiss on her brow.

'Well done.' A huge yawn cracked his face. 'Lady, your timing is lousy.'

She grinned mischievously. 'I thought it was rather good, myself.'

'Hmm.'

The midwife took the babies from Emily, one at a time, and washed and dressed them, then put them in David's arms.

'You sit there with your family while Dr Allen sorts your wife out,' she told him, and he settled back in the big armchair with a baby on each side.

They were all asleep in seconds.

Emily, watching him, thought of Sarah and Philip,

and their son, her son now and David's, and of Jenny Wellcome who had died the night the babies were conceived.

If it hadn't been for Sarah dying, Emily might never have come back to Biddlecombe and found David again, and if she hadn't spent the evening at the hospital checking on Jenny she might not have ended up in his arms that night.

Both women, in their way, had been instrumental in her happiness. It seemed fitting that they should be remembered.

Watching her husband and babies now, Emily settled back against the pillow.

Her marriage was working this time, truly working. They had learned a lot between them, and they wouldn't waste this second chance. Once more, she thought, with feeling. . .

Marion Lennox is country girl, born on a south-east Australian dairy farm. She moved on – mostly because the cows just weren't interested in her stories! Married to a 'very special doctor', Marion writes for Medical Romance™ as well as Tender Romance™ where she used to write as Trisha David for a while.

In her non-writing life, Marion cares for kids, cats, dogs, chooks and goldfish. She travels, she fights her rampant garden (she's losing) and her house dust (she's lost).

After an early bout with breast cancer she's also reprioritised her life, figured out what's important and discovered the joys of deep baths, romance and chocolate. Preferably all at the same time!

STORM HAVEN

by

Marion Lennox

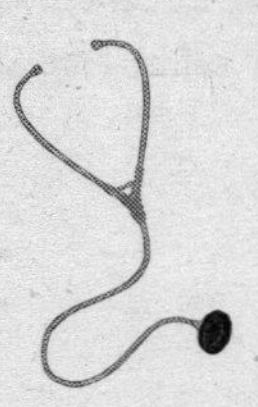

CHAPTER ONE

'NIKKI RUSSELL, you're killing yourself!'

Nikki looked up from her books. The causes of renal failure were swimming around her tired mind, and it took a moment before she could focus on her elderly housekeeper. Beattie Gilchrist stalked forward and planted a mug of hot chocolate on top of Nikki's open text. 'I know you asked for coffee,' she said darkly, 'but I've no intention of helping you stay awake. It's bed you need, Dr Russell, and that's a fact.'

Nikki smiled wearily and pushed her heavy glasses from her nose. 'Thanks, Beattie. I'm coming to bed in a moment.'

'I know. I know.' Mrs Gilchrist folded her arms and glared at her employer. 'In a few hours more like. You delivered the Raymond baby last night, you were up at six to Amy, you had a full day at the surgery today and it's near to midnight now. Odds are you'll be called out again tonight and then where will you be?'

'Exhausted,' Nikki admitted. 'But the exam's only three weeks away, Beattie.'

'And old Doc Maybury told me there's not the least need for you to be sitting the exam yet. He said most doctors wait five years from graduation before even thinking about it, and you've been practising less than that. You'll drive yourself to an early grave, Nikki Russell, you mark my words!'

'Beattie, I'm only twenty-seven.' Nikki smiled placatingly at her housekeeper and pushed stray curls of flaming hair back from her face. 'I'm young and fit. Hard work's not going to kill me.'

'It will if it's all you do.' Beattie sniffed. 'It's no life for a girl, buried here as Eurong's solo GP. You should be out having fun while you're still young. You've a little girl who's growing up without knowing her mother can be fun and happy.' She hesitated. 'Honestly, Nikki, dear, it's been five years since Scott. . .'

Nikki's smile faded and her face closed. 'What I'm doing now has nothing to do with Scott.' She grimaced. 'Or maybe it has. I had fun with Scott. And look where that got me.'

'But——'

'Thanks for the chocolate.' Nikki's eyes told her housekeeper to keep away from the raw spot—the aching pain that had been there for five long years. 'Beattie, I really need to study.'

The housekeeper stared at her young employer in concern. Beattie had known Nikki Russell since childhood and was almost as fond of her as she was of her own family. Nikki's nose was back in her text but Beattie tried one more time.

'While this locum's here,' she started tentatively. 'While he's here, couldn't you get away for a bit? Take Amy and have a few days right away. . .'

'I've employed the locum so I can study,' Nikki said shortly. She shoved her glasses higher on to her nose as she buried her face determinedly in her text. As she did, the front doorbell pealed. 'Damn!' she swore.

'I'll go,' Beattie sighed. 'Oh, my dear, I didn't want you to be called tonight.'

'Leave it, Beattie.' Nikki echoed Beattie's sigh, closed her book and rose. 'You go to bed. I'll deal with it.'

Nikki made her way swiftly through the darkened house to the front door, sending up a silent prayer that whoever was waiting for her had a minor problem. The last thing she needed tonight was major trauma—not when she was so tired.

Still, she might not have a choice. If there was a medical emergency there was only Nikki. On this bleak thought she swung the front door wide—and found herself staring into the most arresting blue eyes she had ever seen.

This was no emergency. The man was standing half turned, as if he had been soaking in the view across the moonlit valley to the sea beyond. There was no panic here.

'Dr Russell?' The man smiled as she frowned across the veranda at him. He held out his hand. 'I'm Luke Marriott.'

Luke Marriott. . . Mechanically Nikki held out her hand and had it enveloped in a much larger one. The stranger's grip was strong and warm, intensely masculine. He stood holding her hand and smiling down at her, and Nikki felt her secure, dull existence shift on its foundations.

She had never seen a man like this. Never. Not even Scott. . .

Good grief! What on earth was she thinking of? Nikki gave herself a mental shake, trying to rid herself of the overwhelming impression of—well, there was no other word for it—of masculinity!

Nikki was tall, but this man was taller by several inches. He was strongly built, with fair, unruly curls that looked in need of a good cut. His face bore two or three days' stubble and his jeans and open-necked shirt were stained with sweat and dust. There was a smudge of dirt across the strong, wide features of his face, and the deep blue eyes laughing down at her in the porch light were creased as though constantly shielded from the sun.

'Luke Marriott. . .' Nikki said blankly.

'Your new locum,' the man explained patiently. 'I know I'm not due until tomorrow but I hitched a lift on a prawn boat rather than wait for the bus.' He grinned ruefully down at himself. 'I hope that explains the dirt—and the smell. I'm not usually so perfumed.'

Nikki wrinkled her nose. Now that he mentioned

it. . .ugh! There was a definite smell of old fish about him.

'The prawn boat was down in Brisbane for a refit,' the man explained ruefully. 'One of the deck hands lives here so I filled his place until we arrived. What I'd thought would be a great two days' holiday turned into a solid two nights working.' He looked down to his grubby sports shoes. 'I hate to think what's on these,' he grinned. 'I'll take them off before I come in. That is——' he raised his eyebrows in mock-enquiry '—if you intend asking me in.'

'I. . .' Nikki shook her head as through trying to dispel a dream. Luke Marriott. She had advertised for weeks for a locum and had been so delighted when this man had rung to accept that she'd asked little further of him except his registration details. But. . .

'But we've organised your accommodation at the hospital,' she stammered. 'There's a room there.'

'There's not,' he told her. 'I've been there and the night sister's apologetic, but Cook's car's broken down and if they want Cook on hand for breakfast she stays. They seemed to think their breakfast is more necessary than I am—and Cook won't share.'

'But. . .but you can't stay here. . .'

'Look, I only take up six feet of floor space.' The man's humour was beginning to slip. Clearly he'd expected a warmer welcome. 'Lady, I've come almost a thousand miles to do a locum for you. Do you expect me to find a park bench?'

'I. . .'

'Your night sister said Whispering Palms had at least six bedrooms and it only held three people. Now, if I promise to rid myself of prawn bait and berley, and not indulge in rape or pillage, can Whispering Palms stretch itself to accommodate me?' The stranger stepped back as he talked, his eyes following the long lines of generous verandas with the rows of French windows opening out to the night breeze. 'Or do you want me to go back to Brisbane?'

Nikki pulled herself together with a visible effort. Of course there was no reason to refuse to accommodate her new locum. If only. . . Well, if only he weren't so. . .

So. . .so she didn't know what! She stood aside and held the door wider.

'Of. . .of course not. Come in, Dr Marriott. Welcome to Eurong.'

'I'm not very,' he said, looking quizzically down at her. What he saw made his deep eyes crease in perplexity. Nikki Russell was a stunner in any man's books. Her fabulous red-gold curls framed an elfin face with huge green eyes which refused to be disguised by her too heavy glasses. She was slender—almost too thin for good health—and her pale skin was shadowed by the traces of exhaustion. The casual jeans and worn cotton shirt she wore accentuated her youth. She looked too young to be a practising doctor. 'And I wonder why not?' he said slowly.

'I'm sorry?' Nikki frowned, trying to make sense of his words.

'You do want a locum?'

'Oh, yes.' Nikki was under control now, moving aside to make way for him. As she did she was intensely conscious of his size—his smell—and it wasn't all fishing-boat smell either. 'It was only that you were so. . . well, unexpected.'

'Because I wasn't due until tomorrow?' he asked.

'Yes,' she said firmly. Why else?

She turned to usher him into the house, but as she did the telephone on the hall table started to ring. Now what? She flashed him a look of apology and went to answer it. It was almost a relief to turn away—to give her confused mind time to settle.

She wasn't granted time. The voice on the other end of the line was harsh and urgent.

'Nikki?' It was Sergeant Milne's voice, Eurong's solitary policeman.

'Yes?' Nikki knew trouble when she heard it. Dan Milne's voice was laced with it.

'You'd better get here fast,' the policeman barked into the phone. 'I've got two kids trapped in a wreck on the beach road and I doubt if either'll make it. They look bloody awful!'

Luke Marriott and a car crash all in one night! Nikki turned from the phone to find her new locum watching her. He'd placed his luggage down on the polished boards of the hall and was listening in concern to Nikki's terse queries.

Behind them, Beattie Gilchrist appeared in her dressing-gown and fluffy slippers. The housekeeper raised her brows in surprise at the strange man making himself at home in the hall, but didn't speak until Nikki put down the phone.

'Trouble?' she said as she saw Nikki's face. What she saw there made her treat the stranger's presence as secondary.

'Beattie, this is Dr Marriott, our new locum,' Nikki said briefly, pushing her hair back in a gesture of exhaustion. 'Can you find him supper and a bed? I have to go. There's a car come off the back beach road and a couple of kids are still inside. Sergeant Milne's there and it looks bad——'

'I don't need supper,' Luke Marriott's deep voice cut across her decisively. He abandoned his battered suitcase and strode back to the door. 'Is the ambulance there?'

'It's on its way. But, look, I can handle——'

'I don't think you can.' The big man was suddenly in control, more assured than Nikki. 'To be honest, you look done in already, and if there are two kids. . . Is there a medic with the ambulance?'

'Our ambulance drivers are volunteers with first-aid certificates,' Nikki admitted. 'But——'

'Then no buts,' the man ordered. 'Let's go, Dr Russell.'

It took five minutes to get to the wrecked car.

Nikki didn't speak but concentrated on the roads, and the man at her side seemed content to let her do so. The local roads were treacherous. The population of Eurong was too small to support major road maintenance and the roads were twisting and narrow.

Above Eurong's swimming beach, the road curved in a sharp U around the headland. The teenagers in the car had tried to take it too fast and a massive eucalyptus had halted their plunge to the sea below.

By the time Nikki's little sedan pulled to a halt at the scene there was a tow-truck and ambulance in attendance, and floodlights lit the wreck from the road above. Nikki left the car and swiftly made her way to the edge of the cliff, abandoning Luke Marriott in her haste. What she saw made her wince with dismay.

The tow-truck driver was securing cables to the rear of the crumpled car. Ernie, the ambulance driver, was half into the wreck and the policeman was behind him. Sergeant Milne looked up and gave a wave that showed real relief as he saw Nikki. He struggled up the cliff to meet her.

'It's bad,' he said briefly, casting a curious glance across at Nikki's companion. 'It's Martin Fleming and Lisa Hay. Lisa's conscious but her legs are crushed between the car and the tree. Martin's unconscious and bleeding like a stuck pig. Ernie's trying to put pressure on now.'

'I'll go down.' Nikki turned to slide down the slope but was stopped by a strong grip on her arm.

'Your bag's in the boot?'

'Yes.' Nikki had forgotten that she wasn't alone. She looked up to Luke Marriott, relief in her eyes. 'If you'll get it. . .'

'There's morphine. . .?'

'There's everything. I. . . We'll need saline. . .'

Luke was already moving. 'That car's stable?' he snapped over his shoulder.

'Now we've secured it, it is.' The policeman grimaced. 'I wouldn't let Ernie in till then. For a while I thought they'd slide right down.'

'We'll need more men to get them out.'

'They're on their way.'

Nikki didn't wait to hear more. She was already sliding.

The car was a mess. The ambulance driver pulled back as Nikki arrived, his face grim and distressed.

'I can't stop the bleeding,' he whispered, his eyes on the conscious girl in the passenger side of the car. Lisa was moaning softly to herself, her body rocking against the savage constriction of her legs. 'And I can't do anything for——'

'Get around to Lisa's side,' Nikki ordered. 'See if you can check those legs for bleeding. And stop her twisting!' She raised her voice, trying to penetrate the girl's pain. 'Lisa, help's here. We'll give you something for the pain while we cut you free. You'll be OK now. Just keep still and let us help you.'

The girl's moans grew louder. She turned wild eyes to Nikki. 'Martin's going to die,' she sobbed. 'And my legs. . . You'll have to cut off my legs. . .'

'No.' Nikki's voice was sharp but she didn't make an impression. She was trying to work as she talked, conscious of the blood pumping through a wound on Martin's scalp. Her fingers searched frantically for the pressure points but her eyes also saw what Lisa was doing to her legs. She was pulling, doing what Nikki could only guess to be more damage.

'I'm going to die. You'll have to cut off my legs. Martin's dead. . .' The girl's voice rose in terrified hysteria and she writhed helplessly against her cruel confinement.

'You're talking nonsense.' A man's clipped, firm voice cut across Lisa's screams. The ambulance driver was edged firmly out of the way and Luke Marriott's face appeared on the other side of the car. His hands came in and caught the hysterical girl's flailing fingers from hauling at her legs. 'Keep still,' he ordered. 'Don't move.' Then, in the fraction of a moment while she reacted to his voice, he produced a syringe, swabbed with lightning speed and plunged the morphine home. 'That's good, Lisa,' he said more gently. 'The pain will ease now and we can cut the metal from your legs.'

'But they're smashed. . .'

'You're cutting them by pulling,' Luke said firmly. 'So don't pull.'

'And Martin's dead. . .'

'Is Martin dead?' Luke looked over to where Nikki had found the point she wanted. Nikki was pushing firmly on a wad of dressing over the wound. At Luke's terse request she looked up.

'No one bleeds this much if they're dead,' she said grimly. 'Ernie, I need a saline drip. If I can replace fluids. . .'

'There you are,' Luke told the frightened girl. He looked down at what he could see of the bottom half of her body. 'Now, if you'll stay absolutely still, I'll see if I can relieve some pressure on your legs.'

It was grim work getting the two from the car, and by the end of it Nikki was despairing for the boy she was treating. Martin was deeply unconscious and the longer he remained unconscious, the worse it looked. The steering-wheel had slammed into his face. He had smashed his cheekbones, but something else was causing the coma. What? She hated to think. All she could do was keep him alive while around them men worked to free them.

Over and over she was grateful for Luke Marriott's presence. What good fairy had brought him to Eurong tonight? Lisa needed attention as much as Martin, and Nikki knew that alone she would have struggled to keep both alive.

Finally the metal panels were ripped from the frame of the car. Martin was freed first. As Nikki, the ambulance driver and the assisting men carefully lifted his unconscious frame on to a stretcher, Nikki turned helplessly to Luke.

'It'll be another ten minutes before we have Lisa free,' Luke told her. 'How far's the hospital?'

'Five minutes.'

'Take him and send the ambulance back for us,' he ordered, and there was nothing Nikki could do but obey.

She didn't have time to think of Luke Marriott for the next half-hour. Nikki didn't have time to do anything but hold desperately to her patient's fragile grip on life. Both she and Martin were fighting, she thought grimly, but only one of them was aware of it.

The nursing staff of Eurong's tiny hospital were out in force—the full complement of five nurses and a ward's maid were all at the hospital before Nikki and her patient reached it. In a tiny community like Eurong, word travelled fast. Everyone knew these two kids, and the nurses were grateful for anything they could do to help.

But there was so little. . . Nikki set up an intravenous infusion, took X-rays and then monitored her patient with an increasing sense of helplessness.

'He's slipping.' Andrea, the hospital charge sister, took Martin's blood-pressure for the twentieth time and looked grimly to where Nikki was adjusting the flow of plasma. 'Isn't there anything we can do?'

'The plane's on its way from Cairns,' Nikki told her. 'It'll be here in an hour. They'll transport him back there.'

'But he's slipping fast.'

'I know.' Nikki looked helplessly down at the boy's pallid face. She suspected what was happening from the X-rays. There was pressure building up in the intracranial cavity. She was faced with an invidious choice—to operate here with her limited skill, or put the boy on the plane, knowing that by the time the plane landed in Cairns he'd probably be dead. 'I can't operate,' she whispered. 'I haven't the skills. . .'

There was so much to this job. She would never be skilful enough to cope with the demands on her. Nikki had done obstetrics, basic surgery and anaesthetics but now—now she wanted a competent neurosurgeon right here and now. And because she hadn't done the training this boy would die.

'I can.' The voice sounded behind her and Nikki spun around. Luke Marriott had quietly entered the theatre and was standing watching her.

He looked more disreputable than he had when she'd first seen him. The travel stains and the marks from catching prawns for two nights had been augmented by an hour trying to free the injured girl. His shirt was ripped and blood-stained. Even his fair hair was filthy, matted with dirt and blood. 'Intracranial bleed?' he asked.

'Yes.'

'I've stabilised Lisa,' he said briefly. 'She'll make it. She has two broken legs but they'll wait for surgery in Cairns. She's out to it now. If you prep, Dr Russell, I'll throw myself through the shower, scrub and operate here.' He turned to the junior nurse. 'Show me where to go. Fast.'

'But you can't,' Nikki said blankly.

'Why not?' The fair-haired man turned back to her and his eyes seemed suddenly older than Nikki had thought. Despite the dirt, he looked hard, professional and totally in control. 'You're wasting time, Dr Russell. Prep, please, and fast.'

'But you're not——'

'I'm a surgeon,' he snapped. 'And I've done enough neurology to get me through. Now move!'

Nikki moved.

The burr hole was the work of an expert. Nikki could only watch and marvel, in the few fleeting moments she could spare from her concentration on the anaesthetic. Luke Marriott's fingers were skilled and sure. It was Martin's good fairy that had sent him here tonight.

What on earth was such a man doing as a relieving locum in a place like Eurong? Luke Marriott's skills belonged in a large city teaching hospital. For him to be volunteering to work for the meagre wage of a locum for three weeks. . .

There was little time for her to question his motives. All Nikki's energy had to focus on the job she was doing. Skilled surgery such as Luke Marriot was performing took every ounce of her anaesthetic skill, and she knew that the nurses too were being pushed to their limits. At one stage she raised her eyes to meet the eyes of her charge nurse. Andrea pursed her lips in a silent whistle of wonder, and Nikki agreed with her totally.

And then, finally, this strange surgeon was done. He dressed the site with care and signalled for Nikki to reverse the anaesthetic.

'We've done all we can,' he said grimly. 'Now it's up to Martin.'

'His parents are outside.' Nikki was still fiercely concentrating. She wasn't going to slip now, when Luke's part had been so expertly played.

'I'll take over the anaesthetic,' Luke Marriot told her, his voice gentling. This was the job all medicos hated—to face parents when they couldn't totally reassure. 'You know them, Nikki?'

Nikki nodded numbly. She stayed where she was until Luke reached her and his fingers took the intubation tube. As they did, their hands touched and

Nikki felt a flash of warmth that jolted her. That, and the gentleness of his eyes. . . He understood what she was facing, and that, on its own, made her job easier.

'I'll go,' she whispered, and left him with his patient.

The few moments with the two sets of parents were as bad as they could be. Nikki tried her best to reassure them. This sort of thing hadn't been so bad before she had Amy, she reflected sadly, but now. . . How would she feel if someone were telling her these things about her lovely daughter?

'We're taking them both down to Cairns,' she told them gently. 'We can take you on the plane but you must be back here in twenty minutes with what you need. Overnight gear for yourselves and a few things Martin and Lisa will want. The hospital will provide the necessities but a few personal belongings make a difference.' She hesitated. 'Maybe a few of Martin's favourite tapes. He may. . .he may be in a coma for a while. Sound is important.'

Martin's dad's eyes filled with tears. 'A coma. . .for a while. . . How the hell long?' he demanded roughly.

'I don't know,' Nikki said honestly. 'Dr Marriott has lifted the pressure but there may have been damage done before that. We can only wait.'

Luke was waiting for her as she returned to Theatre. 'Bad?' he said softly, and Nikki looked up at him. For some stupid reason she felt like weeping. This wasn't Nikki Russell—professional—untouchable.

'Terrific,' she said sarcastically, and her tone was harder than she intended. 'What do you think?'

His face tightened and he turned to the sink. 'Sorry I asked.'

Nikki bit her lip. She followed him across and mechanically started to wash.

'You'll fly to Cairns with them?' she asked tentatively. Normally it would be her making the long flight, and she hated the flights with emergency patients. It left Eurong with no doctor within thirty miles. Still, both Lisa and Martin needed a doctor on the trip, and now there was Luke Marriott ready to go.

Or maybe not. Luke shook his head. 'Your job, Dr Russell.'

Nikki stared at him. 'But if something goes wrong. . . It's you who has the neurology skills, Dr Marriott.'

'And a fat lot of good they'll do me at ten thousand feet. You can take blood-pressure and fix a drip just as well as I can, Dr Russell.' They were being abruptly formal and all of a sudden it sounded absurd. The trough where they were washing was meant for one doctor. They were confined in too small a space and the night was too hot for comfort. The nurses had turned on the air-conditioning but it was still making a half-hearted effort to cool.

'But. . .' Nikki tried again. 'But I've a little girl at home.'

'You've a daughter?' His brows rose as if the news shocked him. Nikki winced, wishing for the thousandth time she looked her age.

'I have,' she told him. 'Amy's four and she worries.'

'But your housekeeper is there.'

'Yes. But——'

'And I'll be there too.' He smiled, and his smile held a trace of self-mockery. 'I'm held to be good with children.'

'But——'

He shook his head and his hands came up suddenly to grip her shoulders. 'Dr Russell, do you know what I'm wearing at this particular moment?'

Nikki stared. His deep eyes were challenging her, and behind the challenge was the hint of laughter.

'I don't know. . .' Nikki looked down, writhing in the unaccustomed hold. She didn't enjoy being so close. Then she gasped. Luke Marriott was wearing a theatre gown. Nothing else. Below the gown hard, muscled legs emerged—naked. Even his feet were bare.

'I'm in my birthday suit,' he grinned. 'Without my theatre gown I'm really something.' His smile deepened, and he released her to turn his back, so that the ties behind him faced her. 'Want to untie me and check it out?'

'No!' Nikki stepped back in horror. He turned back and smiled.

'Well, I'm sure as hell not wearing an operating gown all the way to Cairns. My stuff was caked with dirt. I couldn't wear it in Theatre. And these gowns are meant to fit someone about six inches shorter than I am. Sister's already told me you keep a change of clothes here, Dr Russell. On the grounds that you'd look better in your change of clothes than I would, you're going to Cairns.'

'But——'

He sighed, leaned back and folded his arms. 'What's the matter, Dr Russell? Aren't you happy leaving Eurong and your daughter to my tender mercies? Don't you trust me?'

Nikki stared up at him. The deep blue eyes mocked her with their trace of laughter.

For the life of her, she couldn't answer.

CHAPTER TWO

MARTIN recovered consciousness before the plane touched down at Cairns.

For Nikki it was a weird journey. She felt as if she had been snatched from her nice, safe existence, and only part of that feeling was due to flying to Cairns. She watched over her patients while she tried hard to avoid thinking of Luke Marriott.

'He's nice, isn't he?' Lisa whispered as she stirred from her drugged sleep and found the strength to speak.

'Who?' Nikki asked. She knew already whom Lisa was talking about.

'The new doctor. He. . .he saved my life.'

Nikki shook her head, but part of her acknowledged the truth of Lisa's words. His presence might not have saved Lisa's life but it had probably spared her legs, and as for the boy she was with. . .

Nikki checked Martin for the hundredth time and noticed with satisfaction the lessening of his unconsciousness. He stirred just as they touched down, his eyes flickering open and gazing upwards in dazed confusion.

'You're safe,' Nikki told him gently. 'You and Lisa crashed the car. Lisa's here with you. She's OK. We're taking you both to hospital.'

It was all he could cope with hearing. His eyelids lowered and he slept.

At Cairns Nikki was suddenly redundant. Forewarned, there were ambulances and doctors waiting as their flight landed. Martin's condition was less serious now than they had feared, so Nikki could slip into the background. She was content to do so. By now the cumulative effects of two sleepless nights were showing. It was five in the morning and she was close to exhaustion.

Someone showed her to a sparsely furnished room at the hospital. All Nikki saw was the bed. Somehow she shed her clothes, slipped between cool sheets, and seconds later was asleep.

Nikki woke to heat. There was a big ceiling fan in the bedroom but she'd been too tired to think of turning it on. Now the temperature in the room had risen to the point of discomfort. Nikki opened her eyes, looked automatically at the wristwatch on her arm and sat up with a start. Midday.

Midday! It couldn't be. She stared again and shook her wrist. The daily flight up to Cooktown—her only means of getting home—left at eleven a.m. Now. . . now she was stuck here for another twenty-four hours whether she liked it or not.

She flung back her sheet in distress. Someone should have woken her. They knew the routine. The staff here knew she had a flight to catch. Then a knock on the door made her dive back for the modesty of her bedclothes. The door opened and a smiling face appeared. It was Miss Charlotte Cain, a young surgeon whose friendship with Nikki dated from medical school.

'Hi, Nikki,' Charlotte smiled. 'Welcome to the day.' The white-coated young doctor looked down at her watch and her smile widened. 'I can't say good morning any more, that's for sure.'

'Charlie, what on earth were you doing letting me sleep?' Nikki demanded angrily. 'You knew I had a plane to catch.'

'I'm only following orders,' Charlotte grinned. 'I hardly dared do anything else.'

'What do you mean?'

'Just that Luke Marriott rang from Eurong early this morning,' she told the bemused Nikki. 'He rang to find out how his patients were—*his* patients, mind—I think you've suffered an insurrection in your absence. When we reassured him as to Martin and Lisa's condition, he turned his attention to you. He said you weren't to be woken. He told us he didn't expect you back in Eurong until tomorrow. We are to pass on instructions to you to get some rest. Go shopping, the man said. I am informed everything is under control at Eurong and you are not required. An autocratic male, is our Mr Marriott. Not a man to deny, I'd say.' Charlotte sat down on the bed, raised her eyebrows at her friend and grinned. She had the look of someone who was enjoying herself hugely.

'Mr Marriott. . .' Nikki stared up at Charlotte in confusion. 'So the man really is a surgeon?'

'One of the best,' Charlotte said simply. 'As your young Martin can testify. He's fully conscious and showing no signs of permanent damage.' Charlotte shook her head. 'I wish I could operate like that.'

'I don't understand.' Nikki folded her sheet more closely about her and stared up at her friend.

'What don't you understand?'

'Anything,' Nikki wailed. 'But especially I don't understand why someone with Luke Marriott's skill and training accepts the job as my locum. It doesn't make sense.' She looked desperately at her friend. 'Make sense of it for me, Charlie?'

Charlotte shook her dark hair. 'I can't,' she admitted. 'We were all amazed when you contacted us last night and told us who was operating. Luke Marriott resigned from this place two years ago. We thought he'd gone overseas but no one heard. And then he springs up with you in Eurong—in the nick of time, as far as I can gather.'

In the nick of time. . . It had certainly been that. But why?

'Did anything happen?' Nikki asked slowly. 'I mean, why did he leave here to do locum work?'

'Who knows?'

'There must be something,' Nikki frowned. 'Did something dreadful happen? Was there a lawsuit or medical mistake that would make him give up surgery?'

'Didn't you ask for details of his past when you employed him?' Charlotte asked, amused. 'Surely an outstanding lawsuit would have to appear on his curriculum vitae?'

'I didn't ask for his curriculum vitae,' Nikki snapped, and then at the look on her friend's face she changed her tone. 'I checked he was currently registered and left it at that. Honestly, Charlotte, I was just so tired I thought anyone would do, as long as they were qualified and registered. I mean, I wasn't going to leave the town.'

'You mean you were going to do your usual trick of employing a locum and then doing the work yourself,' Charlotte said drily. 'For heaven's sake, Nikki——'

'Leave it, Charlie,' Nikki said brusquely. She looked up, saw the fleeting look of hurt in her friend's eyes and immediately regretted her words. 'Look, Charlie, it's just that. . .'

'It's just that if you stop working then you have time to think,' her friend retorted. And then a sudden smile flashed over her face. 'Well, you and Luke Marriott should get on famously. Two workaholics and only enough work for one. Dear, oh, dear. . .'

'So tell me about him,' Nikki demanded, anxious to get the conversation away from herself. 'Why on earth is he acting as a locum if he's so darned clever and conscientious? He looks like. . .' She thought back to Luke Marriott's disreputable appearance, and the sudden memory of naked legs appearing from under his scanty hospital gown made her almost gasp. 'He looks like a bum to me,' she said unsteadily.

'Well, he's not a bum.' Charlotte shook her head vehemently, frowning. 'I suppose we're talking of the same Luke Marriott? I don't think I've ever seen the man without imported, tailored suits and amazingly expensive silk ties.' She looked at Nikki. 'What's your Luke Marriott like?'

How to describe naked legs and laughing blue eyes. . .? Nikki couldn't. She opened her mouth and tried but the words stuck. And then Charlotte laughed.

'OK,' she smiled. 'That's our Luke you're thinking of. I know Luke Marriott. There's not many men who could make you look like that, Nikki Russell, but Luke Marriott has to be a good bet. He hasn't changed, then.'

'Hasn't changed. . .?'

'Luke Marriott was the most gorgeous male within jet-plane distance of this hospital,' Charlotte said firmly. 'He had every junior nurse, some senior ones, and a few female doctors besides, making fools of themselves every time he walked past. He's broken more hearts than I care to name.' She peered at Nikki. 'Not yours yet, sweetie?'

'Don't be ridiculous,' Nikki snapped, and to her annoyance found herself flushing.

'No.' Charlotte stood up abruptly. 'I'm not being ridiculous. Nikki, it's five years since Scott——'

'I don't want to talk about Scott.'

'I know,' her friend said grimly. 'You don't want to remember Scott. Well, that's never going to happen if you don't ease up on work and start enjoying yourself a bit more,' Charlotte said bluntly. She looked at her watch. 'Hey, your new locum ordered you to shop,' she smiled. 'And I have the afternoon off. When was the last time you went clothes shopping, Dr Russell?'

'I don't need clothes,' Nikki snapped. 'I can use this afternoon at the library. I need to study, Charlie.'

'The medical library is closed on Wednesday afternoons,' her friend grinned. 'Now isn't that a shame? And you haven't a text with you—and I'm damned if I'll lend you a single one of mine.'

'Charlie——'

'Nikki Russell, you must have more money than you know what to do with. Your parents left you that fabulous house, and you have a perfectly sound income from a too busy medical practice. And I don't see a single sign of frivolous spending. Those jeans you were wearing last night were years old. Now either you come shopping with me or I'll personally ring the airport and cancel your flight home tomorrow.' She put her hands on her hips. 'Coming, Dr Russell?'

Nikki sighed. Well, maybe she could do with some new jeans. . . 'If you're not doing anything. . .' she said reluctantly.

'I'm doing something all right,' her friend grinned. 'I'm spending the afternoon with my closest friend to spend someone else's money. There's nothing I could enjoy more.'

'I have to telephone Amy.'

'There's a telephone beside your bed,' her friend told her. 'You have fifteen minutes, Dr Russell. And then you're coming shopping, whether you like it or not.'

Jeans weren't what Charlotte envisaged when she said shopping. Charlie dragged her friend from one shop to another and there wasn't a pair of jeans in sight.

'Honestly, Charlie,' Nikki expostulated. 'This stuff is crazy.' The shop Charlie had pushed her into was up-market and exclusive, dealing in everything from beautiful imported shoes and designer fashions to the most indulgent of lingerie. Nikki fingered the soft Swiss cotton of the dress her friend had just discovered. The frock was lovely, light and soft, with swirling green pastels which lit the brilliant red of Nikki's hair. 'I wouldn't wear this in Eurong. It'd be wasted.'

'Maybe yesterday you wouldn't have worn it,' her friend grinned. 'But today. . .today Luke Marriott is your new locum. I wouldn't be seen dead in anything less than this dress if Luke Marriott was in the vicinity. Honest, Nikki——'

'Charlie, I am not the least bit interested in Luke Marriott,' Nikki snapped.

'You're lying,' Charlotte said simply. 'My grandmother would look twice at Luke Marriott. And she's been happily married to my grandfather for fifty years!'

'Charlie——'

'Look, just try it on,' Charlie pleaded. She thrust the dress into Nikki's hands and pushed her towards a changing-room. 'You could even wear this to work —with a nice white coat over the top. It's time you gave the bachelors of Eurong their money's worth. I bet you charge top rates even when you wear your mouldy old jeans.'

Half laughing, half exasperated, Nikki gave in. She was fond of Charlie—in fact Charlotte Cain had been a true friend for a long time. It wouldn't hurt to humour her. And these clothes—she fingered the soft cotton with a trace of regret—these clothes could join the rest of the things she had put away five years ago. Her mother's jewellery. Her cosmetics. Her contact lenses. She looked up to her face and grimaced at the too heavy glasses. She knew she was being stupid wearing these but they were a defence against something she no longer wanted.

They were a defence against the likes of Luke Marriott. Unbidden, the thought of Nikki's new locum flashed before her and it was all she could do not to rip the dress she was trying on from her back. The thought of him produced something that was close to panic.

This was crazy. There was no need for her to panic. Luke Marriott obviously had problems of his own and a three-week stint as her locum was hardly going to change either of them. Her panic was inexplicable and needless.

Nikki forced herself to concentrate on the dress. It

was pretty, there was no doubting that. It fell in soft folds around her slim form, catching the colour of her eyes and highlighting her brilliant hair. She should get her hair cut, she thought crossly. There was too much of it. Or maybe she should just tie it back into a severe knot. She shoved her glasses back on and opened the curtain. Charlie and the shop assistant were both waiting.

'Oh, Nikki, it's lovely!' Charlie exclaimed delightedly. 'Don't you like it?'

'It's OK,' Nikki agreed reluctantly. She fingered the fine cotton. 'It feels good.'

'And so it should.' Charlotte took her by the shoulders and spun her around. 'It really makes you look like. . .well, like you ought to look. Apart from those glasses.'

'There's nothing wrong with my glasses.'

'Why do you wear them all the time?' Charlotte demanded. 'You know you only need them for reading.'

'I'm more comfortable with them on.'

'But you used to wear contact lenses.'

'Well, I don't any more,' Nikki snapped. 'I'll take this off.'

'You'll buy it?'

'If you think I ought to,' Nikki said flatly.

The shop assistant had been watching the proceedings with interest. 'It does look pretty,' she said. 'But have a look at it in the full-length mirror before you buy it. There's one just around the corner here.'

'I don't need to.'

'Yes, you do,' Charlotte said, her voice firm. 'Go and look, Nikki.' Then she reached forward towards the objects on Nikki's nose. 'And look without these awful glasses!'

'Charlie——'

'Can you see without them?' Charlotte demanded.

'Yes, but——'

'Then look without them.' Charlotte firmly removed the offending articles and thrust her forward. 'Now go and look at what you should be, Nikki Russell!'

Nikki was propelled firmly forward by the shop assistant. The assistant had obviously taken Nikki's lack of interest as a personal challenge. She stood next to Nikki, chatting cheerfully at Nikki's image in the mirror.

'It looks so good, miss. You should wear that colour all the time. Green really suits you.' She smiled up at her reluctant client. 'And your friend's right. You shouldn't wear those glasses.'

Nikki stared at her reflection and a part of her cringed. She wanted no part of this. To be beautiful. . . Scott had told her she was beautiful. . .

'I'll get changed now,' she said firmly.

'You will take it?' the assistant said anxiously.

'Oh, yes.' Nikki grimaced. Charlotte would give her no peace unless she did, and her friendship with Charlotte was important. Speaking of Charlotte. . . She looked around. Where was her friend?

'Charlie?'

'Your friend must have slipped out.' The assistant frowned. She looked around the shop, visions of shop-lifting clearly flashing through her mind. People who distracted the shop assistant and left were a worry. Surely not. These two women seemed. . .well, classy.

But Charlotte had gone.

And then Nikki parted the curtain to her changing-cubicle and realised with horror that something else had gone as well. All her clothes. Everything. Her sandals. Even her glasses. . .

The shop assistant was right behind her. Seeing what Nikki had seen, she gave a nervous but relieved giggle. 'Oh, dear,' she offered. 'Your friend seems to have. . . to have taken all your clothes.'

'Charlie. . .' Nikki's voice was an angry wail. What on earth was her friend playing at?

'I'm back.' It was the cheerful voice of Charlotte coming back in the door from the street. 'Missed me?'

'Charlie, where are my clothes?' Nikki asked softly. Her tone was low and dangerous.

Charlie grinned, unperturbed.

'I put 'em in a rubbish bin,' she confessed blithely. 'Actually I put 'em in about five garbage bins. I put your jeans in one. I put your shirt in another. One sandal per bin. I wish I'd been able to get your knickers and bra. But you will be sensible and buy some more of those, won't you, sweetie?'

'Charlotte!'

'Well, you were going to buy new clothes,' her friend said innocently. 'You said you were. And you'd never choose to wear those old things when you have lovely new clothes, now would you?' Her face assumed an expression of innocence. 'You weren't buying these just to humour me, now were you, Nikki?'

It was so close to the truth that Nikki gasped. She opened her mouth to say something and then couldn't think of a thing to say. Finally she closed her mouth again and contented herself with glaring.

'That's better,' Charlie said. She turned to the shop assistant. 'You know, this girl has nothing now but the clothes she's standing in. I think we need at least a couple more outfits.'

The sales assistant choked on shocked laughter. 'Oh, yes, miss,' she breathed. She turned to Nikki. 'We have the loveliest linen suit that you'd look smashing in.'

'Wheel it out,' Charlie said firmly.

'Charlotte, where are my glasses?' Nikki said awfully, and her friend threw up her hands in mock-fright.

'Beats me,' she laughed. 'Either Mall Litter Bin 36 or Mall Litter Bin 39. Or was that your left sandal?' She shrugged.

'Charlie. . .'

Her friend put her hands on her hips. 'Nikki Russell,

you are my very best friend.' She smiled, then her face grew suddenly serious. 'You have been vegetating in Eurong for the past five years with no one to appreciate how lovely you really are. Now I find that one of the most eligible males I know is working as your locum. I'm damned if I'll let you go home wearing those glasses. I'd be failing in my friendship if I did. Now try this suit on, Nikki Russell, and let's have no more nonsense.'

'Charlie, I am not the least interested in Luke Marriott.' It was almost a wail.

'Well, that's fine,' her friend said simply. 'All I'm ensuring is that Luke Marriott is interested in you.'

It was a still angry Dr Russell who climbed from the plane at Eurong airstrip the next day. The wind was hot and blustery. The dress Charlotte had chosen hung coolly on Nikki's slim body, fluttering in the breeze. It felt soft, pleasant and frightening. Nikki's legs were bare apart from simple crystal-green sandals. Her hair wisped around her face, no longer held back by the rigid frames of her glasses. Nikki's fingers kept moving self-consciously to her face, but there was no dark shield to hide her. She felt strange, and frighteningly exposed.

'It's only until I reach home,' she muttered to herself. 'I can change immediately.' If only she had more glasses. . .

The pilot had come around to help her from the cabin. As she thanked him he reached down on to the floor and retrieved a package the size of a small suitcase.

'This is for you too, Doc,' he grinned. 'A Miss Cain sent it out to the airport last night. Said we weren't to give it to you until now.'

Nikki looked down at the package and her lips tightened. The package was emblazoned with the logo of the shop she had visited the day before. She had refused to buy anything more than the dress she was wearing, but she knew already what would be in the parcel. Everything Charlotte had pleaded with her to buy, she imagined.

'I suppose these are all paid for,' she said icily, and the pilot grinned as though he too was in on the plot.

'They're bought on approval,' he said.

'Well, here.' Nikki thrust the package at him. 'I don't approve. You can take them right back.'

'Not me, Doc.' The pilot backed off with his hands held up in negation. 'I promised Miss Cain that they'd stay in Eurong for a least a week. If you don't want them after that, she says I can bring 'em back.'

'But——'

'You wouldn't have me break a promise,' he smiled.

'Yes.' Nikki put the parcel down on the tarmac and glared.

His grin deepened and he shook his head in mock-sorrow. 'Tut-tut. What a thing to say. Now, I'm sorry, Doctor, but undermining my moral values is something I don't hold with. Have it here in a week if you want it returned.'

'Fine,' Nikki snapped. 'I will.'

'Now, Doc. . .' Pete was looking anxious and Nikki sighed and relented. It was no fault of the pilot's that she had such a scheming friend.

'Sorry, Pete. It's just that I'm feeling managed.'

'Yeah, she looks managing, that Miss Cain.' The pilot looked behind her across the runway. 'And speaking of managing. . .is this your new locum?'

Nikki spun around. She'd been expecting Beattie to meet her, but striding across the tarmac was Dr Luke Marriott. He was walking swiftly towards them, carrying a parcel in his arms.

It was all Nikki could do not to gasp. The change in the man was extraordinary. Instead of the disreputable vagrant of two days ago, this man was well-dressed, arrogant and assured. It showed in his stride, in his immaculately tailored linen trousers and quality open-necked shirt—and in the way his eyes dropped approvingly over Nikki's figure.

'Well, well, well.' He whistled soundlessly as he neared them. 'A veritable transformation. . .'

'You should talk,' Nikki said abruptly, and then flushed. Her eyes fell away. She didn't know how to react to this man.

He grinned. 'Didn't you like my coating of prawns, bait and blood?' he smiled. He looked up to the pilot. 'Thanks for bringing her back.'

It was as if he were a parent thanking the air hostess for looking after a child. Nikki's flush deepened and she felt anger mounting within her.

'Couldn't Beattie come to collect me?' she asked ungraciously.

'You don't approve of the substitute?' he demanded, his eyes still laughing. He motioned down to the parcel in his arms. 'Beattie and Amy are involved in a most important function at Amy's kindergarten. They said they'd meet you at home. Speaking of Beattie, she asked me to send this down to Cairns.' He handed it over to the pilot. 'Can I leave it with you? The address is on the label.' Then he turned back to Nikki. 'Shall we go?'

'Fine.' Nikki turned away but the pilot stopped her.

'You've forgotten your parcel, Doc,' he said apologetically, looking down at the bulky package still at Nikki's feet. He looked from Luke to Nikki, obviously relishing the undercurrents he was sensing.

'Leave it here until next week,' Nikki snapped. 'I don't want it.'

'I'm not doing that,' the pilot said definitely. 'This building is open to heaven knows who. You'll have to take it.' He turned to Luke. 'Can you take it for Doc Russell?'

Luke nodded and held out his hands to accept it. 'I

get rid of one and I'm given another. What is it?' he asked curiously.

'I gather our Doc Russell went shopping yesterday,' the pilot grinned.

'As per instructions.' Luke Marriott smiled and the smile made Nikki's heart give a sickening lurch. 'Very good, Dr Russell. I'm glad to see you can follow orders.'

'Excuse me,' Nikki said icily. 'I thought I was the general practitioner and you were the locum. Or was I mistaken? Since when has the locum given orders to his employer?'

Luke's smile only deepened. 'For three weeks, you said, I was the general practitioner and you were out of work,' he told her. 'And that's the way it's going to be.'

'Over my dead body,' Nikki said savagely; and then wished she hadn't. Both Luke and the pilot obviously found it enormously amusing.

'Come on, Nikki Russell,' Luke Marriott said kindly, in the voice of one humouring a fractious child. 'Let's take you home.'

'Dr Marriott. . .'

'It's Mr Marriott,' Luke told her. 'I thought your friends in Cairns would have told you that. But you can call me Luke if you like.'

Nikki stood almost speechless. The ground was being swept from beneath her feet. She felt as if every foundation she possessed was cracking. 'Luke Marriott, I don't know what the hell you're playing at. . .' she started.

'I'm not playing at all.' Luke raised his free hand in acknowledgement and farewell to the pilot, tucked Nikki's parcel under his arm and started walking towards the hangars. In the distance Nikki saw her car parked, waiting. He glanced at his watch. 'In fact, I'm late.'

'Late?'

'For afternoon surgery,' he informed her blandly. 'I have patients booked.'

'My patients!'

'No.' He shook his head. 'They're mine. You're not wanted for three weeks, Dr Russell. You can take yourself off to your texts or sleep by the swimming-pool for all I care. But you're not working.'

'But——'

'Beattie has explained things to me,' Luke went on blandly. 'She tells me you're set on passing this exam and it's my responsibility to see that you do. And I'm one to take my responsibilities very seriously.'

'I'm not your responsibility. . .'

'No. But your practice is. For the next three weeks, Dr Russell, you are not wanted.'

CHAPTER THREE

'WELL, we think he's lovely.'

Nikki's housekeeper and her small daughter were smitten. Beattie stood at the big wooden table, mechanically mixing her dough, her eyes far-away. Amy was fixed on her mother's lap, her small fingers fingering the soft fabric of Nikki's dress in blatant admiration. 'Oh, Nikki, he's just the best thing. . .' Beattie continued dreamily.

'Since sliced bread,' Nikki snapped. She was perched on the stool as she held her daughter, sipping tea and feeling stranger and stranger. It was mid-afternoon. Her surgery was crowded, she knew, and she wasn't even welcome there, much less wanted.

'If you come near the place then I'll pick you up and deposit you outside on your very neat bottom,' Luke Marriott had said sternly, and by the look in his eyes Nikki wasn't going to test the truth of his statement. She had the feeling that Luke Marriott didn't make idle threats.

'But what's he doing here?' Nikki asked for the fiftieth time. 'He's a surgeon, for heaven's sake. What's he doing acting as temporary locum in Eurong?'

'I have no idea,' Beattie said, giving her dough a sound pummelling. 'All I know is that's he's an answer to a prayer, Nikki Russell, and you don't ask questions when fate plays you lucky.'

'He might be the answer to your prayers,' Nikki said bitterly, 'but he's not the answer to mine. A more autocratic, overbearing. . .'

'I know,' Beattie sighed. 'Isn't it lovely?'

'Beattie!'

'I don't mean he's rude,' Beattie said, shocked by

Nikki's tone. 'He just knows what has to be done.' She looked down at her pastry. 'And he really likes my cooking.' She cast a look of disapproval at her employer. 'No just picking around the edges. I asked him what he'd like for dinner tonight and he said, "The same as last night—only more!" I won't give it to him, of course. Last night I made a chicken casserole but tonight I'll do a standing rib roast with Yorkshire pudding—and have apple pie to follow. Eh, but it's good to cook for a man again. I haven't since my John died.'

'But he's not staying here,' Nikki said, frowning. 'Isn't he supposed to be staying at the hospital? I'd arranged it.'

'I know.' Beattie eyed her employer doubtfully. 'The thing is, Matron rang while you were in Cairns and asked if we could have him stay on for a while longer. Cook's done the cylinder-head on her car and it'll be a week or more before they can get the part. Meanwhile she'll have to stay at the hospital—and Matron doesn't want to use a ward.' Beattie took a deep breath and her dubious look intensified. 'So. . .so I told her of course we'd have him here.'

'Beattie!'

'We've plenty of room,' her housekeeper told her severely. 'For heaven's sake, Nikki, there are three spare bedrooms. You hardly have to see the man apart from mealtimes.'

'I'll have my meals in my study,' Nikki said angrily and Beattie smiled. 'With Amy.'

'Mummy, why don't you like him?' Amy had been intent on her drink and biscuits. Finished with the serious business of life, she turned to her mother. 'We think he's nice. And he makes us laugh.' She frowned direfully at her mother. 'I'm not eating in the study if Dr Luke's in the dining-room.'

'Dr Luke!' Nikki frowned back down at her daughter. 'Mr Marriott to you.'

'He said I could call him Dr Luke,' Amy announced.

'I said no one would think he was proper if we called him Mister, and he thanked me for the advice. And he agrees. And I showed him the swimming-pool this morning and he said he'd teach me to dog-paddle. Starting tomorrow. So he has to stay here.'

'Well, there you are, then,' Beattie grinned. Her smile faded a little and she looked down at Nikki in concern. 'It's better this way,' she said gently. 'The night calls come here and you'd be going out anyway if he was staying down at the hospital. This way. . .'

'I know.' Nikki threw up her hands. 'This way I have nothing to do except study.'

'Which is what you wanted, isn't it?' Beattie said doubtfully, and Nikki gave a reluctant smile.

'Yes, Beattie,' she said slowly. 'It's what I wanted.'

Nikki left and made her way back to her study. Her text still stood open at the causes of renal failure. Nikki picked it up and frowned at the blurred image. She'd have to put in her contact lenses and part of her didn't want to.

She put a hand up to her face in a gesture of distress. Her heavy glasses were a token of her defence against the world, but they were a comfort to her. Charlotte had thought she was doing her friend a favour depriving her of them. If she had known how distressed it was making Nikki feel. . .

'How exposed, you mean,' Nikki whispered, and then shook her head angrily. She wasn't exposed. There wasn't the slightest reason to believe that Luke Marriott was the least bit interested in her. 'I can wear what I like,' Nikki muttered, looking down uneasily at the attractive dress she was wearing. Still. . .

Still, she would just go and change before Luke Marriott came home for dinner. After all, she had to go to her bedroom to find her contact lenses anyway. . .

Two minutes later she was back in the kitchen.

'Beattie, where are the rest of my jeans?' she asked softly. The housekeeper looked up, startled, from her cooking and turned a becoming shade of pink.

'Oh, Nikki, dear, you startled me. . .'

'Beattie, where are my jeans?' Nikki's voice was dangerously quiet. She stood with her hands linked behind her, staring at the elderly Beattie.

'All of them?' Beattie asked. She sounded flustered.

'All of them.'

'Well, I sent them to Charlotte, of course.' Beattie's expression of innocence didn't quite come off. 'Like she asked me to.'

'Beattie——'

'Now, I know you'll think we're interfering,' Beattie said, paying minute attention to the pastry she was crimping, 'but Miss Charlotte rang and said you'd bought the most lovely clothes and you wouldn't be game to wear them if you didn't get some encouragement.' She flushed even redder. 'So she told me to burn them. And I wouldn't, of course,' she said virtuously as she saw Nikki's jaw drop. 'So then she told me to pack them all up and put them on the aeroplane back down to Cairns. Said she'd look after them until you wanted them again.'

'So. . .' Nikki stared, speechless.

'So I did. I asked your new locum to give them to the pilot when he met you from the plane.'

'Beattie——'

'And Miss Charlotte said you were to yell at her and not me.' And then Beattie smiled a cheeky smile. 'But you can yell at me if you like. My shoulders are broad enough to take it.' She left what she was doing, folded her floury arms and fixed her young employer with a hard stare. 'Miss Charlotte thinks it's time you started living again and I'm not disagreeing.'

Nikki sank on to a kitchen chair. Her anger was palpable. 'So you take my clothes. . .'

'Those things weren't clothes,' Beattie said harshly. 'They were a disguise, is what Miss Charlotte reckoned, and she's right. You're pretty as any girl in

Eurong, Nikki Russell, and you're too darned young to be as bitter and reclusive as you've been.' She sniffed defensively. 'So we've taken a hand.' She buried her hands in her pastry again. 'And if you don't like it you can sack me, but I've done no more than my Christian duty or what your mum would have done if she'd been alive.' She sniffed again. 'I was that fond of your mother! And I've a duty to her too——'

The telephone broke across her words. It was just as well, Nikki thought grimly. In another minute Beattie would be in tears. Flashing a look of frustrated fury at her housekeeper, she crossed to the bench to answer it. It was the last person she wanted to speak to. Luke Marriott. . .

'OK, I said I wouldn't disturb you.' From the other end of the line his voice was clipped and efficient. 'But I've a child here I'm unhappy about. Karen Mears.'

Karen. . . Nikki's anger was placed aside. 'What is it?' she asked quietly.

'It's a greenstick fracture of her arm. But am I right in worrying?'

Nikki sighed. 'Yeah,' she said grimly. 'We'll have to get her to hospital. I'll be right there.'

'No.' The voice was firm and authoritative. 'I just wanted my suspicions confirmed. I can deal with it.'

'But Mrs Mears will never let you——'

'She'll let me.'

'Luke, Mrs Mears has problems. . .'

'None that justifies this. Her problems can wait. For now, all we need to do is make sure Karen's protected. Then we act.'

'But——'

'Nikki, I don't need you. Go back to your study. I'll see you tonight.' The line went dead. Nikki was left holding the useless telephone. She stared down. Karen. . .

At least this showed that Luke Marriott was thinking as he worked. Most children presenting with a greenstick fracture would not excite attention. Karen, though. . .

Karen was eight years old—the eldest of a family of four children. Her father had walked out a year ago, and Nikki was sure Mrs Mears wasn't coping. Karen seemed to be bearing the brunt of it. She'd been a quiet child to begin with but now she was withdrawn to the point where Nikki worried. She had grown thinner, her pinched little face pale and haunted, with her two huge hazel eyes a mirror of misery. The child had one cold after another, but the only time Nikki saw her was during routine school check-ups. The teacher had drawn Nikki aside and confided her worries.

'She's often bruised,' the young teacher had whispered. 'And she "forgets" her lunch most days. I'm sure she's not getting enough to eat.'

Nikki had gone over the little girl thoroughly. There were bruises over the child's body—enough to make her approach Mrs Mears.

'She's just clumsy,' Sandra Mears had said defensively. 'She's always knocking into things.'

Nikki had watched the young woman's hands tremble as she talked. Sandra Mears was younger than Nikki—much younger. To have to cope with the burden she was facing. . .

'Sandra, can I organise you some help?' Nikki had said gently. 'I can get council child care one day a week—some time to give you a break. The four children must make you tired.'

'There's nothing wrong with me,' Sandra had snapped. 'I don't want your charity.'

'Sandra, it's not charity——'

'Well, I don't want it,' the girl had repeated, rising. 'Now butt out of what's not your business.'

'Karen's health is my business.'

'There's nothing wrong with Karen and if she says there is then she's a liar.' The girl had thinned her lips in a gesture of defiance, but still the lips had trembled.

'Now let me get Karen and I'll go home.'

And Nikki had been able to go no further. She'd talked to Karen's teacher again and then, reluctantly, had contacted the state's children's protection services. The social worker had travelled from Cairns but, like Nikki, she had hit a blank wall.

'There's not a lot I can do,' she'd told Nikki unhappily. 'I'm sure Karen's taking the brunt of her mother's unhappiness. Sandra seems deeply depressed, but neither will admit there's a problem.'

At what point should the authorities step in and remove children from a parent's care? Nikki didn't know. Unhappily she stared now at the telephone and accepted that the point might be now.

It took all her self-control not to go back to the hospital. 'I don't need you,' Luke Marriott had said. If he could get Sandra to agree to the little girl's going to hospital. . .

Well, he had as much chance as she did, if not better, Nikki thought bitterly. An autocratic male might succeed where she had failed so dismally. Maybe even egocentric surgeons had their uses! With this cheerless thought she buried her head again in her books, the hated contact lenses in place. If only she could concentrate!

Somehow Nikki managed to do some useful study. She left her books when Beattie called her for dinner, once more uneasily conscious of her new appearance. Her dress felt odd around her bare legs—like a forgotten memory. She wished she could go back to work. A white coat now would be comforting.

Luke Marriott was in the kitchen with Amy and Beattie. Amy was involved in helping Beattie serve, and Luke seemed to be supervising. In his hand he held a glass of wine, and as Nikki walked in he raised it in salutation.

'The worker emerges,' he said drily, and Nikki flushed.

'I would have described you all as the workers.' She frowned at the glass. 'Did you buy wine, Beattie?'

'I bought wine,' Luke told her. He filled another glass. 'Have some.'

'No, thanks. I never do when I'm working.' She was being a wet blanket but the man unnerved her.

'One glass isn't going to interfere——'

'I don't want it!' Nikki bit her lip, ashamed of her outburst. 'I'm sorry,' she managed. She turned to the housekeeper who was regarding her in astonishment. 'Can I help, Beattie?'

'I've all the help I need in young Amy here,' Beattie told her. 'You two go in. Shoo.'

'I'll wait and help carry in the plates.' The last thing Nikki wanted was to be alone in the dining-room with Luke Marriott. Alone anywhere. . .

Nikki ate in silence while Beattie, Amy and Luke chatted amiably over the events of the day. Nikki couldn't join in. Her overwhelming emotion was anger with herself.

Why on earth had she behaved like a tiresome child? Nikki hadn't the faintest idea why this man was making her react like this, and she hadn't a clue what to do about it. Her normal, cloistered existence was shattered. She was having to share her home with a man who made her feel. . .who made her feel like a gauche schoolgirl.

Luke lapsed into silence as Beattie left to clear the table, Amy virtuously helping, but he didn't seem in the least uncomfortable. On the contrary, his deep blue eyes held the trace of a twinkle, as if he was aware of and enjoying the discomfiture his presence engendered in the girl at the other end of the table.

Finally the interminable meal came to an end and Nikki rose. She hadn't tasted a thing and Beattie had gone to extraordinary trouble. It was a shame.

'I'm going to put Amy to bed,' she said stiffly.

'You mean you do occasionally spend some time mothering?'

Nikki bit her lip. 'I spend heaps of time with Amy,' she said hotly. 'And Amy understands how important my job is.'

'Does she?'

'Look, I don't have to answer to you. . .'

'No,' he said slowly. 'Only to Amy.'

Nikki pushed back her chair, scraping it harshly on the polished boards. 'Amy has to understand that life is serious,' she told him. 'And work's important. Now, if you'll excuse me. . .'

'Don't you want to know about Karen?' Luke enquired, raising his brows. 'I thought a bit of professional concern might be in order.'

Nikki flushed bright red and sank down. She was going crazy. Not to have enquired. . .

'Tell me about her,' she said stiffly. 'Of course I'm worried.'

'Are you?'

'Of course I am.' Nikki bit her lip as again her anger threatened to burst out.

'So why haven't you interfered before now? You do know the child is being abused?'

'Abused. . .?'

'There are bruises all over her. And the X-ray shows the arm has been broken before.'

'Not that I'm aware of.'

'Well, it was.' Luke grimaced. 'The fracture is further up the arm from the original break. The bone's calcified around the old fracture. It happened around a year ago, I'd say.'

Nikki closed her eyes. 'I didn't. . . Neither her teacher nor I picked that up,' she whispered. 'It must have happened during the long vacation. I've seen the bruising, though.'

'And turned the other cheek?'

'I contacted community services. They sent a social worker up from Cairns.'

'That did a lot of good, I'll bet.'

Nikki rose. 'So what would you have them do?' she snapped. 'Take the children away? Sandra had Karen when she was fourteen. Fourteen! She's only twenty-two now and she has four children. She married a no-hoper, had one child after another and now he's left her and she has nothing. The community here labelled her eight years ago when she had Karen out of wedlock, and she's been isolated ever since. She struggles on to hold them together——'

'Well, she's not struggling enough,' Luke said grimly. 'I'd say she has a temper and Karen's taking the brunt of it.'

'So we take all the children?' Nikki shook her head. 'Where does that leave them—or Sandra? I asked Karen about the bruises. She told me she kept falling over—Sandra's obviously warned her about telling the truth—but if you gave her the choice of going to a strange foster home or staying with her brothers and sister, then I know the choice Karen would make.'

'So you're proposing we patch her up and send her back to face her mother's temper again.'

'No, of course not.' Nikki subsided again into her chair. Some things were just so hard. 'Not if it's reached the stage of bones being broken. But I don't know. . . I'll have to contact Cairns again.'

'The social worker?'

'Well, what else do you suggest?' Nikki demanded.

He smiled then, the blue eyes challenging. Rising, he came around to her end of the table and placed a hand on the back of her chair.

'I suggest you abandon your studies for a couple of hours,' he said firmly. 'Let's go and see Sandra now.'

'What, now?'

'As soon as Amy's in bed.' He looked at his watch. 'She won't be expecting us. It will give us a chance to assess what things are like at home, and we just might be able to do something constructive.'

'Like bring all the children back here?' Nikki said bitterly, and Luke's smile deepened. He looked around appraisingly, through the French windows to the swimming-pool beyond.

'Well, there's certainly enough room.'

'In case you hadn't noticed,' Nikki said icily, 'this is my home. And I like my privacy!'

'And I wonder why?' Luke said thoughtfully. 'This place is enormous. It needs half a dozen kids to bring it to life.'

'So you propose going and taking Sandra's? Just to keep Amy company, I suppose.'

'Dr Russell?'

Nikki looked up at him suspiciously. 'Yes?'

'Don't be so bloody stupid.'

They stopped at the hospital first. The children's ward was in darkness. The nurse rose to greet them. her finger raised to her lips in a gesture of silence.

'Karen's only just gone to sleep,' she whispered. 'Despite the medication.'

Luke frowned. 'Why? She should have drowsed off hours ago.'

'She was too frightened to go to sleep. She said. . .' The nurse hesitated. 'She kept saying we'd take her away while she was asleep.' She sighed. 'And her mother didn't come.'

'Was Karen asking for her?'

'No. But her eyes never left the door, waiting. Poor wee mite. . .'

Luke crossed silently to the bed and Nikki followed. The child was sleeping soundly in a drug-induced sleep. Her injured arm was flung out at a rigid angle. In the dim ward light her face was a wan pool of dejection. There were shadows under the huge eyes—shadows that spoke of abject misery. Nikki felt her heart wrench within her. Maybe this little one could come back to Whispering Palms for a while. . .

'Professional detachment,' Luke said softly from the other side of the bed, and Nikki raised her eyes as she realised he was watching her. 'It's a bit hard, isn't it?'

'It's impossible,' Nikki said wearily, and turned to go.

Nikki directed Luke mechanically, out past the town boundaries, along the coast road and then inland to an old farmhouse set well back from the road. This had once been the homestead for the sugar plantation it was on, but the owners had long ago wearied of the fight with white ants and age, and had rebuilt a mile further down the road. They were renting this house out for a pittance, waiting for nature to take its course.

It would soon happen. This land was natural rainforest, and without constant clearing the forest was reclaiming its own. Huge palms surrounded the house, so much so that it was difficult to see where house started and garden ended. The veranda was sagging wearily on rotten footings, and vines and the beginnings of coconut palms were shoving up through the boards.

What a place to bring up children! The place must be crawling with snakes, Nikki thought grimly, and it was miles from anywhere. Sandra had been isolated from the Eurong community since she'd had her first child, but by living here her isolation was complete.

There was complete silence as they approached the house. A rusted-out Ford sedan stood forlornly in front of the veranda, and a light showed through a single window. They could see a vague shape through the cracked glass. The figure rose while they watched and came towards the door.

'What a dump!' Luke stood at the edge of the veranda and looked up, whistling soundlessly between his teeth. 'Surely there must be better places. . .'

'What do you want?'

Sandra was standing at the door, the solitary light behind her casting her shadow twenty feet out into the night. She was wearing a worn dressing-robe, and her long hair was matted and wild. Her figure was so thin that she appeared almost emaciated. She stood, bare-foot, her arms folded. Her stance spoke of defiance and a fear so tangible that Nikki felt she could almost touch it.

'You didn't come to see Karen,' Nikki said gently. 'We thought you might.'

'Karen shouldn't be in hospital. She's only got a broken arm——'

'We're not keeping Karen in hospital because she has a broken arm,' Luke said harshly. 'Mrs Mears, may we come in?'

'No.'

Luke nodded. 'Then we'll keep Karen until the social workers arrive from Cairns,' he said firmly. 'We have no choice.'

'But——'

Luke looked up at the woman on the veranda, and in the dim light his eyes were suddenly implacable and hard. 'Mrs Mears, Karen has bruises all over her. She has a broken arm and it's not the first time it's been broken. She flinches when I raise my hand as if she's used to being beaten. And she's malnourished. Hungry, Mrs Mears. Now, are we going to come inside and talk about it, or do we contact the authorities in Cairns?'

Sandra Mears gave an audible gasp and her hand flew to her mouth. She took a step back as if Luke had slapped her.

'We need to talk, Mrs Mears.' Luke's voice had softened but was no less implacable.

There was a long silence. Then Sandra slowly turned as if sleep-walking, and walked inside.

Nikki had expected chaos. Judging from the outside, the house was a ruin and Sandra incompetent. To her amazement the place was almost pathetically clean, the cleanliness accentuating the abject poverty in the place. She looked around in amazement and then down to Sandra. Sandra had sunk to sit at the kitchen table. Her head fell forward on to her arms and her shoulders heaved. This girl was wretched, and despite her anger Nikki felt a wave of compassion. What sort of mess was this girl in?

'So tell us, what happened?'

The compassion hadn't touched Luke. He was standing over Sandra almost like the interrogator in a bad movie. Nikki put up a hand in protest but he silenced her with a look.

Sandra looked up, her tear-stained face a plea, but Luke wasn't interested in pleas. 'Tell us, Sandra,' he said.

'She. . .she broke her arm.'

'No. Tell us.'

The silence stretched out. Outside on the veranda a cane toad started its harsh croaking. The naked light-globe made the effect surrealistic and awful.

'You know,' Sandra said at last.

'No. You tell us.'

Sandra cast a scared look up at him and dashed a hand across her cheek. Luke didn't stir. His gaze didn't waver.

'She was. . .she wouldn't. . .she wouldn't do what I told her. . .' She took a deep breath. 'It's not true,' she said suddenly. 'It was Jamie. My. . .my youngest. He's four. I'd just been to town and bought some biscuits. We hadn't had biscuits for so long but. . .but the kids asked and asked. One packet of biscuits.' She looked up, pleading with them to understand. 'I just couldn't bear not to—so I got them and then I went outside and when I come back Jamie had got at them and eaten six and shoved the rest in the toilet 'cos he was full and he didn't know what to do with the half-eaten packet and was scared I'd find them. And they blocked the toilet and I found them and I hit Jamie, but I couldn't hit him hard 'cos he's only four and he gets asthma, and then Karen started crying and said I shouldn't hit him and. . .and I just——' Her voice broke off into tears.

'So you hit Karen instead,' Luke said, and to Nikki's surprise his voice had gentled.

'Yeah.' The girl's face came up. 'I always do. She's so like me. She just stands there and takes it. She doesn't even cry. She just stands there. The other kids were crying 'cos they hadn't had any biscuits but not Karen. . .'

'She's so like you. . .'

'Yeah.' Sandra's head sank on to her arms and she gave a broken sob. 'I feel so bad. I love her so much and I hurt her. . .' She managed to look up again. 'Maybe it's best if you take her away. I know I'll keep hurting her. And I love her.' She gave a desperate gulp as if to gain strength to continue. 'I know it sounds crazy but I love her more than the rest of the kids put together and yet I hurt her. . .'

'You didn't come to the hospital. . .'

'She'd look at me,' Sandra said brokenly. 'I know she'd just look at me and not say anything. She won't even cry.'

Luke sat down at the bare, scrubbed table and his hand came out to cover Sandra's. 'Mrs Mears, you've reached the point where you accept help or watch your family disintegrate,' he said softly. He motioned backwards to where Nikki was standing, silently watching. 'Dr Russell and I can help, but only if you let us. You've admitted there's a problem. If you love your daughter, then you must admit that you need help. And then accept it.'

Sandra's eyes once more met his. There was a long silence. Even the cane toad outside had hushed. Nikki found she was holding her breath. So much depended on these next few moments.

Then Sandra took a ragged breath, and then another. She looked over to Nikki and back to Luke.

'I'm in trouble,' she whispered. 'I don't know what to do. Please. . .please help me.'

Luke nodded as if he had expected no less. His hand stayed exactly where it was, and Nikki had a sudden sense of how Sandra must feel. To have this man touching her, feeding strength, reassurance and warmth into her through his touch. There was a sudden, crazy moment of irrational jealousy, quickly stifled.

Luke stood, and motioned to Nikki. 'Do we have any sleeping-pills, Dr Russell?'

'Yes.' Nikki frowned. She wouldn't have thought leaving sleeping-tablets for this woman was the most sensible thing. Sandra seemed almost suicidal.

'We'll leave you two tablets for the night,' Luke told Sandra, heading off Nikki's criticism. 'I want you to take them and get a solid night's sleep. Tomorrow morning I want you to get up, wash your hair, put on your nicest dress and bring the children into the hospital. I'll arrange the nursing staff to take care of them for the rest of the day. You'll visit Karen and then meet me in my surgery at twelve.'

'My surgery'. Nikki flinched on the words. This man had taken right over. Still, he had achieved more so far than she had ever been able to with this sullen, frightened girl.

'But——'

'No buts.' Luke was standing, still not taking his eyes from Sandra. 'By twelve tomorrow I'll have a list of options available for you, and I want you to come knowing that every option is better than what's happening now.'

'But there's nothing. . .' It was a frightened whisper.

'There's everything.' Once more, Luke's voice gentled and his hand came down on to her shoulder. 'There's a whole great world out here for you and your children, Sandra, and it's time you started finding it.'

'But Karen. . .'

'Karen loves you.' He smiled then and his smile warmed the bleak little room. 'If I didn't think that, I wouldn't help you. But Karen loves you and she's a smart little girl. She wouldn't love you unless you were worth loving. So let's get to work and repay her trust.'

They left her then, sitting staring out bleakly into the night. Nikki was aware of intense disquiet as they bumped down the overgrown track away from the house.

'You don't think she'll do anything stupid, do you?' she said softly.

Luke flashed her a quizzical look. 'Like suicide?'

'Like suicide.'

He shook his head. 'She loves her family too much.'

'You sounded tougher before you met her.'

Luke nodded as he manoeuvred the little car out on to the road and turned homewards. 'She's OK.' He was talking almost to himself. 'Sometimes life is just too much. I think for Sandra it's reached that point. But now she's said she needs help—well, I reckon there's light at the end of her tunnel, anyway.'

Nikki frowned across at him. His voice had suddenly flattened as if he was doing some sort of personal comparison. Surely this self-confident, overbearing male couldn't have major problems in his life. And yet. . . He was at Eurong for a reason. What on earth was it?

'Tell me why you're doing country locums,' she said gently, and he flashed her a look of amusement.

'Probing into my ghosts, Dr Russell?'

Nikki flushed. 'You're a successful surgeon,' she continued, and was annoyed at the trace of resentment she heard in her voice. 'Why. . .why have you given it up?'

'I haven't given it up.'

'Doing a locum in a backwater like Eurong is hardly a strategic career move,' she said waspishly.

'No.' He smiled across at her. 'Neither is burying yourself here in a house too big for you in a community that's known and labelled you from childhood. And that's what you're doing, Dr Russell.'

Nikki bit her lip angrily. 'Beattie——' she started.

'If you think I can practise for half a day in this place and not learn all the local gossip, you don't know much about the town you live in,' he told her.

'Especially when you ask!'

He grinned. 'Especially when I ask.'

The car slowed suddenly and Nikki looked out. They were still two miles from home on the beach road. Luke was pulling the little car on to the kerb, and coming to a halt.

'Wh-what are you doing?' Nikki stammered.

'I've been in a stuffy surgery all day,' Luke told her. 'And the moon is full and the beach is calling. I'm taking a short walk, Dr Russell. Are you coming or do you intend to sit in the car and sulk while I walk?'

'But. . .'

Luke didn't hear. The car was stationary and Luke had left, striding swiftly around to hold the door open for her. 'Coming, Dr Russell?'

A walk on the beach was how Nikki often ended her day. After hours spent trying to solve everyone else's problems, the sea and the moonlight were often the only way she could calm her tired mind. But to walk with this man. . .

She looked up, and his eyes held a challenge. Afraid? they mocked, and suddenly she knew she was. She didn't want this. She didn't want what seemed to be happening whether she wanted it or not.

'Don't be so bloody stupid,' he said, for the second time that night, and his eyes mocked her.

Nikki took a deep breath. 'I should be in bed,' she said tightly.

He held up the car keys. 'Well, the car's going nowhere,' he said gently. He held out his hand to take hers. Helplessly Nikki felt herself drawn up and out of the car. 'A walk,' he said firmly. 'Nothing else, Dr Russell. Not yet.'

CHAPTER FOUR

THE night was still and warm. A gentle breeze from the sea stopped it being oppressively hot. October on the coast along the Great Barrier Reef was the loveliest of months—the time before the real oppression of the steamy wet season began.

Nikki walked slowly down towards the sea. As she had risen from the car Luke had released her hand and had gone before, leaving her to follow if she would. Now he strode easily across the firm, tide-washed sand, his face lifting to the moonlight as though soaking in its beauty.

Once more Nikki found herself wondering about this man of many parts. How many men took time to soak up the loveliness of a night like this?

What had she expected? That he would use this opportunity to make a pass at her? He seemed now to be oblivious to her presence, and Nikki knew that Luke would have stopped the car and walked even if he'd been alone.

As he was now. He walked alone across the moonlit beach, alone with whatever demons drove him, and Nikki was left to her own demons.

And they were there. The ghosts from Nikki's past were never far from this place. Her parents. Scott. . .

What was Scott doing now? Married again? Of course he'd be married, Nikki told herself bitterly. Scott was charming and personable and desperate for money. He'd be married now to some lady who could support the lifestyle he craved.

Bitterness at the past rose up in her, threatening to overwhelm her. How could he have treated her like that? Men were bastards, she thought bleakly, remembering Sandra Mears' haggard face. She and Sandra both. . .

Why on earth hadn't she been able to see Scott's true colours before she'd been crazy enough to marry him? She'd been so stupid.

Well, it wasn't going to happen again. Not ever. She needed no one and Amy was solely dependent on her. Amy would be brought up with security and love, but no man was needed.

The bitter words Scott had flung at her had stayed in her heart for five long years. He had called her a lying, deceitful whore. He had laughed at her for believing that he had married her for love—he'd told her that no one would ever want her for herself alone.

Nikki took a deep breath and turned her face into the warm night air. The bitterness was all around her, and she was so alone. She looked down to the water's edge at Luke, and a sense of empathy edged into her consciousness. Somehow this man was alone as she.

It was curiously comforting. The soft night wind whipped the fine fabric of her dress around her bare legs. Her hair blew lightly around her face and she drank in the salt air greedily.

Something was happening to her. She didn't know what it was but she only knew that something inside her was being released—just a little—from the bondage that Scott had imposed. Was it Charlotte's crazy, impulsive action in forcing her into attractive clothes? Or was it something else?

Luke was walking slowly back up the beach towards her, his face in shadow with the moon behind him. As he reached her he held out his hands and Nikki took an involuntary step back.

'I'm not going to rape you,' he said easily, and there was a trace of mocking laughter in his voice. 'Oh, so scared, Miss Prim. Why?'

'I'm not scared.' Nikki sounded like a defiant child.

He nodded as though humouring her, then sank on

to the sand and hauled his shoes off. Then his socks. Then. . .

'What are you doing?' Nikki gaped open-mouthed, and then blushed crimson as she realised just what he intended.

'I'm going for a swim, of course.' She couldn't see his face but there was no mistaking the laughter. 'Coming?'

This was something Nikki had done in the long-forgotten past. Eurong beach stretched for miles and the tiny population meant that it was almost always deserted. Eurong was not a tourist destination—the locals kept its beauty as a closely guarded secret—and it meant it was possible to come down here, strip to nothing and swim undisturbed.

The last time Nikki had done such a thing had been five years ago—five years. . .

'Don't be. . .' Nikki turned away with a gasp as she realised her protest was falling on deaf ears. His naked body in the moonlight was breathtaking—and the last thing she wanted to do was look. 'I'll. . .I'll wait for you in the car.'

'It's a magnificent night,' he protested, still half laughing. 'Why waste it on prudery, Miss Prim?'

'I'm not. . .'

'You don't have to strip,' he told her. 'Or are you worried about spoiling your beautiful new clothes?'

'I'm. . .'

'Scared?' To Nikki's horror she felt his hands grip her shoulders. His body touched the soft fabric of her dress, sending a sensuous shiver through her skin. 'Life's short,' he said softly. 'And you're wasting it, Dr Russell. You wouldn't really go back to bury yourself in books tonight, would you?'

'Let me go.' Nikki wrenched herself away but was no match for his strength.

'Why?' His voice softened and the humour faded. 'Nikki, life is for living. God knows what tomorrow holds. Surely you can't ignore tonight?' His grip on her shoulders tightened. 'Look up. The stars are magnificent. The sea is ours. The night is ours, Dr Russell, and I don't intend to go tamely home to bed. And I can't soak it up if I know you're sitting in the car tapping your fingers on the dashboard with impatience. So, as far as I see it, there's only one thing for it.'

'I——'

'You're going to have to come in too.'

'No!' Nikki's cry of refusal was cut off in a staccato shriek. It was ignored. In one fluid movement Luke Marriott had dropped his hands to her waist and pulled her up into his arms.

There was nothing she could do. Nikki was cradled helplessly against him, powerless to struggle. Heedless of the futility of her actions, she crashed her fists into his bare chest. It was as much use as a moth fluttering against a lighted window. Luke's chest showed as little impact, and he strode purposefully forward.

'Put me down.' It was a cry of outrage. No man had touched Nikki Russell for five years and she had no intention of permitting it now. Especially not this man!

'I'll put you down,' Luke promised drily, 'when I'm ready.'

'But——'

'Dr Russell, you are withering into dust with your old house and your elderly housekeeper and your books. Beattie has more life in her than you and she's near seventy. Your housekeeper says you need something to cheer you up, and I've taken it on board as a personal challenge.'

'If you think dumping me in the water will cheer me up. . .!' She pummelled again and her feet lashed out, but he kept right on walking, implacably quiet, towards the water.

And Nikki fell silent, speechless. The feel of Luke's hard body under her was doing crazy, crazy things to her equilibrium. This was mad. Her whole world was mad.

'I'm not dumping you in the water,' he said cheerfully as they neared the shallows. 'I'm taking you for a swim.'

'There are stingers in the water. And stingrays.'

'Beattie tells me the stingers won't be here for another few weeks,' he reassured her kindly. 'And with the amount of noise you've been making, any self-respecting stingray will have lit out for Texas ten minutes ago. Now shut up, hold your nose and enjoy yourself.'

'But. . .'

She got no further. While Luke had been talking he had broached the waves at the water's edge. Now they were surging around his waist, and as Nikki uttered her last word a large crest surged towards them, shoulder-high. Luke simply lifted his burden and deposited her neatly into the foaming surf.

Nikki had forgotten what it would be like. . . She had expected coldness—shock—but. . .the tropical water was almost warm. It had been five long years since Nikki had granted herself the indulgence of a beach swim and, despite her shock and anger, her overwhelming sensation was that of being welcomed back by a friend. She had loved the sea. Now it folded her back into its clasp with a sensual pleasure that was almost a caress.

Involuntarily Nikki felt her body moving into a graceful dive, turning away from the man throwing her into the wave and sweeping under the crest in a lithe arcing of her slim body.

Oh, it was lovely! Why had she stayed away for so long? The salt water surrounded her, encasing her in its cool caress, cooling her overheated body, taking the shards from her anger. . .

What on earth was she doing? She wasn't swimming! There were texts she hadn't opened yet and she was in the water, cavorting. . .

She rose unsteadily to her feet, her feet finding the sandy bottom. Her dress clung and swayed around her legs, pulled by the strength of the water. Luke was only feet from her, his eyes in the dim moonlight amused and appreciative.

'Well, well,' he said slowly. 'The lady can swim. Now, why does Beattie tell me you haven't swum in the sea for years?'

'It's none of your business,' Nikki spluttered, trying to stalk forward. Another wave pounded into her back, making her stumble and spoiling the effect of her damping words entirely. Where on earth was her dignity? Before she could fall, strong arms reached out and held her.

'It's OK to have fun,' Luke Marriott said softly, looking down at the sodden girl in his arms. 'It's OK, Nikki.'

'Well, this is hardly my idea of fun,' Nikki snapped. 'To be half drowned. . .'

'You? Half drowned? You can swim like a fish.'

'You didn't know that when you threw me under!'

'No.' He was staring down at her in the soft light. 'I didn't. But I could guess. As I can guess a hell of a lot about you, Nikki Russell.'

'Well, keep your guesswork for someone else.' Nikki was almost crying. 'I don't want it. I don't want you anywhere near me.'

'Or anyone else,' he said softly. 'At least, that's what you say.'

'It's true.'

'No.' He shook his head. 'You have needs, just like the rest of us, Dr Russell.'

'I don't. . .'

'Well, let's just see.' His grip suddenly tightened. Her body was drawn hard against his naked chest and his blond head sank to kiss her.

Nikki froze. His lips took hers to him, yet they couldn't force her to respond. Her mouth was hard, immobile, and then her hands came up to shove him away.

It was that movement that was her undoing. Her fingers touched his wet, bare skin and a tremor ran through her. Five years. Five long years of nothing. . .

And now this. Lips that searched hers, hands that held her hard against him, making her body feel his strength—his maleness. Her dress might not have existed. Wet and limp, it was a frail barrier between them, and Nikki's body knew his beneath it.

His hands held her tighter, tighter still, pulling her to compliance, moulding her breasts into his muscled chest. Waves of salt foam swept in and out around them but the surging water just deepened the caress, isolating them more against the world.

And to her horror Nikki felt herself respond. The night was magic. This moment was magic. The warmth of the water, the light of the waning moon and the sweeping whisper of the surf all combined to drug her into euphoria. She was powerless to resist. Powerless. . .

Slowly, slowly, her lips parted, allowing his insistent tongue to enter. He tasted of the sea, salt and something else. . .something of the night and the mood and the maleness of him.

Oh, God, she was mad and yet she couldn't stop. It was as if she were indeed drowning and this man's body was the only thing between her and the end of the world. There was the ocean around them. They were an island in the sea and they were stranded forever. His hands fell to her hips, caressing her thighs, pulling her in to feel his maleness, and she felt her body mould to him. If she were to die now, this was what heaven would feel like. She arched back, her neck white and satin-sheened in the moonlight, and from a distance she heard herself moan. The sound held pain and desire and. . .

And what? Who could know?

His mouth fell to the swell of her breasts, and the top button of her dress was suddenly undone. A hand went in to tease the tautness of her nipples and Nikki moaned again.

And then the sea intervened. A surge of surf, larger than the rest, tossed itself at the entwined couple. They staggered together and Luke's hand fell away to save them both from falling.

It was enough. The tiny movement of withdrawal was enough to give Nikki back her senses. With a gasp of horror she pulled away, her hands coming up to cover the gaping nakedness of her breasts. Mad. She was mad. They were both mad.

And then they were staring at each other over the moon-drenched sea and Luke's eyes reflected what Nikki was feeling. There was horror in his eyes as well, and Nikki knew that he too had not intended what had just happened.

'Nikki. . .' Luke's voice was unsteady, uncertain, for the first time since Nikki had met him. Nikki shook her head and turned away.

'I'll be in the car,' she whispered. 'When you're ready. . .'

Luke dressed swiftly on the beach while Nikki sat sodden in the car, waiting. When he came, she was hunched as far away as it was possible to be on the passenger side of the car and, after one swift, hard glance at his companion, Luke started the car and turned for home. They drove home in silence.

Luke's face was set and grim, and his customary cheerfulness seemed to have deserted him. It was almost as though he was as shaken as she was, Nikki thought bitterly, though such a thing was hardly possible. A 'love 'em and leave 'em' man, was Luke Marriott, if Charlotte's information could be relied on.

Which it could be, Nikki thought. To do this. . .to seduce her. . .

He hadn't seduced her. He had kissed her and she had responded. That truth made Nikki hug her arms into her breasts and shiver, and Luke cast a glance across at her.

'My sweater's over the back,' he said impersonally, and another shudder ran through Nikki's body. How could he? How could he act as if nothing had happened?

Maybe it was the only way to act, but some emotion which Nikki could not define was running between them, and to talk—to try for impersonal conversation—would somehow strengthen that emotion. The tension scared Nikki half to death and, by the look of it, Luke also didn't know how to react.

Good, she thought nastily. To get the great Luke Marriott off balance. . .

Curiously the thought didn't help at all. All it did was make her want to cry.

Finally the little car pulled off the road into the driveway of Whispering Palms. Nikki looked out in relief at the sight of her home—her refuge. If only she could turn to Luke Marriott and tell him it was no longer his. That he should find somewhere else—even if it did mean sleeping on a park bench!

She turned to him and found him watching her, but before she could speak he laid a finger on her lips.

'I'm sorry, Nikki,' he said gently. 'I should never have kissed you.'

The great Luke Marriott apologising! Nikki could hardly believe her ears, and yet all it did was make her urge to burst into tears even greater. And then, before she could respond, before she could realise what he intended, his head came down and his lips touched hers.

It was a kiss of contrition—a feather-light kiss that

should have caused no feeling. She had been kissed many times like that before. Instead Nikki felt her heart turn within her. She put a hand up to touch his face but he had already withdrawn.

'And I'm sorry for that, too,' he said unsteadily. 'It won't happen again.'

How was a girl supposed to study after that?

Heaven knew. Nikki didn't. She showered the salt and sand from her body, donned a housecoat, rinsed her sodden dress and then went to tackle her texts. It was the last thing she wanted to do, but she had wasted so much time!

What was Luke doing? The words of the text danced before her eyes in a meaningless jumble. What on earth was she trying to study?

Hearing difficulties. . .problems with the ear. . . She had to concentrate. If she kept going like this, she'd fail.

And then what? A thin, insistent little voice started up in the back of her head. So what if you fail? There's always next year. And your income doesn't depend on it.

What on earth was she saying? This was work she was rejecting, and one thing Nikki Russell hadn't done in the last five years was reject work. It was only a matter of blocking out the thought of Luke Marriott. The memory of his hands. . .his lips. . .

Damn the man. She stared down at her page and started to read aloud, forcing her tired mind back on to track. 'Tinnitus. . .ringing in the ears. . .' What on earth did she know about tinnitus?

'Do you need some help?'

Nikki jumped close to a foot in the air. The house had been deathly still and she hadn't heard Luke come up behind her. Now she nearly dropped her text as he placed his hands on the back of her chair and read over her shoulder. 'You shouldn't be working,' he said conversationally. 'But if you insist, then I'll give you a hand.'

'Thanks, but I don't need it.' It was as much as Nikki could do to get the words out.

'What do you need, then?' he quizzed her gently. 'You tell me you don't need a walk. You don't need a swim. You don't need help.' He smiled down at her, his mobile eyebrows arched upwards. 'I'm a paid employee, Dr Russell. So start employing me.'

Nikki shoved her book down on the desk with a bang and rose unsteadily to her feet. She should be wearing something more substantial than her flimsy housecoat. It was sheer cotton and not respectable in the least.

'I'm employing you to attend to my normal medical duties,' she said tightly. 'And I'm. . . I don't want anything else.'

He wasn't listening. Luke had picked up the text she had just dropped. 'OK,' he said absently. 'What are the three types of tinnitus?'

'Look——'

'What are they, Dr Russell?'

Nikki stared helplessly at him. Arguing was impossible. The man was like a bulldozer. She forced herself to focus on what he was saying.

Tinnitus. Types. What were they?

'Low-frequency noise, like hearing the sea,' she started hesitantly.

'Cause?'

'Typically impacted wax. Or maybe otosclerosis.'

'Good,' he approved. 'Next type?'

'High-frequency noise, like a cicada,' Nikki told him. Her hand was on the back of her chair as if for support, but her mind was steadying as she focused on work. 'Suggestive of inner ear pathology such as ototoxicity, trauma or tumour compressing the nerve.'

'And the last?'

'Look, you don't have to do this.'

'I wasted your time taking you swimming. Now I'm making amends. Next, Dr Russell.'

'I don't——'

'Think, Dr Russell.' Luke's voice was clipped and professional, reminding Nikki of nothing so much as her old professors, grilling her until she was exhausted during final exams. She took a deep breath. She knew. She had to know.

And it was there, locked in the recess of her tired mind. She brought it out and dusted it off. 'Pulsatile tinnitus,' she said hesitantly. 'Noise coinciding with the patient's heart-rate.'

'That's the one. And cause?'

'I don't know.' Then at his look of disgust she changed her mind. 'Yes, I do. Intercranial vascular lesion, for instance jugular tumour.'

'And if you can't treat tinnitus, what do you do about it?' Luke demanded, and Nikki stared.

'I thought you were a surgeon,' she muttered. 'Surgeons never admit you can't treat something.'

He smiled then, his eyes weary but acknowledging a hit. 'This is an exam for general practitioners,' he smiled, 'not for surgeons. Let's assume we've done our worst—all the medical possibilities are exhausted, the surgeons have sent your patient back to you with a "too hard" label on him and your patient still has ringing in his ears. What then, Dr Russell?'

'Antidepressant?'

'It can make the noise more tolerable,' Luke agreed. 'But then what? Do you leave your patient taking pills for the rest of his or her life? The examiners won't like your answer, Dr Russell.'

Nikki flushed. 'Well, the accepted treatment is the use of white noise,' she said stiffly. 'A noise simulator which produces something like the noise of a running stream, or rain on a tin roof. Most unmedical, but effective.'

'And that's what this exam is all about,' Luke told

her. 'How Nikki Russell has learned to dispense medicine in the real world, and knows when to shove the prescription pad aside.'

'It sounds as if you know it all,' Nikki said resentfully.

'And I'm just a surgeon.' He flipped to the next page. 'What next?'

Nikki moved to the door. 'I'm going to bed.'

He shook his head. 'You intended to work for at least a couple of hours before I appeared, didn't you, Dr Russell?'

Nikki nodded reluctantly. 'But I can't now.'

'Yes, you can.' He moved back to block her exit from the door. 'Dr Russell, I am here to ensure you pass this exam, come hell or high water. And it's only come Dr Marriott. So sit down and answer questions. Now, Dr Russell!'

'But——'

'Sit down,' he said quietly, but his low voice held the trace of a threat. 'Sit or I'll sit you down in a way you'll find distinctly undignified.'

Nikki stared up at his face, but the humour was gone. His eyes were stern and implacable.

And she did want to pass this exam. If he could really help. . .

She sat.

To Nikki's amazement the ensuing two hours were the most productive she had spent so far. What had passed between them earlier in the night had somehow been driven aside. It was still there, latent, unresolved, but it was another part of them. The professional part—the part that had put them through stringent medical training—was in play and it produced the most effective study Nikki had done. When the big grandfather clock in the hall struck midnight she lifted her head in amazement.

'Thank you,' she said simply. 'I will go to bed now.'

'To sleep?' The blue eyes watching her saw too much.

'Of course.'

'The shadows let you sleep, then?'

'What. . .? What do you mean?' Unconsciously Nikki clutched the neckline of her housecoat as though seeking warmth from its flimsy fabric. 'What do you mean—shadows?'

'They stand out a mile,' Luke told her. He stood, stretching his long limbs. He was barefoot, wearing light cotton trousers and a soft, short-sleeved shirt, open at the throat. The two of them could be taken for a married couple, Nikki thought suddenly, and then grimaced. It was a crazy scenario—the two of them alone at this hour. Beattie was long since gone to bed and the house was in whispering stillness. The palms along the veranda which gave the house its name murmured in hushed tones in the night breeze.

'You're crazy.' Nikki stood too and then wished she hadn't. The movement brought her too close to Luke. She half expected him to move back, but he stayed, looking down at her.

'Tell me about Scott,' he said softly.

CHAPTER FIVE

SCOTT. . .

The name flashed before them like a cruel sword, knifing at Nikki's heart.

How had Luke. . .?

'Tell me about him,' he repeated gently.

What sort of questioning was this? Nikki's eyes widened. She stared up at Luke with anger flashing, but Luke's eyes were reflective and calm.

'No,' she whispered.

Luke was between Nikki and the door. Nikki put out a hand to shove him aside but he caught and held it. Her hand lay in his, warmth against warmth, and Nikki's anger turned to an overwhelming feeling of distress. She pulled again but the grip tightened.

'Look, it's none of your business,' she managed. 'I don't know how you found out about Scott. . .'

'Beattie,' he smiled. 'How else?'

'Well, Beattie has no right to talk about me. Beattie, Charlotte, and now you!' Nikki's voice rose in anger. 'All of you think you can interfere with my life. Well, I don't want it. I don't need your interrogation. . .'

'You don't need anybody.' Luke's eyes were still calm, the deep blue penetrating into the depths of her heart. His look was like a red-hot torch, burning in. Nikki had never felt anything like it in her life before. This man could see parts of her that had remained hidden for years—that she had sworn would never again be revealed. 'You do, though, Nikki,' he said softly. 'And whatever is hurting needs to be talked of. So tell me.'

'No.'

He shook his head. 'Nikki. I'm only here for three

weeks. Then I get out of your life forever. But for those three weeks I intend getting rid of the shadows—or at least having a damned good try. You need someone to talk to. So talk to me.'

'I don't want to.' It was practically a wail, and Luke smiled.

'Yes, you do,' he told her, and pulled her firmly in to lie against him. His hand came up to run through her mass of golden-red curls and his fingers sent warmth and reassurance through her body. 'Beattie tells me you've been carrying this for five years. It's too long to carry bitterness and hate. So tell me.'

Nikki held her body stiffly, resentfully, but the fingers did their work insidiously. His hand moved against her head, sending messages of reassurance and comfort through her. Let the bitterness go, his hand was telling her. Tell me. Tell someone. Spill it out. And he wouldn't release her until she did. . .

'Scott was my husband,' she said stiffly, reluctantly. 'But I suppose Beattie told you that.'

'And he left you?'

'Yes.' It was crazy talking to this man, cradled against his shoulder like a child needing comfort. She didn't feel like a child, though. Nikki felt every inch a woman and her body was achingly aware of his.

And yet. . . And yet she could talk to him. This was a comfort she had never known—a peace she had never been blessed with.

'Scott and I grew up together,' she said slowly. She was talking into the soft folds of Luke's shirt. His face was above hers. She could feel the beating of his heart. There was no need to talk above a whisper.

'Scott's father was a fisherman,' she continued. 'But Scott hankered for life away from here. We went to university together in Brisbane—Scott to do law and me to do medicine.' She sighed. 'Scott's motives—well, I'm not sure why he wanted to do law—but my mother had severe rheumatoid arthritis and ever since

I was tiny I'd been frustrated by not being able to help. So we went to Brisbane—two kids from a tiny town—and we just kept on together. Scott was always there. Just as he'd been when I was small.'

'Your parents were wealthy?'

Nikki stiffened in Luke's hold but his fingers didn't pause in their gentle stroking. He was way ahead of her. He could read her mind, this man. It seemed that she didn't need to tell him anything. He knew.

'My father was the son of a British peer,' Nikki said bitterly. 'He had a fight with his father, came to Australia when he was a teenager, married my mother and stayed. Money was never a problem for us—or at least it never appeared a problem. Dad was Lord Peter Russell, and he never stopped using the Lord. My mother's family left us Whispering Palms but my father always implied that he was humouring her by living in her childhood home rather than something much more grand. My father didn't work. He spent heaps on my mother and me, and he made it sound as though he had lots for me to inherit. That's why. . .'

'That's why Scott asked you to marry him.'

Nikki writhed in Luke's grasp but his hold didn't ease. Instead it tightened and the waves of warmth and reassurance increased. 'Tell me, Nikki,' he said.

'Of course it was why he asked me to marry him,' Nikki said reluctantly. 'But I was too stupid to see. I didn't realise that the only reason someone so vibrant—so alive—as Scott would want to be with me was because he was on to something he couldn't get any other way.' She shook her head and angry tears started behind her eyes.

'Scott and I were married while we were still at university,' she continued bitterly. 'We were happy for a while. And then, just as I graduated, my mother died. And my father—the man who I always thought was the strong one—couldn't face what was left behind. He took what he believed was the only way out.'

Luke gave an almost soundless whistle. 'Tough!' he said softly.

'It was.' Nikki put a hand up to wipe away angry tears but Luke was before her, his hand taking the tears away from her eyes. 'But it got worse. After his funeral they gave me a note which he'd left with his lawyer.' She took a deep breath. 'My father left a note saying the money had finished a couple of years earlier—that he couldn't face life without money and he was deep in debt. He'd managed to hide it until my mother had died but now. . . Now the only way for him was suicide. . .'

'And Scott?' Luke's voice was grim.

'Scott!' Nikki laughed, a harsh, tight little sound that was caught by Luke's nearness. 'At first Scott was so supportive. He was marvellous when my mother died, and when they found my father. I remember thinking, At least I have Scott. With Scott I can face this. Only then—the night of the funeral—the lawyer gave me the note and Scott and I read it together. And then. . . and then we sat down and went through my father's desk and realised that after coping with the bills there would be nothing.'

'I see.'

Luke did see. From his voice Nikki knew she didn't have to say the rest. It came out, though. It seemed as if it had to.

'At first I thought Scott was just upset for me—but then. . .then I said that at least we still had Whispering Palms. It was my mother's. She. . .she must have known about my father's debts. The house was left in trust for our. . .for my children, so it couldn't be sold. So at least we had a home. . .'

'And Scott wasn't impressed.'

Nikki shrugged listlessly. 'Scott said he was damned if he was working hard for the rest of his life. He said he'd been conned. He said he'd been trapped into marriage—that my father had led him to believe there were millions. And that much was true,' Nikki admitted. 'My father had always talked big. And Scott . . . well, Scott just stood up at the end of it and said "That's it, Nikki. This is where I get off." And he walked out. Just like that. Just like. . .just like my father. "This is where I get off".'

Nikki fell silent. She stood motionless against Luke while his fingers did their work. 'I never saw him again,' she whispered finally. 'He wrote once, to ask for a divorce. But that was all. . .'

'Well.' Luke's fingers had stilled but now they started again. 'That must have been some week out of your life, Nikki.'

She shrugged. 'In that week I had my pregnancy confirmed. In that week. . .well, it was the week I found out what the world is really all about.'

'What Scott was all about,' Luke said grimly. 'You can't judge the world by your father's weakness and Scott's appalling behaviour. You can't, Nikki.' He put her away from him then, his hands holding her shoulders at arm's length, allowing him to look into her tear-drenched eyes. 'Believe me, you can't.'

And for a moment she almost believed him. Nikki looked up into the depths of those eyes and found her world shifting. She could drown in those eyes. She could let herself go. She could be as big a fool over this man as she had been over Scott.

Then from nowhere Charlotte's words came crashing into her head to haul her back to reality. 'Luke Marriott had every junior nurse, some senior ones and a few female doctors besides, making fools of themselves every time he walked past. He's broken more hearts than I care to name.' Charlotte's words echoed over and over again until Nikki came to her senses.

Luke Marriott wasn't breaking her heart. She wasn't

going to make a fool of herself. Not again. She couldn't bear it. With an angry thrust she put herself away from him and whirled to face the door.

'I know I can't keep judging,' she said bitterly, 'but I can make darned sure I'm not such a fool again.'

'If you don't trust, then you can't love,' he said softly.

She turned back to face him. 'Well, who can I trust?' she demanded. 'Are you to be trusted? I don't even know why the hell you're here, Luke Marriott. You should be sitting back in Cairns with your adoring nursing staff and your highly paid surgical career. . .'

'That's right,' he said equitably. 'I should be.'

'So why the hell aren't you?' Nikki had gone past the point of courtesy. This man had left her raw and exposed and she wanted to lash back—at any cost. 'Why aren't you there? What are you running from?'

'I'm not running from anything.'

'No?' Nikki gave a bitter laugh. 'Something had to go wrong in your life to make you give up such a lucrative profession as your surgical career. I've told you my pathetic past, Luke Marriott. Now you show me your shadows.'

Luke's eyes darkened. For a moment Nikki thought he would walk out of the room in anger, without replying. Then his look changed.

'Fair enough,' he said softly. 'You did tell me.'

'So. . .? So why did you leave Cairns in such a hurry?' The words came out slowly as Nikki's anger died. Suddenly she wasn't sure she wanted to know his reason. And when it came, she was sure of it.

'There was a very good reason,' he said slowly. 'I had cancer.'

Cancer. . .

The word echoed around and around the small room. Nikki stared across at Luke as if he had physically struck her.

'Cancer,' she said blankly.

'That's right.'

She took a deep breath. 'What. . .what sort. . .?'

'Hodgkin's disease.'

It had to be, she thought dully. Hodgkin's disease was a cancer of the lymph glands, often presenting in otherwise healthy young males. Nikki had seen a couple of cases in her practice. One had died and Nikki still cringed at the tragic waste.

'Yes.'

'I. . .I see.'

'No.' He shook his head and his eyes were suddenly far-away. 'I bet you don't see, Dr Russell. Only someone who's faced cancer themselves can see what a diagnosis like that can do to you.'

'It must. . .it must have been frightening.'

He shrugged. 'What do you think?' He closed his eyes momentarily. 'I don't think I've ever been so scared in my whole life.'

Nikki moistened her lips, searching for the right words. In the end she found refuge in medicine—a doctor's approach.

'How did you find it?'

'I had night sweats,' he said shortly. 'I'd been working too damned hard and was feeling pretty run down. Then I started waking drenched with sweat. For a while I told myself I was imagining things. Then I found a swollen lymph node in my neck.'

'Weight loss?'

'No.' He smiled without humour. 'I was living too well for that.'

Still. . . Nikki's mind was racing. Without weight loss, he'd caught it early.

'So you had tests in Cairns?'

'No.' Luke grimaced. 'I can put two and two together pretty fast, even if I was hoping to hell I was making fourteen. I was at the end of a job in Cairns. An oncologist friend, Rod Olsing, who worked with me for a while in Cairns, had just moved to Sydney, so I rang him and took myself down there.'

'Why?'

He shrugged again. His habitual smile was gone, replaced with bleak remembrance.

'Cowardice, if you like. In Cairns I'd been successful and totally in control. Suddenly I was badly out of control and I couldn't face it. So I went south and faced it there.'

'And it was bad?' Nikki's voice had softened in automatic sympathy.

'Yeah. It was bad.' He gave a short laugh. 'And there's nothing like lying in a strange hospital thinking you're facing death for making you look at life. Or what you've been calling life.'

'You had radiotherapy?'

'And chemotherapy.' Luke dug his hands deep in his pockets and turned away. 'The X-rays and CT scan were clear, thank God. The glands in the neck were the only ones affected, but the night sweats made me stage 1B instead of stage 1A. Hence they gave me the works.'

Nikki nodded. The appearance of a single tumour would usually be treated just by radiotherapy. The night sweats would mean chemotherapy, though. Involuntarily her eyes went to Luke's shock of blond hair and he caught her look as he turned back to face her.

'It's grown back nicely,' he said grimly, touching his hair. 'That's the least of the side-effects.'

Nikki nodded sympathetically. 'But you've been in remission now for. . .?'

'For close on two years.'

'But that means there's every chance you're cured. The cure-rate for Hodgkin's is. . .'

'Over seventy per cent if it's caught at stage one. I know, Dr Russell; believe me, I know.'

'Well, then.' Nikki took a deep breath. 'Well, then, why aren't you getting on with life again?'

'I am.'

'By running?'

'I'm not running.'

'So what are you doing here? Isn't your career centred on the city? You'll never get anywhere doing three-week locums.'

He shook his head. 'On the contrary, Dr Russell. I'll never get anywhere by being a successful city surgeon.' He touched her hair lightly with his finger. 'And now, if you'll excuse me, Dr Russell, your locum is going to bed.'

To bed but not to sleep.

Nikki lay for hours watching the light of the full moon gradually move across her ceiling. The big ceiling fan whirred lazily, mesmerically, over her head. Usually it soothed her to sleep, but not tonight.

Hodgkin's disease. . . The prognosis ran around Nikki's tired mind as though she were being examined tomorrow. Even with the added symptom of night sweats, Luke's prognosis was good. If he'd been in remission for two years he was nearly out of danger. Nearly. . .

And then something hit her tired mind, making her sit up in bed and turn on her light. Hodgkin's disease. . . Treatment. . .

Was she right? Suddenly it was imperative that she know, and know right now. Now. . .

Padding softly through the darkened house, she found the text she wanted and returned to bed. Where was it. . .? Treatment of Hodgkin's. . . Diagnosis. . . Management. . . Chemotherapy. . .

What regime had they used? Nikki flicked the pages over, missing what she wanted in her urgency and having to return.

There were two chemotherapy regimes listed. The first was MOPP. . . Nikki stared blankly at the printed page. 'MOPP is associated with significant toxicity including infertility. . . MOPP therapy produces near-universal sterility in males. . .'

MOPP wasn't warranted, though. Not for stage 1B. The lesser regime was ABVD: 'Adriamycin, bleomycin, vinblastine and dacarbazine. . . Reduced risk of sterility. . . Recommended in stage 1B. . .'

Surely they'd used ABVD and not MOPP?

Even so. . . Even so, there was a strong chance that Luke Marriott was now sterile—that he would no longer be able to father children.

How would such an outcome hit a man who exuded masculinity as Luke Marriott did? To know that he could never father a child. . .

It was all just too hard. There was too much going on in Nikki's tired mind for her to assess what she had been told. Somehow her eyes managed to close and she fell into a troubled, dream-filled sleep.

She woke to laughter.

Nikki stirred, her eyes moving automatically to her bedside clock. It was close on seven, later than she usually woke, but in her exhausted, troubled state the night before she had not set the alarm.

The laughter sounded again, the high, tinkling sound of Amy having fun. For a moment Nikki frowned, thinking how rarely she had heard that sound lately. Why?

And then she heard a splash, and Nikki rose to her feet before she was aware she was doing so, her feet flying to the door. Amy wasn't allowed in the pool by herself. She knew the rules. It wasn't safe. . . She flung open the French windows, stepped through into the soft, morning sunlight, and stopped dead.

Amy wasn't alone in the pool. Luke Marriott was there too, his arms holding the laughing little girl high above the water and then swooping her down like a bird, so that her body flitted through the water and then swept up again, showering the man beneath her with sunlit water.

'Do it again,' Amy screamed. 'Do it again.' And Luke obliged, laughing with her.

Was this her daughter? Nikki put her hand to her eyes as if to rub the shreds of dreaming from them. Amy was a serious, grave little girl who seldom laughed. She took her life seriously, did Amy.

Or maybe that wasn't true. As Amy had been brought up in a house with an elderly housekeeper and a mother who distrusted the world, maybe there just weren't enough opportunities for laughter.

Amy looked up then and saw her mother. 'Look at me,' she screamed happily. 'Look at me, Mummy. Dr Luke's teaching me to dive. Look at me dive. Do it again, Dr Luke.'

Luke Marriott looked up at Nikki, his eyes quizzing her dangerously. 'Maybe your mummy had better go put on her swimming costume and join us. She'd be more respectable that way.'

With a gasp Nikki looked down. Her nightgown was a short, soft cotton one that was years old, and its age meant that it was almost transparently thin. And the sun was behind her! She put her hands up to cover her breasts and backed away.

'Mummy, do come in.' Amy's voice pleaded with her. 'Please, Mummy. We're having a really, really lot of fun.'

'Amy, I have to work,' Nikki said uncertainly. 'You and Luke are enjoying yourselves without me.'

'I always enjoy myself without you,' Amy said sadly. 'But if Dr Luke is here too. . .'

Oh, help. . . The tiny niggle of guilt which her daughter's laughter caused now rose to overwhelm her. 'I always enjoy myself without you'. . .

They were both watching her now—man and child. Amy was nestled in Luke's arms as though she belonged. She watched her mother with eyes that expected to be rebuffed. Luke's eyes gave away nothing.

'OK.' Nikki swallowed. 'I'll come in.'

She was rewarded instantly with Amy's whoop of joy. 'Yes!' she yelled. 'Mummy's coming in. Mummy's coming in! Hurry, Mummy. The water's beeyoootiful. . .' She arched back and plummeted her small body downwards, under water, and emerged, choking and laughing. 'We'll get Mummy in, won't we, Dr Luke?'

'It's your Mummy's decision,' Luke grinned. 'We have nothing to do with it.'

'Oh, yeah?' Nikki said to herself grimly, stalking in to find her bathing costume. This place had been sane before Luke Marriott arrived. The man was turning their lives upside-down.

Five minutes in the pool, she promised herself. A token to appease Amy. And then work!

Only of course it wasn't five minutes.

The morning sun was hot by the time Nikki slipped self-consciously into the water, and the water was a balm to her tired body. She had slept badly and was thick with bad dreams and self-doubt. Somehow the sun and the water and her daughter's laughter dispelled the black cloud. Luke was teaching Amy dead man's float, taking his duty very seriously. Nikki floated aimlessly on her back, watching man and child enjoy each other.

This was what Scott should be doing. Enjoying his daughter. Loving his daughter. Instead of which. . . She had written to him, but Scott had never even acknowledged that his little girl existed.

It was a bitter thought, but this morning it didn't seem as bitter as it usually did. Somehow the sting was eased.

Because Luke was here? The thought drifted around Nikki's mind as she floated, and she had to acknowledge that while Luke was here she had no place in her mind for Scott. For the first time Scott's face blurred in her mind, as though the memory was fading. The laughing eyes. . .the mocking smile. Where were they?

Gone with Scott. Replaced suddenly with eyes that laughed with a sympathy that was not feigned—that mocked, but mocked with kindness and compassion. She looked to where Luke was bending over the small, wet Amy, holding her still while the child tried desperately to keep her body floating. Kindness. . . This wasn't some errant playboy making a line for her. This was a man who genuinely wanted her small daughter to feel good about herself.

And then his eyes shifted to her and his smile faded a little. 'Feel better for your swim, Dr Russell?'

Nikki found her feet and stood upright, breast-deep in water.

'Thank you. I'd. . .I'd better be settling down to work. And. . .'

She was absurdly shy somehow, having trouble making her voice work. It was so. . .well, so darned domestic, to be in the water—the two of them with the child. 'And you'd better be thinking about morning surgery,' she managed.

'Not yet.' It was Beattie's voice cutting across the morning stillness. Nikki looked up to see the housekeeper smiling down at them. She was carrying a vast, loaded tray. 'Pancakes,' she called. 'I saw you out here and decided you might like a special breakfast.'

'Pancakes!' Amy surfaced from her float, still bubbling with excitement. She looked from Luke to Nikki. 'Pancakes for breakfast! We haven't had pancakes for breakfast—ever.' She looked anxiously across at her mother as if expecting this treat to be somehow snatched away. 'Will you both stay to eat them?' The child was used to Nikki eating on the run. 'Please?'

'Of course we will,' Luke promised, holding out his hand to tow Amy to the side of the pool. 'Won't we, Nikki?' And he held out his other hand.

It would be churlish not to take his hand. Amy stared at her mother, waiting for Nikki to take the proffered hand. Nikki wavered helplessly.

'Come on, Dr Russell,' Luke said gently. 'Pancakes await us. And I'm not one to hesitate where pancakes are concerned. Are you?'

Still the hand was out. To avoid it Nikki had to walk right by, brushing him aside. Amy watched.

The sun was warm on her face. Nikki's body was cool in the water, but all of a sudden the water wasn't enough. It was as if she was flushing all over.

Slowly she brought up her hand. Luke's eyes were still, watchful, the laughter gone. In a slow, considered movement he brought his fingers closer and closed on hers. The three were entwined, man, woman and child.

'Come on, Amy,' Luke said slowly. 'Let's take your mother to breakfast.'

Somehow that morning Nikki managed a little study, but little was the operative word. Even with her contact lenses, her eyes refused to focus on the books, and when she forced herself to read the words aloud they failed to make sense.

What on earth was the matter with her? Amy was at kindergarten. Beattie was shopping and Luke was running morning surgery. She had the house to herself and she had less than three weeks to the exam.

'So work,' she muttered savagely. 'Make yourself work.'

She stared back at the page but all she saw was Luke—Luke lifting her daughter high in the air smiling up at Amy, smiling across at her. . .

'I'm going nuts,' Nikki whispered. 'I can't. . .'

Can't be falling in love? The words suddenly slammed into her head and stayed. Falling in love with Luke Marriott? What on earth was she thinking of?

'You just feel sorry for him,' she told herself

savagely. 'Because of the cancer. . .'

But that wasn't true at all. This morning the fact that Luke Marriott had suffered from Hodgkin's disease had been thrust away into some far recess of her mind. She hadn't been thinking of it while she had been in the pool.

All she had been thinking of was him. All she had been aware of was his body—his presence—binding her to her small daughter, entwining them into a threesome like a family. . .

Oh, good grief! She had to stop this. Luke Marriott was here for another few weeks and then he would be gone—forever. Just like Scott.

Not like Scott. Her mind suddenly rebelled, refusing to link the two men, and she stood abruptly. She was getting nowhere at all. If she went on like this she was going to fail this damned exam.

The phone cut across the silence and she answered it gratefully. Anything to get her mind away from these dangerous thoughts. It didn't help, though. It was Luke on the end of the line.

'Nikki, I'm seeing Sandra Mears at twelve,' he told her. 'I'd like you to be present.'

'But——'

'I know. I'm covering for you. But Sandra needs someone who's going to provide ongoing support. If I persuade her to trust me and then leave, she'll be no better off than before. I've done the groundwork, but I want you to be involved.'

So who was whose boss? Nikki held the receiver back and stared at it. She was used to giving the orders.

He was right, though. Her exam—her studying—was important, but not more important than the long-term happiness of the Mears family.

'I'll be there,' she told him slowly. 'What have you done so far?'

'I've another patient in the waiting-room,' he said

curtly. 'I can't talk now. But I'd like you here at twelve.'

Yes, sir. Nikki thought the words but wasn't given a chance to utter them. The line was dead.

CHAPTER SIX

BY THE time she reached the clinic, Nikki had worked herself up to anger. It was the only feeling she was capable of defining, and it covered a number of other emotions she was trying to dismiss.

Luke Marriott might have been ill but it hadn't stopped him being autocratic. He said jump and he expected the world to jump. He should have asked—not ordered.

Maybe I should dock his wages, Nikki thought humourlessly. On the grounds of insolence.

The thought gave her a fleeting ray of comfort, putting the relationship back on a purely professional basis. She climbed out of her little car, self-consciously smoothed down the next frock from Charlotte's never-ending supply, and made her way indoors. Her receptionist met her.

'Hi, Doctor,' Mary said happily. 'Wow, you look gorgeous.' She grinned. 'I don't blame you. Our new locum's worth dressing up for, isn't he?'

'I'm not dressing up for any locum,' Nikki snapped, but her receptionist simply arched her eyebrows and grinned.

'Mrs Mears is in with him now,' she smiled. 'The children are all over at the hospital. And I've cleared an hour if you need it.' She held up her fingers, showing them crossed. 'Good luck. Sandra's not going to take to interference very kindly.'

'She no longer has a choice,' Nikki said.

Sandra was sitting in an easy-chair in the surgery. Luke had come from behind the desk and was sitting beside her. They looked up as Nikki knocked and entered, Luke giving her a small, professional smile and Sandra looking downright scared.

'I asked Dr Russell to join us,' Luke said gently. 'I'm only here for another two and a half weeks and you'll need Nikki for longer than that.'

'Nikki'. . . The use of her name jolted her, and Nikki flashed Luke a look of annoyance before sitting. He didn't seem to notice.

'How's Karen?' he asked Sandra.

'She's fine.' Sandra's voice was apprehensive. 'At least. . .'

'Did you go and see her?'

'No.' Sandra shook her head defensively. 'I. . .I went and talked to the sister in charge. She says. . . she says Karen's OK.'

'Why didn't you go and see her?'

'She wouldn't want to see me.'

'I think she would.' Luke frowned. 'Sandra, what do you think Karen would say to you now if you went to see her?'

'Nothing.'

'Nothing? You mean, she wouldn't be upset that you hurt her?'

'No,' Sandra said bitterly. 'She'll just. . .she'll just look at me. . .'

'You'd like it better if she yelled at you?'

'Well. . .' Sandra's head sank down so that she was staring at the carpet. 'I. . .I hurt her.'

'So what are you going to do about it?' Luke's voice was unemotional and firm. It was as if he were asking what Sandra intended to have for dinner that night. That she should have something was as inevitable as the fact that she was now forced to take action.

Sandra raised tear-filled eyes. 'I don't know,' she said hopelessly. 'I don't. . .'

'Sandra, why are you living in that dump?' It wasn't a criticism, just a statement of fact, and Nikki's eyes flew to Luke. She would never have been so blunt.

'I. . .I can't afford anything else.'

'But you've the supporting mother's benefit. I've been on to the Department of Social Security here. They tell me what you get should cover one of the Housing Commission homes down near the river. They're basic but they're clean and well-kept—and with your skill as a housekeeper you'd get one looking great in no time. And they're right in town. The children could walk to school and you could walk to the shops.'

'But. . .'

'But what?'

Sandra swallowed. 'My husband. . .my husband ran up debts before he left. I'm paying them off but so far. . .so far I've done no more than cover the interest.'

'Does your husband pay any child support?'

For the first time Sandra's dark eyes flashed anger. It was as if something deep within her was hidden—and as though she was afraid of exposing her hatred.

'Of course not,' she said bitterly. 'He and his girlfriend are further south—he's a cane-cutter and makes a heap, but I'm left with nothing but his debts. His debts and the kids.'

Luke nodded. 'But you'd like some help?'

'I've no hope of getting it.' Sandra's voice flattened again. 'He spends as fast as he earns.'

'No.' Luke smiled then. 'The new rules require all employees—even casual workers—to register tax file numbers with employers wherever they work, and there's no way your husband can be working without doing that. All we have to do is ask Social Security to place a garnishee on his wages. You'll be paid before he is. And we'll ask for his debts to be transferred to his name. If you've sole responsibility for the children there should be no problem there.' He grinned. 'And he'll find his debtors have no trouble garnisheeing even more of his wages. Your husband might find himself with a little less easy money in the future, Mrs Mears.

And you might find things a whole lot easier.'

Sandra stared, hope and disbelief warring visibly in her tired eyes. 'If. . .if I lived in town I could sell the car. . .'

'That's right.'

'But——' Sandra swallowed '—folks around here think I'm a tart. Because I got pregnant before I was married. They'd give me a hard time. . .'

Nikki moved then. She rose and walked around the table. 'Sandra, there are lots like you in the town,' she said gently. 'Everyone has their ghosts. You can either move to a bigger city where you can be anonymous or stay here, look people in the eye and ride it out. You'll find history is forgotten as long as you act as though it's forgotten. Honest!'

Sandra looked up and smiled. 'You had a hard time too, didn't you, Doctor?'

'I sure did,' Nikki said ruefully. 'But I still wanted to stay. A small town has some good things going for it when it comes to raising children.' She touched Sandra's shoulder. 'And there are supports here that you won't find in the city. If you accept them.'

'I should have before this.' Sandra hesitated, looking from Luke to Nikki. 'If I'd admitted I was in trouble earlier, I could have got help. . .I wouldn't have hurt Karen maybe. . .'

'You're asking for help now,' Luke said gently. 'That's all that matters.' He rose as well, handing Sandra a slip of paper. 'The Housing Commission tells me there's a house vacant at the moment. Go and have a look before you commit yourself.'

'But. . .'

'But what?' He was smiling down at the girl, daring her with his eyes. 'This is going to take courage, Sandra. But you have it. I know it, and so does Karen.'

'Karen. . .'

He nodded. 'Your little girl has faith in you. You're all she has, Sandra.'

'Can I take her home?'

Luke shook his head. 'Not yet. You need time to sort yourself out, and Karen needs you at your best. Until you move you'll be worried and anxious, and that's the time when Karen is most likely to be at risk, isn't it?'

Sandra hung her head. 'Yes,' she whispered. 'But I wouldn't. . .'

'We can't risk that.' Luke's voice was firm. 'Karen doesn't need hospital but she does need care. I'm not fussed about involving community services and sending her to Cairns for foster care. I suggest that she spend the next couple of weeks with us at Whispering Palms.'

Nikki's eyes widened. She opened her mouth to protest but Luke's eyes were on her, hard and challenging.

'We have a great housekeeper, a comfortable bed and a little girl who'll enjoy your daughter's company. You can pop in and see her once a day, but you can have two weeks' time out from each other.' He smiled. 'It'll make you realise just how much you do care for your eldest daughter, and how much you risk losing if you don't put her first.'

'I don't risk losing——'

'Yes, you do.' Luke's smile faded. 'Sandra, if I reported this break to community services, they'd have no choice but to place Karen in foster care. Now, what we're offering is an alternative. Do you accept?'

Sandra looked wildly from Nikki to Luke and back again. 'But. . .but you don't want my daughter. She'll be a nuisance. . .'

'We'd love to have your daughter as our guest,' Luke said firmly. 'Whispering Palms is built for children, isn't it, Dr Russell?'

Nikki took a deep breath. She looked down at Sandra, and read the desperate need in her eyes. This woman had reaped a harvest more bitter than Nikki's from her relationship with her man. And Nikki could help. Luke was right.

'Whispering Palms is built for children,' she repeated slowly. She smiled at Sandra and her voice firmed. 'We'd love to have Karen.'

'You could have asked me!'

Nikki barely waited until Sandra had closed the door behind her before her anger burst forth. 'For heaven's sake, Luke Marriott, who do you think you are? It's my house!'

'And Karen needs it.'

'And you need it. And so does half the population of North Queensland, as far as I know. And you intend inviting them home. Home! My home. Not your home, Luke Marriott, my home!'

'Nikki Russell, do you know how extraordinarily beautiful you are when you're angry?'

Nikki slumped back into her chair and gazed up at the man before her in fulminating fury. 'If you think you can worm your way around me with your insincere compliments to get you what you want. . . You don't care, do you?'

'For your privacy?' He smiled. 'Not a lot. It seems you're taking enough care of that for both of us.'

'Just because I like keeping to myself——'

'And blocking the world out.' He shook his head. 'Nikki, Amy needs the rest of the world, even if you don't.'

'Luke Marriott, I am not your patient.'

'No?'

'No!'

'Well, then.' His smile deepened and he pulled his white coat from his shoulders, hanging it behind the door. 'If you're not my patient, then you can come to lunch with me. Hungry, Dr Russell?'

'No.'

'Liar,' he said equitably. 'Coming, or do I have to sling you over my shoulder and take you by force?'

'You wouldn't dare!'

Once more the irrepressible smile.

'Try me, Dr Russell. Maybe we'd both enjoy it.'

Nikki glared. Luke's smile didn't slip. She placed one foot tentatively forward and Luke's smile deepened even further. He would enjoy it, Nikki realised. He'd enjoy carrying her past her patients and receptionist with no thought at all for her dignity. . .with no thought for the fact that she was here forever in this town and had her reputation to consider.

'I'm going back to Whispering Palms for lunch,' she said half-heartedly, but he simply shook his head and took her hand.

'Beattie packed me enough lunch for three,' he told her. 'I want sea, sun, sandwiches and swim in that order. Let's go, Dr Russell.'

'I don't——'

'If you're worried about your precious virtue, you needn't worry,' he smiled. 'We're taking Karen.'

'Karen?' Nikki said blankly. 'But she's in hospital.'

'For the next three minutes,' he agreed. 'We're taking her to the beach for lunch and then you're taking her home to Whispering Palms.'

'Luke Marriott, do you have any idea what you're doing to me?' Regardless of listening ears on the other side of the door, Nikki's voice rose hysterically. 'I have exams in two and a half weeks. My house is filling with strangers. I never allow my work to impinge on my private life. To take a child home. . .'

'So what would you do, Dr Russell?' The hand holding Nikki's suddenly tightened, and Luke's smile slipped. 'Would you send Karen home to her mother before Sandra's been given a chance to sort her life out? Or would you put her on a plane to Cairns to be put into a foster home there? She knows you and she trusts you. Sandra can pop in and see her when she feels like it. . .'

'More people in my home!'

'Yes.' The smile crept back. 'With any luck, by the time I leave that place will start feeling like a home. Let's go, Dr Russell.'

Karen was still in bed when they reached the hospital, propped up by so many pillows that her wan little face all but disappeared. She didn't smile as they approached—just watched them gravely.

'How's my girl?' Luke smiled as he reached his small patient. His hand came down and ruffled the short, cropped hair. 'Feeling better?'

'Can I go home?' Karen's voice was lifeless and uninterested. Her eyes flicked over to the door as though she was expecting someone else to come.

'Karen, we're going to hold on to you a while longer.' Luke sank down to sit on the bed. He took Karen's small hand in his and his body blocked her view of the door. He looked down, silent until he was sure he had her full attention. 'Karen, your mum broke your arm, didn't she?'

The child stared up, silent, and Luke nodded.

'You don't have to tell us,' he said. 'But it's not you who needs the treatment—it's your mum.'

'You're taking her away. . .'

'No.' Luke's hands came up to grip Karen's slight shoulders. 'Karen, you've seen a balloon burst, haven't you? What's happening to your mother at the moment is very much like what happens when you blow a balloon up too far. She has so many worries—and each one is like a puff into a balloon. The worries build up and build up, until the last little puff makes her explode. That little puff might be just a child coughing at the wrong moment—or tea burning—or even just a draught from an open door. It's not the person who caused the tiny puff who's at fault, but the explosion comes just the same.'

'You mean. . .you mean when she gets angry. . .'

'I mean that's what happens when your mum hurts

you.' Luke's eyes didn't leave the child. 'Your dad isn't giving your mum the money she needs to support you. She can't afford to buy the food you need. The littlies are causing her too much work. She's lonely and she's worried and all these things are just building up and building up to the point where she hurts you. She feels dreadful about it, Karen.'

'But. . .'

'I know. She doesn't come. It's because she's ashamed, Karen. Can you understand that?'

Karen's big eyes filled with tears. She looked wildly up at Nikki, the doctor she knew and trusted. 'She doesn't have to be ashamed. And she shouldn't be worried. I can look after her. I try. . .'

'I know you do.' Nikki moved swiftly to give the little girl a hard hug. 'But you've been trying on your own for long enough. Now it's time for Dr Marriott and me to take a turn. What your mum needs now is a rest and a chance to sort herself out. So while she does that she's agreed to let you come to stay with us for a holiday.'

'Us?' Karen looked through her tears from Nikki to Luke and then back again.

'Yes.' Nikki's voice firmed. She didn't look at Luke. OK. He was right. This little girl needed Whispering Palms more than Nikki needed her privacy. 'You know Amy—my little girl—and Mrs Gilchrist. We've a swimming-pool and lots of toys and books. Your arm can heal while your mum finds a new place for you to live.'

'A new place. . .?'

'Yes.' Luke grinned and pulled back Karen's covers. 'A perfectly splendid new home where you and your mum and brothers and sister can all live happily ever after. Now, Miss Mears, we have a picnic lunch to eat and a quick swim before Dr Russell takes you to your temporary accommodation.'

'But——' Karen looked up wildly '—I won't be able

to swim. I haven't got my bathers and. . .and you said I mustn't get my plaster wet.'

Luke shook his head solemnly. 'No problem.' He glanced around to the ward nurse. 'Sister here will provide us with a large plastic bag and a rubber band for your arm, and as for the rest—well, if you're wearing a plastic bag you can't be accused of skinny-dipping, can you?'

Karen looked from one doctor to another. Her tear-drenched eyes widened. And then, very softly, she giggled.

So what was happening to her nice, quiet study period? Nikki sat in her study and gazed out over the pool. Amy and Karen were sitting under the vast grape-vine discussing the merits of alternative ways of dressing Barbie dolls. It was evidently a very solemn topic—both little girls were taking the matter very seriously. Despite herself, Nikki smiled. It hadn't occurred to her to have children here to play with Amy, and now—now she saw how much pleasure Amy could get from it.

And Karen too. Karen had enjoyed her picnic to the full, laughing at Luke's silly jokes and thoroughly enjoying frolicking in the shallows with him. Later, though, as Nikki had tucked her into bed for an after-noon sleep, the shadows had come back over her face. 'I want to go home,' she'd whispered.

'Not yet, sweetheart,' Nikki had told her. How to tell a child that her mother was still so tense that she might strike her again? They couldn't risk it. Then, as tired tears had welled in Karen's eyes, Amy had appeared clutching her teddy and a battered stuffed monkey.

'I have to have an afternoon sleep too,' she'd announced. 'And I thought I could sleep with Karen if. . .if I let her use Monkey.'

It was the perfect solution. Karen had moved over

in the big bed and the two little girls cuddled down together. They were asleep in minutes.

So Luke was right. Luke Marriott was always right, Nikki had thought bitterly. He could organise everyone's life except his own.

She had picked up her abandoned text and stared at it uselessly. She'd still been staring two hours later when the sounds through the house had announced that the girls were awake and ready for fun.

The exam was starting to seem irrelevant. So what if I fail it? she'd asked herself, and then blinked. What had she just said? She looked out of the window as the two little girls emerged to the poolside. As she watched, Beattie brought out a tray of lemonade and biscuits. Nikki saw her glance doubtfully across to Nikki's window. She'd be wondering whether to disturb her, Nikki knew, and suddenly Nikki threw her text aside. It was time for a few minutes with the children, she decided. Some things were more important than exams.

A few minutes? An hour and a half later Nikki was still by the poolside. Amy's entire collection of dolls was dressed to the young ladies' satisfaction and the young ladies themselves were clothed in a variety of evening wear supplied by Nikki. They looked amazing. Both had high heels, stockings down around their ankles, mock pearls and diamonds and enough make-up to supply an entire chorus line. Luke arrived home just as Nikki was lining up the giggling girls and assorted dolls to be photographed for posterity.

'Wow,' he said reverently, emerging from the French doors to the astounding sight. 'A real bevy of beauties.'

'We're gorgeous, Dr Luke,' Amy announced importantly. 'Aren't we?'

'You certainly are,' Luke grinned. He picked Amy up and swung her high, causing her stockings to fall down around his face. 'Ugh. What are these?'

'They're my pantyhose,' Amy said indignantly,

making a futile clutch as they fell. 'I don't know how Mummy keeps 'em up.'

'Mummy has hips,' Luke said, grinning wickedly across at Nikki. 'Ample hips is what you need, my girl.'

'Are Mummy's ample?'

'They certainly are.'

Nikki gasped. Without thinking she abandoned her camera, scooped down and brought up a huge handful of pool water, directing it straight at Luke. It hit him full in the face.

Karen's jaw dropped but Amy crowed in delight. 'Yay, Mum,' she yelled. 'Do it again.'

'I'm not sure I could,' Nikki said nervously, backing away from the pool.

Luke grinned. He picked up a towel and carefully wiped his face. His shirt-front and tie were sodden.

'Mummy growls at me when I get my clothes wet,' Amy giggled. 'Are you going to growl at Mummy?'

'Of course I am,' Luke said severely. He frowned direfully down at the two children. 'What do you think I should do to her?'

'Nothing,' Karen said nervously, but Amy was made of sterner stuff.

'I think she should be spiff. . .spifflicated,' she pronounced.

'Oh, yes?' Luke's straight face broke. 'And what exactly is spifflication?'

'I'm not sure,' Amy confessed. 'I think. . .I think it's sort of like tickling.'

Luke grinned. 'I can do that,' he agreed. He turned back to Nikki. 'Prepare to be spifflicated, Dr Russell.'

'Don't you touch me——'

'In front of the children,' Luke finished for her smoothly. 'Of course not. You have your dignity to maintain. I only ever spifflicate in private. Beattie!'

The housekeeper appeared from nowhere. She had obviously missed nothing of the proceedings. 'Yes?'

Beattie Gilchrist was close to laughter, fighting to keep a straight face.

'Is dinner something that will spoil?'

'It's casserole, Dr Luke.'

'Would it ruin your day if I told you I was taking Dr Russell off to dinner and hence to a fate of spifflication?'

Beattie chuckled delightedly. 'Of course not,' she beamed. 'The casserole will taste better than ever tomorrow night, and me and the girls will cook ourselves hamburgers. You won't mind, will you, girls?'

'No way,' Amy shouted, but Karen looked troubled. Luke crossed to the little girl and knelt down.

'What is it, Karen?' he asked gently.

'You won't. . .you won't hurt Dr Russell, will you?' the child asked tremulously. 'She didn't mean to get you wet.'

'Don't you believe it. Our Dr Russell did so mean to get me wet.' Luke took Karen's hands in his and gave them a reassuring squeeze. 'But no, Karen. I may tickle Dr Russell until she screams for mercy but I won't hurt her. Not now. Not ever. I don't hurt people. That's a promise.'

The laughter had gone from his voice. He met the little girl's eyes, and what she read in his seemed to reassure her. The corners of her mouth struggled to smile. 'I like hamburgers,' she said simply.

'Then that's settled.' Luke turned to Nikki. 'Go and get yourself into a pretty dress, Dr Russell. I'll take off one sodden shirt and then. . .then prepare to meet your doom!'

'But I like hamburgers too,' Nikki said weakly. This was going too fast for her. She had no intention of going out to dinner with this man.

'Beattie, if you were doomed to spifflication, where would you want to eat your last meal?' Luke demanded, ignoring Nikki's protest and turning to the housekeeper.

Beattie chuckled. 'Only one place to eat out hereabouts,' she told him. 'The fishing co-op runs a club. The dining-room looks out over the harbour. It's real pretty and the food's not bad either.'

'It sounds just what the doctor ordered,' Luke smiled. 'OK, Dr Russell. You have ten minutes to prepare yourself. Let's go.'

The man was like a bulldozer, Nikki thought grimly. She stood in her bedroom and gazed helplessly at the mirror. A meal out. . . To be taken out by a man. . .

To be taken out by Luke Marriott! Nikki closed her eyes as a wave of confusion ran through her. What was happening? She should be staying at home studying. She should put her hands on her not so ample hips and tell Luke Marriott exactly what she thought of him.

If he hadn't been ill, she would do, she decided, but it was hardly fair when he'd been through such a bad time.

'That's not the reason and you know it,' she told her reflection out loud. 'You want to go out.'

No, you don't, a little voice inside her protested.

'Yes, you do.'

Nikki thought back to Luke Marriott kneeling before the troubled Karen, and a feeling of warmth flooded over her. This man was kind and caring and. . .

This man was trouble. Capital T. Trouble.

He would be gone in a couple of weeks. He was transient—a transient presence in a life which so far hadn't been all that much fun.

'Why shouldn't I go out, then?' Nikki demanded of her reflection. 'Seize the day. Live for the moment.'

You're talking rubbish! that inner voice asserted.

'Oh, leave me alone!' Nikki turned her back on her wiser self and stared into the wardrobe. She had hung the clothes Charlotte had sent her and then ignored all that she could. Now she crossed to pull the racks apart.

Charlotte was never a girl to do things by halves. She

had taken Nikki's wardrobe as a personal challenge, omitting nothing.

And there was something just right for tonight. Something just right for a first and last date. A night to forget she was Dr Nikki Russell who took the world seriously. A night to forget the loneliness of the rest of her life. . . Taking a deep breath, Nikki slipped the fabric over her shoulders.

The dress was soft white silk, loose-fitting but clinging with the sheerness of the fabric. It hung low across her breasts, the soft sleeves cut away so that they exposed her slender arms. The dress fell in delicate folds around her thighs and down to swirl around her long legs. A ribbon of palest green looped around the waist and down to hint at its presence among the folds as she moved.

The dress turned her into someone she wasn't. Or someone she had once been but had forgotten existed. Nikki stood before the mirror and stared. Unconsciously she brought her hand up to gather her hair into a loose, curling knot of flame. The action made her seem younger, and more vulnerable. She let it fall, and then in swift decision put it up again. Before she had time to change her mind she pinned it and turned from the mirror. She had done it. She was ready.

'Wow!' It was Amy, bursting through the door, her new friend tagging behind. 'Wow, Mummy, you're beautiful. Isn't she beautiful, Karen?'

'My mum's prettier,' Karen said stoutly. 'But. . .but you're really pretty, Dr Russell.'

'Is she ever!' Luke Marriott was standing in the passage. He too had changed, into a dark suit which made Nikki see just why he had caused so many problems among the nursing staff in the city. Drop-dead handsome, the man was. She looked up, blushed and looked away again. What on earth was she doing?

'Have a really good time, now,' Amy ordered them. 'What time will you be home?'

'By midnight, Mother,' Nikki laughed, swooping her small daughter up to give her a kiss. 'Don't wait up for me.'

'Don't spifflicate her too hard, will you, Dr Luke?' Amy warned.

'I make no promises,' Luke grinned. His arm came around Nikki in a proprietorial gesture. 'Vengeance is mine, Dr Russell. For tonight, you're at my mercy.'

CHAPTER SEVEN

IF THERE was to be only one evening left in the world, this could well be the evening. It was a night to forget the past, forget the future and just be.

Something had snapped inside Nikki's controlled head. Who knew what had caused it? Was it the culmination of long years of work and worry, Charlotte's lovely dress floating around her slim form, the balmy tropical night, or the presence of the man at her side—a man whose smile made her heart do crazy jumps inside her body and made her forget that she was Dr Nikki Russell with the weight of the world on her shoulders? Which of these things was causing the feeling of euphoria creeping over her? Nikki didn't know, and she no longer cared. The night was hers.

And somehow for Luke it seemed the same. The world was put on hold. They were alone together and nothing else mattered.

Miraculously there was a table available in the best part of the club—a sheltered alcove with windows looking out over the lights of the harbour to the sea beyond. The waiter showed them to their seats with an astonished second look at the town's transformed lady doctor. I didn't know you existed, his glance said, and Luke's hand tightened on Nikki's waist as he guided her forward.

The lady's mine for the night, his hand said. Keep off. Nikki should have shrugged the hand aside but she wouldn't. Not tonight.

Afterwards Nikki couldn't remember a thing they'd talked about. Inconsequential nonsense, she suspected. Luke kept her in a ripple of laughter as they ate. The tiny pieces of calamary still tasted of the sea, and of the lemon groves in the hills above the town—and the grilled whiting melted in Nikki's mouth, blending in with her perfect night.

He made her seem the most desirable woman in the world, Nikki thought, and wondered fleetingly how many other women had been given the same treatment. It didn't matter. Not tonight. Tonight was hers.

They ate huge red strawberries and farm-fresh cream, drank their coffee and then rose reluctantly to leave. Miraculously the beeper in Luke's pocket stayed silent. It was as if the world were holding its breath.

'A walk, I think,' Luke told her as they emerged to the star-filled night. 'I'm not ready for bed yet, Dr Russell, and I don't think you are either.'

'N-no.' It was true. Nikki didn't want this evening to end. In the morning she would be back with her books, and Luke would be back to being her locum, and the world would have shifted on to its rightful axis. But not yet. . . So they walked along the sand, barefoot, with shoes dangling in their free hands. One hand of each was in use, linked unconsciously with the other.

They walked far from the lights of the jetty and of the town, around the headland where the beach stretched out for mile upon endless mile of deserted sand. The moonlight played on their faces. From somewhere a long way off Nikki heard herself talking of her childhood—telling this man things she had told no one—of a lonely childhood with eccentric parents in a house too big for her—but with love and laughter always present. And Luke talked too—a little—of his family in Melbourne and his life before. . .before he knew he had cancer.

It was as if the last few years were taboo. They weren't spoken of. The night was magical, and ugly realities weren't allowed to intrude.

And finally their wandering feet came to a halt and Nikki's voice fell silent. Luke let his shoes drop to the sand, removed Nikki's sandals from her grasp and then took her shoulders, turning her to face him in the moonlight.

'So what now, my lovely Nikki?' he said softly. 'Are you going to let the world in again? Is your life going to have ended when Scott walked out the door?'

'I don't. . .'

'You can't let that happen,' he told her, his fingers tightening on her shoulders. 'I'm pushing you hard, but when I go, will you close the door on life again? Retire back into your parents' house and shut the world out?'

'When I go'. . . The words hung between them and Nikki was aware of a rush of desolation sweeping through her. This was a transient thing. This moment was just what she knew it must be—a dream—a fantasy of something that could never be.

'It's none of your business what I do when you go,' she managed to whisper.

'But it is.' His hands came up to cup her cheeks. Tilting her face, he looked deeply into her troubled eyes. 'I care about you, Nikki.'

'Yes, you care,' she agreed bitterly. 'The way you care about Karen. And the way you care about Sandra. Like all the other waifs you've decided to adopt as part of your healing process.'

It was unfair. Nikki's accusation was contemptible and she knew it, but somehow. . .somehow it was so important that she be different.

And she was. She saw it in the sudden blaze of anger in Luke's deep eyes and the tightening of his mouth. His hands held her harder.

'Why do you do this?' he said softly, his voice dangerously low. 'Why do you want to lash out at me?'

'I don't. . .' Nikki's voice fell away. 'I don't know,' she whispered miserably. 'I'm sorry, Luke. . .'

Her words trailed away. Between them there was a long silence, broken only by the rush of the sea in its constant washing of the vast stretch of beach.

Luke gave a low, savage moan and turned to stare out to sea. Nikki's hands came up to touch her face where he had held it. What now? What?

And then slowly, as though driven by something he didn't understand and couldn't fight, Luke turned. He reached out to take her face again, and when she tried to pull away his hands gripped harder. For a long, long moment he stood looking down into her bewildered face, and then, infinitely slowly, he stooped to kiss her.

It was a harsh, demanding kiss. It was a kiss of confusion and pain, and of punishment. You've hurt me, the kiss said, and I take my revenge. . .

But then it was more than that. The lips that demanded possession of her mouth were asking something more than appeasement of anger.

They wanted her. They wanted to know her mouth—know the secrets of her tongue—possess the smooth contours of her even teeth. They wanted. . .

It wasn't the lips that wanted. It was the man. And the woman wanted in return. Nikki felt the hardness of Luke's body against hers, and a flame started deep within her. This was a sweetness that she had never known. She could smell him, taste him, feel him, and she wanted more! She wanted to be closer than she had ever been to a man in her life before.

Where were the memories of her long-gone husband? They were certainly not here. In fact they no longer existed—blown away by the sensation of these hands holding her, these fingers caressing the smooth contours of her thighs, pulling her closer to feel the urgency of his want—his need.

'Luke. . .'

She wasn't sure that she whispered the name aloud but it crowded her consciousness. It was a cry of desperate loneliness, need, and the start of some crazy hope. Soon this man would be gone, but if only. . .if only. . .

It didn't matter. For tonight there were the stars and the sea and this man holding her as if she were the most precious thing in the world. Nikki arched herself against him and felt his head drop to her breast.

Somehow the loose silk of her dress was put aside and Luke's mouth covered the taut wanting of her nipples. The sensation was so sweet that Nikki cried aloud and tears of joy coursed down her face.

Oh, God, it had never been like this with Scott. She had thought Scott was a friend and he turned into her husband. This man, though. . .this man was no friend. This man was her mate—her soulmate—her love. . .

Her love. The word swept through and through her and she knew with absolute certainty that it was true. She loved Luke Marriott with every ounce of her being.

She loved. She loves. She will love. Forever and ever and ever. And then as Luke's arms came around her, cradled her and gently lowered her to lie on the warm sand beside him, she knew that whatever he wanted was right with her. If he only wanted her for this moment, then this moment would have to last forever.

And then, from some far-away place, came the sound of a harsh, electronic beep. It grew into a crescendo, splitting the night with its awful insistence. Luke's mouth stilled where he had been exploring the valley between her breasts. As Nikki grew rigid in his arms, he swore unsteadily and rose.

'Fate worse than death,' he said unsteadily. 'I think we're wanted, my love.' He put down a hand and pulled her to her feet, his arm pulling her to his body. Kissing her roughly on the mouth, he put her from him in bitter resolution. 'The world calls. Let's see what they have to say.'

'The world calls'. . . Nikki stood, confused, as Luke searched his trouser pocket for the beeper. He lifted it high to see its faint light in the moonlight.

'McDonald baby arriving,' he read. 'Assistance required.'

'McDonald. . .' Nikki frowned. 'But. . .but Mrs McDonald's only seven months pregnant.' She thought back to the last time she had seen Lara McDonald. Last week. And she was only twenty-nine weeks then. . .

'I'll have to go fast,' she said unsteadily. 'We'll have to try to stop labour until we get her to Cairns.' She was already searching in the sand for her sandals.

'We'll walk faster without shoes,' Luke told her. 'Come on. Ready for a run, my love?'

They covered the distance back to the car in a time Nikki would have thought was impossible. Luke, however, was in a hurry, and with his hand holding hers anything was possible. He gave Nikki's feet wings. It was a desperate run, with both knowing the need for urgency, but somehow. . .somehow it was still part of the magic night. Whatever the night held, Nikki was as one with Luke Marriott. If he ran fast then she was part of him, carried along by emotion.

She was gasping for breath as they neared the car, but as Luke stopped to find the key she started laughing.

'I feel like a naughty child trying to get home before they find I'm missing,' she laughed. 'Oh, Luke, I hope we can stop this labour.'

He looked down at her curiously in the dim light, and his mouth twisted into an answering smile.

'So do I,' he murmured. 'But whatever we do, we need to do it fast.'

It was an enigmatic statement which Nikki didn't follow. There was no need to say the obvious, she thought, but then they were in the car, with Luke's hand on the horn as they turned back out on to the main road towards the hospital.

Nikki turned her face towards the ribbon of bitumen, forcing her thoughts savagely away from the man beside her. Lara McDonald didn't need a love-struck girl, she needed a competent doctor, and that was just what Nikki had to be.

Nikki was out of the car almost before it had come to a halt at the front door of the hospital, running swiftly up the tiled steps and through the glass doors. The night sister came out to meet her.

'She's in the labour ward,' the sister said. Behind her, a big man in denim work trousers and generous flannelette shirt materialised out of the shadows. He was literally wringing his hands, but ceased momentarily as he reached to clutch Nikki's arm.

'The baby'll die if it comes now,' he said hoarsely. 'Doc Russell, it's too early. And Lara's had three miscarriages already. This. . .this is our last chance——' He broke off to run his hand across his wet cheeks. 'Oh, God, Doc, you gotta stop it. If this baby doesn't make it. . .'

'Sister, could you find Mr McDonald a cup of strong, sweet tea?' Nikki said. 'And then come straight back to the ward. Have you examined Mrs McDonald?'

'I didn't like to,' the sister told her. 'I thought I might make matters worse.'

'Good.' The nurse was right. An internal examination might hurry things even further. She turned to the labour ward and found Luke by her side.

Two doctors. . . At least there were two doctors. If the baby was born it would have a much better chance if it could have the undivided attention of Luke while Nikki attended the mother. She smiled gratefully up at Luke as he swung the door wide.

Lara McDonald was a small, wiry woman in her late thirties. She and her husband owned a small sugar farm just out of town, and struggled to make ends meet. Lara's face reflected it, weathered and lined from years of too much sun and hard work.

Her face was further lined now, creased in agony as a spasm ripped through her. Her eyes were wide with terror, and as Nikki approached she reached out to clutch her hand.

'Stop it,' she whispered frantically. 'You've got to stop it.'

Nikki kept hold of the hand until the worst of the spasm passed. Out of the corner of her eye she could see Luke scrubbing and getting into gown and gloves. Once more she was grateful for two doctors. It meant she could stay where she was.

'Let's not panic,' she said gently. 'Wait until we see what's going on. When did you start having pains?'

'After dinner. About. . .about an hour ago?'

'Have you had a show? Any bleeding?'

'No.' A fresh spasm hit and the hand clutched again.

Then Luke was at the table. The night sister had returned, and together she and Nikki lifted away Lara's cotton dress. Nikki frowned as the fabric fell to the side. Lara was mid-spasm but her swollen abdomen was smooth and still. Nikki put a hand on the firm flesh. Nothing. This wasn't a contraction.

She looked a question to Luke. Swiftly he performed a gentle examination, his face clearing as he did.

'There's no dilation at all,' he told Nikki. 'Mrs McDonald, what did you have for dinner?'

'I. . .' Lara was wincing through pain. 'I don't. . .' Then she paused. 'Curry,' she said suddenly. 'We had curry.'

'Do you often have curry?' Luke's voice was clipped and professional, demanding the woman's attention.

'No. . .' She managed a faint smile. 'But. . .but I really wanted it. So Bill went down to Innisfail to get some for me. He got three tubs. . .'

Luke grinned. 'And you ate the lot.'

'Well, Bill didn't like it.'

Luke shook his head. Nikki found herself relaxing, the tension oozing out of her. Three tubs of curry when unaccustomed to it. . .

'Mrs McDonald, you're not in labour,' she said

gently. 'I'm sure of it. What's happening to you is caused by your system reacting to curry. Probably your pregnancy has made you a bit more prone to tummy upsets than usual, and the curry is making itself felt.'

'Is that all?' The woman's eyes widened. She stared wildly from Nikki to Luke and then back to Nikki. Slowly the frantic terror behind her eyes faded. Still clutching her stomach, she fell back on to the pillows, exhausted. 'Oh, my God,' she whispered fervently. 'Oh, thank you.'

'Any time.' Nikki grinned. She looked up to see Luke's smile reflecting her own. Relief was making her light-headed, she thought suddenly. She felt like singing. Or maybe. . .maybe it wasn't all relief.

'We'll give you an injection to settle your tummy, and we'll keep you overnight,' Nikki reassured her patient, forcing her attention away from Luke. 'But you'll live to eat curry again.'

'And. . .and the baby. . .?'

'It seems he's enjoying the new sensations you've been causing him too much to want to leave,' Luke grinned. 'I bet he emerges in two months demanding more vindaloo and chapattis.'

'Ugh. . .' Lara McDonald moaned. 'Don't even mention them. . .'

A few minutes later they left their patient resigned to an uncomfortable night. Nikki had kept a straight face as she'd administered medication, but as she climbed into the car she broke into delighted chuckles. It wasn't often that dramas turned so nicely into farce.

'Unsympathetic wench,' Luke growled. 'Did you never have food cravings in pregnancy?'

'I was desperate for oysters and beer one night,' Nikki confessed. 'But I made myself a cup of hot milk instead.'

'A very restrained young lady,' Luke nodded. His hand came over to her side of the car. Starting from the tip of her knee, his fingers gradually worked their way upwards. 'Keep your eyes on the road, Dr Russell,' he advised kindly. 'Just remember how restrained you are.'

Nikki gasped. 'Don't. . .'

'Why?' The fingers were touching the soft flesh of her inner thigh through the flimsy fabric of her dress. 'Why stop, Dr Russell?'

'Because I'll crash the car if you don't,' Nikki managed.

He grinned. 'Point taken. How long until we get to Whispering Palms?'

The house was in darkness when they arrived home. A solitary lamp burned in the hall, but Beattie and the children had long gone to bed. Nikki locked the big front door behind them and then turned uncertainly to the man beside her. All of a sudden she felt very young, and very shy.

'G-goodnight, then,' she stammered.

He flicked her cheek with his finger, lifting an errant wisp of flaming hair. 'Do you want it to be goodnight, my Nikki?'

Of course she did. Of course she wanted to walk along the passage to the solitude of her own room. She could even do an hour's study before she slept.

So why was she slowly shaking her head, as if mesmerised by Luke's slow smile—the look of understanding and care in his hypnotic eyes? Hypnotic. . . It was the right word, she thought ruefully. It was as if she were drugged. Her eyes held his and she smiled uncertainly up at him.

'N-no.'

'Are you sure?' He took her shoulders in his hands and held her at arm's length. 'Nikki, I make no promises about tomorrow. I'm here for two and a half weeks and after that. . .well, after that, who knows where I'll be? But for now. . .'

She could hardly accuse him of deceiving her. He was laying his bitter cards out for her to see, and if she didn't like them she could leave right now—walk through the house to her bedroom and close the door hard behind her.

But he wasn't lying. This man was telling her the truth, and, no matter how unpalatable it was, the truth was what she wanted. Scott's lies and deception had been with her for too long for her to want anything else.

And she wanted Luke. His eyes held her, mesmerised, and Nikki knew that if two weeks of this man was all she could have, then two weeks would have to be enough. It would have to suffice for the rest of her life.

She lifted her hands to hold his face, and stood on tiptoe to touch his lips with hers. 'If tonight is all we have,' she whispered, 'then tonight is all there is.'

For a long moment he stood motionless. Nikki felt a moment's searing panic. She had thrown herself at him. Would he react in disgust?

And then his hands came around her body, and tenderly she was lifted up to lie cradled in his arms. He held her hard against him and his lips deepened the kiss.

'My bedroom has the double bed,' Nikki whispered as the kiss came finally to its sweet end, and Luke chuckled.

'Ever the practical one, Dr Russell.' He pushed the door from the hall open with his foot. 'Well, Dr Russell, what are we waiting for?'

It was the sweetest night Nikki had ever known.

Five long years she had been without a man, and her body had forgotten just how good it was. Or maybe her body had never known. Luke held her tenderly in his arms and the world was forgotten. All she knew was the feel of his skin against hers, his warmth embracing her, making her feel the most desirable woman in the world.

And when tenderness turned to urgency it was Nikki's desperate need that drove her on. She wanted this man so much. She wanted to be closer to him than she had ever been to another person in her life before. She wanted to be part of him, one with him, and when they climaxed together she soared on a pinnacle of ecstasy that made her feel the night was exploding around her.

Oh, God, she loved him. She loved him so much. . .

Nikki drifted towards sleep in his arms, his face cradled in the rise of her breasts, and her heart swelled in a rush of pure tenderness. She would do anything for this man. Anything. And he was only hers for two and a half weeks.

They hadn't taken precautions. Nikki's eyes suddenly widened in the dark as the thought struck. Suppose. . . Suppose she was wrong about Luke's infertility. . .?

He felt her sudden stiffness, and stirred to lift her face to his. 'What is it, my beautiful Nikki?' he asked sleepily.

'Luke. . .' Nikki said unsteadily. 'Luke, I'm not. . .I'm not protected. I didn't think. . .'

'There's no need.' Luke's voice was suddenly bitter. 'You know the ramifications of the treatment for Hodgkin's disease as well as I do, Dr Russell, and as for anything else. . .well, I haven't been with a woman since I was ill. You're quite safe.'

'Oh, Luke, I'm sorry.' Nikki could have bitten her tongue from her head.

'Yeah, well, leave it,' Luke said roughly. 'Go to sleep.'

She didn't straight away. As Luke slept, Nikki lay in the dark and tried to come to terms with what she was feeling. She couldn't. The emotions crowding through her mind were those she had never felt before and had no idea how to cope with.

'I haven't been with a woman since I was ill. . .' Where had he been? Had he moved from locum position to locum position since then? And if so, what was he trying to escape?

It was too much. For now, he was here and she could somehow assuage the barrenness of the past. And he could do the same for her.

Nikki nestled her head against Luke's bare chest. He stirred slightly in his sleep and pulled her closer.

She slept.

Luke woke at dawn. Gently he disengaged himself from Nikki's arms, but the slight movement woke her. For a moment—just a moment—she wondered where she was, and then the tender memories flooded back. Her hands reached out to hold him to her. He couldn't leave. Not yet.

'It's nearly morning.' Luke smiled tenderly, leaning over to kiss the smooth skin behind her ear. He entwined a golden curl in his finger and then replaced it reluctantly where it had been lying on the pillow. 'Do you want your daughter to burst in on her not so respectable mama, Dr Russell?'

Nikki chuckled and her hands tightened. Luke's chest was broad and muscled and warm. A tremor went through her as the flame started to spread without volition through her naked body. 'Amy's a heavy sleeper,' she whispered. 'And she's under strict instructions not to wake Mummy until seven.'

Luke shifted slightly so that he could bring his arm up from under Nikki's supine form. 'Give me back my watch, woman,' he growled. Finally he held it up. 'Six-fifteen,' he announced. 'That gives us forty-five minutes.'

'Forty-five minutes for what?' Nikki asked breathlessly. She knew, but to ask was heaven.

'If you don't know, then I'm not the man to tell you,' Luke told her sternly. He moved to pull his body up and over her. The flame in Nikki's thighs was building to an inferno.

'You. . .you won't tell me?' she managed.

'Lady, what use is talking?' he muttered. He leaned down to take first one nipple and then the other between his strong teeth. It was all Nikki could do to stop herself crying aloud. 'What use is telling, when I can show you?'

CHAPTER EIGHT

LUKE left her with five minutes to spare.

Luckily Amy chose this morning to sleep late, so Nikki was able to shower and pull her disordered mind back into some sort of control before her daughter and their visitor burst in.

'Luke's in the swimming-pool,' Amy informed her. 'Beattie says we can swim too, but will you come as well?' Then she frowned at her mother. 'You look different.'

'I wore this dress a couple of days ago,' Nikki said self-consciously. It was one that Charlotte had sent. 'Don't you like it?'

'I remember. It's a pretty dress,' Amy agreed. She eyed her mother up and down. 'It's not that that's different. It's. . .' She stopped. 'I don't know what it is.'

'Your mum's smiley,' Karen announced suddenly. 'She's not usually smiley.'

'Well, I hope your mum's smiley today too,' Nikki said softly, stooping to give Karen a swift hug. The hug did more than show affection to the little girl. It also enabled Nikki to hide her mounting colour. 'She's coming to see you today, and maybe she'll take you for a walk to show you your new house.'

'Will I go back home today?'

'We'll get you moved into your new house first,' Nikki promised. 'Karen, it might be a week or two before your mum's got things under control. Do you think you can put up with us for that long?'

Karen nodded solemnly. 'I like it here,' she said seriously. 'And if you think Mum needs a rest. . .'

'I think you both need a rest,' Nikki told her. 'When

your arm's a bit better and you can go back to being your mum's best helper then we'll send you home so fast we won't see you for dust. Faster than a speeding bullet. . .'

'Faster even than Superman. . .' Amy giggled. 'I like having Karen here. Mummy, are you coming swimming with Luke?'

Nikki shook her head. 'No.' She dared not. The thought of Luke in the swimming-pool. . . The thought of Luke anywhere at all was enough to turn her knees to water. She needed strong black coffee and some distance between them. 'You girls go,' she ordered.

'But Luke's waiting!'

'Let him wait!'

Once again they breakfasted by the side of the pool. Whispering Palms was transformed, Nikki thought fleetingly as the children's laughter sounded across the water. Beattie was beaming and affable. She kept looking from Luke to Nikki and back again, and Nikki knew exactly what was in her mind.

'You need to find yourself a nice new man,' Beattie had told Nikki over and over again, and now, seemingly, one had found her cherished Dr Nikki. And such a nice young man! Beattie handed out extra pancakes and her smile broadened.

'Are you staying home to study all day?' Beattie asked Nikki, refilling her coffee-cup, and Nikki nodded.

'Though I'll have to go in to the hospital first,' she told the housekeeper. She was carefully avoiding Luke's eyes. 'I need to check Mrs McDonald.'

'I can do that,' Luke told her lazily.

'No.' Nikki flushed and stared intently at her cup of coffee. 'Lara's my midwifery patient and I should see her.'

'Suits me.' To her surprise Luke didn't argue. He pushed back his chair. 'Thanks for breakfast, Beattie.'

He lifted his brows at Nikki. 'Coming, then?'

He could as well have kissed her. His eyes smiled at Nikki as he moved to help her rise and she felt herself flush to the core of her being. She felt beautiful and desirable and. . .and loved. Oh, if only she were. . .

There was a minor hiccup. Luke had been using Nikki's car and Beattie needed the house car to take the girls to school and kindergarten. 'It's no problem,' Luke told her as Nikki voiced doubts. 'I'll drop you back after the hospital rounds. You'll still be home in time for enough study to suit your rigid requirements.'

Nikki looked up at him suspiciously but he wasn't laughing. He wouldn't laugh at her, she thought suddenly. He'd laugh with her maybe, but not at her.

They found Lara McDonald perched up in bed eyeing her breakfast dubiously. 'Do you think I should?' she asked as Nikki and Luke entered.

Luke grinned. 'I don't see why not, do you, Dr Russell?'

'Not too much,' Nikki advised. She crossed to the bed. 'Feeling better, then?'

'A hundred per cent.' Mrs McDonald took a deep breath. 'You know, maybe some of the pain was just fear. I thought the baby was coming and it got worse.'

'It happens.' Nikki lifted the chart and smiled at what she saw. 'Everything's fine, then. I see no reason why your husband can't take you home this afternoon. Stay until after lunch, though. We'll see how your tummy responds to breakfast first.'

'He won't want me home.' The woman smiled shyly. 'He cossets me that much! If he had his way I'd stay in hospital for the next two months.' She sighed. 'I can't blame him. This baby means so much to both of us.'

'I know,' Nikki said gently.

'Well, maybe you don't,' the woman said. 'You had

your baby young, if I remember right. My husband and I, though—well, we've been trying for ten years. Ten years is a lot of time to be without a baby when you really want one.' She bit her lip. 'I don't know how people cope when they can't have children. I think. . .I think I might have gone mad.'

'Or maybe you would have found the strength to cope,' Nikki said gently, trying hard not to look up at Luke. 'There's more to life than having children.'

'You say that, but then you have your daughter,' Lara said firmly. 'And maybe I'll say that when I've got my brood safely round me. But not until then.'

A slight sound made Nikki turn. Luke had quietly left while the woman talked, closing the door behind him.

'Oh,' the woman in the bed said. 'He's gone. I guess he's in a hurry and I was wasting your time with my small talk.' She looked up at Nikki. 'Such a nice man,' she smiled.

'Yes,' said Nikki dully. 'Such a nice man.'

There was little else for Nikki to do. All the other patients in the hospital had been handed over to Luke. She spent ten minutes in the office going through correspondence and then made her way back out to the car. Luke appeared fifteen minutes later.

'There should be a taxi service in this town,' Nikki said lightly as he lowered himself into the car beside her. For once, Luke's face was set and grim. Nikki turned away, not wanting to see the etching of pain in the lines around his eyes.

'It's no problem to drive you back.'

'No. But it'll make you late for surgery.'

'Will you dock my pay if I'm late?' Luke demanded, and Nikki swung back towards him, surprised by the intensity of his tone.

'Don't be daft.'

He laughed without humour. 'It's happened before. Being a locum is the pits.'

'So why do you do it?'

Luke's mouth tightened even further. He swung the little car out of the car park and was silent for the rest of the drive home.

That was the last time they talked for the day. Back at Whispering Palms, Nikki left the car without a word. For the life of her she couldn't think of a thing to say. Tackle what's really wrong, her medical training told her. Probe the hurt. And yet. . . And yet this was the man she loved and she couldn't do it. She couldn't hurt him further.

She spent the rest of the day desultorily studying, but to her surprise she achieved a lot. 'I'm in danger of passing this blasted exam,' she told her reflection as she dressed for dinner. 'Which makes Luke Marriott's arrival well worth while.'

The thought held no comfort at all. Nikki stared bleakly at her reflection and then turned away. What on earth was happening to her nice ordered life? She had no idea.

Luke wasn't in his customary position in the kitchen when she appeared. Beattie shook her head disapprovingly at Nikki's questioning look. 'He won't be in,' she said tightly. 'Rang and said he had a case out the other side of town. It's only Verity Birchip. I told him if he spent his life running all the way out to Birchips for every one of Verity's imaginary ills he'd have his work cut out for him, but he wouldn't listen. Said he'd grab something to eat in town and be home late.'

'Maybe there really is something wrong with Verity,' Nikki said mildly.

'That'll be the day,' Beattie snorted. 'You mark my words—Verity Birchip'll go to her grave swearing she has something the medical textbooks haven't even heard of and demanding to know why the heck the doctors are worrying about her dying of old age when she's got something far more interesting.'

Nikki managed a chuckle and Beattie looked at her closely.

'What's the matter, then, lass?'

'Nothing.' Nikki crossed to the cutlery drawer to avoid Beattie's penetrating gaze.

'Something is. And it wouldn't be why Dr Luke had suddenly decided to spend tonight out, would it?'

'Beattie Gilchrist, you're out of line!'

'You'd say that to your own mother.' Beattie crossed her arms and fixed Nikki with a look. 'And it's your substitute mother talking now. Nikki Russell, if you play your cards right——'

'Beattie, be quiet.' Nikki clapped her hands on her ears and glared at her housekeeper. If only Beattie knew that Nikki was playing every card she had—and it wasn't going to be enough.

There was a long silence, and then, thankfully, the door burst open and two small girls tore in.

'We're starving,' Amy said breathlessly. 'Mummy, where's Dr Luke?'

'He's out on a call,' Nikki told her abruptly, stooping to kiss her small daughter. She smiled down at Karen. 'How was your day, Karen?'

'Good,' the little girl said seriously. She appeared to consider the question. 'Mummy picked me up after school and took me around to see the house she's been offered. We think. . .' Despite her solemn tone the child's face suddenly twisted into a smile. 'We think it will be satisfactory. It has one bedroom for Mummy, one for the girls, one for the boys and. . .and one left over. And it's nice! It's even got an inside toilet!'

'That's great.' Nikki swooped to give Karen a hard hug. 'And when does Mummy think she might be able to move?'

'The lady at the hospital has offered to look after the littlies.' Karen was back to being solemn—an eight-year-old matron. 'Mummy says it will take her a week to have everything sorted out. She said if I was able to help she'd be much faster, and she really misses me.' Karen looked up anxiously. 'She said she's really sorry she hurt me. She said she was so worried she went a bit crazy, but you and Dr Luke are fixing it up so she'll never get like that again. She cried, and she hugged me and. . . I. . .I don't think she'll do it again.'

'I don't think she will either,' Nikki told her, with a small rush of relief. Sandra was talking to her child. The lines of communication were open and, by the sound of it, Karen still considered them friends. Sandra was still only twenty-two and her relationship with her daughter might always be more one of friendship than mother-daughter—but then, that was OK too.

'Can I go home when she's moved in?'

'Of course you can, sweetheart,' Nikki assured her, and made herself a promise to contact Sandra the next day. By the look of things the situation was improving rapidly, but it needed to.

It was a long night. Nikki read the girls to sleep, and then went back to her study. Every time a car came up the road she let her book fall as she listened, but it was close to midnight when Luke finally came home. Nikki listened to the brisk tread of steps along the hall and then his bedroom door closing firmly behind him.

She was being shut out. Whatever intimacy had existed between them last night had ceased to exist now.

She prepared herself for bed and climbed between cool sheets in her lonely bed. Last night Luke had been here. Last night. . . The memory of him was all around her and he was so close. . .

The night was hot. Above her head the wooden ceiling fan lazily stirred the air but it wasn't enough. Nikki tossed and turned as she struggled for sleep, but it wasn't forthcoming.

Finally she could bear it no longer. She slipped out

of bed and padded along the bare wooden boards of the hall. Her naked feet made no sound.

There was a light shining underneath Luke's door. Nikki hesitated for a moment and then, taking a deep breath, softly knocked.

Silence. Had he gone to sleep with the light on? Then, as she turned reluctantly away, afraid to go further, the door opened inwards.

Luke was still fully clothed. He had been working. The desk behind him was strewn with papers, and a pen had been tossed hastily aside. All this Nikki saw before Luke moved to block her view.

'What is it?' he asked abruptly, and Nikki flinched.

'I. . .I couldn't sleep.'

He looked down at her for a long moment, his eyes inscrutable as he took in her slim form scantily clad in her wispy cotton nightdress. 'I dare say you have sleeping-tablets in your bag,' he said roughly at last.

Nikki drew in her breath. 'I don't need a sleeping-tablet,' she managed angrily. 'I need to talk.'

'What about?'

'Luke Marriott, what the hell is going on?' Despite her struggle for dignity and control, Nikki's voice rose. Her words echoed down the darkened corridor and instinctively she looked towards the door behind which the children slept. 'Luke, can I come in?'

'No.'

'Why the hell not?' Suddenly Nikki's fragile hold on her temper snapped. 'What are you playing at? Last night you treated me as the most desirable woman you knew and tonight. . .tonight you don't even want to talk to me. What have I done to deserve being treated like a one-night stand?'

Her voice was a whisper, intense, angry and wavering. To her fury she felt hot tears slip down her cheeks, and she brushed them away angrily with her hand.

Behind them she heard the sound of a child stir in her sleep and cough. Nikki winced. Luke stood before her, implacable and immovable. Remote.

'Damn you, Luke Marriott,' she whispered brokenly, and turned away.

He moved then. In two swift strides he caught her, seized her shoulders and swung her round to face him.

Away from the light of the open door Nikki couldn't make out his expression. Not that she looked. She was aware that her body was trembling as she tried to stay rigid in his grasp.

'Hell,' he muttered savagely.

'It is,' Nikki whispered. 'Maybe you'd better let me go, Luke.'

'Nikki. . .'

The child coughed again and Luke swore. Seizing Nikki's hand, he pulled her forward into his bedroom and closed the door behind him.

Silence stretched out between them. Within the small room, Luke released her. Nikki stood numbly against the closed door, her hand idly rubbing her arm. There would be bruising there where he had pulled her.

'God, Nikki, I'm sorry.'

The words were wrung from him. Nikki looked up at him, her eyes dull and heavy. 'For making love to me?' she asked flatly.

'I never meant to.'

'No.' She kept rubbing her arm as if by doing so she could assuage some of the hurt in her heart. 'I don't suppose you did. Charlotte said. . .'

'Charlotte?'

'My friend in Cairns. She said you couldn't help yourself where. . .where women were concerned.'

'God, Nikki, last night was different.' He turned away, his voice agonised. 'I'd say that anyway, wouldn't I?'

'Yes.'

'It's the truth.' He turned back to her and grasped her shoulders. 'It's the truth but it still can't make a difference to the final outcome. The truth is that I was mad. I forgot. . . I don't want you, Nikki. I don't want a woman. Not now. Not ever.'

'That's not how it felt last night.'

'No. But last night. . .last night I was crazy. Just for a little. . .'

'You forgot that you can't father a child?' Nikki took a deep breath. 'Is that what it is, Luke?'

'No. Yes.' He thrust her back from him. 'God, Nikki, you're so lovely. You stand there and all I want to do is make love to you and. . .'

'And what?' Nikki said gently. 'Luke, you accused me of shutting the world out. Aren't you doing the same thing?'

'Leave it, Nikki,' he said roughly.

'No.' Nikki shook her head, her red-gold hair tossing from side to side. 'You've hauled me from my splendid isolation and now. . .now you're telling me I'm really alone after all.'

'You're not alone. You have your daughter. . . Beattie. . .this town. . .'

'Oh, yes. That's not what you said a week ago.'

'Nikki, it doesn't matter.' Luke's eyes hardened. 'Whatever I said, whatever I've done doesn't alter the fact that I want no one. I should never have made love to you, because, of course, you want more. . .'

Nikki's green eyes flashed. She took a deep breath. 'You arrogant toad!' she spat.

'I meant. . .' He rubbed his hand wearily through his hair. 'Nikki, I didn't mean that to sound. . .I just mean that lovemaking implies emotional commitment and I can't give that. Not now. Not ever.'

'Not ever'. The phrase echoed harshly around them. Nikki took a ragged breath and leaned against the door. At least he was honest. Last night. . . Last night she had thought it would be enough. Now. . . Now she hated his damned honesty.

She hated him. He was avoiding the issue. Running. Just like her father. Just like Scott. . .

So what was left? Their professional relationship. She could tell him to get out of her house now—or somehow she could act professional. One doctor to another. . .

'How was Mrs Birchip?' she asked suddenly.

'Mrs Birchip?' Luke looked blank.

'The lady you spent the night with.'

'I beg your pardon?'

'You did a house call to Verity Birchip,' Nikki said coldly, striving desperately for a return to normality. 'And it kept you all night.'

'Oh.' Luke's blank look suddenly faded and he managed a smile. 'Mrs Birchip thinks she has heredity.'

'Heredity?' It was Nikki's turn to sound blank.

'She read somewhere that heredity can cause all sorts of problems, so she thinks she's got it. I suspected a bad cold, but she's sure it's heredity.'

'You know, I wouldn't be the least bit surprise if she's right,' Nikki said slowly. 'It would explain a lot.'

And Luke managed to grin. 'Yeah. . .'

So this was all there was. Over. A fine romance, Nikki thought bitterly. Gone the way of all the loves in her life. Walking away from her.

Nikki drew in her breath. 'I guess. . .I guess I'd better go to bed, then.'

'I think you should,' Luke said gently. His smile faded. 'Nikki, I'm sorry.'

'Don't.' It was practically a cry. She bit her lip and then gestured to the pile of papers on his desk. 'I'm. . .I'm sorry I interrupted you. What. . .what were you doing?'

'I'm writing a newspaper column.'

Nikki's eyes widened. 'A news. . . What sort of newspaper column?'

'"Who Cares?"'

'"Who Cares?"' Nikki stared in amazement. In disbelief she crossed to the desk and stared down. There were loose sheaves of handwritten pleas for help, and attached to each was a neatly written paragraph. Nikki picked up and read the first note.

Dear Doctor,
My fifteen-year-old daughter has one breast bigger than the other and I can't get her to agree to visit our family doctor. I know she's scared stiff she'll be like this forever. . .

Then there was the response, carefully worded under the major heading 'Who Cares?'.

And Nikki didn't have to read the response. She had read 'Who Cares?' every week for the past eighteen months with a growing sense of admiration for the measured, careful and caring responses given by the anonymous answering doctor. She knew just what the reply would be—a careful reassurance, amusing anecdotes of 'lopsided adolescents I have known' as well as a plea to back up the reassurance by a visit to the girl's own doctor.

Nikki let the sheaf of papers fall to the table. 'You're the doctor behind "Who Cares?",' she whispered. She stared. This was making less and less sense. The column must pay well. Why then was he doing locums?

'Yes.' He came abruptly forward and pushed the papers into a folder. 'I started doing it while I was ill.'

'For the money?'

He laughed without humour. 'You guessed it. And besides. . .'

'It's a job you can do without people.'

'Nikki, I'm not trying to avoid people.'

'Only involvement.'

'Look who's talking.'

'You still think I'm trying to avoid involvement?' Nikki demanded. She put her hand wearily to her eyes. 'I think. . .I think I'm cured.'

He looked hard at her then, his eyes narrowing. 'Nikki, I——'

'You don't want to hear,' Nikki finished for him. 'Well, you're going to. You came up here for God knows what reason, but whatever your motive you decided on a nice, Boy Scout objective. Get Dr Russell out of herself. Involve her with the human race again. Teach her to love.'

'Nikki, I didn't mean——'

'I don't care what you meant.' Tears welled up in Nikki's eyes and she turned away. 'And I don't care what you were trying to do. All I know is that I love you. . .'

There. The words were said. She could do no more. This man was all she wanted in life and she had laid her heart on a plate for him to take. If he wanted it. . .

It seemed he didn't. He stood motionless for a long moment and then came to turn her gently towards him. 'Nikki, don't,' he said gently.

'Cry? Why the hell not? Isn't falling in love with yet another man who doesn't want me something to cry about?' She wrenched back away from him, her fingers searching for the doorknob while she watched his face. It was bleak and hard. Whatever she said would make no difference.

'Nikki, I'm sorry,' he said softly. Implacably. There was no love for her in the words.

'I'll bet you are,' Nikki whispered. She shrugged. 'And so am I.'

Her fingers found the knob and twisted. Nikki turned and walked out of the room. Regardless of sleeping children and housekeeper, she slammed the door. Hard.

She hadn't stalked more than three feet from the door when the front doorbell rang.

Nikki stopped dead. Now what?

Her hand flew up to her tear-stained face. Great. If she was needed now. . .

Luke's bedroom door opened again as he too heard the bell. 'I'll go,' he said roughly. 'You'd better wash your face and pull yourself together.'

Great. Professional caring and sympathy. And to make it worse he was right. Nikki watched him stride along the passage and if she'd had something in her hand she would have thrown it. Something hard and big, she thought savagely. Something that would break into a million fragments and release some of the awful tension within her.

Instead of which she went meekly back into her bedroom to repair some of the ravages of the last few minutes.

She had hardly started before Luke was back. His knock on her door showed as little respect as Nikki had for the still sleeping occupants of the house.

'Nikki, I need you.'

Like hell you do, Nikki thought bitterly. You don't need anyone, Luke Marriott. She didn't say it, though. Instead she let her robe slip to the floor, hauled on the dress she'd been wearing that afternoon and opened the door. 'What's wrong?'

He narrowed his eyes. 'Are you fit to operate?'

'Of course.' Nikki's hands were fumbling to fasten the front buttons on her dress, and once again she cursed fate at having sent Luke to stay in this house. She was forced to be intimate in such surroundings.

'We've a nasty tear and fracture to repair A fisherman got his hand caught in a cray-pot rope. It's darn near torn off his thumb.'

Nikki nodded. It happened. The fishermen worked fast and often didn't stop the motor when they dropped the pots. Occasionally one fouled on a propeller. There had been a couple of nasty accidents since Nikki had started practising.

'I usually send them down to Cairns,' she said quietly, trying to make her voice sound professional and detached. 'I can't. . .I don't have the skills. . .'

'I do.' He was striding away. 'Ring the hospital and

tell them to prepare Theatre. Then come. I'll drive him down.'

'He's here?' Nikki's eyes widened.

'He's currently making a mess of Beattie's hall,' Luke said grimly. 'His mates were set on a night prawning and wouldn't interrupt to take him to the hospital. They dropped him at the wharf and he walked up here because Whispering Palms is closer than the hospital.'

'Good grief.' Nikki frowned in disbelief.

'Hurry,' Luke told her, turning away. 'The kid's lost a lot of blood and the thumb's hanging by a thread. The faster we get it sewn back, the more chance he has of keeping it.'

'The kid. . .'

'He's not much more than a teenager. . .'

It was a fiddly, delicate operation. Once more Eurong was in luck having Luke as acting locum, Nikki thought reflectively, knowing that if the boy had been sent to Cairns his thumb would have been well and truly dead by the time they got him there.

As it was he had a good chance of keeping it. Luke meticulously cleaned the shattered bone, inserted a tiny metal pin which would hold the bones together and then slowly stitched the mass of torn muscle and flesh back into the shape of a thumb. He used skills Nikki could only wonder at.

It took hours. The first trace of dawn was showing through the big south window of the operating theatre as Luke finally raised his head.

'That's it,' he said wearily. 'The best we can do.' He moved to adjust the intravenous line. It was feeding antibiotics through, which hopefully would keep the wound free of infection. Infection now would mean all their work was wasted.

It was considerate of Luke to include Nikki in his assessment of what had been done, but the work had been Luke's. Nikki's job as anaesthetist had been relatively easy, keeping a fit and healthy nineteen-year-old asleep for the time it had taken.

'Well done,' she said softly to Luke, signalling one of the nurses to assist him with his gown. He looked exhausted, and Nikki suddenly remembered that the man had been ill himself. Was he completely recovered?

'Is Mr Payne here yet?' she asked the charge sister. Jim Payne had given permission for himself to be operated on—at nineteen he was able to do so—and in response to their enquiries he had replied that his dad didn't give a stuff anyway. Beneath her hands the boy stirred as he took over his own breathing.

'Not as far as I know,' Andrea told Nikki. 'We telephoned home but no one answered. I guess his dad will still be at sea.'

Luke frowned down at the boy. 'Does he have any other family?' He had been scrubbing while Nikki had questioned the boy earlier.

'Only his father here,' Nikki said grimly. 'His father owns the boat Jim works on. He would have been the one to put Jim off last night.'

'With instructions to walk to hospital.' Luke stared down at their still sleeping patient. The boy was pale beneath his weathered complexion. At nineteen he still looked very young—and very vulnerable. 'Some people don't deserve to have children,' he said softly.

'No.' Nikki shook her head. 'There are some cases where parents can't seem to help mistreating their children—like Sandra Mears. It's just the build-up of hardship that proves too much for them. But Bert Payne's different. . . He's always been rough and uncaring. Jim's mum took off when Bert's roughness finally got too much for her, and since then Jim's had to cope with it alone.'

Luke's mouth twisted into a grimace. 'Poor bloody kid,' he said softly. 'I've given him back his thumb, but what sort of chance does he have?'

'He'll survive,' the nurse told them. 'The Paynes are tough.'

'Yeah. And toughness breeds toughness. Next generation. . .'

'Well, maybe he'll marry a nice girl who gives him all the cuddles he's missed out on,' Nikki said roundly.

'Ah, yes. The happy ending.' There was no mistaking the derision behind Luke's words and Nikki flushed.

'I'll finish up here,' she said tightly. 'You're tired.'

'Feeling sorry for me, Dr Russell?'

Nikki's eyes flew up to his and flashed fire.

'No,' she said between her teeth. 'I just want to get rid of you.'

CHAPTER NINE

THE days that followed were endless. Somehow Nikki managed to study but afterwards she never knew how. It was a defence mechanism, she thought dully. Immersed in her texts, telling herself they were important, somehow she could block out Luke's presence in the house.

Not that he was there often. He worked longer hours than he needed to, and Nikki suspected that many house calls were simply an excuse to be away from Whispering Palms. Away from her. . .

'I don't know what's eating the man,' Beattie puzzled one day as they ate yet another dinner without him. 'He was so darned cheerful when he came—like a breath of fresh air through the place—and now. . .'

'He's like a bear with a sore head,' Amy announced. 'Isn't he, Karen?'

Karen nodded solemnly and then carefully replaced her knife and fork on the plate. 'Mummy says she'd like me to come home on Saturday,' she announced. 'She says. . .she says the house is ready. She says it's really pretty and we've got a nice garden I can help look after and. . .'

'What else will she let you help with?' Beattie said darkly and Karen flushed, hearing the implied criticism.

'I like gardening,' she said in a small voice. 'I want to grow carrots. And. . .and flowers. And Mummy says I can. . .'

'I'll drop in tomorrow and see your new house,' Nikki intervened, sending her housekeeper a dark look. 'And if your mum's really ready, then I don't see any reason why you can't go home.'

* * *

It was yet another way of blocking her thoughts from Luke—and no way was entirely successful. After lunch the next day Nikki walked around the river to Sandra's new home. It was quite a distance and by the time she arrived Nikki was regretting her impulse to leave the car at home. Especially as she rounded the corner and saw her own second vehicle parked outside. Luke. . .

Oh, no! She stood irresolute in the sun as she tried to decide what to do. The last thing she wanted was to walk in on Luke. . .

Then the door opened and Sandra saw her. Before she could move, Sandra lifted an arm and waved. 'Dr Russell. Hi! Come and see.'

So there was nothing for it but to cross the road and enter the sparkling clean home. Luke had obviously just been leaving. He was standing in the hall as Nikki entered.

'Two doctors,' Sandra said, smiling nervously. 'Do I get charged for two house calls?'

'Of course not.' Nikki tried desperately to ignore Luke as she smiled reassuringly at Sandra. 'I just thought I'd drop in for a look.'

'Let me show you——' Sandra started eagerly, but Luke interrupted.

'I have to be getting back for afternoon surgery,' he told them. He didn't look at Nikki. 'I'll leave you two alone.'

Sandra nodded. She looked up at him and then suddenly stretched out her hands to take his. 'I don't know how to thank you,' she told him. She turned to Nikki. 'Did you know Dr Luke has located my husband?' She whirled suddenly into the kitchen and returned carrying a slip of paper. 'And look! I don't know how he did it but it's a cheque. For child maintenance. And they say. . .they say there'll be more coming.'

'It wasn't me that found him,' Luke told her. 'It was the Department of Social Security.'

'I've been to them before,' Sandra said darkly. 'And

nothing's happened. And then you two move in and. . .'

'And your husband gets to shoulder his responsibilities,' Nikki said warmly. 'I'm so glad.'

Sandra smiled. For the first time in years she seemed young. 'This will mean—oh, everything. We'll have enough to eat for a change, and there'll be money left over. I'll be able to buy them new clothes, and take them to the pictures sometimes.' She giggled. 'And my husband. . .he's not going to have all that great a time with his new girlfriend now,' she chuckled. 'Not with his wages being garnished for maintenance for the kids. Plus,' she ended triumphantly, 'all the stuff he bought on credit cards and I've been paying off. Some of it he's still got and the rest he's sold. His girlfriend was there when the social welfare people came around and she told them without thinking, "Oh, yeah, he bought that. . . That old stereo," she said, "he sold it," and things like that. And they told the credit people and the credit people transferred the debt. I don't get to use the credit cards any more but I never did anyway. So now. . .so now he's got to pay for the lot and I don't have a single debt. I feel. . .I feel fantastic.'

'Ready for Karen?' Nikki said quietly.

Sandra's smile faded. She met Nikki's look without flinching. 'I'm ready for Karen,' she said. 'I think. . .I think I've come to terms with what I've been doing with her. I just felt so darned useless. . . And Karen's so like me. So when I felt like punishing myself I took everything out on her.' She took a deep breath. 'But it won't happen any more, I promise you that. Karen. . . well, Karen's going to be a little girl again. And I'm going to be a proper mother.'

'You know there won't be any more chances,' Luke said heavily. 'You know that, don't you, Sandra?'

Sandra nodded. 'I know you two have given me a second chance,' she agreed. 'I know that and I'll be grateful forever. And I won't mess it up.'

'Karen can come back to Whispering Palms at any time,' Nikki promised. 'Use us as a safety-valve. If you feel the tension's mounting then send her to us.'

'To us'. . . Because she was standing beside Luke it sounded as if the invitation was from both of them and Sandra took it as such. She smiled at both of them in turn.

'I'll take you up on that if I ever need to,' she promised. 'But I won't. I know that now.' Suddenly she leaned forward and kissed Nikki on the cheek. 'And Dr Russell?'

'Yes?' Nikki was flustered and it showed in her mounting colour.

'I'm really glad you've been given a second chance too.'

Luke left them then, much to Nikki's relief, and Sandra showed her around the house. It looked lovely. Finally Sandra walked her to the refrigerator and opened the door. The interior was crammed with the sort of food most children would die for—lemonade, cocktail sausages, chocolate éclairs, lamingtons. . .

A small boy sidled up beside Sandra as they looked and pulled his thumb from his mouth to announce, 'No one's allowed to eat anything until Karen comes home. It's Karen's welcome-home party 'cos we're glad she's better and we missed her. Mummy's put me in charge of seeing no one cheats.'

And this was the little boy who'd triggered the scene that had ended with Karen's broken arm. Nikki smiled down at him and wondered just how she'd react, given the scenario of not having enough food to feed her children. She looked back to Sandra and saw that Sandra guessed her thoughts.

'It tore me apart,' she whispered. 'To be hungry myself and still watch Karen be hungry—and for her not to complain. . .'

'It won't happen again,' Nikki said softly. 'It's over.'

'I know.' Sandra smiled happily. 'And guess what?

I've got a spare room and Dr Luke suggested I might take in a boarder. It'll mean even more money, and I'll have someone—some adult—to talk to.' She grimaced. 'I know I've been treating Karen too much like an adult—but then, I've needed to. I've been so darned lonely.'

'I know the feeling,' Nikki said softly, and their eyes linked in a moment of understanding. And Nikki knew in that moment that Sandra would ask for help if she needed it. There was a bond between them which both recognised.

Nikki left then, her heart a little lighter because of the family's obvious happiness. She glanced at her watch as the door closed behind her. It would take her half an hour to walk home, which left her with a solid afternoon to study. On Sunday—in two days' time—she had to climb on to an aeroplane and face the exam in Cairns.

It no longer had meaning. It was a meaningless milestone she was aiming for because she had nothing else to do. Nothing but face a future which was bleak and empty.

'I still have Amy,' she said aloud. 'And Beattie. And Whispering Palms. And a good job.'

And it sounded empty. There was a void that only Luke could fill.

She looked up towards the road and her heart stilled. Her car was parked on the corner. Luke was waiting.

He got out of the car as she approached, and watched her walk towards him.

'I thought you were late for surgery,' she said nervously.

'So sack me.'

She shook her head, and unbidden tears threatened behind her eyes. 'You know. . .you know I wouldn't.'

He shrugged. 'I thought you could do with a ride, seeing as I'm using your car. It's bloody stupid walking so far in the midday sun.'

'I know,' Nikki said bitterly. 'I'm bloody stupid.'

He glanced over at her as he started the car, and his mouth tightened. It was as if he was agreeing with her.

'You leave for Cairns on Sunday,' he said evenly.

'Yes.'

'Your exams are on Monday and Tuesday.'

'Yes.' She couldn't think of anything further to say.

'And you'll be back here on Wednesday.'

She nodded, unable to trust her voice.

'I'll leave here first thing Thursday, then.'

'Fine.' She hardly recognised her voice. It was tight, young and forlorn. She sounded about Amy's age, lost, desolate and alone.

Once more he glanced at her and then stared determinedly back at the road. 'It's better this way,' he said finally.

'Why?' It was all she could do to whisper. 'Where. . .where are you going?'

'I'm not sure. Maybe I'll go back to Sydney for a while. Spend some more time on my column.'

'Fine.' She couldn't think of anything else to say. Instead Nikki sat with her hands clenched tight in her lap and waited to be deposited home.

There was little more preparation she could do for the exam. If she didn't know what she needed now, she never would. Nikki desultorily packed and stared aimlessly at her books for the rest of the weekend. On Saturday she took Karen home to be welcomed by a tearful Sandra and her joyful brothers and sister, but that was the only cheerful spot in the day.

'When you get back there'll be no Karen and no Dr Luke,' Amy said dolefully as she hugged her mother goodbye on Sunday. 'Mummy, what are we going to do?'

'We survived fine by ourselves,' Nikki told her daughter, forcing a smile.

'But we weren't happy,' Amy reminded her. 'Dr Luke makes me laugh.'

He doesn't make me laugh, Nikki said to herself sadly. She clenched a tight wad of paper in her hand—a note left on the kitchen table when Luke had left this morning on one of his interminable house calls.

'Good luck,' the note read. 'Love, Luke.'

'Love. . . You don't know what love is,' Nikki whispered to the absent Luke as she made her farewells. 'You have it. If you want it, it's yours. . .'

Nikki stayed in the staff residence of the hospital while she sat her exams. It was the same hospital she'd stayed in the night she'd come down with her two casualties. She took the opportunity of visiting them and her spirits lifted a little as she found both recovering well.

'It's the last time I drive a car fast,' Martin told her and Lisa, settled in a wheelchair beside Martin's bed, agreed with him.

'I was egging him on,' she said sadly. 'We were fools. Lucky fools.'

'At least you're both alive to learn a lesson from it,' Nikki smiled. The pair were now inseparable, their hands linked tight while they talked. A happy ending if ever she saw one.

And she was so jealous she could cry. Nikki turned from the bed as her friend Charlotte came into the ward.

'Oho.' Charlie grinned. 'Back in town. Need some more clothes, do we, Dr Russell?'

'No, I do not.' Despite her cross tone Nikki couldn't suppress a smile. Charlotte was incorrigible.

'So it's just exams that's brought you to town. How boring. I suppose I can't persuade you to join me for dinner tonight?'

'Are you kidding?' Nikki linked arms with her friend and they walked out together. 'My last night before the exam. . .'

'And this exam is so important!'

'It is to me.'

Charlotte shook her head. She glanced across at Nikki's strained face and wisely decided to hold her peace.

'Would you have half an hour to spare from your hectic exam preparation, though?' she asked slowly.

'Charlotte, I can't. . .'

'Not to spend in riotous living,' her friend assured her drily. 'But there's someone in town who badly wants to see you.'

'Who?'

'Luke Marriott's sister.'

'Luke's sister.' Nikki turned and stared at her friend. 'What on earth. . .? Why would Luke's sister want to see me?'

'I suspect to ask after Luke.'

'But. . .'

'Look, don't ask me.' Charlotte spread her hands. 'I'm only the intermediary. I only know that this girl's from Melbourne. She told me about Luke's illness—apparently she hasn't seen him since then. She's worried sick about him and came north to try and locate him. I heard she was asking the staff if anyone had heard from him—I stuck my oar in and told her where he was and I told her you were coming down. She was due to fly back to Melbourne today but has held over to try and talk to you. Will you see her?'

Nikki frowned. 'I suppose so.'

'So what's the story?' Charlotte linked arms again and kept walking. 'Has he murdered someone?'

'Who? Luke Marriott?' Nikki tried to laugh. 'I wouldn't think so.'

'So why's he running?'

'Who knows?' Nikki said lightly, much more lightly than she felt. 'Who knows?'

* * *

Luke's sister, Megan, was a more petite version of Luke, in a feminine form. She was blonde, blue-eyed and beautiful, and her smile would turn men's hearts. Her smile was tentative when she met Nikki, as though she was afraid of what she might be about to hear.

'I hope you don't mind me bothering you,' she started awkwardly as Nikki ushered her into her sparsely furnished little bedroom an hour later. 'Miss Cain says you have exams tomorrow.'

'It doesn't matter.' Nikki pulled out the hard chair from the desk, motioned her guest into it and then perched on the bed. 'How may I help you?' They were both so nervous, the air was brittle, she thought.

'I thought. . .I just wondered if you could tell me about Luke.' The girl gripped her hands together and held them hard. 'We. . .we were so worried. My company sent me up here for a conference and I thought I'd try to find out about him while I was here.'

'You haven't heard from him for a while?'

'No.' Megan bit her lip. 'Oh, we heard about his illness. He rang from Sydney and my oldest sister flew up to be with him during the worst of it. But then. . . then he just seemed to withdraw. Since he left Sydney we've received the occasional postcard from different places and nothing else. It's as if. . .it's as if he doesn't want us any more.'

Join the club, Nikki thought bitterly, but she didn't say it. Instead she looked sympathetically across to Megan. The girl was young, maybe only twenty or so, and looked miserable.

'You're fond of your brother?' she asked.

'We all are.' The girl took a deep breath. 'We're a really big family, Dr Russell. I'm the second youngest of eight children and Luke is the oldest. My father died when I was two and my mum died three years ago. Luke. . .well, Luke's been more a parent than a big brother. . .to all of us.' She looked at the floor.

'We know he's not working—at least, until I heard about you I didn't think he was. My young brother's still at university, though, and the cheques keep arriving from Luke to keep him there. I don't know how he's doing it.'

Nikki did. This explained why he had to do the locum work. But. . .

'But why doesn't he contact you?' Nikki was talking almost to herself.

'We. . .we wondered if he was still ill. If his cancer had come back. If he didn't want to face us?'

Nikki shook her head. 'It hasn't,' she said gently. 'He's fit and healthy and I'd be willing to bet he's going to be one of the lucky ones who's in for a complete cure.'

'And is he happy?' Megan asked tremulously. 'It's driving us crazy not knowing. Last Christmas. . .well, we all got together—all of us and husbands and wives and children—do you know that Luke now has eleven nieces and nephews with two more on the way? And the only one not there was Luke. The only one. And you know——' she lifted a woebegone face '—I would have said, of all of us, to Luke the family was the most important.'

And maybe it still is, Nikki thought slowly. Maybe the sight of his brothers and sisters marrying and producing their own families when he can't is just too painful for him to face.

She didn't say that. She couldn't. Instead Nikki leaned forward and gripped Megan's hands.

'Megan, I can't answer your questions,' she said gently. 'I don't know the answers myself. All I can do is assure you that Luke seems healthy. If you like I'll tell him I've seen you, and tell him you're worried. That's. . .that's all I can do.'

'But he is at Eurong?' Megan's tear-stained eyes met Nikki's. 'I can't extend my stay now, but one of my brothers or sisters will come up. I know they will.' She grimaced. 'Maybe if you don't tell him we're coming. . .'

'Megan, he won't be there.'

Megan paused. 'N-no?'

'No. Luke's doing a locum for me and he leaves on Thursday. And I don't know where he's going.'

Something in her tone caught Megan's attention. She stared. 'You. . .you care for him too,' she said slowly.

Nikki nodded. 'I do.'

'Well, then. . .'

'Megan, Luke won't let me near him. He won't let anyone near him.' Nikki closed her eyes, with remembered pain. 'For now. . .for now Luke wants to be alone, and I think. . .I think we have to respect that.'

'Do you think it's because he's sterile?'

Nikki looked up sharply. 'You know about that?'

Megan nodded. 'My sister was so worried, she made a special trip to Sydney to see Dr Olsing six months ago. He's the one who looked after Luke when he was ill. Dr Olsing thought that might have something to do with why. . .why he's avoiding the family.'

'Luke would have been fairly upset when he found out,' Nikki said carefully and Megan nodded again.

'Dr Olsing said there was some reason Luke couldn't bank sperm. . .and almost as soon as the last chemotherapy session was over he asked to be tested and his count was really low. Dr Olsing said if Luke hadn't been a doctor he would have pushed him to counselling but. . .well, if you know Luke you'd know he wouldn't take to counselling very well. He'd reckon he could cope. Luke hasn't been back to Dr Olsing since then. We assume he's getting his regular check-ups—but he could get them done anywhere, couldn't he?'

'I'm sure he is,' Nikki said gently. 'Luke's sensible, Megan. He'll be being careful.'

Careful and remote as the South Pole, she thought bleakly.

Megan left soon after, and Nikki faced a long and sleepless night.

In the morning she sat the first of her exams. They seemed easy, or maybe that was just because Nikki's mind was elsewhere. She answered perfunctorily and if sometimes one of her examiners seemed annoyed, well, Nikki couldn't help it.

She was nervous, though. She must be. Nikki had sat down in the hospital cafeteria for breakfast on the Monday morning only to be nauseated by the sight of so much food. She'd been ill before she'd gone into the exam. Her stomach had settled as she worked, but on Tuesday morning it happened again.

Nerves? It was almost as if. . .

The thought struck Nikki out of the blue halfway through an oral examination on bone-structure on the Tuesday afternoon. Strange sensations suddenly slid into frightening place.

Somehow Nikki managed to answer the professor's questions. There was one other written exam, which she completed in not much more than half the time stipulated. She walked out of the examination-room and didn't stop until she reached the hospital pharmacy.

An hour later Charlotte knocked on Nikki's door. Hearing no response, she turned the knob to find it unlocked. Nikki was sitting on the bed staring out of the window.

'Hey, what's this?' Charlotte chided her. 'I thought you'd be out painting the town red.' She plonked herself down on the bed beside her friend. 'Or did the exam go badly?'

'It went OK,' Nikki said listlessly.

'Well, what——?' Charlotte broke off. Her eyes caught sight of what lay on Nikki's bedside table. A small bottle, a plastic box and an eye-dropper. Charlotte leaned forward and picked up the box. The paper in the window on the front of the box showed a firm, definite cross.

Charlotte glanced across to where Nikki was still staring intently out of the window, and then looked back at the box.

'A cross,' she said conversationally. 'Who's the lucky girl, then?'

'Charlotte, don't.' Nikki put her hands up to her face and her shoulders heaved. With a gasp Charlotte leaned over to grasp her friend.

'Hey, honey, don't. This isn't the end of the world. How far. . .?'

'I'm only just,' Nikki wailed. 'I'm only a week overdue. I just couldn't. . .'

'Luke?'

Nikki closed her eyes. 'Of course Luke,' she whispered. 'Who else?'

'Who else indeed?' Charlotte whistled silently over Nikki's tumbled curls. 'Holy heck, Nikki, love, I thought you had more sense.'

'I did. I do. He's supposed to be sterile. . .'

And then the whole story came tumbling out while Charlotte's frown deepened and her hold on her friend's shoulders tightened.

'Well,' she said at last. 'What now, Nikki Russell?'

'I don't know,' she said bleakly. 'I can't think. . . I. . . He was so sure that he was sterile. . .'

'When was he tested?'

'I don't know,' Nikki wailed. And then she remembered what Megan had said. 'Just. . .just after the last lot of chemotherapy. He was very anxious.'

'Too anxious,' Charlotte said grimly. 'If he tested too soon. . .'

'Surely he would have re-tested if he'd been negative,' Nikki whispered. 'When it was so important to him. . .'

'Maybe that's why he didn't re-test.' Charlotte shrugged. 'To submit yourself to a sperm count when you think you're sterile must be pretty darned demoralising. If he got a really low count he would have assumed it would stay low. The chances of it rising are pretty darned small.'

'Small but possible,' Nikki said bleakly. 'And guess who wins the prize?'

Charlotte shook her head. 'You always were the lucky one. Nikki. . .Nikki, you realise it's early enough to do something about the pregnancy?'

'No.'

'Just like that?'

'Just like that,' Nikki told her. 'I could have done the same when I was pregnant with Amy. I was broke and frightened and much younger. And if I had, I would have missed out on my lovely daughter, and besides. . .'

'Besides?' Charlotte prompted.

'This is Luke's child.'

'I see.' Charlotte looked hard at her friend and her heart sank. Luke Marriott had claimed another victim, then. 'So tell Luke,' she said heavily. 'I've never heard that Luke Marriott didn't take his responsibilities seriously. Maybe. . .maybe he'll want to marry you.'

'For a happy-ever-after ending?' Nikki gave a short, harsh laugh. 'Is that what you think?'

'If he thinks he's sterile he'll be delighted about the baby.'

'Yes.' Nikki nodded. 'He's taken his sterility hard. And family is important to him. You're right, Charlie. If I told him, then Luke would marry me.'

'And you don't want that?'

Nikki shook her head. 'Not. . .not on those terms.'

'But he made love to you. He must feel. . .'

'He made love to me out of some crazy, stupid scheme to shake me out of my isolation and misery. For the same reason as you pinched all my clothes. Well, it worked only too well. I'm not isolated any more. I'm going to be the mother of two.'

'Oh, Nikki, will you cope?'

'Sure I'll cope,' Nikki whispered. 'The town will talk behind my back—but they always have. Beattie will stand by me. And I have my career. Isn't it lucky I've just done this damned exam?' Her voice broke on a sob and she buried her face in her hands.

'Nikki. . .' Charlotte held out a hand helplessly to her friend and then withdrew it. 'Nikki, you'll have to tell him. It's not fair. . . Apart from anything else, he has to know he's not firing blanks.'

Shaken, Nikki looked up sharply and Charlotte shrugged and grinned. 'Well, he does. . .'

'If he had a low sperm count he must only have marginal fertility,' Nikki said slowly. 'He could try for twenty years and not father another child.'

'Or he could do the same tomorrow.'

Nikki nodded. 'OK,' she said slowly. 'I'll tell him.' She took a deep breath. Her face was set. 'But not yet. I'll let him get right away from Eurong and then I'll write to him, care of the medical board. They'll forward a letter. But it won't be for a while yet. I'll give myself time to have the strength to tell him to go to blazes when he demands that I marry him.'

'That's really what you want to do?'

'He'll love our baby,' Nikki said bleakly. 'But he doesn't love me. So. . .so it's what I really have to do.'

CHAPTER TEN

NIKKI arrived back at Eurong the following afternoon to find Beattie and Amy waiting for her at the airport. Amy raced across the tarmac to envelop her mother in a bear-hug.

'Mummy, guess what? We're going to have a Luke party!'

'A Luke party.' Nikki buried her face in her daughter's chubby shoulder for longer than usual, finding comfort in that small person's presence. Another Amy? Maybe. . .maybe someone who looked like Luke. . .

'A Luke party,' she said again unsteadily, bringing her face up to smile at Beattie. 'What's a Luke party?'

'Luke's going tomorrow,' Amy told her, her face momentarily clouding. 'But Beattie said tonight we're having a party to say welcome home Mummy and goodbye Dr Luke. Only. . .only I think it would be nicer if Luke thought the party was just for him. If you don't mind?' she asked anxiously.

'I don't mind.' Nikki set her daughter back on to her feet. 'And what delicacies have we planned for such an event?'

'All the food he'll like best,' Amy said proudly. 'Little red sausages. Bread and butter and hundreds and thousands. Jelly beans. Red lemonade. Sausage rolls. . .'

'Wow!' Nikki grinned. 'What man could ask for more?'

'Exactly.' Amy skipped beside her, her hand clinging to her mother's. 'Maybe—maybe if he sees what really good food we have sometimes, maybe he'll stay.'

'I don't think that's possible.'

'No.'

Beattie glanced across at Nikki's set face and then looked away. There was real pain there.

Nikki drove down to the hospital just before dinner. Luke, it seemed, was leaving in the morning and Nikki needed to know what hospital patients were in and what their medications were while he was still available to answer questions. She did a slow ward round, methodically going through each patient's chart. There were no problems. Luke had written each patient's history with meticulous care, knowing that he was soon handing over.

The young fisherman was recovering nicely and Nikki was pleased to see his impatience to be home. 'I dunno why he's keeping me so long,' the boy complained. 'I've only got a sore thumb.'

'You wouldn't have any thumb at all if it weren't for Dr Luke,' Nikki told him severely. 'And if you risk infection by going home you can still lose it.'

'Yeah, well, I've got nine more,' the boy grinned and Nikki shook her head.

'You don't know how much you'd miss your right thumb until you're without it,' she warned him. 'So just lie back and let us take care of you.'

'It is nice,' the fisherman admitted. He smiled shyly up at her. 'The nurses here are great. And the food is something else.'

'I guess it beats your dad's cooking.' Nikki hesitated. 'Has he been in to see you?'

'Yeah, once.' The boy's face closed. 'Just wanted to know how long he'd have to hire someone else for. I dunno. . .I dunno that I'll go back to living with him. I might get private board or something.'

'Does your mum know you're in hospital?'

'No.' Jim bit his lip. 'Mum. . .well, Mum left a couple of years back and I chose to stay with Dad. It was a mistake, I guess, but. . .but I didn't know where she was going and. . .I know Dad would hang up if she rang, or would burn any letters she wrote.'

Nikki nodded. 'If you give me her full name and birth-date, I might be able to contact her,' she offered. 'If you like.'

'Could you?' Jim's eyes brightened and then clouded again. He lay back on his pillows. 'She's probably glad to be shot of us both.'

'Let me try and see,' Nikki told him. 'It can't hurt to try.'

She left him then and spent a fruitful half-hour on the telephone. At the end of it she was practically certain that the Brisbane police would contact Mrs Payne. 'Just let her know her son's in the Eurong hospital after suffering an accident,' she told them. It made it sound a little more serious than it really was now, but Jim—well, Jim was only nineteen and he still needed someone.

Everyone does, she thought bleakly. She looked up as the door of her office opened and Luke entered.

'Welcome back.' His tone was formal and his smile was forced. 'How did the exam go?'

'Fine.' Nikki rose to her feet and stood awkwardly. How would it be, she wondered, if I just told him? Luke, I'm carrying your child. For a moment—just a moment—she felt a crazy impulse to do so, but he was looking at her with eyes that were distant and formal.

'You've come for hand-over?'

'I thought I should.'

'Fine, then. Let's go.'

So they walked through the hospital again, this time with Luke going through the notes as they visited each patient. The process was professional, efficient and cold.

The patients must think we can't stand each other, Nikki thought, and bit her lip. Maybe for Luke it was true. Nikki had made him drop his guard and let the world in. Luke had done the same for her, but for Nikki the world, in the guise of one Luke Marriott, was more than welcome.

'Is there anything else I should know about?' she asked in a tight voice as they reached the end of the patient list.

'No. I've left notes in the surgery.'

'Fine.' She nodded hopelessly. 'I'll be getting home, then. I've. . .we've a party to organise.'

'Nikki, don't go to any trouble.'

She turned then. 'You do intend to show up?' she demanded.

'I have. . .there's a house call.'

'Luke, Amy's counting on this party.'

'Nikki, Amy has you and Beattie. . .'

'And she has you.' A surge of anger rose in Nikki. That he could hurt her was enough, but to hurt Amy. . . 'My daughter cares for you, Luke Marriott. She's as big a fool as her mother in that regard. I'd stop it if I could but I have no control over my daughter's decision to give her affection. She's sad to see you go and she's pressed us all into giving you a party that you don't deserve.'

'Nikki. . .'

'You don't care who you hurt, do you, *Mr* Marriott?' she demanded. 'You'd hurt Amy. . .you'd hurt me. You're hurting all your family—— Oh, yes, I forgot to tell you—I saw Megan while I was in Cairns. She's another whom you've hurt with your introspective nurturing of your damned pain. Just because you've been sick, Luke Marriott, you think you can trample on the feelings of others and you don't give a damn.'

'Nikki, I do. . .'

'You don't or you wouldn't do it. Amy is a lovely little girl, Luke Marriott, and she's going to cry herself to sleep tonight if you don't come to this damned party. So you can put yourself second for a change and come and eat little red sausages and party cakes and you can look as if you're enjoying it or. . .'

'Or what?' Luke's face was still.

'Or I don't know,' Nikki ended up lamely. 'Or I'll think you're even more selfish than. . .than my ex-husband!'

If it hadn't been for the children, the night would have been impossible. As it was, Sandra came with her four and the party was a riot. If Nikki was quiet and Luke's smile was forced, then the children more than made up for it. Sandra's brood were making up for past deprivation with a vengeance. They ate like miniature vultures while Sandra made futile protesting noises in the background and Beattie looked on with an indulgent smile.

'It does me good to see Whispering Palms full of children,' she beamed. 'It's like it ought to be.'

She glared then at both Luke and Nikki in turn, as if they were deliberately withholding its due from the old house.

Afterwards the children dived *en masse* into the pool and Luke joined them. Amy looked a question at her mother but didn't voice it. It seemed she sensed Nikki's reluctance to be with them. And tonight Amy was going to enjoy her Dr Luke and her new friends to the fullest. For tomorrow, her doubtful look at her mother said, we'll be back to being by ourselves.

Not for long, Nikki thought grimly. Eight months?

At the thought of what lay ahead, blind panic filled her. She had assured Charlotte that she could cope, but could she? When Amy was a baby she had suffered at the hands of Eurong's gossips. Now? All Eurong would count back and know whose baby this was.

And how would Luke react when he finally found out? He won't find out for months, Nikki told herself desperately. It can't be until I have the strength to say I won't be part of a family for a baby's sake. I won't. . .

And finally the interminable evening ended. Luke

left to drive Sandra and her children home and Nikki wearily carried an exhausted Amy up to bed.

'It was nice, wasn't it?' Amy asked sleepily, snuggling into her mother's arms.

'Yes, it was.' Nikki pulled back Amy's bedcovers and deposited her daughter on to the pillows. 'A special night.'

'Dr Luke's special,' Amy said seriously. 'Mummy, I don't think Dr Luke should go away. I think he should stay here and be our daddy.'

And so say all of us, Nikki's heart replied. Instead, though, she kissed her daughter goodnight and made her way back down to the kitchen. Beattie had already left for bed. Nikki made herself coffee and then went to sit out by the swimming-pool. She needed time to think.

Think of what? The next few years? The rest of her life? She closed her eyes as loneliness engulfed her. The responsibilities ahead were awesome and she couldn't face them. Not alone.

There were footsteps behind her and she turned. Luke was there, his body outlined in the light of the doorway. He saw her and came across.

'Satisfied?' he asked her.

'That you came to my daughter's party? It was very generous of you,' she whispered.

'I even ate little red sausages.'

As an attempt at humour it was pretty appalling but Nikki managed a smile. She rose. 'Well done. A manly effort.' She made to go past him but he stopped her with his hand.

'Nikki?'

'Let me go, please,' she said steadily. 'I'm tired.'

'Nikki, I'm sorry it had to end this way. Before God, I never meant to hurt you.'

'What did you mean to do?'

He sighed. 'I don't know, my Nikki. I saw you so damned alone, and I thought—well, I thought it was time you came out of your shell. So I dragged you out.'

'And now I'm exposed,' she whispered. 'Without a shell. And I'm supposed to be grateful.'

'Nikki. . .'

'I'm going to bed,' she said wearily. 'Let me go, please, Luke.'

'Not yet. . .'

'Please. . .'

'Nikki, tomorrow I'll be gone. I can't stay here. We both know that.'

Nikki shook her head. 'I don't know that. I don't see why you have to keep running.'

'I'm not running.'

'No?'

He closed his eyes. His face was haggard in the moonlight. 'Nikki, I'm just trying to come to terms with myself—with what's happened. Can't you see that?'

'With the fact that you can't have children.'

He nodded. 'Yes. It's important to me.'

'Luke. . .'

It was so close. The words were so close. Instead Nikki drew in her breath. She wouldn't buy this man's love. She wouldn't. It had to be for her. . .

'Luke, I love you,' she whispered. 'Isn't that enough? Can't that be enough?'

He stood motionless in the still, tropical night. Around them even the cicadas fell to silence, waiting. And then Luke shook his head.

'I don't think it can be,' he said roughly. 'God knows it should be. But I can't make it work. Even though I want you. . .'

'Do you want me?'

'You don't know how much.' He opened his eyes and stared across at her. She stood motionless, waiting. She was playing with every card she had. There was only tonight. There was only now.

'I'm yours if you want me, Luke,' she whispered. 'If you want me. . .'

She could do no more. She closed her eyes and waited.

And he would have had to be less than human to resist. In the moonlight, her soft white dress floating around her and her tousled curls gold-red in the moonlight, she was almost ethereal. Luke groaned and half turned away. Nikki didn't move. Please, she was whispering over and over in her heart. Please. . .

And he came to her. He had to. It was as if they were two parts of a magnetic force that only had attraction for each other. He came and gathered her into his arms as though he were drowning. His lips took hers and Nikki gave herself to him with joy.

She could never recall how it happened, but somehow. . .somehow they were inside, in her big, cool bedroom, and he was kicking the wide French windows closed behind them. Nikki's dress was somehow falling on to the polished floorboards and she was being lifted to lie on the smooth sheets, to wait. . .to wait for her love.

This was her place. This was her rightful home in the universe. She was with her man—of her man—one—and her body responded with all the joy that was in her heart.

This man was her love. This man was the father of the child she carried in her body, and her whole being reacted with light and love. Her hands took him to her, greedily, hungrily. She wanted to know every part of him, forever and ever and ever.

They were mad that night. They were two hearts, wounded and somehow made whole for the blessing of one magic night. In each other's bodies they found joy and peace and love. They made love and slept and woke and made love again and Nikki tried to keep awake in Luke's arms, so that she could savour it—this night that she wanted to go on for the rest of her life.

'I love you,' she whispered over and over again as

he loved her body—as he made her feel the most loved and wanted woman on the face of the earth. She ran her fingers over his muscled frame and sought to make him hers—sought to melt her body into his. 'I love you,' she whispered, but he didn't respond.

He didn't reply.

His lovemaking told her that he wanted her—that he needed her—and that when he was gone he would be desperate for the comfort of her body.

His tongue tasted her and loved her, but didn't say the words that would tie him to her forever.

Nothing.

And, finally, Nikki slept.

She woke at dawn as Luke stirred beside her, disengaged his body from hers and rose.

Sleepily Nikki looked up, loving the strong curves of his muscled body. Her eyes sought to know every inch of him. Instinctively she knew that there was to be no more. This was the end. The end. . .

She didn't speak. She couldn't. Instead she lay in the weak dawn light and watched the man she loved prepare to leave.

Finally, clothed, he turned to face her. Wordlessly she watched, waiting. Silence stretched out between them. It went on and on, as if neither was willing to face what had now become inevitable. Finally Luke swore softly and crossed to the bed to look down at her.

Nikki lay still, her red-blonde hair tumbled on the pillow around her too pale face. Her eyes were enormous as she looked up at him, waiting for the hurt.

And, sure enough, it came.

'Last night shouldn't have happened,' he said quietly, his eyes pain-filled. 'These whole three weeks. . .'

'Should never have happened,' Nikki agreed. 'I know. But they have, Luke. And. . .and I've changed forever because of it.'

He touched her hair as if it hurt to do so. 'I'm glad. . .if it means you'll get out more. Meet people. Find someone. . .'

'Someone who'll love me. . .' Nikki's voice broke and she turned into her pillow. 'Luke, how can you say that? How can you say that when you know I love you?'

'God, Nikki. . .'

She turned back to him then and rose to a sitting position, the sheet falling away to reveal her lovely nakedness. Her hand came out to touch his—a wordless pleading.

'Luke, why don't you want me?' She shook her head. 'I don't. . .I don't understand. You don't feel what I feel?'

'Hell!' Luke pulled his hand from hers and turned away to stand and stare out of the window. 'I want you, Nikki. God knows. . .'

'But not enough to ask me to stay with you.'

'For a while, yes,' he said bleakly. 'I want you. At this moment I want you more than anything I have ever wanted in my life. But I want more than that, Nikki. I want things I can't have. I want a family. . .'

'And I'm not enough.'

'No.' He stared sightlessly out of the window. 'For a few crazy moments here I thought it might be. I thought that with you and Amy I could be at peace. But I don't think I can ever be at peace, Nikki.'

'So the fact that you can't father a child is more important than your love for us?'

Nikki's heart shrank from what he was saying. She could have this man, she knew, just by opening her mouth and promising him his child. And it would be no better than what she had had with Scott. Scott hadn't wanted her unless she had money. Now Luke had no use for her unless she had his child.

'Nikki, it seems unfair. . .'

'It is unfair.' Nikki took a deep breath and rose,

pulling her sheet after her. She wound it around her as if it were some sort of defence against him, but her defence had come too late.

'You made love to me as if you loved me,' she whispered. 'You made me feel. . .you made me feel as if I was part of you. And I gave myself to you. Not just my body, Luke Marriott, but myself. My love. My heart. And now. . .now you tell me that because of your damned past—because of an illness that's robbed you of the ability to bear children—my love's not enough.'

'Nikki. . .'

Anger came then, as some sort of in-built defence against the pain. It gave her strength to lash out one more time. 'You've got a damned nerve.' Nikki's eyes flashed fire. 'You want me if I can bear your children, but not otherwise. What the hell does that make me, Luke Marriott?'

'I know. It's unfair. . .'

'Too damned right it's unfair.'

He shook his head. Luke's hands came up as if to touch her and then fell away uselessly to his sides.

'Nikki, my family is important. . . Look, it would be so easy to take you. To take what you're offering. And then, in five years. . . Well, in five years, if my inability to have children were as important to me as it is now, we'd be in a real mess.'

'Because it would hurt for me to have Amy, and your brothers and sisters to have children, and you not.'

'Yes. Damn it, yes.'

'And that's more important than my love. . .'

'Yes. No!' Luke was as angry as Nikki now, his eyes almost black with frustration and fury. 'It's easy for you to say it's not important. . .'

'And if magically you could have children. . .what then. . .?'

He shook his head, the flash of anger slowly fading. 'I don't know,' he said quietly. 'Nikki, if I could have children with you. . . Oh, God, Nikki. . .'

'So you'd want me as a mother to your children?' Nikki's voice was flat and lifeless. 'But not otherwise.'

'Nikki, that's not what I'm saying.'

'Well, it's what it sounds like from here,' Nikki spat. 'It's just as well you're going, Luke Marriott. It's just as well you're getting out of my life. Because I think your cancer has done more damage than you know.'

'I don't know what you mean.'

'You should,' Nikki said bleakly. 'I think. . .I think it's destroyed your capacity to love.'

'Nikki. . .'

'Just go,' she said.

CHAPTER ELEVEN

THE weeks that followed were desolate. Without Luke the house fell silent. Amy became once again a solemn child, and even Beattie forgot to sing as she did the housework.

Beattie watched her young employer with concern, her shrewd eyes taking in the tell-tale shadows on Nikki's face. If she heard Nikki wandering the house late at night, or saw her lonely figure standing out by the swimming-pool staring at nothing for hours on end, she said nothing.

Somehow Nikki managed to work. Her results came through for her examinations—'a magnificent result', the letter said. 'Congratulations!' She felt nothing. Nikki laid the letter aside and Beattie found it underneath a pile of advertising literature the following morning. Once more Beattie's forehead wrinkled into a frown of concern but still she said nothing.

It was fortunate for Nikki's sanity that there was plenty of work. She drove herself mercilessly, shoving aside the lethargy of early pregnancy. There was no time to think of the child she was carrying. She didn't want to know.

And yet, in a way, she was intensely aware of the new life starting within her. It was a little of Luke left to her. The baby would bring Luke happiness when he heard, she knew. Once he knew he was not sterile he could find someone else—one of the women who had loved him when he was back in Cairns, or someone else—someone who'd be prepared to accept him on the terms he offered. A woman who wanted to be the mother of his children first. . .

The mother of Luke's children. . . Nikki touched her

still flat stomach self-consciously as she acknowledged herself as such. That was what she was whether she wanted it or not. The mother of Luke's child. So why not accept the joy as well?

Because she wanted more. For once in her life, Nikki wanted to be loved for herself—wanted for herself—and if Luke didn't want her on those terms, then she couldn't let him near.

She began to plan the mechanics of the next few months as she went about her work. At about five months she would write to him care of the medical board, she thought—or care of the newspaper he wrote for. She would have to write before there was a possibility of his hearing via the medical grape-vine. It would be a formal little note, passing on the news of her condition and also letting him know it could make no difference to their relationship. Even if he came storming up here in another three months, then she must be strong enough to cope with that. She must be strong enough to tell him there was no place in her life for him.

'Is there anything wrong, Doc?'

Nikki looked up swiftly from what she was doing. She was re-checking Jim Payne's healing thumb. He had been released from hospital the week before, with no complications anticipated. It was healing beautifully, thanks to Luke's expert care, and Nikki forced a smile.

'Nothing's wrong, Jim,' she reassured him. 'This is looking really good. You might have some residual stiffness, but I'll give you some exercises to do once you get rid of the plaster and it'll slowly get back to almost a hundred per cent.'

'I meant——' the young man frowned down at her '—I meant with you. You're not. . .well, you're not as cheerful as you used to be.'

'I'm not a really cheerful person,' Nikki told him, somewhat taken aback at his forthrightness.

'You were when Doc Marriott was here.'

Nikki shook her head. The town would be talking about her and Luke, she knew. How much would the talk grow as her figure filled out?

'It was good to have him here,' she said simply. 'He was a very skilled surgeon.'

'Don't I know it.' Jim looked ruefully at his thumb. 'I guess I'll be grateful to him for the rest of my life.'

'You haven't heard from your mother?' Nikki asked, trying to turn the subject.

'Yeah.'

Nikki frowned. She picked up the scraps of the bandage she had been fixing and tossed them into the rubbish bin. 'So what gives?'

The boy was silent for a moment, staring at his bandaged hand. 'I dunno,' he said at last.

'You don't know.'

Jim shook his head. He looked up. 'Did you know I'm boarding at Sandra Mears's? That's. . .that's why I was saying you were more cheerful when Doc Marriott was here. Sandra said you were. She reckoned. . .she reckoned you had something going between you.'

Nikki shook her head. 'Sandra's on the wrong track,' she said tightly. Then she looked up. 'How are you finding it at Sandra's?'

'It's great. She's a real good sort. And I like the kids.'

'Mmm.' Was this going to work? Nikki turned it over in her mind, replaying the conversation she'd had with Sandra the week before.

'We advertised and Jim replied,' she'd said happily. 'And I've always felt sorry for Jimmy. I reckon he's had almost as bad a deal as me.'

'Do you think you can cope with the extra work?' Nikki had frowned and Sandra had laughed.

'I like housework,' she'd grinned. 'Call me daft if you like, but now I've a decent house to look after it'll be no trouble. The kids like Jimmy and his board money will be handy—well, I'm going to start thinking we're rich.'

So Nikki had smiled and agreed, knowing Jim was reluctant to go home to a father who didn't seem to give a damn about his only son. But if Jim's mother were to come. . .

'She telephoned me in the hospital,' Jim said slowly. 'And. . .and she asked me to go to Brisbane to stay with her.'

'Oh, Jim, that's terrific.'

He shook his head. 'Maybe not.' He looked up. 'She's remarried. Her new husband's a widower with three kids. I dunno. . .'

'You don't know where you fit?'

He shook his head. 'I know Dad seems a selfish bastard,' he said directly. 'But Mum. . .well, she left and maybe if she really wanted to contact me she could have. And here. . .well, here at least I know the people and I know I've got a job.'

'On your father's boat.'

'Yeah, well, maybe I'll go back to working for him and maybe I won't,' Jim said uncertainly. 'There's other boats. But fishing's all I know.'

'It's going to be quite a change, living with Sandra.'

'It is and all,' Jim said happily. 'Those kids. . .' He shook his head. 'They're great kids, Doc Russell, and do you know, the boys have never even been taught to kick a football?'

'No!' Nikki breathed in mock-horror and Jim grinned.

'Well, I'm going to teach them,' he said resolutely. He took a deep breath. 'Sandra's taken a risk taking me in. I know this town and I know it'll talk even more about her. But we talked it over and reckoned we could ignore it and maybe make it work.'

Nikki sat back on her heels and looked thoughtfully at the young fisherman. He sounded as if he was taking on more of a responsibility than a decision to rent a room for a few weeks. And when the door opened for Jim to leave the surgery and Nikki saw Sandra and the two youngest children in the waiting-room she saw what was happening.

A family was forming out of mutual need. The children came forward to greet Jim as their personal property and he took a hand of each and turned to go. 'Thanks a lot, Doc,' he told Nikki over his shoulder. 'Thanks for everything.'

Nikki watched them walk away—Sandra at twenty-two with the lilt of a girl back in her step and Jim at nineteen playing the father. For heaven's sake. . .

She smiled suddenly. It might. . .it just might work. Crazier things had happened.

And then her receptionist handed her the next card and Nikki turned her attention to Mrs Alphington's neuralgia. She didn't have time for reflection—and that was the way she wanted it.

The days dragged on. Nikki found herself staring stupidly at the calendar, as though it had some meaning. Three weeks since she had seen Luke. . . Four. . .

'When will he come back?' Amy asked for the hundredth time and Nikki strove for patience.

'Luke isn't coming back,' she said gently.

'He will,' Amy said stubbornly. 'Even if it's just for a visit. Maybe he'll come for Christmas?'

'Don't count on it.' Nikki winced at the thought of Christmas. She hated it. Christmas—the time of families. Beattie left them every Christmas, flying down to Brisbane for her once-a-year visit to her daughter, and there would only be Amy and Nikki. Some Christmas!

Maybe she should employ another locum—get right away for a few weeks. If she could get somewhere cooler, maybe this awful cloud of oppression would lift.

Summer had arrived with a vengeance—the real

tropical rainy season. It rained unceasingly, the rain turning to steam in the blistering heat. Nikki never enjoyed the rainy season and now—it was as if the sky were crying in sympathy with her.

'It's real cyclone weather,' Beattie said darkly as the first week of December neared its end. 'We're in for one, you wait and see.'

'Don't say so,' Nikki groaned. The last cyclone near Eurong had passed five years before, cutting a swath of damage. There were still scars in the rainforest from its passing.

Beattie sniffed. 'Well, there's no warnings yet. But it'll come soon.'

She was wrong. For the next few days Nikki worked with her eye on the weather and her ear constantly tuned to the local radio. Cyclone Hilda threatened them for a little, but swerved right away from the coast and blew harmlessly out to sea. There were no other warnings.

Finally Nikki ceased worrying and her thoughts went back to Luke. Where was he? How would he spend Christmas? As she and Amy put up their little Christmas tree she thought of Luke's family gathering in Melbourne. Would he visit them this year?

What would his reaction be if he knew that a child of his was on its way? That next year he would be a father. . .

A father *in absentia*, she reminded herself, and then winced. What if he demanded access? How would she cope seeing him every time he wanted to visit their child?

It didn't bear thinking of. She made herself concentrate on the silver baubles she was tying to the tree.

'It's lovely, Mummy,' Amy said in satisfaction, and then paused as Beattie hurried into the room. The housekeeper had been packing her suitcase ready for her afternoon flight south.

Something was wrong. The elderly housekeeper's

face was pale and she was obviously distressed.

'I knew it,' she said tremulously. 'It's a cyclone.'

'Oh, no.' Nikki rose, her eyes creasing in sympathy. Beattie had been filled with excitement at the thought of seeing her newest grandchild for the first time. If a cyclone was threatening between here and Brisbane then flights would be cancelled. 'How close?' Nikki asked. It wouldn't have to be too close for the plane to be cancelled.

'We're dead centre,' Beattie said grimly. 'I just heard it on the radio.'

Dead centre.

Nikki stared at Beattie in dawning horror. Dead centre of a cyclone. . . The damage cyclones did was enormous, but Eurong had never been directly in one's path. The destruction caused by being close to the cyclone path was bad enough.

'But. . .but there's been no warning of one imminent. There's only been Cyclone Hilda, and it's right out to sea, hundreds of miles north.'

'That's the one.' Beattie was practically wringing her hands. 'It's swung inland for some reason and there's a red alert. They say. . .they say it'll hit here in three hours.'

Three hours! Instinctively Nikki looked out of the window. The palms were swaying in a rising wind, but there was nothing to suggest an impending disaster.

This was no time for panic. Amy was watching with enormous eyes, and if Nikki showed she was frightened it would communicate fast to the child.

'OK,' Nikki said evenly, striving for calm. 'Let's get the storm covers up.'

'Does this mean you're not going away for Christmas, Beattie?' Amy asked, and Beattie and Nikki looked at each other. If that was all it meant they would be lucky.

'I guess it does. I. . .I think I'll take some things down to the storm cellar,' Beattie said nervously, and

Nikki nodded. They hadn't used the storm cellar for anything but storage for years. Nikki's father had installed it as a safety precaution and Eurong had decreed him mad. Totally unnecessary, they'd said, but now. . . Now, it made Nikki feel that there was at least one safe place where she could leave her daughter.

'We need to open the windows on the lee side a little,' Nikki said quietly, trying to remember the precautions she'd been taught. 'If the pressure builds up. . .'

'I know.' Beattie nodded, putting her personal disappointment aside. 'I'll do that now.'

'I'm going to have to go down to the hospital.'

'I know that too,' Beattie said grimly. She took a deep breath and looked down at Amy. 'Come on, then, young lady. You and I have got work to do.'

'Can we telephone Karen and her mum and ask them to share our cellar?' Amy bubbled. The cyclone sounded like a wonderful adventure from a four-year-old's angle.

Nikki nodded slowly. 'It's not a bad idea. Sandra's house is fibro-cement with no protection. Our cellar's big enough. . .'

'I'll telephone,' Beattie told her. She nodded decisively at Nikki, and Nikki silently blessed her good fortune at having such a competent housekeeper.

'OK.' She stooped to give Amy a quick hug. 'You promise you'll both be in the cellar an hour before the storm's due to hit—whatever happens?'

'We promise,' Beattie told her. 'And you, Nikki Russell. . .' She sighed. 'Well, take care of yourself. Don't go taking any damned fool risks.'

'Who, me?' Nikki smiled, with a bravado she was far from feeling. 'I'm not one for damned fool risks. I was born a coward.'

* * *

The hospital was at peak, bustling efficiency when Nikki arrived. There were three internal rooms that had no windows—the hospital had been built with storms in mind—and when Nikki arrived the nurses were moving their patients into safety.

'One room will have to be left free as Theatre,' Nikki said grimly.

'We've had enough warning for people to be prepared,' Andrea, the charge sister, said. 'Surely there won't be. . .'

'People do darned stupid things.' Nikki grimaced. 'Especially when they're frightened. And if we really are in the eye of the storm then many of these houses won't make it.'

'But most are built under regulations for cyclones.'

'Yeah.' Nikki piled boxes of dressing to carry to the makeshift theatre. 'But there's still no guarantee they'll survive the eye of a cyclone. Remember Darwin. . .'

They both did. The city had been struck on Christmas Eve several years previously and hardly a house had been left standing. The force had been as great as a major earthquake.

'It can't be as bad as that,' the nurse said nervously. 'Can it?'

'Heaven knows. I don't. Is the fishing fleet in?'

'There weren't any boats too far out to get back into harbour,' the nurse told her. 'They're all back.'

'Well, that's something.'

Nikki worked steadily, setting up her makeshift theatre as best she could. With luck the work she was doing could be totally unnecessary. To operate on seriously injured casualties. . .

She might not have a choice. Even after the cyclone passed it would be hours before the wind died enough to evacuate casualties. Nikki thought fleetingly, longingly, of Luke. She felt desperately alone, knowing the next few hours would bring more casualties than she could cope with.

'Everyone's being warned?' she asked anxiously. Her mind raced over her scores of elderly patients who lived alone. Many wouldn't have heard the radio warning.

'The State Emergency Service are doing a door-knock now,' the charge nurse told her. Andrea was linked to the emergency services by two-way radio. 'Anyone they're worried about they'll bring in here or to the school.' Like the hospital, the school also had reinforced rooms.

Fine. Everything that could be done was being done. So now there was only time to sit and wait. And hope. . .

'I don't suppose Dr Maybury could come?' Nikki said uncertainly. If she didn't have an anaesthetist there was little she could do if there were serious casualties. The elderly doctor was Nikki's nearest colleague and he was within driving distance if he came at once.

'I doubt it,' the charge sister told her. 'Penrith is thirty miles south, but by the sound of the radio warnings they're expecting damage there as well. He'll have to stay.'

Nikki nodded. She knew it already. She was on her own.

The wind rose with relentless fury.

How would Amy and Beattie be coping? Nikki tried to block out thoughts of home as the storm gathered strength. Her attention was needed here. Half an hour before the eye of the storm was due, every one of the occupants of the hospital deserted the outside rooms and the inner doors of the little hospital were wedged closed.

The telephone lines were already down. There was no way Nikki could contact home, even if she wanted to. Eurong was isolated until the storm was past, and every home was also completely isolated.

As they closed the big inner doors and Nikki saw the outside world for the last time, she wondered how on earth the storm could get fiercer. The huge coconut palms around the hospital were bending almost double in the shrieking wind and, beyond the headland, the sea was a seething white fury.

But grow worse it did. Locked behind their doors, the hospital occupants couldn't see but they could hear. The wind screamed around the little building and every now and then a crack rang out like gunfire—the sound of a palm giving up its fight for life.

There was little time to listen. Within the room Nikki's patients were terrified—not so much for the immediate danger but at the thought of what lay ahead when those doors were opened again. Nikki moved from bed to bed, comforting as best she could and listening to nameless fears. She sedated one elderly lady as her fears brought on angina. A full-scale heart attack was the last thing Nikki wanted now. She would have enough to deal with when the doors opened.

The wait was interminable. The sound of the screaming wind went on and on, and when it finally eased Nikki knew that the doors had to stay closed.

Now they were in the eye of the cyclone—and there was a rim to the eye. They had passed through one side of the rim, and the other was yet to come.

If only she knew what was going on at home. . . The thought of the cellar was infinitely comforting. And Beattie knew about the eye of the storm. She knew not to come out yet. The little radio owned by one of the patients and listened to by all was blazing out warnings of the danger to come. 'Stay where you are,' it warned over and over again. 'Don't think the danger is over. Stay behind closed doors. Use rooms with the least windows. Think of the pantry—or the broom closet. The bathroom is often the safest room. Stay where you are. . .'

As long as people were listening. Nikki sent endless

silent prayers up to whoever would listen. Please let people stay put. Please let no one be hit by falling trees or flying pieces of corrugated iron. . . It was a useless prayer but she sent it anyway.

'I won't have a house any more,' an elderly man said flatly as she paused by his bed. 'My place is old and run-down, and it won't stand up to this racket.' His gnarled old face creased into tears. 'You'll have to put me in a home after this. My house'll be matchsticks.'

There was little comfort Nikki could give. Outside the storm struck again as the eye passed and each fresh blast made her wince. To stay here while Eurong was blown to bits. . .it was the hardest thing she had done in her life.

And then, finally, the worst of the storm was past. The screaming wind settled to howls, and then to a dull whine. The nurses looked at each other fearfully and then at Nikki. Nikki nodded in silent acquiescence. It was time to open the doors.

Maybe it would have been better to stay inside. The nurses and the ambulatory patients walked outside to a deathless hush. It was a frightening new world.

The hospital had survived. The building was intact, but every window had been blasted out. The rooms were full of debris and rain water. Torn curtains lay shredded on the floor in sodden heaps. The wind still whistled in through the broken windows, bringing rain in with it. Steam rose from everything.

Soundlessly they moved outside. The veranda posts had crumpled under the strain and the roof sagged under the weight of a huge coconut palm. Luckily the two posts over the door had held so it was safe to move outside.

If one wanted to. Nikki took one look and decided she might not want to see the rest of the devastation. The hospital gardens were in ruins. Nikki's car lay where she had parked in the hospital car park, turned up on to its side. It was covered with a mass of torn and twisted debris.

'Dear God.' Andrea was beside Nikki and her hand came up to grasp Nikki's arm. 'Dear God. . .'

There was nothing else to say.

Around them the rest of the staff were slowly coming to terms with what they were seeing. They had little time for reflection. As the patients saw and guessed at the damage elsewhere it was as much as the small nursing staff could do to control the rising hysteria.

Nikki conquered it by ordering everyone to work, patients included.

'I want everyone fit enough to move to start getting the water out of the wards,' she demanded. 'I want plastic over the windows. I want the beds made up again dry and ready for whatever comes. Mrs Fletcher. . .' Nikki eyed a patient who'd been in hospital with a broken hip. Mavis Fletcher was in tears already and her tears were turning to noisy sobs. 'Mavis, can you hear me?'

Mavis looked up tearfully. 'Oh, me dear,' she gasped. 'What are we going to do? What are we going to do?'

'I don't know about you but I intend to start working,' Nikki said grimly. 'If I'm not mistaken there'll be people out there who are a lot worse off than we are. If I put you in a wheelchair, can you supervise sandwich-making? Mr Roberts might be able to help. What do you say?'

Mavis gave a tearful gulp. She looked around at the mess and then back to Nikki. To be needed. . .

'If you think I can, dear,' she whispered.

Nikki grinned. 'I'm sure you can,' she said solidly. 'I'm sure we all can.'

It was the last time Nikki had to ask anyone to help. The whole hospital was galvanised into action, even the patients doing what they could to clear the mess and prepare for the onslaught.

And onslaught there was. Five minutes after they emerged from the inner rooms their first casualty arrived—a man carrying his three-year-old daughter. She'd been hit by a block of plaster falling from the roof. The child was concussed and needed stitches to a nasty gash on her head, and by the time Nikki had attended her there were three more patients waiting.

Amazingly there seemed little serious injury. As each casualty arrived Nikki braced herself for tragedy, but, although the stories of property damage were heartbreaking, as yet there were no reports of loss of life. There were a couple of fractures and dozens of lacerations caused by falling debris. Nikki held her breath as she worked. If this was all. . .

'The new regulations seem to have worked,' Andrea told her in a break between patients. 'And the warnings which everyone's had since Darwin. People haven't taken risks, and they haven't been seriously hurt.'

Nikki nodded. 'Andrea, could you find out about Whispering Palms?' she said tightly. The girl working beside her flashed her a look of understanding.

'Oh, Doctor, I'm sorry. I'll contact SES. They'll go around now.'

'There's no need to make a special trip,' Nikki managed. 'But. . .but I'll work better if I know it's still standing.'

'Of course.' Andrea turned to go but before she did they heard footsteps racing along the debris-strewn hall and the door to their inner sanctum burst open.

It was Sandra.

Sandra was soaking wet, her dress was torn and a gash dripped blood slowly down across one eye. She was wild-eyed and gasping for breath.

'Nikki,' she burst out. 'Doctor. . .Nikki, can you come. . .?'

Nikki turned from the wound she was dressing. The colour drained from her face. Sandra had been in the cellar at Whispering Palms.

'Amy,' she whispered. She clutched the edge of the examination table. 'Sandra, where's Amy?'

Sandra caught herself with a visible effort. She took a ragged breath and then another. Silently Andrea moved forward and took the girl's arm. She looked as though she was about to collapse.

'It's not Amy,' she managed. 'I'm. . .I'm sorry. I didn't think. . .'

'You were in the cellar at Whispering Palms?'

Sandra nodded. Andrea pushed the girl into a chair and she sat gratefully, her knees buckling under her. 'Th-thanks.'

'OK.' Now that Nikki's worst fear had been relieved she could be calm again. She knelt in front of Sandra and took her hands. 'Tell me what's happened,' she said gently.

'It's Jim. . .'

'Jim Payne.'

Sandra nodded. 'He was with us at the beginning. Helping with the kids. Then, when Beattie rang, he said it was sensible that we all go to Whispering Palms. So he took us.'

'But he didn't stay?'

Sandra shook her head. 'He wouldn't. He. . .he made sure we were all safe and made us promise not to leave the cellar. And then he said he had to go to his father. . .'

His father. Nikki thought of Bert Payne's tiny run-down house down by the beach. Whatever regulations the council had introduced, she could be a hundred per cent sure that Bert wouldn't have introduced them. He'd tell any official to mind his own damned business.

'So Jim's down at his father's.'

'No. Yes.' Sandra looked up, her face a tear-stained plea for help. 'As soon as we got out of the cellar I went to try to find him. Whispering Palms is OK and Beattie said she'd be fine with the kids. And. . .and Jim's been so good to us. I had to leave the car a quarter of a mile from the house and walk in. There's trees down all over. And then. . .then I came to the house.' She looked up. 'It's down.'

'The house has collapsed?'

'Yes.'

'And Jim and his father are inside.'

'Yes.'

Nikki's grip on the girl's hands tightened. 'Are they dead, Sandra?'

The shock tactics worked. Sandra's eyes flew open and she fought for some sort of control. She shook her head. 'Not. . .not yet. I. . . Will you come?'

'Of course I'll come.' Nikki was already rising, pulling Sandra after her. 'Are they trapped inside?'

'I don't. . .' Again a ragged gasp for breath. 'Yes. There's a huge tree over the house. And Jim's inside and his father's stuck fast. And Jim says he'll bleed to death if he leaves him, but the tree's going to come all the way down any minute, and. . .'

'Let's go.' Nikki turned to Andrea. 'Let the emergency services know. I want able-bodied men there as fast as possible. Tell them I want shoring timbers and as much help as I can get.'

'Do you want me to come?' Andrea asked.

Nikki shook her head. 'You're needed here, Andrea. I'm needed here too, come to that, but if Bert Payne's bleeding. . .' She turned back to Sandra. 'Does anyone else know?'

Sandra shook her head. 'I. . . It was closer to run to the hospital than go back for the car. I didn't meet anyone. . .'

'OK. Let's go.'

They arrived at what was left of Bert Payne's fishing shack ten minutes later. The road was impassable with Nikki's little car, but just as they came to a halt three men in a State Emergency four-wheel-drive vehicle came racing up behind them. They moved Nikki's equipment over to their Jeep and kept on going.

'Good grief,' Nikki muttered, holding on to her seat for dear life. The Jeep bucketed over the debris, strewn as if it were a deliberately placed obstacle course. 'You'll kill this car.' She blinked forward, trying to see what was ahead in the pelting tropical rain.

'Better the Jeep dies than Jim Payne,' the driver said grimly and Nikki nodded. Jim. . . There was concern for the boy but not the father. Bert Payne had made few friends in this town.

Then what was left of Bert Payne's house was in view and the condition of the Jeep was forgotten.

The house was flattened as if it had been a house of cards, blown flat. Nikki stared at the wreck in horror. There were the remains of a chimney-stack in one corner and nothing else. There was nothing higher than chest height. That someone might still be in there. . .

The driving wind and rain were almost blinding her, whipping her sodden hair around her face. Nikki pushed it back in frustration. Before the Jeep came to a halt Sandra was out of the vehicle, running to what was left.

'Jim!' she screamed. 'Jim. . .'

'Sandra. . .' It was a hoarse cry from somewhere under the ruin, barely audible above the sound of the still whistling wind. 'Sandra. . .'

'I've got help,' Sandra yelled hoarsely. 'Dr Nikki. And men. . .'

Already the men were in action, following the sound of Jim's voice. Nikki dragged her bag from the car and then stood helplessly. Where on earth were they?

'They're right under the tree,' Sandra said hopelessly. 'Oh, God. . .'

The tree was enormous. It was a vast strangler fig, which had grown originally around a coconut palm. The coconut palm had long since died and the fallen fig now resembled a huge hollow log after the rotting of its host. It was almost twenty feet wide at the base—a mass of thick, twisting wood, smashed down on the tiny house.

'We're going to have to cut through,' the SES chief said grimly. 'We'll never lift the thing.'

'It's going to come down further,' Sandra told him. 'Look. . .'

They looked. Where the tree had snapped was about eight feet from the base. It had fallen but the base of its broken part had caught on the shattered stump. There was maybe a two-inch rim where the weight of the huge tree rested.

'My God. . .' the SES chief whispered. He swung around to his second-in-command. 'The shoring timbers we've got won't hold that. Get back to base. I want more men and stouter timbers. If that goes down. . .'

There was no reason to finish the sentence. They all knew.

'Jim, where are you?' Nikki was moving along the trunk of the tree, stepping over debris.

'In here. . .' Jim's voice was hoarse and tight.

'Are you hurt?'

'Yeah. . . I've. . .I think my arm's broke. . . And my head. . .I keep blacking out. . .'

'And your dad?'

'He's here. He's unconscious but he's still alive. He's bleeding, though, Doc. I'm holding his leg but. . .I can't keep the pressure up.'

'Are you trapped?'

'There's a bit of space behind me. I reckon. . .I reckon I could crawl back out. But. . .but Dad's stuck and if I leave him he'll bleed to death.'

Nikki was standing almost over the voice now. She looked around to where the debris subsided. The old doorway was just here. . .

Clambering down, she peered through. There was a gap in here. If she crawled. . .

'Jim. . .?'

'Yeah. . .'

She could see a shape stir slightly in the blackness. The beams of the doorway had slipped down but had afforded protection to a small area—a tunnel of no more than eighteen inches in diameter. Jim seemed about fifteen feet in through this tunnel.

'Your father's bleeding from the leg?' she asked. Behind her, the SES men and Sandra were staring in horror as she wedged herself into the gap, trying to see.

'The top of his thigh. He's. . . The tree's over his chest. I can't budge. . .' Jim's voice trailed off. He sounded close to unconsciousness himself.

'And you've lost blood too?' Nikki spoke loudly and insistently. She didn't want him passing out now.

'Yeah. . . It. . .it doesn't matter. . .'

'Oh, Jim.' Behind Nikki, Sandra had started to cry. She clutched Nikki's arm and pulled her backwards. 'He's got to come out. If that tree slips. . .' Then she raised her voice. 'Jim, you've got to come out. Your dad doesn't give a stuff about you. You've got to——' She broke off and turned away.

'Jim's not like his father,' Nikki told her, rising and putting her hand briefly on Sandra's shoulder. 'And if he were. . .if he were then you wouldn't be crying.' She took a deep breath and lowered her voice. 'Sandra, have you told Jim how dangerous the tree is?'

Sandra shook her head. 'I didn't see until now. Oh, Nikki. . .'

'Jim, we're shoring up the entrance to where you are.' Nikki gave a warning look to Sandra and the men as she raised her voice. 'I want you to come out.'

'I'm not leaving. I told you. . . Dad'll die.'

'He'll die if you stay,' Nikki said brutally. 'You sound as though you're drifting in and out of unconsciousness. 'Do you have the strength to maintain pressure on that leg, or is it still bleeding?'

'It's still bleeding,' Jim managed.

'But you can move?'

'Yeah. . .but. . .'

'Jim, I can't get in unless you come out,' Nikki said harshly. 'And your father needs me.'

Sandra gave a gasp. 'But Nikki. . . You can't. . .'

She was stopped by Nikki's fierce grip on her arm. 'Sandra, Jim's hurt and I don't know how badly. This is the only way he'll come out.'

It was. Nikki had known it since she saw the entrance. It was unpalatable but true. She bent down and peered into the recess. One of the SES men was directing a flashlight through the rubble. 'OK, Jim,' she ordered. 'Start moving slowly backwards. Now!'

'But Dad'll die. . .'

'The faster you get out, the faster I get in,' Nikki said ruthlessly. 'Move, Jim.'

Three minutes later Jim emerged to daylight. Nikki did a lightning check on the dazed young man, satisfied herself that she could leave him to the care of the people around him, and then stooped down. The SES man stopped her as she placed her hand on the door-beam.

'Doc, this is just Bert Payne you're risking your neck for,' he said uncertainly. 'I. . .I don't like this. . .'

Nikki nodded. 'I know it's just Bert Payne,' she whispered, looking over to where Sandra was holding Jim. 'But he's dying in there, and I'm a doctor. I haven't a choice.'

'He wouldn't do the same for you,' the man said brutally.

'No.' Nikki shook her head. 'But then he doesn't seem to have passed his cruel attitudes on to his son, thank heaven. . . And we can't afford to be like him.' She took one last look at Jim and Sandra, took a deep breath and lowered herself into the makeshift passage.

Jim had been wearing heavy denim jeans, which had protected him a little from the worst of the jagged splinters and nails, and for the first time in weeks Nikki regretted that she wasn't wearing the same. Charlotte's pretty clothes had become part of her—a legacy of her time with Luke. Now the dress she was wearing ripped three feet into the tunnel and she felt a nail jab into her bare leg. She swore and kept going.

I'll ring Charlotte and give her a hard time when I get out of here, Nikki thought grimly as she felt her way forward through the mass of broken timber. The thought of Charlotte—of Cairns—of somewhere other than this hell-hole—was somehow steadying. She had to think of something other than the tree poised above.

Where on earth was Bert? Jim had backed out this way. Bert Payne must be somewhere here. . .

She shoved forward, her hands groping in the dim light, and her hand met something soft. Here he was. . .

Nikki could see nothing. What she was feeling seemed to be a leg. She'd attached a rope to her waist before coming in, and now she turned to tug it after her. Her bag came sliding roughly through the debris, and attached to its handle was a flashlight. Nikki looked back along the tunnel and saw daylight being blocked by anxious faces. She flashed her light at them and then turned back to her patient.

And her heart sank. Bert Payne lay half crushed by the huge tree. It held his body in a vice, and Nikki couldn't see his left arm or leg. His face was near her, his skin devoid of any colour, and his breathing was shallow and uneven. Nikki's hand slid down the exposed leg, and met the warm ooze of blood.

Instinctively Nikki felt for a pressure point, but she knew already that her action was useless. There must be massive internal injuries. With her free hand she felt for a pulse, and as she did Bert's eyes flew open.

'Jim. . .' he whispered.

'We've taken Jim out,' Nikki said gently. 'He has a broken arm, but he's safe.'

'But. . .' The man's eyes concentrated in a sheer

effort of remembrance as Nikki groped in her bag for morphine. 'But he was here. . .'

'Yes.'

'He came back to see I was all right. . .'

'Yes, he did.' Nikki twisted her body to a position where she could fill the syringe. She turned and drove it home, wondering as she did so whether there was time for it to take effect.

'I was. . .I was a bastard to him,' the big man muttered. He reached forward with his one free arm and gripped Nikki's hand. 'You're sure. . .you're sure he's all right?'

'He's safe.' Nikki was no longer worrying about the oozing blood. It was too late for that now. She gripped Bert's free hand in hers and held it.

'Tell him. . .tell him I'm sorry.'

'I'll do that,' Nikki told him evenly. 'I promise.'

'And tell him. . .' The elderly fisherman closed his eyes as if he had reached a point where he could go no further. His words were an almost superhuman effort. 'Tell him he's been a good kid and I'm. . .I'm proud of him. Tell him. . .'

'I'll tell him.'

It was the last thing Bert Payne ever said. Five minutes later he died.

There was nothing more for Nikki to do. She let Bert's hand rest on the pile of rubble, and pushed her bag back out of the way. There was no point in her staying. Not now. . .

But as she moved so did the tree. Nikki looked up in fear as the massive trunk started slowly to settle. She flung herself backwards, but it was too late.

The mass of rubble in the tunnel behind her came down in a dust-laden roar. The dust filled her head, blinding her. She put her hands instinctively to her head and waited.

And it came. The huge mass of debris above her head shifted downwards. Nikki felt a blow to her shoulder and then a massive, crushing weight on her head. She tried to cry out, but no sound came. The weight. . .

'Nikki!' The sound came from outside the shifting rubble. 'Nikki. . .'

'Luke. . .' Nikki whispered a response uselessly into the shifting, tearing dark. It was Luke. He had come back to her. . . 'Luke. . .'

Then she knew no more.

CHAPTER TWELVE

THERE was something gripping her head. It was an iron vice, clamping behind each ear and slowly squeezing. . .

Nikki opened one eye and then shut it again fast. Whatever was holding her gripped a thousandfold tighter with light. She lay absolutely still, not daring to move. Whatever vice her torturers were using might stay in abeyance if she only kept still.

'There's my girl. Come on, Nikki, love. You can do it. Come on, my love.'

She was dead and was dreaming. Nikki's eyes stayed firmly closed while she thought about the voice.

It was Luke's. It was Luke's voice. Her love. . .

Maybe it was. . . Maybe. . . Maybe if she opened her eyes she would see him, but then again, maybe not. Maybe she was dead and dreaming.

'Come on, Nikki, love.' There was no mistaking the voice. Nikki felt her hands being taken between two strong ones, and gripped. And somehow Luke's hold on her hands lessened the gripping pain surrounding her head.

'Come on, Nikki, love. You can do it. Come back to me, Nikki.'

'Come back to me'. . . Still Nikki didn't stir. She lay and let the voice drift around her.

It was Luke. He was here, with her, and his voice held love.

If she opened her eyes then she might find it was all a dream. That it was all some cruel joke. Her head hurt so. . .

A tear crept down her cheek and she tasted it as it

reached her lips. She was dead and dreaming that Luke was here. . .that Luke had come back to her. . .

And then the hold on her hands tightened and a mouth covered hers, kissing away the salt tear. 'Come on, Nikki, love. Come back to me. I love you so much. . .'

And she opened her eyes.

It was no dream. He was here—her Luke. He was holding her as if she were the most precious thing in the world, and his kiss held the tenderness she had only dreamed of.

He must have felt her slight movement. Luke's head lifted from her face and his troubled eyes looked down. And he saw her eyes on his.

There was no mistaking the joy in his face. It lit him within, blazing down on her like a blessing.

'Nikki. . .' His voice was hoarse with strain. 'Nikki. . .'

'Luke. . .' Nikki wasn't too sure where her voice came from. She only knew that somehow the nightmare had receded. The pain in her head was still there but so was Luke—and who could feel pain with so much happiness inside?

Tears slid helplessly down her face. 'Luke,' she whispered again, and he closed her lips with his fingers.

'Don't try to speak, Nikki, love. You're safe. Amy and Beattie are fine. And you're safe. That's all that matters.'

'You came. . .'

'Too damned right I came,' Luke said grimly. He gathered her tenderly to him, holding her tight while leaving her carefully still on the white hospital bedclothes. 'And I'm never leaving you again. Not ever. And that's a promise, my love.'

'My love'. . . Nikki closed her eyes again as the words drifted round and round her. 'My love'. . .

It was with her still as she drifted into sleep.

* * *

When next she woke the pain in her head had all but disappeared. Nikki lay for a moment staring sightlessly up at the hospital ceiling. The pain had gone, but so had Luke.

Had she dreamed the whole thing? Had it been some crazy nightmare. . .?

She put her hand tentatively up to her head. A large bandage covered her forehead. She'd been hit on the head and had been dreaming.

The disappointment almost made her cry out, but as her hand dropped to the pillow the door opened and Andrea bustled in.

'Well, well,' the charge nurse smiled. 'So you're awake, Dr Russell. About time too.'

Nikki tried to focus. 'How. . .how long have I been asleep?'

'Oh, about two days.'

Two days!

'Well, not all of that time asleep,' Andrea told her, lifting Nikki's wrist and looking down at her watch to check her pulse. 'You were unconscious for twenty-four hours.' She grimaced down. 'You gave us the fright of our lives,' she confessed.

'I gave me the fright of my life,' Nikki agreed weakly. She put her hand back up to her bandages. 'What's. . .?'

'A fractured skull and twelve stitches,' Andrea told her. 'But it's a simple fracture and there doesn't appear to be any internal bleeding. Dr Luke says——'

'Dr Luke. . .?'

'Dr Luke says you'll live.' Andrea grinned happily down at Nikki. 'And Dr Luke seems a whole heap happier since he made that announcement, I can tell you.'

'So he really is here. I. . .I thought I dreamed it.'

'He's here,' Andrea told her. 'He's checking a plaster at the moment or he'd probably be beside you right now.' She smiled again. 'He's spent a fair amount of time next to this bed over the last two days.'

'I. . .I thought I heard him when. . .when the tree came down.'

'You did,' Andrea told her. 'I gather he was in Cairns and when the cyclone warning came through he moved heaven and hell to get back here. He came storming in here about fifteen minutes after you left for Bert Payne's. He got a helicopter to Port Douglas, but heaven knows how he got through the blocked roads to here. The call came from the SES people about two minutes after he arrived, asking for more men and longer shoring timbers and telling us why. They told us you were in the ruins with Bert, and Dr Marriott. . .well. . .' She shook her head. 'I think Dr Marriott seemed a little crazy.'

'So he was there. . .'

'He got there just as the tree came down,' Andrea told her. 'The SES men told me he worked like a madman.' She hesitated. 'Have a look at his hands next time you see him. They're torn to bits. He didn't stop until they got you out, and even then. . .well, even then I think he was a little crazy.' She shook her head. 'You looked awful. You were deeply unconscious and there was so much blood. . .'

'But Bert Payne. . .'

'Bert Payne's dead,' Andrea told her. 'But Jim's alive, thanks to you. The SES people say it was a miracle you weren't crushed to death. Anyone as big as Jim would be dead for sure.'

'Jim's. . . Jim's OK?'

'Jim's OK. It's his plaster Dr Marriott is checking now.'

'It's checked.' The strongly masculine voice came from the doorway, making the charge nurse twist around with a start. Luke was standing there, his stethoscope swinging from his fingers and his eyes on Nikki. 'He needs a new sling, though, Sister,' he said without taking his eyes from Nikki. 'If you could.'

The charge nurse looked from Nikki to Luke and back again. She smiled broadly. 'I was just taking Dr Russell's obs,' she said demurely. 'But if you think my services are wanted elsewhere. . .'

'I think your services are wanted elsewhere,' Luke confirmed.

'You won't disturb my patient, will you, Doctor?' the nurse grinned. Luke picked up the observation chart threateningly.

'Get out of here, you insolent baggage,' he smiled. 'Dr Russell, I'm sorry to inform you that you have a very insubordinate staff.'

'It's hard to command respect when Andrea and I went to kindergarten together,' Nikki whispered, and Luke crossed swiftly to the bed to take her hand. Behind him Andrea made her departure, still grinning.

'Don't you worry about that, my love,' he said gently. 'The staff'll fall in line now I'm back working here. Together we'll pull this place into shape.' He smiled down at the bed in a way that made Nikki's heart almost stop beating.

'Together'. . . And Luke was looking at her as. . . as she had always dreamed a man would look at her.

Not just a man. Her Luke.

'We. . .' she whispered.

'This medical service is damned inefficient,' Luke complained with mock-severity. He sat on the bedside chair and possessed himself of her other hand. 'Leaking roofs. Draughty corridors. Nurses wearing torn jeans and swearing their uniform blew out the window when I complain. A hospital kitchen with a living pot-plant wedged right through one wall. I like a bit more antiseptic and sparkle myself. A staff who say, "Yes, Doctor, no, Doctor, three bags full, Doctor."'

'You don't stand a chance in a million,' Nikki smiled. 'But. . .but, Luke. . .'

'Yes, my love?' His eyes were twisting her in two.

His eyes were making love to her all by themselves.

'You're not staying?'

Luke frowned. 'Nikki, Whispering Palms is one of the few undamaged houses in the district. You don't have any reason to leave.'

'I. . . N-no.'

'Well, there you go, then. You're staying. I'm staying.'

'Luke. . .' Nikki looked helplessly up at him. Her head was spinning in a dizzy haze of light. 'Luke, don't. . .don't say it. . .'

'Don't say it isn't true,' he finished for her. He nodded and his smile faded. His grip on her hands tightened. 'I shouldn't. But I can be happy here. There's enough medicine to keep me content, and I can keep my journalism going as well. But whether I stay depends.'

'Depends?'

'On whether one crazy, courageous, beautiful girl-woman will find it in her heart to forgive me for walking away on the most precious gift I've ever received. On whether my heart. . .my life. . .my lovely Nikki will marry me.'

Nikki drew in her breath. 'Luke. . :'

'I know I left you,' Luke said softly. 'But, Nikki, I almost went out of my mind. I thought. . .I thought family was so damned important. My masculinity was such an issue that I couldn't cope. And then. . .then I walked away and I realised you and Amy were my family already, whether you agreed to marry me or not. Because my heart is yours, Nikki Russell. For now and forever.'

Nikki took a long, shuddering breath. Tears of weakness and joy were sliding down her face and Luke swore as he bent to kiss them away.

'You don't have to say anything yet,' he told her gently. 'God, Nikki, I shouldn't be saying this. But. . . but I thought I'd lost you. And I thought there was nothing as bad as that. The cancer. Infertility. Nothing. To lose my lovely Nikki. . .' He shook his head and then kissed her lightly on the lips. 'You need to sleep. We can talk about this later.'

'Yes. . .' It was a sleepy murmur. Nikki's hand didn't relinquish her grip, and her hand was not relinquished in turn. She was where she wanted to be for the rest of her life.

'Nikki, love. . .'

'Mmm?'

'Nikki, before you sleep, can you do a wriggle for me? Test your fingers and toes.'

Nikki thought about this for a moment. It was sensible, and it didn't interfere with her euphoric happiness. She tried.

'Ouch,' she said softly.

'Where?'

'I've got full movement,' she told him sleepily. 'But my lower back feels as though it's been kicked by a horse.'

'You've got a thumping bruise there,' Luke told her. 'It looks like just bruising, but maybe I'd better take an X-ray to make sure.'

Nikki's eyes flew wide suddenly. 'Luke. . .Luke, I haven't been bleeding, have I?'

He frowned. 'No. Apart from your head.'

She closed her eyes in thankfulness. 'Thank God,' she whispered.

'Thank. . .' Luke let her hands fall and he bent forward. 'Nikki, what the hell. . .?'

She smiled faintly and her eyes opened again. This was right. There would never be a better time.

'I was just thinking maybe you shouldn't do that X-ray,' she whispered.

'Why not?' Luke's eyes were dark with anxiety.

'Because pelvic X-rays on unborn babies are contra-indicated.'

'Unborn babies.' Luke sat back hard in his chair.

'You mean. . . My God, Nikki, you're not pregnant?'

'Only a little bit.' She smiled shyly.

'Only. . .' He seized her hands again and his grip wasn't gentle. 'How far?'

'You tell me,' Nikki smiled. 'Or don't you remember?'

There was a long, long silence. Nikki watched as Luke's face twisted. His eyes closed, as though in pain.

But when they opened there was no pain. There was joy. There was love. And there was peace.

'My Nikki. . .'

He gathered her to him and held her close. Around them the insistent rain battered the roof and the wind whipped around the building searching for entry in the makeshift repairs.

Neither noticed. No storm could touch them where they were.

They had come home.

Josie Metcalfe lives in Cornwall now with her long suffering husband, four children and two horses, but as an army brat frequently on the move, books became the only friends that came with her wherever she went. Now that she writes them herself she is making new friends, and hates saying goodbye at the end of a book – but there are always more characters in her head clamouring for attention until she can't wait to tell their stories.

FOR NOW, FOR ALWAYS

by

Josie Metcalfe

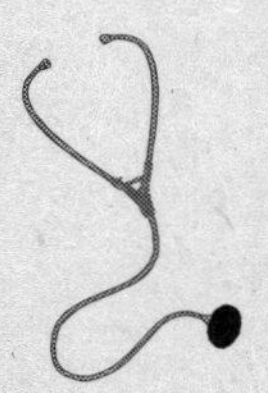

CHAPTER ONE

'WHEN will the pain end. . .?'

Leo sat down heavily on the edge of the luxurious king-sized bed and, lifting the glass to his lips, threw the contents to the back of his throat. He grimaced at the unaccustomed taste even as he welcomed the fiery bite of it sliding down.

With a rock-steady hand he poured another generous inch into the hand-cut crystal, not appreciating the quality of the glass or the brandy in his search for anaesthesia.

'Here's to you, Andreas, with my grateful thanks,' he toasted his absent friend with the beautiful glass which had accompanied the expensive brandy to his hotel room, hardly noticing the gleams struck from the facets by the last rays of the dying sun as he sent the contents swiftly after the first dose.

He reached for the jacket of his silvery grey suit, dragging it towards him across the bed with no regard for the excellence of the tailoring.

'Where is it. . .?' he muttered as he fumbled one-handedly for the inside pocket to retrieve his wallet, letting the jacket drop heedlessly to the floor between his feet as he flipped the dark leather open to slide out a small photograph.

A sad smile barely lifted the corners of his mouth and came nowhere near his steely grey eyes.

'Happy birthday, Nico,' he whispered as he traced

the smiling face with a trembling finger and a solitary tear slid down his cheek.

Maria couldn't remember when she'd ever felt this tired. Not even during the nightmare years of her training had a week piled on the agony like this.

The taxi lurched round the corner, almost seeming to tilt onto two wheels before the driver began weaving in and out of the other traffic again, the oncoming headlights glaring into eyes already sore from lack of sleep and at least one bout of weeping.

As her purse slid off her lap and on to the floor, Maria grabbed for the door-handle just in time to prevent herself joining it.

'Please, God,' she murmured through gritted teeth, nearly at the end of her tether. How she was supposed to be able to concentrate in the morning if she didn't get to the hotel soon, she didn't know, but there was no way she could have made the right flight; no way that she could have left any earlier when Cara had needed her there. . .

As they finally drew up outside the entrance to the hotel she surreptitiously crossed her fingers that her room would still be available in spite of her late arrival.

She dredged up a tired smile for the rather flustered-looking elderly man behind the desk, knowing that she looked less than her best. Her skin felt sticky and shiny and she could tell that her dark hair had begun to straggle untidily down the back of her neck.

'Good evening.' She deposited her suitcase gratefully at her feet. 'My name is Maria Martinez. I'm terribly sorry I'm so late but. . .'

'*Scusi, Signorina. Non parla inglese.*' He was

shaking his head dolefully, his large dark eyes making him look almost like one of those toy dogs she sometimes saw in the back windows of cars.

'And I don't speak Italian...' For a moment Maria was astounded that a hotel of this size would have staff on Reception who couldn't speak English and then she dragged her concentration back to her predicament. Her shoulders slumped as she tried to cudgel her tired brain into life.

It took several minutes of pantomime and the comparison of the name in her passport with the list of reservations he held at the counter before the penny seemed to drop and he let loose with a barrage of Italian that hit her aching head like bullets from a machine-gun.

The only sense she could make of it all was that the room she had booked was no longer available but, if she didn't mind, there was another one she could have elsewhere in the hotel.

At least that was what she hoped he was saying.

When he seemed to be trying to tell her that there was some problem with this other room, too, she hastily held both hands up as she shook her head.

'No problem. No problem,' she assured him, too tired to try to work out what he was saying and too tired to care, even if he was offering her the broom cupboard. All she needed was somewhere to sleep before she fell down where she stood.

'*Grazie*.' She murmured the sum total of her Italian vocabulary as she hastily scribbled her name in the register and prepared to follow him to the lift.

When she finally managed to shut the door on his voluble attempts at a further explanation Maria slumped back against its welcome support and blearily tried to focus.

'Wow,' she breathed, her tired eyes widening in disbelief as she surveyed her sumptuous surroundings. 'Talk about luxury. . .' Her gaze slid from the mouldings on the ceiling, highlighted by the subtle positioning of the peach-shaded lamps, to the acres of thick cream carpet.

The bed itself must have been nearly the size of her whole flat back in England and just the sight of the mountain of soft peach-coloured pillows was enough to make her yawn.

She deposited her solitary suitcase on the ornate stand at the foot of the bed and flipped the lid open to retrieve her washing kit, stumbling as she kicked off her shoes on the way to the bathroom.

With a mental apology to her foster-mother for the untidy pile of clothing she dumped beside the shower she climbed under the soothing stream. For several minutes she allowed the warm water to pound the stiffness out of her neck and shoulders before she shampooed her long hair with practised ease and rinsed her body off.

She didn't have the energy to do much more than towel-dry the dark mass and run a wide-toothed comb through it, even though she knew that she was encouraging it to revert to its natural wild curliness.

A quick glance confirmed the fact that she'd forgotten to bring her nightdress to the bathroom with her but she couldn't focus her concentration enough to worry about it.

'The hotel's warm enough for me not to catch a cold and I'll sort my hair out properly in the morning,' she mumbled around her toothbrush.

Within seconds she was reaching out to turn off the light as she opened the door to her room.

'Oh.' She paused in the darkness, her hand searching for the light switch while she strained her eyes to get her bearings. 'I don't remember turning the lights out. . .'

Catching sight of the corner of the bed in the gloom, she gave up her quest for the switch and padded silently across the velvety soft carpet.

The covers appeared to have been turned back in her absence and she felt a momentary pang of guilt for the poor maid who'd had to stay on duty so late before she slid bonelessly under the covers.

Maria just had enough time to be grateful that her exhaustion would enable her to sleep in spite of the events of the day before the world faded into oblivion.

She must have been sleeping very deeply because the dream slid so gently into her mind that she wasn't aware of the beginning. . .

She knew that she felt warm and comfortable, the way she had the first day she'd met her new foster-mother and had been swept up against Anna Martinez's pillowy bosom in a loving hug. She'd been seven years old and it had been the first time that she'd ever remembered anyone wanting to hold her. . .

This dream was different because she wasn't wearing the slightly dingy pink dress which was all the orphanage could find to fit her tall thin body. This time she wasn't wearing any clothes at all but instead of feeling cold she felt warm. . .as warm as if she was curled up in front of a fire with the flickering fingers of firelight playing over her shoulders and arms and warming her breasts.

'Mmm,' she murmured her approval as she stretched out and arched as languidly as a basking cat to allow the heat to play over the rest of her body. 'Nice. . .'

The fire was getting hotter, even seeming to reach inside her, spreading, growing fiercer and wilder until her whole body turned to searing liquid—like molten lava consuming everything in its path as the volcano erupted.

Maria drifted in strange peace after the explosion, for the first time feeling totally content and without a trace of the lingering loneliness which had always permeated her life.

'Thank you.'

The sound of the husky voice in her ear was enough to drag her out of her drowsy lethargy and back to full consciousness in a hurry. Every muscle tensed in terror, her horrified eyes flying wide open to stare blindly into the darkness trying to see the owner of that voice—trying to see whose body was pinning hers to the bed.

This *wasn't* just a dream brought on by exhaustion; this was really happening to her. There was a man in her bed and she had no idea who he was or what he was doing there. . .

'Oh, God, thank you. . .'

Her frantic thoughts scattered as his husky heartfelt words were followed by the gentle touch of his lips tracing the outline of her features with the delicacy of butterfly wings.

'You'll never know how much this means to me.' There was such agony in his deep voice that Maria paused even as she braced her fists against the powerful male body looming over her in the darkness, the frantic scream trapped in her paralysed throat.

'Sometimes it feels as if the pain will go on for ever. . .as if I'll never escape the memories. . .' His husky voice broke on that desolate note, the spicy heaviness of expensive brandy on his breath playing over her face as she felt his fingers spear through her hair and fan it out across the pillow.

'So silky,' he whispered in a wondering tone. 'So healthy and full of life. . .' His hands traced the shape of her head, his fingertips hesitantly outlining the curves of her eyebrows and cheek-bones before he slanted his mouth over hers in a kiss of such stunning sensuality that Maria was mesmerised, hardly able to remember why she had been prepared to fight him.

All she knew was that in his words, in the very tone of his voice, she had heard all the agony of emptiness and loneliness that she felt inside.

In the end the only thing that counted was that he shared the same pain as she did. It didn't seem to matter that she was going against a lifetime's convictions—all she wanted to do was comfort him and draw consolation in return.

Instinctively she uncurled her hands to run her fingers through his curls and over the warm, smooth skin of his chest and up around his neck, exploring the warmth and strength of the powerful muscles and the heavy silk of his thick hair.

Her tentative response drew an answering groan from deep in his throat. Convulsively his powerful arms wrapped around her and she delighted in the physical contact after the emptiness of this awful day.

Fleetingly she remembered the situation that she'd dragged herself away from back in England.

It had been little comfort to the grieving parents to

know that everyone had done their best for their beautiful daughter. Maria knew, intellectually, that it was true. But she also knew that it was her emotional response to losing a favourite patient that was turning her inside out; that, in spite of everything she'd been able to do for Cara, her frail body hadn't been able to take any more.

Despite all their antibiotic armoury Cara hadn't had the reserves to fight off that last overwhelming infection. . .

'Sometimes it seems as if death always wins. . .' she whispered through an aching throat as she wrapped empty arms around him and relished the comfort of a warm male body against hers, strong and full of life.

'Not always,' he vowed. There was desperation in his tone as he gathered her tightly against himself. 'Sometimes life is too compelling to deny. . .'

This time Maria knew where the searing heat was coming from; knew that the touch of his hands and his body on hers were an undeniable primitive force—an affirmation of the triumph of life over death which turned her to liquid fire until all she could do was hold him tight as the world exploded around them.

'I've overslept!'

Maria sat bolt upright in the middle of the bed, her heart pounding furiously as she tried to sort out her frantic thoughts.

She was in Italy to take part in a conference and if she didn't get moving she'd be late for the presentation of the first paper.

She'd swung her feet over the side of the bed and taken several steps towards the *en suite* bathroom before the subtle aches in her hips and thighs brought the memories of what had taken place last night flooding over her.

She stopped in her tracks as if she'd hit a brick wall and swung round to stare back at the bed.

'Oh, my God!' Her hands came up to cover her horrified mouth as she took in the rumpled state of the bedclothes.

The fact that half of the sheets were hanging off the side of the bed could have been put down to a bad night's sleep but the imprint of a second head on the pale blue pillows was something that she couldn't ignore.

'Who. . .? Where. . .?' Her eyes feverishly examined every corner of the room and her brain didn't know which question it wanted answered first.

This wasn't her room.

She gazed at the pale, mossy-green carpet and the blue draperies accenting the room. The décor was just as opulent but the colour scheme was totally different.

Her heart was racing unevenly as she searched for some evidence of what had happened during the night. She *knew* that it had happened; knew that she had contributed to the disarray of that luxurious bed with a man she'd never seen.

There was no time to check around the room but, as far as she could see, he didn't seem to have left anything behind. There was certainly no note and not a trace of his belongings—nothing to suggest who he had been or where he had gone.

Heat seared her cheeks as she realised that in the dark of the night she had shared the most intimate of delights with a stranger and she wouldn't even recognise him if he stood in front of her.

The sound of a car horn somewhere outside the hotel window brought her back to her present concerns as she glanced at her watch.

'Oh, no!' she wailed as she dived towards the bathroom. 'Five minutes to go. . .'

Her shower was so swift that the water hardly had time to land on her body before she was switching it off. There wasn't time to do anything with her hair except drag a comb through it and subdue it at the back of her neck with an ornate clasp and she had the feeling that her face would never need blusher again. . .

This time she took note of the fact that there were two doors leading into the bathroom and left by the one which took her back to the peaches-and-cream room she remembered from last night and the familiar suitcase waiting at the foot of the pristine bed.

'Where have you been?' Lena Harper hissed when Maria finally slid into the empty seat beside her. 'You've missed the first session completely.'

'I can't have!' Maria muttered to her colleague as she checked her watch. 'I'm only ten minutes late.'

'Add an hour,' she was advised wryly. 'You forgot to change your watch.'

Maria groaned and rectified her mistake immediately.

'What did I miss?' she demanded under her breath while she tried simultaneously to listen to the venerable gentleman who was reading an introduction to a slide presentation. 'What did he cover in the first session?'

'Not him. It was Leo da Cruz. Thalassaemia,' her friend supplied cryptically.

'Damn,' she swore under her breath as she realised that she had missed one of the key presentations she had wanted to attend. 'Was he good? Did you manage to get any notes?'

'Superb in a very intense kind of way. He's very much into early diagnosis and counselling. . .' There was a brief delay as the lights were dimmed and Lena took advantage of it to flick back several pages in her spiral-bound notepad to show Maria the notes she'd taken. 'I'll let you have what I've got at the next break.'

The first slide flicked up onto the giant screen at the front of the specially appointed conference room and as the professor began to point out the salient features Lena and Maria turned their attention towards the purpose of their attendance.

By the time they joined the stream of people making their way towards the dining-room they were deep in a discussion of what they'd seen, hardly noticing the press of bodies around them as they reached for trays and filled them with food from the selection available.

Maria was halfway through her meal before she had the uncanny feeling that someone was staring at her. The fine hairs at the back of her neck began to prickle as they stood on end in the classic warning of danger.

'Do you know any of the other delegates?' Lena broke into Maria's distracted thoughts.

'Apart from the names of some of the people presenting papers, I don't think so,' she frowned quizzically, her fork halfway to her mouth. 'Why?'

'Are you certain? Only Leo da Cruz has been watching you ever since he sat down.'

'Has he?' Maria blinked. 'Which one is he? Perhaps he's miffed that I missed his lecture this morning.' She allowed her eyes to scan the section of the dining-room she could see but didn't immediately recognise anyone.

Suddenly her gaze was caught by a pair of steely grey eyes set under frowning dark brows. A strange shiver slid its way along her spine, lifting all the hairs to attention as she was trapped by their intensity, almost unable to drag herself away.

'Do you know him?' Lena's voice broke into the frozen tableau and the spell was broken.

'Who?' Maria's brain seemed to be moving at half-speed.

'Leo da Cruz,' Lena repeated in an exasperated tone as though she was talking to a particularly dim-witted child.

'Which one is he?' She gratefully seized the opportunity to look around the rest of the room, careful not to let her eyes meet a certain pair of steely grey lasers.

'Obviously you don't know who he is or you'd know that Leo's the gorgeous one with the dark curly hair,' Lena teased as she nodded towards the very table that Maria had been carefully avoiding looking at.

'H-he was the first speaker this morning?' She was certain that Lena would see through her pathetic attempt at nonchalance, especially as she had no idea why she was reacting in this way. It wasn't as if she was totally unfamiliar with the fact that men found her attractive and she could hardly have gone through all her years of medical training without learning how to cope with the occasional brush with male appreciation.

. . . Except, somehow, *his* interest didn't seem quite like appreciation. Maria was strangely aware that in spite of the fact that he appeared to be observing her like a cat watching a mouse he didn't seem to be regarding her as juicy prey.

There was more than a hint of disapproval in his attitude towards her and she wondered if Lena had any idea why.

'Lena. . .?'

'Are you sure you haven't met him?' the older woman interrupted as she murmured out of the corner of her mouth, a familiar matchmaking gleam in her dark eyes. 'He certainly seems to be interested in you.'

'Lena!' She felt the heat rise in her cheeks as she prayed that her friend's voice hadn't carried as far as the other table. 'It's all very well joking like that back on our own turf but you could end up embarrassing everyone if we're overheard here! What if he's a married man? You could start all sorts of rumours with comments like that.'

'He's not married; he hasn't been tamed yet,' Lena continued incorrigibly. 'You mark my words. You'd better be ready because he'll make a move on you before the conference is over.'

Maria wasn't certain whether the sudden leap in her pulse was as a result of anticipation or trepidation at the thought of being confronted at close quarters by a man with such a powerful presence. Lena was certainly right about the fact that he didn't look tame. . .

What if he was the man in the room next door? The thought flashed through her brain like a lightning strike as her eyes fixed helplessly on his handsome face.

She felt the colour leave her face as she frantically traced his features one by one. Was that the thick silky hair that she'd run her fingers through? Were they the cheek-bones she'd explored—the lips she'd kissed?

Was that the powerful body that she'd held in her arms and allowed—no, actively *encouraged*—to perform intimacies that she'd never known before?

'I'm sorry,' she gasped as she stumbled to her feet. She couldn't bear to stay under his stern grey gaze for another minute, especially when there was a chance that he might be the one who. . . 'I. . .I left something in my room. I'll see you in a minute. . .' and she fled from the dining-room, desperate to get to the suite.

The lifts were all occupied when she reached them but she couldn't face waiting in the small group. The emotions inside her were so strong that she felt that the whole world must be able to read them on her face.

Until she had herself under control again she needed to be alone so she whirled towards the stairs and sped swiftly up the first flight until she was out of sight at last.

For a second she thought she could hear an echo of the deep voice she'd heard in the dark of the night but she shook her head violently and started up the next flight of stairs, concentrating on putting one foot in front of the other until she was finally able to shut her door behind her.

There was a fatal fascination in the way her eyes were drawn towards the connecting bathroom and she was powerless to prevent her feet taking her in that direction.

Would the room on the other side still be as empty as it had been when she'd left it this morning or would *he* be there? Perhaps, this time, the door would be locked so that she would never find out who the mysterious stranger was. . .

She hesitated in the quiet coolness of the bathroom,

her hand hovering fearfully over the doorhandle for several long seconds before she silently turned it.

The door swung easily on well-oiled hinges and the sight that met her eyes made Maria draw in a sharp breath.

The room was pristine. Everything looked as fresh and clean as if it was new—as if it had never been used at all, never mind as recently as last night.

She was shaking her head as she slowly backed out of the bathroom, pulling the door shut again and turning the key.

She knew, now, that there was no point in trespassing any further into the other room. If there had been any evidence to point to the identity of the man who had slept there last night the very efficient chambermaid would have removed it while Maria had been attending the conference.

Suddenly the enormity of the situation hit her as she realised for the first time the possible long-term consequences of what had taken place.

Her legs were trembling as she sank down onto the edge of the bed that she should have occupied alone last night and she clasped her hands together tightly on her lap to still the nervous fidgeting of her fingers.

As she'd never had the time nor the inclination to indulge in any form of promiscuity she'd never needed to worry about such things as contraception or 'safe' times. Now, with the speed of a bullet, her armour had been shattered and she was left trying to remember whether, in the heat of unexpected passion, her lover had thought to take any precautions of any sort.

Her lover. . .

Maria's shudder was partly due to the unwilling

arousal that her memories brought with them and partly the result of self-disgust that she could have behaved in such a thoughtless way. She knew better than to take stupid risks with her precious health. . .

Think. . .! She sank her teeth into her bottom lip as she tried to cudgel her brain into action.

The most important thing was to find out the name of the man who had shared the other half of this very luxurious suite last night. Without his name she had no way of asking those vital questions.

Unfortunately she also needed to find a way to make her enquiries without anyone knowing why she wanted the information. In spite of the more relaxed attitude towards doctors' private lives, if so much as a hint of what had happened last night became public knowledge it could still have disastrous repercussions on her professional reputation.

Maria waited impatiently until the rest of the delegates were all on their way towards the conference suite before she approached the reception desk. She was dreading the difficult task she would have in making herself understood if the day staff were as ignorant of English as the elderly man had been last night.

'May I help you, madam?' The young man at the desk smiled whitely as he pronounced the attractively accented words and she breathed a sigh of relief.

'I wonder. . . Could you tell me who is occupying the other half of the suite I'm in? They seem to have left some things in the bathroom and. . .' She bit her tongue as it threatened to run away with her. She never had been able to look someone in the face and tell a lie.

'And your name, madam?' He turned towards the hotel register.

'Martinez. Maria Martinez. I've come here for the conference. . .'

'Ah, yes. You're in room number. . . No. . .' His eyebrows drew together as he bent forward to decipher the writing.

'I arrived late last night,' Maria volunteered helpfully. 'There was an older gentleman at the desk but I'm afraid I don't speak any Italian and I couldn't understand what he was saying. . .'

'My father,' the young man smiled widely. 'He came in to sit at the desk while I took my wife to hospital. We had a baby boy last night.' There was immense pride in the pronouncement and Maria couldn't help congratulating him on their good fortune.

'As for your room—' he finally remembered the reason for their conversation '—my father has written the new number of your room against your name but there is no one occupying the other half of the suite.'

'Not today,' Maria agreed. 'But last night there was a man. . .someone who left some things in the bathroom. . .' It was so frustrating having to think carefully about every word in case she gave any hint of what had happened.

'There is no record of anyone being in that room for the last couple of days, madam,' he said soothingly. 'If the room is going to be empty for a while now I'll get the chambermaid to check the bathroom and remove anything which shouldn't be there.' He smiled again, his teeth very white in his darkly tanned face. 'I'm sorry if you've been inconvenienced.'

'But. . .' Maria realised that there was no point in

pursuing it any further. 'There's no urgency,' she smiled wanly. 'Tomorrow morning when she comes to clean the room will be soon enough.'

In spite of the importance of the conference Maria was unable to concentrate properly for the rest of her stay, every fibre strained by the tension that filled her.

It seemed as if every few minutes her mind would return to the well-worn groove as she tried to solve the problem of finding out who the stranger was.

It seemed impossible.

She wasn't even able to take any pleasure in the fact that Lena's prediction had come to nothing.

'Well,' her motherly colleague was still trying to justify herself as they boarded their return flight together. 'I still say he would have approached you if he hadn't had to leave the conference early.'

Maria laughed. She'd been so concerned with her failure to find out the identity of her mystery man that she'd almost forgotten Lena's words.

She made a joking reply as she settled back in her seat ready for take-off but was surprised to feel a lingering disappointment that she hadn't had a chance to meet the elusive Leo da Cruz.

In the last few years he had become something of an authority on the diagnosis and treatment of inherited haematological diseases and it would be at least another year before she could reasonably expect to hear him speak at such a conference again.

The thought of next year's events stopped her thoughts in their tracks. Who knew where she would be by then or what she would be doing? It would all depend on what happened in the next few weeks.

CHAPTER TWO

'MARIA!'

The sharp concern in the voice was the only thing which helped her to hang on to consciousness as she gripped the edge of the desk, a piece of paper crackling against her clammy palm.

'I've got you.' The words coincided with an arm wrapped around her shoulders. 'You can let go now.'

Maria concentrated on releasing her fierce grasp on the desk and sank gratefully onto the chair which nudged the backs of her legs. She didn't think her shaky legs could have held her up much longer.

'Don't tell me this damn flu has got you, too.' Peg Mulholland's voice surrounded her as she sat with her eyes tightly closed. 'You look dreadfully white. I think you'd be better off at home.'

'No,' Maria whispered when she realised that shaking her head only made the ache worse. 'Ian Stanton didn't make it in last night so I ended up working straight through and then. . .' She stopped abruptly as her hand tightened convulsively around the piece of paper and she felt the cold sweat beading her forehead.

'Well, you're in no fit state to stay here,' Peg said decisively, the caring side of her nature showing through.

Maria heard the familiar sound of the buttons on the telephone then listened while her friend organised for a taxi to be ready for her in fifteen minutes.

It wouldn't have been so bad if it had been a quiet night. She could have coped if she'd been able to snatch a few hours' sleep just to recharge her batteries but there'd been no time for that.

Within hours of each other there had been an admission from a car crash to set up on traction after Orthopaedics had finished patching him up and drips and analgesia to regulate in the sterile side ward for two young burns victims from a house fire.

She'd never managed to work out why it always seemed to take ten times longer to get everything organised at night when they were trying not to disturb the rest of the patients already on the ward.

Then, when she finally thought she could curl up and close her eyes, one of her special patients had spiked a temperature during a blood transfusion and she'd spent several hours sitting beside her bed to keep her company while her mother snatched some sleep.

'Are you feeling faint?' Peg's voice demanded. 'If it's safe to leave you I'll get your things and the porter can bring you a wheelchair.'

'No.' Maria's voice sounded rusty as she forced the sound through her dry throat. 'I'll be all right in the lift.' She pushed herself up in the chair, straightening her shoulders and lifting heavy lids. There was nothing to be gained by giving in to the overwhelming load that had landed on her shoulders. The only thing she could do was what she had *always* done—grit her teeth and keep going.

'You look as if a puff of wind would blow you away,' Peg frowned. 'Are you sure it isn't this bug?'

'I'm sure,' Maria smiled wanly. 'I'll go straight to bed when I get home and sleep the clock round. I'll be better by the morning.' She couldn't meet Peg's eyes, certain that a ward sister with her experience would be able to tell that her near collapse had been caused by something far worse than mere tiredness. Would she be able to detect the guilt and shock which Maria was sure must be written across her face?

'Well, you'd better not come anywhere near my ward if you aren't in better shape tomorrow,' Peg warned sternly. 'I can't have you giving things to my patients.'

'It isn't anything contagious.' Maria was seized with the desire to laugh wildly at the thought then felt the ominous prickle of tears building up behind her eyes. 'I'm sorry to leave everyone in the lurch like this. Can I get you to notify the appropriate administrators?'

'Of course you can,' Peg agreed briskly. 'You just concentrate on taking yourself out of here and getting some sleep.'

Maria slumped back in the corner of the lift and closed her eyes, mentally counting the floors as she waited for the quiet ping which would tell her that she'd arrived at the ground floor.

She was only halfway there when the lift slid to a halt and the doors swished open to admit someone else into her quiet space. The best way she'd found to discourage conversation was to avoid making eye contact so she kept her eyes tightly closed and waited for the journey down to continue.

'Are you all right?' a deep voice demanded and for several seconds Maria's heart seemed to stop beating, all the tiny hairs on the back of her neck shivering to attention. Slowly she raised her eyelids, unwilling to believe what she was hearing. It had been over three months since she'd last heard that voice but it had haunted her mercilessly.

After all her efforts at tracking him down had failed in Italy she had believed that she would never know who he was. It was impossible that he should suddenly step into the same lift. . .and on today of all days.

'You!' she breathed as her eyes finally focused on the tall dark-haired man in front of her. 'Dr da Cruz.'

She'd never been able to forget those steely grey eyes boring into her that day at the hotel but she'd never dreamed that they belonged to the tortured soul she'd held in the night.

'Dr Martinez,' he nodded curtly. 'Is there somewhere we can talk?'

'Talk?' Maria echoed weakly.

'Are you on your way to the staff canteen? Perhaps I could get you something to eat.' There was a frown on his face as his glance slid over her as though he disapproved of the weight she had lost in the last three months.

'No, I'm not. . . I mean. . .' Her stammered reply was halted by the final jerk as the lift arrived on the ground floor.

'Come,' he ordered as he grasped her elbow firmly in one lean hand and drew her out of the path of the people trying to enter the small space, leading her towards the cafeteria which the hospital provided for visitors.

'I'm on my way home,' Maria objected as she tried to pull her arm out of his grasp. 'I've got a taxi waiting for me outside.'

'So much the better,' he pronounced as he altered

direction and marched her towards the entrance doors. 'We can share the taxi.'

'I. . . But. . . You. . .' Maria spluttered in his wake but she might as well have saved her breath for all the notice he took.

It wasn't until he released her to open the door that she was able to stand her ground.

'We can't share the taxi,' she said fiercely, all too aware of the interested gaze of a group of staff leaving the hospital at the end of their shift. She knew just how quickly gossip could spread in their enclosed world. 'Everyone will think that I've invited you to come home with me.'

'We shared more than a taxi in Italy,' he growled in a low voice as he leant towards her. 'The least you can do is allow me to apologise for. . .for what happened.'

To Maria's astonishment she saw a tide of dusky red wash over the lean planes of his cheeks and she was certain that she was witnessing a rare occurrence.

'Please?' his dark lashes lifted suddenly and she was speared by the brilliance of his gaze. 'I need to speak to you. To explain.'

She hesitated only briefly before she nodded her agreement and ducked inside the waiting vehicle, sliding all the way across the seat to leave a space between them when he joined her. Even in her exhausted state she was aware of the electric current which seemed to pulse between them and she knew that it was imperative that she kept a clear head. Too much depended on it.

'Alma Road,' he directed the cabbie and Maria drew in a sharp breath.

'How did you know where I live?' she demanded, an uncomfortable feeling settling in the pit of her stomach.

'I asked your colleague, Lena Harper,' he said with a reminiscent frown. 'She seemed only too willing to tell me—as if she'd been expecting me to ask.'

The words were almost an accusation and Maria subsided into a guilty silence.

Now it was her turn to feel the heat build in her cheeks as she remembered Lena's knowing looks and her prediction that the good-looking doctor was interested in her.

The fact that she wasn't speaking didn't mean that her brain wasn't working. Questions were multiplying in her head faster than the flu virus currently decimating her colleagues but before she could sort them out into any kind of coherent order the taxi was drawing up in front of the house where she rented the ground-floor flat.

'Have you got your key?' He paused with one foot on the doorstep and held out his hand.

'I'm perfectly capable of opening my own door, thank you.' Maria fixed him with a steady gaze, the key held tightly in her hand. She had the instinctive feeling that the next few minutes were going to be very uncomfortable and she needed to feel that she had some measure of control over the situation.

With a brief nod he conceded and stepped aside to allow her to reach the door and followed her into the flat.

'Would you like a drink?' Maria walked straight through towards her compact kitchen, desperate to have something to occupy her hands. She'd always thought that the hallway of her little domain was pleasantly spacious but as soon as she closed the front door she had the impression that there wasn't enough air to breathe.

At a shade under six feet and with a slim, agile build, it wasn't the size of her visitor that made the space seem crowded; it was the powerful presence of a man driven by silent demons which was making her flee.

'I've got tea or coffee,' she called over her shoulder. 'I don't think there's anything stronger—I only have brandy in at Christmas. . .' She bit her tongue but it was too late. The memory of the taste of brandy in his kisses must have been so close to the surface of her mind that the words came out by themselves.

'Coffee will be fine, thank you.' He paused, then added quietly, 'I very rarely drink alcohol.'

The flat tone of his voice drew her eyes towards him in time to see his mouth twist in a grimace of self-disgust. 'I don't suppose that's something you find easy to believe after our last encounter.'

Maria was silent while she finished placing their cups on a tray but her mind was busy. Finally she turned to face him, her chin raised just a little higher than usual.

'Actually, I would find it very easy to believe,' she said as she met his combative gaze calmly. 'I think you were under a great strain for some reason and had a little more brandy than you should. If I hadn't come into your room by mistake you'd have slept it off with little more than a hangover to show for it.'

She turned away and drew in a shaky breath before she picked up the tray and led the way through to her tiny lounge.

As she settled herself in her favourite armchair she had time to marvel at the resilience of the human body. An hour ago she had been so tired that she was close to collapsing. A hefty shot of adrenaline in the shape of Dr da Cruz and she was even alert enough to cross swords with him.

'Thank you for your generosity.' The deep voice interrupted her musing as he lowered himself onto one end of the settee and reached for his cup. 'Not many women would be so calm about what happened.'

Maria hoped that her shrug conveyed nonchalance. There was no way she was letting him know how desperately she had wanted to find out who he was and how frustrating it had been not to be able to find out.

First she had been blocked by the hotel manager's insistence that the room had been unoccupied and then there had been her concern that she would only be drawing attention to what had happened if she'd asked him to check further. . .

'Tell me,' he began, 'why didn't you say anything when you saw me the next day?'

'Because I didn't know who you were,' she replied, puzzled by his question.

'Do you mean to tell me you were waiting for a formal introduction?' His laugh was incredulous.

'No,' she drew in a calming breath, 'I mean, I had no idea who you were.'

'Your friend knew,' he pointed out. 'I heard her tell you my name.'

'But she didn't know what had happened the night before and I didn't know that you were the person in the other room.' Her patience was becoming a little frayed. She wasn't accustomed to having her word doubted. 'I did try to find out who it was but the hotel didn't seem to have any record of anyone being booked there that night.'

His steely grey eyes travelled over her face as though

he could see inside her head, and she didn't like the vulnerable feeling that his intensity caused.

'Is it my turn to ask a question?' She relinquished her cup and wove her fingers together on her lap as she turned the spotlight on him. 'If you knew who I was, why didn't *you* say something the next day?'

'Because. . .' He hesitated, his dark eyelashes sweeping down to hide his eyes from her for a moment before he continued, almost belligerently, 'Because I thought you'd been paid to come to my bed.'

'What. . .?' For several seconds Maria couldn't breathe with the shock of his words. She could feel the colour draining from her face and her eyes grew impossibly wide. 'How *dare* you suggest such a thing about me? I'm not a. . .I would never. . .'

'Please!' His own cup clattered as he hurriedly deposited it on the tray. 'I *know* it isn't true now.'

'What do you mean? ''Now''?' Indignation made her voice rise. 'It's *never* been true.'

'But I only found out a few days ago when I caught up with Andreas.'

'And who's Andreas? Your pimp?' She poured scorn into the word as the acid of betrayal ate away at her. How dared he think that she would stoop to such a thing? She was no prostitute—to be paid for her favours. . .

'He's the friend who supplied me with the brandy that night.' He hurried into speech as though he knew what course her thoughts were taking. 'Then, when I turned over in the middle of the night and I found you next to me in the bed, I thought he'd arranged that, too. Look—' he sat forward on the edge of the settee '—as soon as I found out that I'd completely misread the situation I set out to track you down.'

'Why?' Maria was deliberately blunt. 'If you didn't think it important enough to speak to me the next morning why bother to look me up now?'

'Firstly because I wanted to apologise.' He was strangely vulnerable in his embarrassment, unable to meet her eyes. 'As you've gathered, I'd had too much to drink and I know I don't hold alcohol well. I was afraid. . .I didn't know how. . .forceful. . .I was. I doubt that I was capable of much finesse. . .' His words died away as he gazed down at his hands linked together between his knees, the colour darkening over the tanned skin of his cheek-bones.

No finesse? Maria could have laughed aloud. Even on a bad performance it seemed that this man could exceed all her wildest fantasies about sex. . . And he'd been worried about it. . .

'No,' she murmured, her own cheeks flaming at her vivid memories of the pleasure he had brought her. 'You weren't too forceful.'

'I'm glad,' he said softly. 'I would have hated for you to think that I didn't appreciate. . .'

'Please!' If her face grew any hotter she would burst into flames. 'You said there was another reason why you came. . .'

'I just wanted to reassure you that you didn't have to worry that you might have caught anything from me.' There was a gravelly tone to his voice. 'I hadn't been with a woman since. . .for a couple of years so you were quite safe.'

There was a grim irony to his words and for a moment Maria contemplated asking him to explain. But that would imply that she was willing to tell him her own secrets and she couldn't face that yet. The realisation was too new—too fresh to reveal to someone who was, after all, little more than a stranger.

Suddenly her tiredness returned with full force and her eyelids felt weighted with lead. With her brain function slowed to near zero, she knew that she wasn't fit to cope with the problems that talking to him would cause. Not today.

'I'm sorry, Dr da Cruz,' she began as she dragged herself to her feet.

'Leo,' he prompted as he stood up effortlessly and offered her a helping hand. 'I'm sorry we had to have such a traumatic first meeting, especially as we're bound to be running into each other.'

'Are we?' Maria blinked owlishly.

'Specialising in the same field, it seems inevitable.' He smiled briefly and Maria blinked again at the difference the change in expression made to his face. 'Especially,' he continued, 'over the next year or two while I'm based just a few miles down the road. . .'

With those innocent-sounding words he'd delivered a bombshell.

Maria's pulse began thudding uncomfortably at the base of her throat as she contemplated the difficulties which could arise if she kept bumping into Dr da Cruz—Leo—for the next couple of years. There was no way that she could avoid seeing him—not if she wanted to take advantage of his expertise in their special field. Her shoulders slumped as she caught a glimpse of the scale of the problems ahead of her.

'I'm sorry, Dr. . .I mean, Leo. I'm dead on my feet; I've got to get some sleep.' She rubbed both hands over her face.

'I'll leave you in peace, then.' He led the way to her door, turning back towards her at the last moment just as she reached out to release the catch.

Suddenly they were mere inches apart, her eyes on a level with the mobile perfection of his lips as he opened his mouth to say goodbye and a strangely intimate silence grew between them.

'Maria?' The huskiness in his voice drew her eyes up to meet his. 'I'm sorry we met the way we did but I'm not sorry that we met.' She watched as his gaze flicked from her eyes to her mouth and back again and she felt the heat as clearly as if he'd touched her. Her own fingers ached to trace the features that she'd only known in darkness and she had to clench her hands into fists inside her pockets to make sure that she didn't succumb to temptation.

There was a subdued crackle as she found the piece of paper that she'd deposited in one pocket before she left the hospital and suddenly she remembered what was written on it.

She didn't know whether he expected her to say anything further but her head was so full of the knowledge of what was contained on that piece of paper that it was empty of words. She contented herself with a nod of acceptance as she finally opened to door for him.

'I'll be back in a couple of weeks,' he said as he stepped out onto the front path. 'A semi-official invitation to visit your department.'

Through the racing thoughts filling her head Maria vaguely remembered being told about the visit. At the time she had thought of it as a golden opportunity to ask the questions she'd never had a chance to in Italy but now the whole significance of that had altered, too.

'We've been looking forward to it.' She managed to dredge up a polite smile for him but the effort needed to maintain a calm front was getting greater every minute.

'I'll see you, then.' He gave a mock salute and finally set off down the road.

Maria pushed the door shut and leant back against it, her legs so rubbery that it almost felt as if she'd had the bones removed.

Slowly she took the piece of paper out and smoothed it carefully between her fingers to flatten the creases—not that she needed to read the words to know what it said. The message was burned into her brain for ever.

It had taken months for her to finally admit that there was something wrong with her since her trip to Italy but with her steady weight loss the lab result was last thing that she had expected.

'Pregnant,' she whispered, the thought still enough of a shock to set her pulse racing as she looked down at the too-slender flatness of her body. 'I'm over three months pregnant.'

'He's arrived.' Ian Stanton beamed as Maria stuffed her heavy coat in her locker. 'The whole department is in a flap. The poor nurses are just about falling over their feet trying to be helpful!'

'What on earth for?' Maria demanded crossly. 'He's only a man. It's what's inside his head that's important.'

She dragged a comb through the straggly mess the wind had made of her hair and swiftly subdued it into a tight coil at the nape of her neck. A quick glance in the mirror showed her that her pasty complexion was paler than ever. It could do with a liberal application of blusher and some lipstick to make her look as if she was at least halfway alive but she refused to take the time to do it.

'He'll only think I did it for his benefit,' she muttered under her breath, knowing, deep inside, that he would have been right.

It had been a full month since she'd last seen Leo da Cruz, his visit having been postponed twice in the interim, and she was very much aware that the time hadn't been kind to her.

She'd heard that some women sailed through pregnancy glowing with health and energy but you couldn't prove it by her. The intermittent nausea which had eventually led to the discovery of her condition hadn't gone away when she'd completed her first trimester. In fact, it seemed to have worsened. Even her dark, honey-coloured eyes seemed dull when set in a face that looked permanently grey and drained.

She compromised over her refusal to resort to cosmetics by biting her lips and pinching each of her cheeks but the effects, while they lasted, left her looking like a badly painted doll.

The only good thing about her poor health, she thought wryly as she made her way towards the paediatric ward, was the fact that she was now halfway through the pregnancy and her condition was still unnoticeable enough to be a secret between herself and her obstetrician.

As she half turned to shoulder her way through the first set of double doors she pushed her hands into the pockets of her fresh white coat so that the unbuttoned edges were drawn together as a form of camouflage.

'Good morning, Doctor.' Peg Mulholland looked up

to greet her from the bedside closest to the door as Maria closed the child-proof doors behind her. 'If you'd like to go straight through Dr da Cruz is in my office waiting for you.'

Maria raised her hand in acknowledgement, knowing that Peg would be joining them as soon as she had finished supervising the junior nurse's work.

Meanwhile she altered direction, swallowing hard and drawing in a deep, steadying breath before she entered the room.

He hadn't heard her come in and for several seconds she was able to gaze down on the closely trimmed, thick, dark curls on the head angled towards her as he concentrated on the paperwork spread out on the desk he'd appropriated.

'Good morning, Dr da Cruz,' she said quietly as she sat herself in one of the extra chairs which had been brought through for this initial meeting.

She smiled inwardly as he jumped with surprise at the unexpected sound of her voice and looked up.

'Maria?' The smile he wore when his eyes met hers faded slowly as his gaze travelled swiftly over her. 'My God, what have you done to yourself? Have you been ill?' He straightened up out of the chair so fast that it scraped noisily over the floor and rocked back onto the back legs before righting itself.

'What's happened? Have you seen a doctor? Are you fit enough to be at work?'

By the time he had finished firing questions at her he had circled the desk and had reached the other side of the room, dropping suddenly to one knee beside her so that he could look at her more closely.

Maria found the proximity almost suffocating and

couldn't stop herself leaning away from him in spite of the fact that her first impulse had been to throw herself into his arms.

'I'm fine,' she said, her voice sounding too quiet when heard through the thunder of her pulse. 'The hospital's had a particularly nasty flu bug going round. . .' She shrugged one shoulder as though that half-answer was enough to explain her pale face and limp hair and the fact that she could count her ribs in the mirror of her bathroom.

'At a guess you've been filling in for sick colleagues and then conveniently forgetting to take time off for your own recovery,' he hazarded. 'You look as if you could do with a large meal and a week's sleep.'

'I'd heard Italian men were good at sweet-talking women but I don't think that's quite what they meant,' she teased, hoping that the humour would persuade him that she was well.

'Perhaps it doesn't work when only half of you is Italian,' he returned as he straightened up again, the smile he gave her not entirely hiding his concern.

'And which half is that?' She drew in a surreptitious breath of relief that he was putting a little more space between them.

'The half that isn't Greek.' The smile was wider that time.

'So, how much of you is English?' She frowned at the mathematics.

'None of me.' He held his hands away from his sides. 'Before you you see a pure-bred Mediterranean mongrel.'

Their wary laughter was interrupted by the arrival of the rest of the group and their meeting got under way.

'. . .With co-operation between our various disciplines—' Leo was drawing the hour-long discussion to a close '—we can look forward to the time when not only are all babies routinely checked for sickle cell disorders at birth, so that parents can be informed and proper follow-up arranged, but all mothers are routinely checked for the disorders during pregnancy to pick up any who don't know that they are at risk.'

'One of the difficulties with population migrations is that many people these days don't know what their genetic inheritance is because they don't know where their ancestors came from,' one of the registrars commented. 'You can't tell just from a person's colouring whether they're from a high-risk Eastern European background with excellent spoken English or whether they're low-risk English with a taste for foreign holidays and suntans.'

There was a round of laughter but they all knew that he'd pointed out a valid problem.

'I sometimes think the American idea of having to have a blood test before you can apply for a marriage licence is a very good idea,' one of the midwives commented. 'Except, of course, not everyone waits until they're married before they start producing children.'

'In the end it all comes down to the individual,' Maria contributed. 'We can take the blood tests and tell the parents that they're both carriers of, for example, sickle cell trait and arrange counselling. If they then decide to take the one-in-four risk of having a child with the disease we can do the various tests up to the twentieth week of the pregnancy to find out if it's a sufferer.

'But, even if we find out that the child has inherited

sickle cell disorder, it's still the parents' choice if they want to continue with the pregnancy.'

The meeting broke up soon after that but her thoughts were still on Marco, her little brother who'd been born with the form of sickle cell disorder called beta thalassaemia major.

'You're looking sad.' The deep voice spoke softly beside her and Maria looked up to discover that they were the last two left in the room.

'I'm sorry. That was very rude of me.' She avoided looking at him by concentrating on closing her notepad and capping her pen. 'My mind must have wandered.'

'It didn't seem like a very happy thought. . .' His tone invited her to explain but it was something that she was wary of speaking about. She still became emotional, even after all this time.

'Just some old memories,' she said as she dredged up a smile. 'Sometimes I make the mistake of allowing the work I do to become too personal.'

'I don't think anyone can avoid it when they're working with children,' he said quietly. 'Especially something potentially lethal such as the sickle cell disorders. From the first moment of conception the child is doomed to go through years of pain and medical intervention, with some form of limitation on nearly every aspect of their lives.'

'It doesn't all have to be doom and gloom,' Maria objected. 'With the advances in early diagnosis and improved blood transfusion, and especially now that we can remove the accumulated iron, many of them can lead a nearly normal life. Many of them are going on to marry and. . .'

'*Normal*,' he scoffed, unexplained bitterness colouring his voice. 'I sometimes wonder if they would agree? If they knew that they could have been spared the unremitting pain of the condition, let alone the treatment—all the transfusions, all the injections and medicines and all the restrictions. Would they have preferred their parents to have terminated the pregnancy? Would it be fairer if they'd never been born?'

CHAPTER THREE

MARIA was very subdued during the rest of her shift.

She still managed to smile for her patients, cheering up their newest patient by drawing happy faces on the plaster casts immobilising both of her broken legs.

'Have you thought of names for them?' she queried with a serious expression.

'Names for what?' Five-year-old Jemma was mystified.

'For your casts, of course,' Maria replied as though the answer was obvious. 'You can't moan about them if you haven't given them names. How will they know which one you're telling off?'

As she continued on her way around the ward she left a more cheerful child trying out the names of her favourite television characters to see which she preferred—and a pair of very bemused parents.

'Hello, Dr Maria,' piped up a cheeky young voice from the next bed. 'I'm beating Hussein this time. Look.'

Hassan Rehman's big dark eyes beamed up at her, his hand clutching one of the controls for the computer game they were playing.

'No, you're not,' his identical twin brother denied from the next bed. 'You cheated when the nurse was checking the blood.'

Hassan and Hussein were two of her regular patients: eight-year-olds whose thalassaemia meant that they had to come in regularly each month for transfusions of washed, packed red cells to correct their anaemia.

Just a few minutes in their lively company was enough to reinforce her feelings that the life of a child with beta thalassaemia was far from the gloomy prospect that Leo had painted.

As she glanced back at the two of them on her way out of the ward she was determined that she was going to introduce them to him at some time before they were due to go home later in the afternoon.

She was just reaching out her hand for a plate of salad when a familiar sandalwood fragrance warned her that Leo was there just before he spoke.

'You'll never put weight on with that.' One lean, tanned hand reached past her for the roast meal on offer and tried to slide it onto her tray before she could put the salad there. 'This would give your system something to fight back with,' he advised.

When Maria turned to let him know that she was perfectly capable of choosing her own meals she caught a look of open concern on his face and was so surprised that the sharp words remained unspoken.

'I haven't got my appetite back yet.' She made her explanation vague, aware that his weren't the only ears which could be listening.

'Will you give it a try if I entertain you while you eat as much as you can manage? You'll never keep the pace up without cracking if you don't get a bit more meat on your bones.'

'That depends what you mean by "entertain".' She chose her words carefully for maximum effect. 'Do you sing or dance? Perhaps you tell jokes?'

'Smart alec,' he muttered in her ear as he reached

for a large glass of orange juice with one hand and her elbow with the other, escorting her across to the table where his own food waited.

'Ah!' Maria smiled, the bubble of pleasure that he was going to be eating with her lifting her spirits. 'I hadn't realised this was an invitation to dine out in style. . .!'

She managed to eat half of the meal in the time he cleared his own plate before she suddenly remembered the Rehman twins.

'Leo, have you got a few minutes free this afternoon?' She crossed her fingers surreptitiously under the edge of the table. 'Or have the powers that be managed to arrange back-to-back meetings right through?'

'Let me check.' He slid a clipboard across the table towards himself. 'Any particular time?'

'Before six o'clock this evening?' She knew the twins' parents would be coming to collect them at that time so it would be too late for her purposes.

'It looks as if I'm getting some time off for good behaviour at about five-thirty. Was it something special you wanted me to see?'

'Yes,' she smiled secretively. 'Very special. But I'm not giving you any hints.'

The rest of the afternoon flew by with a full outpatients clinic to attend and the usual mountain of paperwork to complete before she could hurry back up to the ward.

'Right on time.' His deep voice reached her as she released the child-proof catches and he followed her through the doors and into the ward.

'As you know,' Maria prefaced his visit with a brief

résumé, 'we already do a sickle cell check on every patient who comes in for surgery in case of problems with anaesthetics and cross-matching and we also check all pregnant women and their newborns.'

'And your counselling service is absolutely first-rate,' he commented approvingly. 'If only there were more like it. . .'

'We also see a number of children with the various sickle cell disorders on a regular day-care basis for blood transfusions and when they have crises and we teach their parents how to cope with setting up the drugs regimen at home. Also, with the advent of bone marrow transplants. . .'

She watched as his expression changed, the smile almost disappearing as his eyes took on the pained expression that she'd seen before.

'Leo—' she paused and reached out her hand spontaneously to touch his wrist '—I know your specialisation means that you've seen far more of the problems than I have and I know there are some cases where the children go through hell but, you must admit, they're far fewer these days. . .'

She stopped, knowing that all the words in the world wouldn't have the impact of the Rehman brothers. 'Come with me,' she invited and led the way across the ward.

'Hassan. Hussein. I would like you to meet Dr da Cruz.'

Two pairs of identical dark eyes swung away from the electronic mayhem they were creating to look up at him, their ready smiles as broad as ever.

'Hi.' It was cheeky Hassan who spoke first. 'Are you Dr Maria's boyfriend?'

'Hassan!' Hussein's horrified voice broke in before Maria could find her tongue.

'I don't know,' Leo countered, managing to sound suitably worried. 'Do you think she'd like me to ask her out?' Maria saw the sly wink he shared with the two boys, drawing attention to her rapidly pinkening cheeks. 'She's very pretty, isn't she?'

'She's *beautiful*,' Hassan corrected Leo then tilted his head to one side in a considering way. 'I don't know if she'd go out with you, though. She might not have time. She has to look after all us kids cos we're special.'

'Why are you special?' His smile told Maria that he was enjoying his encounter with these pint-sized charmers.

'Because—' Hussein took over the conversation '—we're some of her regular customers.' He rolled the syllables around on his tongue as though he enjoyed using the phrase.

'That's cos we have to have blood transfusions,' the irrepressible Hassan butted in, pointing up to the IV stands at the sides of their beds. 'We've both got beta thalassaemia.'

Maria watched as Leo's smile dimmed but there was no time for the fact to register with her charges as their parents arrived just then.

'Dr Martinez.' Mr Rehman greeted her with a smile. 'How have they behaved today? Are you desperate to get rid of them yet?' He tousled their thick dark mops of hair affectionately.

'They've been good as gold,' she confirmed. 'In fact, I've just been introducing them to Dr da Cruz who's a specialist in sickle cell diseases.' She stood back to allow them to shake hands and watched as the Rehmans' open pleasure in their sons and their continued good health worked their own special magic on Leo.

It wasn't until the nurse came to remove the IVs that Maria caught sight of the clock on the wall at the end of the ward.

'Look at the time!' she exclaimed, grabbing Leo's sleeve. 'You're supposed to be going to another meeting in a minute, aren't you?'

'And you're supposed to be going off duty,' he responded with a meaningful glance at his watch. 'It looks as if you're just as poor a timekeeper as I am and we're both going to be late.'

There was a smiling round of farewells and promises to 'see you next month' from the two boys as the family left the ward and then they were left standing together just outside the double doors.

'Well. . .' Maria clenched her hands into fists inside her pockets '. . .I suppose you'd better be on your way to your next meeting. Where is this one?'

'That rather depends on you,' Leo said quietly.

'Me?' Maria's voice came out as an undignified squeak.

'I'm hoping I can persuade you to have dinner with me.' He paused as a visitor walked past them to let herself through the double doors into the ward.

'Well, I suppose there hasn't been very much time for the two of us to discuss the ramifications of. . .'

'Maria. . .' The single word silenced her frantic babble and she bit her lip as their eyes met. 'I don't want to have a business meeting; I want to take you out for a meal.'

'Why?' The word came out as a breathy whisper as her heart caught in her throat.

'Several reasons.' He settled his shoulders against the wall as though he was prepared to stay as long as it took to persuade her, one foot nonchalantly crossing over the other. 'First, as those imps in there said, because you're a beautiful woman and, second, because I enjoy your company but mostly because we haven't had anything to eat since that cafeteria meal at lunch-time and I'm starving but I don't like to eat alone. . .'

He attempted to look pathetic but failed miserably, his eyes far too full of devilment to carry it off, and Maria couldn't help laughing.

'Well, in the face of such overwhelming logic how can I possibly refuse?' She tucked her hand in the crook of the elbow he offered, her fingers relishing the heat of his muscular arm through the fine cloth of his suit.

The warmth inside her owed little to the scant physical contact between them, being a direct result of the glow that she'd felt when he'd called her a beautiful woman. It might have been a throw-away line echoing what Hassan had said but it was something that she'd needed to hear—something every woman craves to hear from the man who has fathered her child.

Her footsteps faltered as the thought registered.

God! How could she have forgotten?

Her obstetrician had explored with her the possibility that her continued malaise during her pregnancy was due in part to the mental stress she was under. Maria had to admit that she thought he was right, her stomach tying itself in knots every time she remembered that at some stage she was going to have to tell Leo that she was carrying his child.

'Do you need to go home before we eat?' Leo's voice drew her back to the present and she was torn between running as far and as fast as she could to avoid the inevitable and getting the job over with.

'We might as well eat straight away,' she said decisively, raising her chin and squaring her shoulders as though preparing for battle. She'd never been brought up to be a coward and had no intention of starting now.

The restaurant that she directed him to was just around the corner from the hospital. She'd walked past it almost every day on her way to and from her flat and had heard from other members of staff that it was well worth a visit.

This evening, because of the unfashionably early hour, they were unlikely to encounter any colleagues who might have raised eyebrows at their apparent intimacy.

Of course, she thought as they were seated in a quiet corner in the nearly deserted room, it could be a positive boon to have the place empty if his reaction to her news was too violent.

A squadron of butterflies began formation-flying in her stomach as she tried to concentrate on making her selection from the menu.

'Need some help deciding?' Leo teased when the waiter returned to take their orders and she still hadn't chosen.

'I only want something fairly light,' she said faintly, worried that the morning sickness which had plagued her morning, noon and night might make a disastrous appearance if she had anything too rich.

'Would Madam like some melon for a starter and then perhaps chicken breasts poached in white wine sauce to follow?' The waiter's smile was nearly as wide as his waistline.

'That sounds wonderful,' Maria replied and managed to return his smile as the decision was made for her and she drew in a steadying breath while Leo ordered his own meal.

'So,' he turned his attention on her as soon as they were alone again. 'What made you decide to go into medicine? Is it a family thing?'

'I don't know,' she admitted openly, having long ago come to terms with the events of her childhood. 'I was fostered when I was seven by a wonderful couple called Anna and Luiz Martinez. Over the years they had a round dozen of us and the love they gave us just seemed to grow the more there were.' She couldn't help the warmth of the smile which took over her face at the happy memories.

'They must have been very proud of your achievement. It's a long haul to qualify as a doctor.'

'They always told us that the only thing they wanted was that we were the best we could be. Dustman or doctor didn't matter to them as long as we did the best we could.'

'Why the interest in haemoglobinopathies? Inherited disorders of haemoglobin structure aren't a particularly common specialisation.'

'Because my brother, Marco, had beta thalassaemia.'

'Had?' he questioned softly, his silvery eyes intent on hers across the candle-lit, linen-clad table.

She nodded. 'He died when he was eleven.'

'So, first you lost your parents and then your brother.' His soft voice spoke of sympathy but she couldn't allow the misapprehension to continue.

'We didn't lose our parents so much as they lost us,' she said wryly. 'When Marco was born my father had the son he always wanted. He was devastated when he found out that his precious son had beta thalassaemia and when it was confirmed that it was incurable he made my mother dump the two of us in a hospital waiting-room. Apparently they were on their way to the airport on their way back to Italy for good.'

'Couldn't the authorities do anything?' He sounded appalled.

'They did,' she smiled. 'They took us to Anna and Luiz.'

'But what about your parents? They should have taken responsibility for their own children,' he insisted.

'I think Marco and I had the best deal,' Maria said confidently. 'Feeling the way they did, our parents wouldn't have done nearly as good a job of raising us and loving us as Anna and Luiz did.' She smiled as she remembered her foster-parents' pleasure when she'd asked to be allowed to adopt their surname.

'So, what happened to Marco? Was he particularly badly affected by the disease?'

'I was too young at the time to realise the full extent of what was going on but apparently our parents tried for a long time to deny that there was anything wrong with him. By the time he reached Anna's care his whole system had been weakened by neglect, although I didn't realise the implications of what I'd seen until I began my medical training.' She looked off into the distance as she called the details to mind.

'He was severely anaemic so he had no energy; his spleen was massively enlarged so he had very little appetite; his bone-marrow was hyperactive and this had caused deformities to his skull and his long bones—virtually all the classic complications of untreated thalassaemia.'

She looked up at him and caught sight of that same haunted expression that she'd seen before.

'What about you?' she prompted before he had time to hide behind his self-protective barriers, intuition telling her that his pain went even deeper than her own. 'What made you specialise in this field?'

He was quiet for so long that Maria began to think that he wasn't going to answer.

'It's a similar story,' he said at last, his voice a low rasp as his eyes focused on the design he was tracing with the tines of his dessert fork. 'But, instead of a brother, I lost a son.'

'Oh, Leo,' she breathed, her heart going out to him in sympathy. 'Why? What happened?'

'There are so many similarities with Marco's story that it makes me feel ill,' he murmured in a deep rumble, the fork abandoned as he linked his fingers tightly together.

'No!' Maria was surprised into an instinctive denial. 'I don't believe you would ever abandon your child.' She reached out her hand and laid it over his tortured knuckles to reinforce her support but he drew his hands away and raised his eyes to meet hers.

'I might just as well have,' he said harshly. 'I was so busy being a doctor that I hardly had time to see him. He was just a little bundle asleep in bed.'

'What about your wife? Wasn't she there to look after him?'

'Just until he was six weeks old. Then she organised for someone to stay in the house with him so that she could go back to work. She told me she was only going back part-time but that was another of her lies. By the time I realised there was something wrong. . .' He shrugged helplessly.

'What about the blood tests? Why weren't they done?' Maria frowned. Something didn't seem quite right.

'They were but, as a haematologist, it was my dear wife who did them herself and didn't bother to tell me what she found.'

'But. . .'

'He had a stroke and died in my arms on his first birthday.' Leo's eyes were liquid with unshed tears as he gazed at her. 'I didn't know that I was a carrier of beta thalassaemia trait and Sophia had never bothered to tell me she was. Between us we doomed that little child to hell on earth. . .' His voice died away as his throat closed up and Maria felt her own eyes stinging in sympathy.

'Do you want to stay for dessert?' Maria murmured into the fraught silence. 'I can offer you some coffee back at my flat if you'd rather leave now.'

'Thanks.' He drew in a deep shuddering breath and nodded. 'I don't think either of us is in the right frame of mind to enjoy any more food. I'm only sorry I spoilt your meal.' He signalled to their waiter for the bill.

'You didn't spoil it.' She took a chance and covered his hand as it lay on the table, his tanned skin seeming even darker against the stark contrast of the white cloth. 'Sometimes the only time you can talk about the things that really matter is when you meet someone who's gone through similar experiences. I doubt if you've told anyone else what you've told me tonight.' She threw the words at him as a challenge and saw him blink then shake his head.

'You're quite right,' he admitted. 'My colleagues knew that my son had died but I couldn't bear to tell them any more than that. I just felt too guilty.'

He held her chair for her with innate good manners and they left the restaurant to find a thin cold rain falling.

'Let's go back in and call a taxi. It's miserable out here.' He leaned protectively over her to shelter her from the misty drizzle as he directed her back towards the door of the restaurant.

'It's not worth it,' she said impulsively. 'It's only a couple of minutes away. Let's walk.'

'Are you sure?' He turned towards her and carefully pulled the collar of her coat up around her ears to protect her from the weather, his hands coming to rest on her shoulders.

Maria nodded, glad that he wasn't able to read her mind as she admitted to herself that she was grasping at any opportunity to spend a little more time with him. Somehow she *had* to tell him her secret tonight. There was no knowing when she might have some time alone with him again.

She'd hoped that having a chance to talk to each other over a meal and learn a little about each other's lives would help her to find the perfect opportunity—would give her an idea how to go about it.

The only problem was that now she felt that she had even less idea how he'd react to her news.

All she could do was hope that, in spite of the shock, he would see that the child she was carrying could help to heal the scars of the past.

'Maria?' His voice was a low rumble in the quiet wetness of the deserted streets.

'Yes?' Tiny drops of water sparkled on her eyelashes as she angled her head to look up at him in the glow of the street-light, her arm tucked securely in the crook of his elbow as they made their way steadily through the darkness.

'Is there. . .?' He paused and she saw the droplets of rain in his dark hair strike pinpoints of diamond fire as he angled his head towards her. 'Are you seeing anyone from the hospital?'

She felt the tension in his body through her contact with his arm and wondered for one heart-stopping moment whether he had guessed why she had gone to see the obstetrician.

'Seeing anyone?' she repeated. 'What for?'

'A boyfriend, for want of a better word.' He pulled a face at the inappropriate phrase.

'Oh.' Relief that he hadn't guessed made her laugh breathlessly. 'No. As Hassan said, I don't really have time for much of a social life.'

'You must find it rather lonely—to go from the responsibility of the hospital to the quiet of your little home without anyone to talk to about what's happened during the day.'

She thought about it for a moment, playing his words over in her head and hearing his own loneliness behind them.

'I hadn't really thought of it like that before,' she admitted. 'I'm surrounded by so much hustle and bustle all day that the silence when I got home was like an oasis where I could recuperate.'

'And now?' he prompted.

'I suppose you're right about the lack of contact,' she said slowly. 'Sometimes it would be wonderful to unwind after a particularly gruelling shift by being able to talk to someone who understands what I'm talking about.'

'Would I do?'

His words hovered in the air in front of them and sheer surprise made Maria stumble over the edge of a paving slab.

Instantly Leo pulled his elbow to his side, trapping her arm against the warm security of his ribs to steady her.

'Do?' There was a quiver to her voice as she tried to keep her emotional responses under control in the face of his physical closeness and his apparent wish to be with her when she wasn't at work.

What exactly did he mean? Was he suggesting that the two of them should become 'an item', as the current phrase went, or did he just mean. . .?

'I could be the person you could talk to,' he clarified, then continued swiftly before she could answer almost as if he was afraid of hearing her reply. 'Now that I'm moving just a few miles down the road I'll be close enough to phone for a chat or for the two of us to go out for the occasional meal. We could act as a sort of safety valve for each other for when the pressure becomes unbearable.'

'A safety valve,' she repeated as her heart sank at the anti-climax. Why on earth had she leapt to the conclusion that he might be suggesting the start of a relationship between them?

'Well,' his voice sounded so calm and logical that she could have screamed, 'I know you aren't interested in a serious relationship at the moment—you're too wrapped up in your career. And I won't be making any commitments—not after my last disaster. Perhaps we could just start off with a sort of. . .friendship?'

What irony!

Maria was tempted to laugh out loud. Here she was walking arm in arm through the misty drizzle of a winter evening with the most attractive and interesting man she'd ever met and he was suggesting that they could develop some sort of friendship between them. The only trouble was that with her vivid memories of the most erotic night—the *only* erotic night—of her life there was little chance that she could ever see him as just a friend.

Still, she gave a swift sigh of regret, it was unlikely that his offer of friendship would survive the announcement that she intended to make before they parted company this evening so the whole question was all rather academic.

'No answer?' he prompted as he drew her to a halt outside her front door and she realised that her silence had stretched out too long.

'It's. . .difficult to know exactly what to say.' She found herself fumbling for words to convey her thoughts. 'After the way we met do you think it's feasible that we could start as if we'd only just met?'

He was silent for a moment, his eyes scanning her face as if he was trying to see her very thoughts and she found herself unable to look away, her own gaze locked on the planes and shadows of his enigmatic expression.

'I know what you mean,' he murmured at last, his voice sounding deeper in the hush as the rain finally stopped falling. 'I only have to hear your voice and I remember the sound of it the first time we met—your soft words in the darkness. I see you and my hands remember how unbelievably silky your skin felt against them and I want to take your clothes off to see if it feels as good as my memories tell me; to see what you look like in the light. . .'

'Leo. . .!' Suddenly her heart was in her throat, strangling any hope of speech as it beat out a frantic tattoo.

So, she wasn't the only one who remembered that night with pleasure; who remembered the soft words and softer caresses. . .

'Maria. . .' His voice was little more than a whisper as he drew her unresisting body towards him and circled her with his arms. 'I remember your kisses. . .' His lips were moving against hers as he spoke. 'After so long alone their softness brought me back to life with their sweetness and generosity.'

His palms cradled her chilled cheeks, his long fingers spearing the damp curly tendrils of hair as he tilted her face up for the full power of his kiss.

Maria melted against him, her arms circling his lean body when her legs refused to support her any longer and her hands unconsciously tracing the long muscular back she had first explored in all its naked glory so many weeks ago.

'Ah, sweetheart.' There was a trace of laughter in his voice as he tore his mouth away from hers and he captured her hands with his and she suddenly realised that she had feverishly begun to unfasten the buttons on his shirt.

When had she become so desperate to feel the supple heat of his body? She didn't know. All she did know was that she was standing on her front doorstep under the glare of a nearby street light in full view of any neighbour who happened to glance out of their window, trying to take Leo's clothes off.

'Oh, my God.' She drew her hands away as fast as if they'd touched a live wire. 'I'm sorry. . .I didn't mean. . .'

'I'm not,' Leo said firmly as he recaptured her hands and drew them back to his chest, holding them over his pounding heart with his own hands. 'The only thing I'm sorry about is that we have to stop long enough to get inside the front door.'

The increasing huskiness of his voice was proof enough that he meant every word but by the time she'd rummaged in the bottom of her bag for the key and turned it in the lock Maria had begun to regain control of her senses and turned to face him in the softly lit narrow hallway.

'Leo. . . We can't just. . .' Her words were lost in the renewed passion of his kiss as soon as the door closed behind them and Maria was overwhelmed by the heat of her response.

Never had she responded this fast or this wildly to *any* man but, with Leo, he only had to kiss her; only had to *look* at her to raise her temperature to flashpoint.

It was several moments before she realised that the heat she was feeling wasn't just due to her reaction to Leo's kiss. She'd been chilled by their leisurely walk in the drizzle and the sudden transition to the warmth of her centrally heated flat was too much for the disturbed equilibrium of her system.

'Leo,' she wailed distantly as everything slipped out of focus and the world went black.

CHAPTER FOUR

MARIA swam slowly to the surface of a dark echoing well. In her ear was the deep rumble of indecipherable words, the tone one of worry as they gradually separated themselves out into speech.

'Maria? Sweetheart, what's the matter?' She felt the warmth of his hand on her forehead and his fingertips at her wrist as he checked her temperature and pulse.

The hint of a smile crept over her lips as she hazily took note of the care he was lavishing on her and then a frown pleated her forehead as she tried to work out what was going on.

'Leo?' She tried to lift her head but his hand cradled her cheek and persuaded her to lie back again.

'Stay still for a minute,' he ordered softly. 'You're still very white.' His fingers smoothed the wildly curly tendrils of hair away from her temple as she gazed up at him out of puzzled, dark honey eyes.

He must have carried her through from the hallway to lay her down on her bed—she knew that she had been in no fit condition to walk here herself. . .

'You're not taking proper care of yourself.' There was an undertone of anger in his voice but his expression was gentle as he finished unfastening her coat and helped her to slip her arms out of the sleeves. 'You shouldn't let yourself get to the stage where you pass out from exhaustion.'

'I think it was the heat,' she offered in a shaky voice,

remembering how hot the hallway had felt when she'd walked into the flat. 'It was too much of a contrast after the cold outside.'

'It's a lot warmer than this in the hospital and it didn't seem to affect you.' There was a frown pulling his dark brows together as he returned from draping her coat over the back of her chair and sat down on the side of the bed. 'And you were fine in the restaurant. . .'

He took possession of her wrist again, his keen grey eyes scanning her face as he noted the rapid tripping of her pulse, and Maria found herself unable to meet his gaze, afraid that he would be able to read her guilt over the secret she still had to tell him.

'What's going on, Maria?' He turned her back to face him with an unrelenting hand on her cheek, his eyes boring insistently into hers. 'What's the matter with you?'

She was peripherally aware that there was a strange note of fear in his voice, as if he thought that there might be something seriously wrong with her, but she dismissed the idea as fanciful as she finally found her tongue.

'Actually,' she began and had to clear the huskiness from her throat before she could continue—an awful premonition of disaster suddenly seizing her.

'Leo, there's something I should have told you. Something that happened. . .that's happening. . . It doesn't mean that I'll expect you to do anything. . .that I want you to be there when I. . .'

'Maria.' He was laughing at her incoherence as he captured the slender hands which were alternately wringing each other and waving agitatedly about.

'Slow down. I haven't the faintest idea what you're talking about.'

'Oh, Leo,' she subsided with a sigh and worried her lower lip between her teeth but there seemed to be no way to lead up to the subject, not when his silvery grey eyes were concentrating so hard on her. 'I'm pregnant,' she whispered at last.

She might as well have screamed the words at him for the effect they had.

'What!' His eyes darkened with a mixture of shock and dismay as he gazed rapidly from her face to her all-but-flat belly and back again, the shaking of his head signalling his disbelief as he began to fire questions at her faster than she could answer.

'When? I mean, how far. . .? *Who*?' This question was more insistent—almost an accusation. 'Who's the father? You said you weren't going out with anyone.'

'I wasn't. I'm not.' She felt terribly vulnerable, lying there under his angry gaze, but there was no way she could have found the energy to sit up; no way she *could* have with his broad shoulders looming over her that way. 'I'm four and a half months pregnant,' she said quietly and left him to draw his own conclusions.

'No. . .! Dear God, no!' His voice was filled with horror as he leapt up from the side of the bed to glare down at her and then began to pace furiously backwards and forwards across the width of the small room like a caged panther.

His instant rejection was so much more violent than anything she had imagined and her eyes filled with anguished tears as they followed him helplessly, each passage making the walls seem to crowd in closer together and the atmosphere grow more tense.

'Why didn't you tell me?' he demanded as he paused briefly at the foot of the bed, throwing the words at her like weapons before he continued on his agitated way. 'You knew about this months ago. You *must* have known last month when I came to find you and apologise. . .'

'*That* was the day I found out,' Maria interrupted bravely. 'It never occurred to me that the reason I wasn't feeling well was. . .'

'Why didn't you say something? I was here in your house—you should have told me then.' His glare was accusing as he stood over her, one clenched fist planted adamantly on each hip.

'Too much had happened that day.' Maria closed her eyes, unable to cope with the sight of his shirt stretched tautly across the broad chest she'd been exploring such a short while ago. She had to concentrate—to remember what had happened that other day or he'd never understand. . .

'I'd just had the shock of finding out I was pregnant by a man I'd never seen and had no means of finding when you turned up out of the blue. All that was on top of thirty-six hours of duty and covering for sick colleagues. I wasn't in a fit state to think straight,' she pleaded in the face of his closed expression. 'I needed time to sort out my. . .'

'Time!' he exploded. 'If you're already eighteen weeks pregnant time isn't a luxury we can afford!'

'W-what?' Maria frowned as she struggled to push herself up against her pillows, heartily sick of lying there like a stranded fish. 'What has time got to do with anything? I've still got another four and a half months before the baby's due. That should be plenty of time to make all the arrangements for. . .'

'You've got beta thalassaemia trait?' The sudden question sounded far more like an accusation and stopped her reassuring words instantly.

'Yes,' she confirmed. 'I probably mentioned that when I told you about Marco. . .'

'So have I,' he barked.

'I gathered that when you told me about your son's. . .'

'Have you been tested?' he demanded abruptly.

'I've had all my antenatal checks, if that's what you mean. I went along as soon as I was told I was. . .'

'No. I mean the chorionic villus sampling before you reached the tenth week,' he interrupted her again.

'I didn't even know I was pregnant until the twelfth week and, anyway, the CVS couldn't be done without a blood sample from both parents.'

'And you didn't know who I was.' He grimly nodded his understanding. 'What about foetal blood sampling? Have you had a percutaneous umbilical blood sample taken yet to find out whether the baby's positive?'

'No. . .'

'But you've arranged for it to be done in the next two weeks.' The words weren't intended as a question.

'No,' she repeated steadily.

'No? Why on earth not?' His growing anger was evident in the clenching and releasing of his fists, his eyes cold steel as they pierced her accusingly. 'You must realise how irresponsible that is. You know more about the curse of beta thalassaemia than most.'

'There's no point in being tested just for the sake of it,' she returned spiritedly, her chin coming up at the attack. She didn't like the way that he was constantly interrupting her. 'For a start there's always a chance that the test could cause a spontaneous abortion but. . .'

'What do you mean, "just for the sake of it"? There's a damn good reason for testing the baby and you know it.' He looked as though he wanted to shake her. 'We both carry the trait and, because of that, there's a one-in-four chance that the baby has inherited the disorder.'

'And a three-in-four chance that it hasn't but. . .' she held up a shaky hand to prevent him breaking in, determined that this time she would finish what she wanted to say '. . .it doesn't matter either way because I wouldn't even contemplate an abortion.'

Her fierce avowal silenced him but only momentarily.

'That's totally selfish and irresponsible,' he raged, his face quite white in the subdued light of her bedroom and his eyes dark coals just waiting to spit fire at her. 'Have you thought for a minute about the child's rights—about *my* rights as the child's father?'

There was just time for Maria to register a pang that the first time Leo mentioned his role as her baby's father was in an argument over his right to decide whether it would be allowed to live at all when her staunch beliefs flooded in to support her.

'Of *course* I've thought about the baby—I've spent the last month thinking about it constantly.' Suddenly she was the epitome of a lioness defending her cub. 'As far as *your* rights are concerned—' she allowed scorn to weight her tone '—not long ago you were at great pains to tell me that you're not interested in any permanent relationships. Well, that might be all right for you—it sounds as if a one-night stand is about as much as you can handle but whether it lives for a day or a full lifetime a baby is permanent.'

She saw the dark colour surge into his cheeks at her slighting reference to what had occurred between them but it hardly slowed the speed of his renewed attack.

'Have you thought about how you're going to cope if the baby *is* born with the disease?' he demanded, putting the ball straight back into her court.

'I'll probably cope just as well as any other mother will—probably marginally better. Considering the nature of my job, I know more than most about the physical and emotional needs of a child with beta thalassaemia.'

'Except you're not in the same position as any other mother, are you?' he accused coldly. 'You're not married so you won't have anyone there to help share the burden; to take their turn at sitting through a crisis so you can catch up on your sleep. If the way you collapsed this evening is any indication you aren't managing to take care of yourself properly *before* the baby arrives so how can you hope to do so afterwards?'

Maria gazed at him silently, holding all the hurt inside the way she'd learned to do so long ago when it had been her parents attacking her for her defence of her sickly little brother.

'So much for your offer of friendship,' she muttered under her breath as she rolled over and swung her feet to the floor. 'I can do without fair-weather friends.'

The sadness inside her heart was overwhelming but there was no way that she was going to let him know how much he'd wounded her.

She straightened up to her full height, swaying briefly as she got her balance rather than acknowledge the hand he reached out towards her.

'I think it's time you left,' she said quietly as she led the way towards the hall on shaky legs. 'I need to catch up on my sleep.' It was a petty dig at him but she wasn't feeling very noble at the moment.

'Maria. . .'

'No doubt we'll be bumping into each other at intervals.' She took great delight in cutting across his attempts at speech to deliver her final challenge. 'I shan't bother passing on any bulletins about the baby—unless you particularly want me to?'

She didn't know how she managed to keep her voice so calm and unemotional when all she wanted to do was scream and rail at the unfairness of it all.

It wasn't that she'd expected him to greet her sudden announcement with cries of joy—how could he when they barely knew each other and the whole situation had come about by accident? But she hadn't anticipated his demand that she have the baby tested to see whether he wanted it to be aborted, nor the attack on her capabilities as a mother.

She felt very small and alone as she stood in the hallway holding the front door open for him, shivering as the chilly wind whipped her clothes around her and teased out the newly dried strands of hair while she stared stonily out into the night.

'For God's sake, woman. We've got to talk about this. Throwing me out doesn't solve anything.' His frustrated voice came from a point right behind her shoulder but she refused to turn and face him, not certain how well she would be able to hide her feelings from him if he didn't leave soon.

'Neither does ranting at me,' she said softly as

she tightened her chilly fingers around the catch. 'Especially when I won't be changing my mind.'

'Well, neither will I,' his voice grated over her raw nerves, his words a heartbreaking mixture of determination, frustration and despair. 'Dammit, I've already been through this once. I couldn't bear to see it all happen a second time.'

Maria watched silently as he stepped past her and out of her flat, turning his shoulders so that there was no chance of any contact between them. She waited for him to turn back; waited for some sort of farewell before he left but he strode away from her, his shoulders hunched defensively inside his jacket as he disappeared into the shadows of the night.

'Dr Martinez?' the young nurse hailed her just as she was making her way out of the ward and Maria sighed tiredly.

'Yes, Nurse?' She waited by the door, unwilling to walk any further than she had to on her aching feet.

'There's been a message up from Emergency. Shabana Saleh is on her way up.'

Maria nodded, her shoulders slumping in spite of her best efforts as she realised that there was now no chance of getting home early. Shabana was one of her 'special' children and the only reason she would be coming in like this when she wasn't due for a transfusion was that she was having a sickle cell crisis.

'Oh, Doctor, I'm so glad you're here.' Mrs Saleh managed a small smile but most of her attention was on her little daughter.

'How is she?' Maria asked while she began her

examination. 'Have you any idea what brought the crisis on this time?'

'It's all my fault,' the poor woman wailed softly as she comforted the little girl on her lap. 'But all her new friends at school had been invited to the party, too, and I hated to have to say no.'

'What sort of party was it, Shabana?' Maria questioned while she noted the six-year-old's paleness in spite of her raised temperature.

'A birthday party for Amy,' she whispered weakly. 'We went to the swimming pool.' She paused to wince as Maria examined her painful joints and then continued gamely. 'Then, afterwards, we had cake with candles.'

'In the swimming pool?' Maria demanded in careful mock amazement. 'How did you get the candles to stay alight?'

'Not in the water!' She pulled a face at Maria's silliness. 'Afterwards. When we finished swimming.'

'Did you all get dressed up in party dresses to have your cake?' she prompted.

'No. We had our swimming costumes on.' Her eyes closed as she rested her head against her mother's shoulder, a small grey rabbit clutched tightly in the crook of one arm.

'So,' she murmured to the worried parent. 'It was a case of too much strenuous exercise and excitement, followed by standing around and getting chilled.'

'Yes, Doctor. If only I'd realised that they weren't going to get dressed straight away. . . She never has this problem after her swimming lessons because the teachers make sure she doesn't stand around. They send her off to change straight away then go to her next lesson.'

Maria saw the woman's eyes stray to a point just behind her but she had no need to look to see who was there. Even if she hadn't recognised the individual mixture of soap and musky male which had been imprinted on her memory for ever one dark passionate night the tiny hairs on the back of her neck had lifted at his proximity in spite of her determination not to respond.

'Well, Mrs Saleh, we'll get Shabana on a drip straight away to dilute her blood and we'll give her something to take the pain away. If I could get you to make sure that she drinks plenty of fluids?'

'What would be best to give her?' The poor mother was only too willing to help.

'Whatever she wants—fruit juice, water, milk—the same as you would give her at home. Just ask the nurses and they'll get whatever she prefers to make sure she'll drink plenty to get her levels up.'

'Have you found anything in particular that helps your daughter to cope with the pain?' Leo's deep voice joined in the discussion. 'Some children prefer to lie still with the painful areas supported on soft pillows; others need to be distracted by someone reading to them or watching a favourite film.'

'Shabana likes me to rock her and sing to her.' Maria watched, unsurprised as Mrs Saleh responded shyly to Leo's charisma. 'She just likes to curl up on my lap with her rabbit and wait for the pain to go away while she listens.'

'She's a lucky girl to have a mother who can sing her pain away,' he said with a gentle smile for the two of them and Maria's heart ached at the evidence of a gentler side to his nature.

It was another half-hour before Maria felt happy about leaving the ward but Peg Mulholland had come on duty and she trusted her to know when to call for assistance if Shabana didn't respond as anticipated.

She half expected to find Leo waiting for her outside in the corridor but it was nearly as deserted as the rest of the hospital corridors at this time of day as she walked towards the main entrance and out into the dark evening.

As she made her weary way home she tried to remember what she'd been doing during the day to make her feel so exhausted but couldn't pinpoint anything out of the ordinary. As far as she could see there were only two major differences in her life these days—her slowly progressing pregnancy and her lack of sleep—either one of which could be responsible for the fact that she just wanted to curl up on the nearest flat surface and sleep for a week.

Unfortunately, as soon as she closed her eyes she was plagued with thoughts of Leo da Cruz; with memories of the incredible pleasure he'd brought her interspersed with his fury at her refusal to consider that the baby they'd created might not be worth carrying. . .

'What the hell do you think you're doing, woman?' an angry voice sounded in her ear as she turned towards her front door and she uttered a strangled shriek as she nearly leapt out of her skin.

'Leo!' she breathed as her pulse thundered in her ears. 'You startled me. What are you. . .?'

'You shouldn't be wandering about the streets on your own at this time of night. Haven't you got the sense God gave a goose? Where's your car?'

'What car?' she snapped back, her sudden surge of pleasure at seeing him totally destroyed by his autocratic attitude. 'I only live a few hundred yards from the hospital. What on earth would I need a car for?'

'But. . .what do you do when it's raining?' He sounded nonplussed by her logic.

'I'm not made of sugar—I don't dissolve,' she pointed out sarcastically. 'And walking's good for the baby.'

She turned away from his steely gaze and concentrated on getting her key out, pausing directly in front of him until he stepped aside for her to reach the lock.

'Has your purpose in coming here been satisfied by shouting at me or do you want to say something more?' She threw the barbed question over her shoulder as she entered the hallway.

'Of course I want to say something more,' he ground out through gritted teeth. 'I told you last time that we needed to talk. . .'

'And *I* told you there was nothing to talk about,' she reminded him as she walked calmly towards the kitchen, leaving him to close the front door for her.

He must have paused in the hallway to regain control of his temper because the kettle was almost boiling by the time he arrived in the doorway.

'Tea or coffee?' Maria offered without looking up from the mugs she was setting on the tray.

'I haven't come here for a teaparty,' he said in a voice that was a chilling mixture of ice and gravel. 'I came to talk some sense into you.'

'Well.' She threw a bland smile at him as she opened a packet of biscuits and fanned them into an expert semicircle on a matching plate. 'I'm sure you'll feel far better if you get something warm inside you first. You must have got quite chilled waiting for me on the doorstep.' She poured water onto instant decaffeinated coffee granules in each of two mugs. 'Milk and sugar?' she demanded brightly.

'For God's sake!' he exploded, throwing both hands theatrically up in the air in one of the first really 'foreign' displays Maria had seen from him. She smiled as it drew to mind fond memories her of her foster-father in one of his volcanic Italian tantrums—the sort that his wife had been able to defuse with nothing more than a kiss even when she was the cause of it.

For all that Leo had told her that he was half Italian and half Greek until now the only evidence she had seen of it was his Mediterranean colouring and his charm. She found it fascinating to discover this whole new facet of his personality.

'I'm glad you find the situation so amusing,' he snapped as he reached for the tray. 'I presume you want this taken into the lounge?' He turned and marched out, leaving Maria hovering over the milk jug and sugar bowl.

'Blow it,' she muttered. 'He can just have his black,' and she followed him through to the other room.

He'd made himself comfortable at one end of the settee, the tray on the table he'd pulled in front of it. When she collected her mug and settled herself in her usual chair on the other side of the room he scowled blackly but refrained from making any comment, even when he tasted his coffee and pulled a face.

The silence between them took on a life of its own, growing denser and more menacing the longer it went on. Finally Maria couldn't bear it any longer and took the initiative.

'You said you wanted to speak to me?' she prompted as she curled her feet up under her on the seat. For the first time she was aware that it wasn't quite as easy to fold herself up so small and she realised that after months of being a secret presence inside her the baby was finally making his or her presence felt.

Her heart gave a little lift as she realised that any day now she would be able to feel real signs of movement—not just the faint flutters she'd been aware of for the last few weeks.

'What. . .?' She suddenly realised that Leo had been speaking and in her preoccupation with the development of the baby she'd completely missed it.

'I said,' he repeated drily, 'have you thought any more about what I said?'

'What in particular?' Maria enquired, refusing to rely on any guesswork. This whole situation was far too important to disintegrate in misunderstandings.

'About having the baby's blood tested,' he said, his voice sharp with tension.

'No.'

'But. . .'

'Leo,' she broke in firmly before he could get in his stride, 'I will *not* be having the baby tested for beta thalassaemia before it's born. That is my choice and it's my *right* to make that choice.'

'And what about *my* rights?' he countered. 'What if I go to court to make you have the test?'

'You could try—and you might even be able to persuade a judge that the tests are a good idea.'

She wrapped both hands round the mug of rapidly

cooling coffee to steady her shaking fingers as she watched the surprised expression cross his face.

'Of course I would oppose the idea on several grounds, the first being that the test could provoke premature labour.'

'You know as well as I do how rare that is these days.' There was open disgust in his voice.

'But do the solicitors and judges? Would they want to be responsible for forcing me to have a non-essential medical procedure which precipitated the death of my baby?'

'It wouldn't take long to produce the statistics to prove my case—both for testing the baby's blood and for the safety of the technique.'

'It might not take long but would it take too long?' she threw the words back at him. 'Every day that it takes to persuade a judge to see your point of view is a day closer to the legal deadline.

'Then,' she continued inexorably, 'when you add in the length of time it takes to do the necessary tests on the blood sample you've still got to go back to court if it turns out to be positive and persuade the judge that it's your right to kill the baby that I'm carrying inside my body.'

She was trembling all over by the time she finished, her knuckles gleaming white under the central light as they clenched tightly around her mug.

'You make a pretty good case, based on emotions,' he admitted bleakly. 'But, luckily, the law doesn't care about that. It's more concerned with justice and legal rights.'

He stood up suddenly, as though he couldn't bear to sit still any more, his long legs eating up the space backwards and forwards between her furniture.

'Oh, don't think I couldn't put forward an emotional argument just as heart-wrenching as yours,' he said bitterly. 'Apart from my professional evidence I could tell them at first hand what it's like to watch your son die of the complications associated with beta thalassaemia; of the agony and frustration of watching his pain and holding him in my arms as he died.'

'But that isn't a fair comparison with what would happen to this child,' she objected furiously as she protectively cradled the slight bump below her waist with one palm. 'He didn't receive the treatment he should have had. . .'

Like a cornered panther, he turned on her with a snarl.

'And can you give me a guarantee that the baby won't have a stroke or a heart attack or its lungs won't collapse? By what right do you decide unilaterally that you will put an unborn innocent through that? Half of his genetic inheritence comes from my genes and that means I have the right to share in making the decisions that concern him.'

'What right?' she demanded very softly, knowing that her next argument would make him more angry than ever. 'If I cast doubt on the possibility that you're the father of the baby you can't prove it without testing the baby's DNA.

'*That*,' she stressed, 'will take you back even further than where you started because unless you can prove you are the baby's father you have no right to demand *anything* and if I deny it you'll have to wait until the baby's born before I agree to the DNA testing.'

He stared at her in silence, his face nearly grey with shock that she would go so far.

'That would be professional suicide for you,' he whispered in horror, obviously realising for the first time just how determined she was. 'The publicity the case would collect would guarantee that the newspapers would drag your name through the mud.'

' "Promiscuous paediatrician",' Maria mimicked a tabloid headline. ' "Respectable lady doctor in a series of one-night stands. Doesn't know who her baby's father is." '

'It's not a bloody joke,' he snapped furiously.

'Matters of life and death rarely are,' she said soberly and sighed. 'So, where does that leave us?'

'God only knows.' He ran his fingers through his hair and cradled the back of his neck as though it ached. 'Who would have thought that a few minutes of forgetfulness could cause such upheaval?'

Maria snorted. 'I wonder how many people have said the same thing when they discover an unexpected pregnancy?'

Leo's attempt at a smile was more like a wry grimace but it was evidence that he was beginning to calm down a little.

'Look. . .' he paused to extract his wallet and take out a small white card '. . .this is the number for an answering service. If you need to get hold of me they'll know where I can be contacted.' He started to hold it out towards her then changed his mind and put it down on the table beside his empty coffee-mug as though he didn't want to get any closer to her.

'Where will you be?' Her voice was strangely husky as she looked up at him and contemplated the very real possibility that this might be the last time that she would see him in anything other than a professional context.

'I need to do some thinking,' he said sombrely, his hands pushed deep into his trouser pockets as he contemplated the muted pattern on the carpet. 'I've got about a month to go on my present contract; then I was going to do a couple more lectures before I took a holiday. You can expect to see me back at St Augustine's in about six weeks—if you don't hear from me in the meantime.'

He paused briefly on his way out of the room and looked back at her as she sat in her chair, stunned by the speed of events. Her eyes travelled greedily over him, trying to store his image as clearly as possible so that she could recall it over the next six weeks, and then he was gone.

CHAPTER FIVE

'CHAOS,' panted Peg Mulholland as she helped one of the more junior nurses moving the ward furniture around.

'All in a good cause, though,' Maria reminded her. 'It will mean that Katy and Laura Johnson can be in adjacent beds.'

Peg's expression softened. 'Poor kids,' she murmured, making sure that only Maria could hear her. 'One of them in for leg-lengthening and the other has her leg broken in an accident on her way here to visit her. No wonder they're desperate to stay close to each other.'

Maria had spent a frustrating afternoon trying to sort the problem out.

After the ward round to review the children hoping to go home she'd spent a long time between the computer and the telephone trying both to empty beds and to move children around to enable the Johnson sisters to share one side of the little four-bedded ward.

It had been just one more task at the end of a crippling day, the fact that it had been her turn to be on call today meaning that she'd been up and down between the ward and the accident department answering bleeps more times than she could remember.

It hadn't helped that the closest bank of lifts to the paediatric ward was undergoing major safety repairs.

After the first circuitous journey around the rabbit

warren of corridors and down to the ground floor she'd decided that it was faster to use the stairs than take the long way round to the next set of lifts. It was only now, hours later, that she was realising just how exhausting it was to spend so much time running up and down stairs.

The one thing that was keeping her going was the hope that Leo would contact her soon.

Each morning she woke up with the conviction that today was the day that she'd look up from tending a patient or reassuring worried parents and there he'd be, smiling his heart-stopping smile just for her.

Unfortunately it hadn't happened yet and, as a result, she still wasn't managing to get a good night's sleep and the drain on her system was beginning to tell.

Then, last night, she'd ended up staying on so late at the hospital with one of her 'special' children that it wasn't worth going home at all. She'd only got through by snatching a couple of hours' sleep on the narrow bed in the on-call room before it was time to start another day.

Meals were another problem which weren't helping her situation, with her erratic visits to the cafeteria or the staff canteen sometimes forgotten altogether. Even when she did manage to get her food on time there was no guarantee that she wasn't going to lose it all in another episode of lingering morning sickness.

'You're not looking so good,' Peg commented in her usual outspoken way as Maria made her shaky way into her office after her latest bout of nausea had robbed her of her tea. 'If you don't put on a bit more weight we'll have to start nailing your feet to the floor or you'll blow away in the breeze.'

'Jealousy gets you nowhere,' Maria teased, knowing

the ward sister was fighting a permanent battle with her weight.

'Seriously, though,' Peg insisted after she'd stuck an impudent tongue out at her. 'Have you been for a check-up? You look as if you could do with some vitamins or something.'

'If the ''or something'' is an all-expenses-paid trip to somewhere warm with nothing to do but laze around in the sun I might take you up on the prescription.' Maria smiled then pulled a wry face as her pager bleeped yet again. 'If you want to know why I don't put on any weight blame this thing.' She waved the offending electronic gadget aloft as she reached for the telephone.

'Another trip downstairs,' she sighed. 'Child without a seat belt in a multiple car shunt. See you later.'

She let herself out of the ward and set off along the corridor at a fast clip, the journey towards the echoing stairwell second nature to her by now.

'Jeremy? Can you hear me, love? Can you give my fingers a squeeze?' Maria smiled her relief as she felt the distinct increase in pressure. 'Good boy,' she praised as she went on with her examination, detailing one of the casualty staff to warn the appropriate department that Jeremy would shortly be coming up for a scan.

'Do we know who's on duty in Neurosurgery?' she demanded as she checked the child's pupil dilation again, her mouth pursing with worry. 'Depending on the results of the scan, this young man might have to pay him a rapid visit.'

'Do you want to have a quick word with the parents?'

Staff Nurse looked at her hopefully. 'I put them in the little interview room.'

'There's not much I can tell them yet but I'll give them what I've got,' Maria agreed, waiting until Jeremy was on his way for the scan before she went out to find them.

'Mr and Mrs Tolliver? I'm Dr Martinez.' She shook hands with each of them, knowing how important that brief physical contact could be to terrified parents. 'I've just examined Jeremy but he needs to have some tests done before I can be sure whether there's any damage.'

It took some time to calm the pair of them down, their guilt at not insisting that their spoilt only son stayed strapped in his seat belt making them alternately aggressive and apologetic.

By the time she'd managed to track the neurosurgeon down for an opinion on the brain scan and checked to see that Jeremy had been settled safely into ICU she had begun to feel quite strange, her head almost feeling as if it was floating several inches above her body as she made her way, yet again, up the stairs.

She'd nearly reached the top when her pager went off, the bleep startling her as it echoed eerily off the bare walls so that she almost missed her step.

In slow motion she watched her hand reach out for the hand-rail and grasp it and felt her feet tread almost silently from one step to the next until she got as far as the landing.

By concentrating all her energy she succeeded in touching the doorhandle leading to the corridor beside the lifts and even managed to pull it open part-way and step into the opening.

The last thing she remembered going through her

bewildered mind was that there was a black hole opening up at her feet. Suddenly she was convinced that somehow she had managed to open the wrong door—that, instead of walking out into the corridor, she had stepped into the lift before the men had finished the repairs and she was about to fall to the bottom of the empty shaft.

'Maria. . .?'

She knew that she must be dreaming because that was Leo's voice and these days he only ever spoke to her in her dreams. She squeezed her lids tightly shut, knowing that if she allowed herself to wake up properly it would be the start of just another day without him.

'Come on, Maria. Open your eyes.'

This time she felt gentle fingers smoothing the unruly tendrils of hair away from her face and she breathed in the indefinable mixture of soap and man that was Leo's alone.

'Leo?' she croaked as she looked up at him. 'What. . .what are you doing here?'

She couldn't see his expression—his head was outlined against a bright light as he leaned over her and gazed into her eyes with professional detachment.

'I'm checking you over, you stupid woman,' he muttered under his breath out of deference to the nurse hovering just behind him.

'What are you checking me over for? I'm perfectly all right.' She glared indignantly up at him, feeling like an upturned beetle under a microscope.

'Ha! So perfect that you passed out in the corridor,' he scoffed.

'That's. . .that's only because I ran up the stairs from

the accident department. I. . .I must have taken it too fast.'

'For God's sake, woman. Why didn't you take the lift? It's not as if you need the exercise.' She could almost feel the lightning glance over her body. 'You're nothing but skin and bones.'

'I would have taken the lift if it was working,' she returned with an air of long suffering. 'As it is it takes longer to go around to the next bank of lifts than to go down the stairs.'

'Couldn't you have sent one of the nurses instead?'

'Hardly. I'm on call today.'

'On call? You mean you've been dashing up and down those stairs all day?' He sounded appalled.

'It feels as if I've been doing it for a month,' she admitted wryly. 'Thank God, tomorrow's my easy day—consultant ward round in the morning and diabetic clinic in the afternoon.'

'That's if you're fit enough to come in at all,' he said grimly.

'What do you mean?' She batted away the hand resting on her shoulder so that she could roll herself over and sit up. 'Of course I'll be here—I'm on duty.'

'We'll see about that.' He nodded to the silent nurse that she wasn't needed any more and she left the room, her reluctance to leave the fascinating discussion evident as she looked back over her shoulder.

'For goodness' sake,' Maria hissed as she watched the door swing closed on her avid face. 'The whole hospital will be talking if you carry on like an overprotective husband. What are you doing here, anyway?'

'Taking care of you as you don't seem to be doing a very good job of it yourself.' He paused to steady her as she slid off the high bed and fumbled her feet into her shoes. 'If you tell me where to find your bag you can wait here while I fetch it and then I'll take you home.'

'You certainly will not!' Maria glanced at her watch. 'I've still got several hours of work to do before I go off duty. In case you've forgotten I'm on call today.'

'That's all taken care of,' he said firmly. 'Now, just tell me where your. . .'

'What do you mean, it's "all taken care of"? What have you done?' There was an awful sinking feeling in her stomach. So far only her obstetrician knew about the baby. Had he unwittingly broadcast the reason why her health seemed to be so precarious at the moment. . .?

'I spoke to the registrar—Ian Stanton? He said he was only too willing to take over for you—said he owed you for several favours you've never let him repay.'

'But. . .'

'No more.' He held up both palms to stop her arguments. 'I'm going to be taking you home as soon as we collect your belongings and you're going to smile and say, "Thank you, Leo," with your best party manners.'

Maria subsided with a heavy sigh. As she ungraciously told him where her coat and bag were she resigned herself to being the object of the latest round of gossip and speculation. As long as the hospital grapevine never got to hear about what had happened in Italy she would be able to ride it out but if *that* ever became public knowledge. . .

She cringed at the thought, only then wondering

whether Leo was going to insist that she go all the way around to the next bank of lifts and if he would try to force her into the indignity of using a wheelchair.

As is the way with such things by the time she was ready to leave the department the repairmen had finished their job and the lift was back in full operation, whisking them swiftly and silently to the ground floor.

Once outside, instead of the waiting taxi she expected, he led her towards the consultants' car park, stopping beside a gleaming white BMW.

'Whose is this?' She gazed admiringly at the powerful lines of the car, thinking how well it suited him. 'Is someone lending you their car to take me home?'

'It's mine.' He opened the passenger door for her and waited until she was settled before he closed it again and went round to get behind the wheel. 'You wouldn't have seen it before because it was being serviced last time I came down.'

He secured his seat belt and flicked a glance across at hers before he switched on the engine and pulled out.

'Maria, I. . .'

'Leo, you. . .'

They began simultaneously then broke off and laughed.

'Ladies first,' he offered, concentrating on the traffic as he turned towards Alma Road.

'You said you weren't coming back for six weeks. . .' She allowed the words to die away, hoping that he would take it as a hint to explain why he had come so much sooner.

'I wasn't going to but when I heard that you'd collapsed I came straight. . .'

'Just a minute,' she interrupted indignantly. 'What

do you mean? *How* did you find out?'

He pulled a wry face, like a young boy caught out in a mischievous prank, but her blood began to boil and she pressed for an answer.

'You haven't been near the hospital for weeks so how have you been keeping tabs on me? How could you possibly know I'd been taken ill?' A sudden thought struck her. 'You've set someone to spy on me!' she cried, horrified at the very idea.

'I asked someone to let me know how you were in case you needed me,' he said stiffly, colour darkening his cheek-bones. 'I wasn't certain that you would call me yourself.' He drew the car up outside her house and leant forward to turn off the engine.

'You needn't bother doing that,' Maria sniped. 'I'll get out and you can be on your way.' She released her seat belt and swung the door open but he was there before her, his hand outstretched to assist her out of the contoured seat.

'I can manage,' she snapped, motioning his hand away.

'I'm sure you can but why not take advantage of the help when it's there?' He grasped her elbow and steadied her with an encircling arm when she found that her legs were still unsteady.

Her half-formed plan to be inside her flat before he'd finished locking the car came to nothing when he pointed a little gadget and the locks clicked simultaneously.

'Go through and put your feet up while I put the kettle on,' he ordered when he'd closed the door behind himself and turned towards the kitchen, for all the world as if *he* was the host. 'Decaffeinated coffee or tea?'

'Please, *do* make yourself at home!' Maria muttered sarcastically as she slid her feet gratefully out of her shoes and padded towards her favourite chair.

If she was honest it was wonderful to have someone there to make her a drink while she waited for her batteries to recharge. It was a novelty that she could grow quite accustomed to. . .

'Maria?'

'Oh.' She'd completely forgotten to answer. 'Tea, please. Not too strong and no sugar.'

'Are you sure you don't want some sugar to boost your energy?' His head appeared around the corner, one eyebrow raised questioningly.

'Not if you want me to be able to drink it. I can't stand sweet tea.' She shuddered at the thought. 'There's a packet of chocolate biscuits behind the. . .'

'Found them,' he interrupted.

'*How* did you find them? They were hidden away so I'd have something in case of visitors.'

'I think it's a system rather like radar,' he called back, his voice coming closer as he brought the tray through. 'Only in my case it works on chocolate biscuits!' The accompanying grin was infectious and Maria had a glimpse of how he must have been as a boy.

With a sudden leap she wondered if their child—the boy or girl she was nurturing inside her as they spoke—had inherited that grin. She found herself hoping fervently that they had, in spite of the fact that it would make it very hard to forget Leo once he had gone out of their lives.

'How's the tea?' his deep voice floated into her thoughts and she glanced down at the half-empty cup in her hand, suddenly aware that her mental meanderings hadn't prevented her from accepting the tea and beginning to drink it. 'Perfect.' She smiled distractedly, her mind still half-occupied with thoughts of the uncertain future.

'Maria?'

Once again she was called back to the present by his deep voice and this time she made an effort to pay attention.

'I'm sorry. I was wool-gathering.'

'Are you feeling any better?' There was honest concern in his voice. 'Peg Mulholland said you were unconscious for a good half-hour.'

'Probably the best sleep I've had in a long time.' She pulled a wry face. 'But I still don't understand how you got there so fast. You must have been sitting in your car just waiting for something to happen.'

'Not quite.' He laughed, his teeth gleaming whitely against the permanent tan of his Mediterranean ancestry. 'I had decided to pay a visit to the hospital and was just about to leave when the phone rang.'

'And who is your mole? Is it someone I know?' She had calmed down enough to smile at the cloak-and-dagger feel to the situation.

'Yes, but I promised I wouldn't be the one to tell you. They want a chance to tell themselves—if you'll excuse the scrambled grammar—I don't want to give away the person's gender.'

Suddenly she was secretly glad that whoever it was had contacted Leo. Now that she'd had time to think about it it had been a wonderfully comforting feeling to be taken care of and cosseted this way.

'Leo?' She spoke before she could get cold feet.

'Thank you for coming. It's nice to know that someone cared.'

'I think you'd be surprised exactly how many people care about you,' he said seriously. 'Not just your "special" kids and their families but everyone on the ward, too. They're worried about you.'

'Worried? But why?'

'Because they can see there's something wrong with you and don't know what to do or what to say.'

'And I don't know how I'm going to tell them.' She busied herself putting her empty cup down on the table and then reached out to switch on the corner lamp. The evening had become quite dark while they were sitting talking.

'I think the bigger problem is going to be *when* you tell them,' he suggested.

'Why? The pregnancy's hardly showing yet and I've still got several months before I start my maternity leave.'

'If you carry on the way you're going it'll be much sooner than that,' he warned seriously.

'But I can't afford to leave any sooner. There are all those patients who. . .'

'Unless you don't care about the baby's health?'

The open challenge in his words made her subside instantly.

'Of course I care about the baby,' she said softly, gazing at him steadily across the room. 'I wouldn't have dared to stand up to your bullying last month if I hadn't cared.'

They were both silent for a moment, remembering the confrontation, before she continued in a worried tone.

'But, Leo, I don't want to have to leave work early. I'd probably go mad with boredom if I just had to sit here for several months waiting for the baby to arrive—apart from the fact that the hospital won't have had a chance to find a replacement for me. And it wouldn't be fair to my colleagues or the patients if I leave them without adequate notice.'

'Can I offer a suggestion?' He was watching her closely as if trying to judge how she would take his words. 'I could take some of the pressure off you by arranging a temporary job-share. I'm sure the hospital management won't mind as long as they're getting the same number of hours' work for the same pay.'

'It couldn't possibly work,' Maria objected, after taking a startled moment to think about it. 'You'd end up killing yourself if you had to drive all those miles backwards and forwards day after day. It's a wonderful idea but it just wouldn't be practical with you living so far away.'

'It's a little over ten miles,' he said quietly.

'Ten. . .? But. . .' Her brows drew together in confusion as she tried to remember exactly how far away the Waverley hospital was.

'I moved into a place of my own last week from the staff flat. It just happens to be on this side of the Waverley.'

She pinpointed the area in her head. 'So you're actually living between the two hospitals,' she confirmed.

'That's right. And the roads are quite straightforward so, logistically, it could work, especially as I've also got some holiday time coming up.'

'But what would we say to St Augustine's? What reason could we give?'

'I take it you still haven't told anyone yet?'

She looked down at her fingers and found herself twining them together in her lap, unable to meet the laser intensity of his eyes as she shook her head. 'I don't know how,' she whispered. 'I know it happens all the time these days and people hardly take any notice but. . .' She drew in a shuddering sigh.

'But Anna and Luiz didn't raise you that way.' He supplied the missing words then he, too, fell silent.

Maria was beginning to feel uncomfortable under the fierceness of his gaze when he abruptly straightened out of the corner of the settee and began to pace.

As she watched him travel backwards and forwards she smiled inwardly. She'd watched him doing this before and recognised his action as evidence of stress.

Suddenly he stopped in front of her, leaning forward to place one hand on each arm of the chair as he fixed her eyes with his.

'We could get married,' he said without warning and her heart leapt into her mouth as she gazed up at him so close in front of her, a strange warmth spreading inside her at the thought of marriage to Leo.

'It would protect your reputation from the gossips,' he continued persuasively, unaware that those extra words were the icy blast that killed the little blossom of hope she hadn't been aware of nurturing along with the baby deep inside her.

'You can't get married just to stop gossip. Marriage is too precious to treat it like a coat of whitewash.' Her voice was harsh in her sudden disappointment and, even as she spoke, she realised how stupid she was being. There had never been any question of a permanent relationship between them so why should she be feeling cheated that he was making a suggestion based on logic?

'It would also give the baby a name so it wouldn't be born illegitimate,' he pointed out soberly, straightening away from her to resume his pacing.

'But. . .' Her thoughts were whirling. 'You don't *want* to get married. You said you wouldn't go through it again. . .*and* you don't want to have anything to do with the baby.'

He was on the other side of the room when he stopped pacing and stared across at her as if he was seeing her for the first time. A whole range of emotions crossed his face as she watched, the mixture far too complex for her to decipher.

'The situation has changed,' he said at last, his voice strangely rough. 'Whatever the rights and wrongs of how we arrived at this point, you're carrying my baby and it's up to me to take care of you.'

In his words Maria heard the echo of his insistence that it had been her parents' responsibility to stay to take care of Marco and herself and she felt another fragment of her dreams shatter. Once she'd longed to be a part of a real family—a family that loved each other and cared for each other because of that love.

Leo's offer, generous though it was, didn't have the same ring to it.

'I need to think about this,' she said into the stillness of the room and watched his shoulders stiffen, his face becoming expressionless as if he'd just put shutters up to stop her looking in.

'Maria, you. . .'

'Please, Leo,' she silenced him. 'Too much has happened today for me to think clearly. This has come at me out of the blue and I don't want to say anything for a few days. *You* might go home and realise that there are other, less drastic, solutions to the problem.'

'All right,' he agreed. 'If you think we need a short cooling-off period I'll back off but, while you're doing your thinking, don't forget that the baby needs a healthy mother and not one who's permanently exhausted. Whatever you decide the present situation can't go on for much longer.'

He'd left soon after, apparently unable to relax with so much unspoken tension between them. His final words before he let himself out of the front door were an order to get herself into bed as soon as possible to catch up on some of the sleep she needed.

'As if I'm going to be able to go straight to sleep after he delivers a bombshell like that!' she complained aloud as she tried to relax in a deep soothing bath filled with her favourite bubbles. 'Right out of the blue without a single word of warning. ''We could get married,'' he says, as calmly as if he was offering me another cup of tea.'

The indignation had long gone by the time she was curled up in bed and she rested her hand over the gentle curve of her belly.

'What should I do, little person? I don't know what's the best course. If we *have* given you beta thalassaemia between us, would it be better for you to have two parents to help to take care of you, even though one of them is only going to be there out of a sense of duty? Or would it be better if it was just the two of us—our own little loving family?'

She heard the echo of her wistful words and it reminded her of all her long-ago dreams.

Oh, she and her brother had started off with all the right ingredients for the perfect family but how quickly that had fallen apart. Then, such a short time later, she'd lost Marco, too, and it was only Anna's and Luiz's care that had helped her to survive.

The trouble was that she'd had to share them with so many others and, for all their loving attention, they hadn't been her own family.

She pulled a face in the dark as she realised that since Anna and Luiz had died she'd all but lost contact with the other members of their 'family'—but somehow it was hard to feel guilty. They'd been brought up to be strong and independent so it was hardly surprising that they had all gone their separate ways.

Now she was expecting a baby of her own—the start of her very own family—but the joy was tempered by the gap in the circle where a loving husband should be.

Leo had offered to marry her and, if she accepted, that would go part-way towards completing the circle—but how could it be the same without love to bind them together?

'Peg? What's Dr da Cruz doing here?'

'He's cheering the Johnson girls up,' Peg said far too innocently as she glanced across the ward. 'With the two of them under the weather and their parents both working they need the extra attention.'

Maria could hardly argue with that but why was *Leo* the one doing the visiting? She'd been expecting to hear from him so that they could arrange to have their talk but for over a week there'd been no message and she'd begun to wonder if he *had* changed his mind after all.

Her pager bleeped as she was halfway across the ward and she had to leave the tall, dark-haired man sitting comfortably on the edge of one bed while he chatted easily to the two enthralled young girls.

It was her day on call again but at least this time the closest lift was working properly and it was easy enough to go backwards and forwards to the accident department without exhausting herself.

Luckily the awful lingering sickness seemed to have disappeared at last and, with it, the drained greyness of her face. At last she was able to look in the bathroom mirror and see that she was beginning to look more like her old self—just before she finally lost her figure.

The only trouble was that while she was steadily regaining all the weight she had lost the progress of her pregnancy meant that she was also feeling more and more exhausted by the end of each day, especially the days when she was on call and hardly had two minutes to sit still.

That afternoon it was especially frustrating, with Leo always just too far away for her to talk to him before she had to dash off somewhere else.

It wasn't until she was called back downstairs three times in succession without even reaching the ward in between that she began to admit to herself that Leo had been right.

'I can't go on like this,' she muttered breathlessly, her white coat flapping as she trod swiftly along the corridor towards the paediatric ward. Her stomach was complaining loudly that she hadn't fed it for far too long and she was beginning to feel distinctly light-headed.

'Here.' Peg held out a cup of tea and a slice of freshly buttered toast as she slipped back into the ward. It was almost as though she had known that Maria was on her way. 'Sit down and get that inside you before you end up on the floor again. At least, this time, the poor man wouldn't have so far to come. . .'

She stopped speaking but it was too late.

'It was you, wasn't it!' Maria pounced, speaking round a delicious mouthful before swallowing hurriedly. '*You* told him.'

'Well, *someone* had to.' Her chin came up defensively. 'He said you were heading for a disaster and he was right.'

'But. . .I thought you were my friend, Peg,' Maria said, her voice a mixture of puzzlement and hurt. 'Why did you have to tell him I'd collapsed?'

'*Because* I'm your friend,' she replied staunchly. 'You give so much to everyone else and never expect anything in return. When he asked me if I'd be willing to keep an eye on you I was only too glad that someone else cared about you too.'

Maria felt the swift sting of tears gathering and blinked hard to control them as she managed a watery smile. 'Ah, Peg, my friend. What would I do without you to. . .?'

She never finished the sentence as her pager cut in yet again with its shrill summons.

'*Enough*!' The deep voice startled her as it growled fiercely in her ear, two hands settling firmly on her shoulders to stop her getting up. 'You can just sit still and finish your tea while I take this call for you.' He straightened up and, out of the corner of her eye, Maria saw him take in Peg's bemused expression. 'Well. . .' he smiled roguishly in her direction '. . .I can't have my wife collapsing through overwork, can I?'

CHAPTER SIX

'WIFE?' Peg squeaked as soon as he left the room, her eyes growing enormous. 'And you thought *I'd* been keeping secrets!'

After its initial startled leap into her throat Maria's heart sank into her aching feet. She only had to look at her friend's expression to know that she wasn't going to be allowed to escape until Peg had heard everything.

The only trouble was that there was nothing to tell and she had a strong suspicion that Leo's parting comment had been a deliberate manoeuvre designed to force her hand.

'Come on, Maria,' Peg coaxed excitedly, 'tell me what's been going on. When did the two of you get married? Why didn't any of us know before now—or am I the last to know?'

The fleeting look of hurt in her friend's eyes made Maria want to curse out loud at autocratic Dr Leo da Cruz. How was she supposed to answer her? If she told Peg the truth it would make Leo look a fool for claiming that they were married but if she supported Leo's claim it could destroy her friend's trust in her.

'Sister Mulholland?' The tentative voice was accompanied by a knock on the partly opened door and Maria breathed a silent sigh of relief at her temporary reprieve when Jeremy Tolliver's mother answered the invitation to come in.

'Hello, Mrs Tolliver,' Maria greeted her with a

heartfelt smile. 'I'll just get out of your way.'

'I'm sorry to interrupt, Doctor.' The poor woman became flustered when she recognised the white coat. 'I can wait outside if you're busy talking to Sister.'

'No need.' Maria was on her feet. 'Sister Mulholland has just saved my life with a cup of tea and some toast so I've got no excuse not to get back to work now.'

As she left the room she looked back just long enough to wave silently to a frustrated Peg and mouth the word 'Later'.

Hidden in the depths of the pocket of her white coat she crossed her fingers in the hope that before she saw Peg again she'd have a chance to grab Leo by the throat and find out what game he was playing.

'Laura's been telling me about her leg-lengthener,' Leo told Maria as she joined him in the ward at the end of her shift, her coat and bag clutched in the crook of one arm.

He was smiling at the shy youngster and, as Maria watched, the pale blue eyes begin to sparkle with new light.

'Dr da Cruz said he hasn't seen one working before so I had to tell him how it works.'

'And did he understand?' Maria prompted, feeling guilty as she determinedly ignored the surreptitious beckoning signals she could see Peg making from the door of her office.

'He wanted to know why I only needed to have one leg done. He asked if I was going to live on the side of a hill so I needed one leg longer than the other.' She giggled as her cheeks became coloured a pretty pink.

'And then I thought it was because she wanted to

walk round in circles,' Leo added and Katy Johnson joined in her sister's laughter.

'I told him that I had my leg broken when I was pushed over by a bully just after I started at school,' Laura continued when she'd regained her breath. 'And when it was in plaster the other leg started growing so the broken one got left behind and it couldn't catch up.'

'And, then,' Katy joined in, determined not to be left out of the telling, 'they put her to sleep and one of the doctors broke her leg again.'

'Ah, but he put pins either side of the break to join it to the fixators, didn't he?' Maria smiled at the younger girl's gruesome delight in telling her part of the tale.

'And now we have to turn the screws one millimetre each day to stretch my bones where they're mending.' Laura pulled a face. 'It makes my leg ache like toothache, especially after the physiotherapist makes me do my exercises to stretch my muscles.'

'I don't have to do fizzy-ferapy,' her little sister gloated with a grin.

'You will,' Laura warned. 'Won't she, Doctor? Otherwise her leg won't get strong again.'

'Then *Katy* might be the one walking round in circles,' Leo pointed out. 'Or she might have to move to a house on the side of a hill. . .'

There was the familiar sound of the ward doors opening and they all turned in time to watch Mr and Mrs Johnson hurry through.

'Mummy. Daddy,' the two girls chorused through their renewed laughter and Maria watched the worried expressions on their parents' faces disappear in an instant.

'Hello girls. Katy. Laura. You're looking happier this evening. . .'

Leo and Maria had moved aside so that the little family could share hugs and kisses and, with the briefest of farewells, Leo made their excuses and grabbed Maria by the elbow.

'Quick,' he muttered out of the corner of his mouth, 'before Peg sees you're free,' and they scooted out of the ward door like a pair of truants.

'Hey, slow down.' Maria panted to a halt when they turned the corner by the lifts.

'I'm sorry.' Leo was immediately penitent, apologising under his breath as they joined the small knot of people so that his voice wouldn't carry. 'I'd forgotten about the baby.'

'It's got nothing to do with the baby.' Maria whispered the words fiercely as the doors slid shut, thankfully enclosing the two of them in a private box for the few seconds it would take to reach the ground floor. 'My legs aren't as long as yours. And, anyway,' she added, 'it was your fault we're running away from Peg in the first place. What on earth possessed you to say such a thing?'

'You mean about getting married?' He raised one dark eyebrow imperiously.

'You implied that I was already your *wife*,' Maria reminded him breathlessly as he hurried her out of the lift and across the reception area. 'How could you say something like that when we haven't even had time to talk about it, let alone make a decision?'

'Well, it was only a little premature. You *will* be my wife as soon as we can arrange it.' The words were reaching her over his shoulder as they made their way towards his car, his tone as decisive as ever until he abruptly turned to face her in the middle of the consultants' car park and took her hands in his, capturing her with his shadowy silver gaze. 'Won't you, Maria?'

It was the first time that Maria had seen him show a sign of uncertainty and suddenly she realised that the revelation of this facet of his character had just sealed her fate.

Just those few words spoken in that hesitant husky voice had made her realise that she was falling in love with him—this outwardly contained, self-confident man whose intimidating manner hid a battered heart of gold which only his patients were allowed to know.

'Yes,' she whispered, knowing that there was no longer anything to think about. She wanted to be with this man who was the father of her unborn child for however long she could. 'Yes.' Her voice was stronger now that the decision had been made. 'I'll marry you, Leo.'

All the way home the cacophony in her head grew louder as doubt piled on doubt.

She'd just agreed to marry Leo but what did she know about him? Only the barest minimum, apart from his excellent professional reputation added to what she'd seen of him with her own eyes in his time at St Augustine's.

By the time he drew up outside her flat in Alma Road she was shaking, convinced that she must have lost her mind. Just because she had realised that she was falling in love with him was no reason to suppose that he had changed *his* mind about anything.

A sudden black thought struck her and she tensed in horror, feeling the blood drain from her face just as he opened her door and offered her a helping hand.

'Maria? What's the matter?' He crouched down beside the open door so that he could see her more clearly, his hand automatically reaching for her wrist and checking her pulse. 'It's racing. . . Are you feeling ill?'

She shook her head dumbly, unable to voice the awful thoughts which filled her head.

'Can you move?' He released her seat belt, his arm almost enclosing her in an embrace as he reached across her for the catch. 'We'd better get you inside.'

Maria felt like an old lady as he supported her all the way into her sitting-room. She was furious to find that she couldn't even control her fingers well enough to unfasten the buttons on her coat and had to stand like a helpless child while he took it off for her.

The whole time one strong arm was wrapped around her shoulders until she was safely seated in her favourite chair.

'You need a cup of tea,' he decided and whisked her coat away to hang it up before she heard him moving about in her kitchen.

While she listened to him setting cups out on the tray she concentrated on breathing deeply and slowly, pleased to feel her pulse rate grow steadier and the tremor in her hands calm down until it was barely noticeable—until Leo came back into the room.

'Here.' He moved a small table beside her chair and carefully placed her cup within easy reach. 'I suppose recent events finally caught up with you,' he said with an understanding air.

If only that was true, Maria thought as she flicked a nervous glance towards him. What would he say if he knew the real reason I've got a fit of the shakes? She reached out for the cup, carefully cradling it between her palms as she absorbed the warmth and gratefully accepting the brief respite before she had to voice her fears.

'When would be the best time to organise this wedding?' His deep voice broke into her muddled musings. 'Have you got a couple of days off in the near future or will we just have to take our chances on getting away together later on?'

Maria found herself silently shaking her head, unable to think about dates and time away when her head was still too full of panic.

'I don't. . .I can't. . . Oh, Leo, I don't think we're doing the right thing. . .' She looked up at him fearfully, expecting an explosion but he began laughing softly.

'I think you've got a bad case of cold feet.' He smiled easily, his voice calm and unworried. 'I promise it will all be all right. We've got so much in common that. . .'

'How do you know?' the words burst out of her. 'You don't know anything about me. Not really. So, how can you possibly know that everything will be all right?'

'But, Maria. . .' She ignored his attempted interruption and forged on.

'It was only a few weeks ago that you were determined to go to court to force me into having tests done on the baby to try to make me have an abortion.' She could hear the shrill tone to her voice but she was no longer in control, the words spilling over like water out of a breached dam.

'*Now* you're saying that we're going to be successful at playing happy families just because we work in the same field of medicine and have so much in common. It's such a radical about-face that it makes me wonder if you've got an ulterior motive behind all your tender attention.'

She ended the accusation with a glare and saw the invisible shutters come down to hide his startled expression. For just a fleeting second she thought that she'd seen hurt in his eyes but it was the brief blaze of anger which had lingered longest before he ruthlessly controlled it.

'And what motive might that be?' he said quietly, the air in the room seeming to grow chilly around her.

'Well, how should I know?' she blustered, already regretting her outburst. 'First you say you don't want to get married, then you do; then you say you don't want the baby and the next moment you're going to take care of it—or are you. . .?' She left the final words hanging in the air.

'And what, exactly, do you mean by that?' he said very precisely, his eyes spearing her like twin lasers as he sat as immobile as a bronze statue.

'Perhaps it was just a coincidence that soon after I threaten to deny that you're the baby's father you suddenly came up with the idea of marriage. You can hardly deny that if we were married it would give you far greater legal power over what happens to the baby.'

'So,' he acknowledged coldly, his face drawn into a scornful mask, 'you think I suggested that we get married so that I would have a better chance of forcing you into having the baby tested?'

'It's perfectly logical,' Maria said defensively, quivering in the face of his obvious fury.

'I suppose it is—apart from one fundamental fact.'

There was a sting in his voice like the lash of a whip as he spoke. 'Even if I *did* want to force you into having the baby tested as soon as we were married there would be no point because it would now be illegal to perform an abortion.'

Maria felt sick.

She had completely forgotten that time had been marching on at an alarming rate while she'd waited for Leo to contact her—all she had been worried about was *why* he hadn't spoken to her. It hadn't occurred to her to remember that she had now entered the third trimester of her pregnancy.

If only she'd taken a moment to think things through before she'd spoken. . .but she'd been too panic-stricken at the sudden realisation that she'd become so emotionally vulnerable; too afraid that she was racing blindly into a relationship too fast to see the pitfalls.

'I'm sorry,' she whispered. 'Oh, Leo, I. . .'

'At least we won't be going into this arrangement with our eyes shut,' he said crisply as he stood up and fished in his pockets for his car keys. 'Although I must admit I hadn't realised you thought me quite so devious.'

'No,' she cried, suddenly scared. He was so angry—angry enough to walk out of her life? 'Leo, please let me. . .'

'Don't worry about it, Maria,' he interrupted as he tossed the small bunch of keys up in the air and caught them again with a vicious swipe of his hand. 'As you said, we don't know a great deal about each other but at least we'll have had the opportunity to remedy that by the time the baby arrives—that's if you still want to go ahead?'

Maria gazed numbly at his composed face but there was no expression there to give her a clue as to his own feelings.

All she knew was that he was more important to her than any other man in her life and she had hurt him deeply with her suggestion that he would have married her just to have the power to decide the baby's fate.

'Yes,' she whispered, her eyes falling to her entwined fingers lying so still and silent in her lap, hoping to hide the gathering moisture behind her thick dark lashes. 'I still want to go ahead.'

'Good,' he said briskly, as though this was some mundane business discussion drawing to a close. 'If you let me know when you're next due for some time off I'll make the arrangements. Any preference as to where it takes place?'

For just a second she had a mental vision of the wedding she had once dreamt of, the way most young girls do—of walking up the aisle in a white dress to join the man she loved. . .

'Well. . .' She paused. Old dreams died hard. 'Would you have any objection. . .? No.' She shook her head dismissively.

'What?' he demanded.

'It doesn't matter—I'd forgotten for a moment that you'd been married before.'

'What difference does that make? Ah—' he suddenly realised the significance '—you wanted a church blessing?'

'It doesn't matter. The registry office will probably be able to fit it in more easily.' She hid her disappointment behind logic.

He was silent for a moment, the power of his gaze

reaching her right across the room, before he gave a little nod as if he'd come to a decision.

'Right, then. As soon as you let me have a list of suggested dates I'll get back to you and let you know which one.'

He left her sitting in her chair feeling as if she'd been run over by a juggernaut, her brain so scrambled that she couldn't think straight.

'Where are we going?' Maria fished inside her cuff for her handkerchief and wiped her hands. She didn't dare touch the skirt of the outfit Leo had insisted on buying for her or the beautiful ivory-coloured fabric might spoil. 'Isn't the registry office back the other way?'

'Don't worry about it,' Leo said calmly, capturing one clammy hand between the warm strength of his and pressing it reassuringly. 'I'm sure the cabbie knows where he's taking us.'

'But what if we're late? Would the registrar wait for us?' There were a million butterflies in her stomach and the baby must be reacting to her tension because she was certain that she was going to have bruised ribs from the frantic activity going on inside her.

'Maria.' He hooked one lean finger under her chin and tilted her face up so that she was looking straight into his silvery grey gaze. 'There isn't going to be a problem so relax.'

'I'm sorry, Leo. It's just. . .I'm still not sure we're doing the right thing. . .'

'Shh. . .'

He touched her lips with the tip of one finger and she went silent, savouring the gentle contact.

'You look beautiful and everything will go

smoothly,' he repeated as the car slowed down.

She missed the warmth of his finger when he took his hand away and turned hurriedly to hide the wash of heat in her cheeks, gazing blankly out at the building they were drawing up outside.

'Leo? What are we doing here? What's happening?' She stared out of the window in bewilderment then looked back at him. 'We've stopped outside a church. *My* church. . .'

'This was what you really wanted. . .wasn't it?' His dark brows were drawn together as an uncertain expression filled his eyes.

'Oh, Leo, yes.' A fragile smile trembled on her lips as she suddenly realised what he had done. She had no idea how he'd managed to arrange it, especially in such a short time, but her heart filled with pleasure that he'd even thought of trying. 'Oh, yes. This is what I wanted.'

'Well, then. What are we waiting for?' He reached forward and flung the car door open then turned back to help her to the path. 'We've got an important appointment in there so let's get moving!'

Suddenly her heart felt as light as a helium-filled balloon and, tucking her hand in the crook of his arm, she walked beside him into the little church.

It wasn't until hours later that her head stopped spinning long enough to sort out all the impressions that had bombarded her as they'd walked together into a church full of guests.

Peg had been waiting for them just inside the door with a spray of freesias and fern and Leo's friend, Andreas, had arrived from Italy in time to stand up as his best man. She didn't have time to look at the rest of the guests in the few seconds it took to reach the altar steps, their faces just a blur as she walked the short distance at Leo's side.

And then they didn't matter. As far as Maria was concerned, she and Leo could have been the only two in the church as she concentrated on the heart-stirring promises they were making to each other.

In the brief pause after Leo was told that he could kiss his new bride she wondered mistily if fate would be kind enough to make him fall in love with her, too, but then his hands were on her shoulders as he turned her to face him.

'Hello, Dr da Cruz,' he whispered intimately, his grey eyes very serious as his glance roved over her face.

'Hello, Dr da Cruz,' she returned as a smile blossomed under the touch of his eyes. She was certain that her feelings must be as obvious as words on the open pages of a book but then he was concentrating on her mouth.

Although it had been months ago that she'd experienced them, she remembered all too clearly what his kisses were like and her lips tingled in anticipation so that the tip of her tongue flicked out to moisten them.

'Maria,' he murmured with a tiny groan as he touched his lips to hers and her heart leapt at the contained passion in his voice.

His arms slid round her shoulders and pulled her into the sheltering curve of his body. As her softness yielded to the hard-muscled power of his lean frame the gentle swell of her belly pressed against him just as the baby gave an enormous kick.

Leo tensed as if he'd been stung, his eyes suddenly dark with comprehension as they gazed down into hers.

Under the cover of her edge-to-edge jacket he slid

one hand over her and was immediately rewarded with another violent contortion of the little person contained inside.

'And hello to you, too, baby da Cruz,' he whispered and Maria's heart sank when she saw the solemn expression on his face.

How could she have allowed herself to forget the reason why this marriage was taking place?

As Leo released her and stepped back the organist began the first few bars of Maria's favourite hymn but all the excitement and anticipation had gone, even when he took her hand and led her through to the sacristy to sign the register with Peg and Andreas as witnesses.

At a small hotel nearby Leo stood with his arm around her shoulders as they greeted their guests but this time she knew better than to allow herself to think foolish thoughts about love and for ever. This time she knew that the gesture was just for the benefit of their guests.

When she'd seen them in the church it had looked as if there were dozens of them, especially as Maria had expected to find just their two witnesses waiting at the local registry office.

She had already counted twenty people when Leo's arm tightened reflexively around her and she glanced towards the latecomers just entering the room.

'Theo. Sophia,' he said coldly to the elegant couple who stood in front of them, every inch of his bearing telling Maria that he didn't want them here.

She shifted briefly in his hold and he seemed to remember that she was beside him, his fingers stroking her shoulder almost in apology as he lessened the pressure of his arm.

'Maria. May I introduce my brother Theo and his wife Sophia?'

Maria had known from his startling good looks that Theo must be some relative of Leo's but, although he might be aesthetically more handsome than his brother, he didn't have the indefinable aura of power that made Leo stand out in a crowd.

Sophia, too, was beautiful, uncannily like a *haute couture* picture, everything about her so perfect that when she turned towards Leo Maria almost expected her to be a cardboard cut-out just millimetres thick.

'Leo, darling,' she greeted him in a saccharine voice, her smile never reaching her coldly calculating eyes. 'When Andreas told us you were getting married we just had to be here to wish you well.'

There was nothing overt in anything that the three of them had said or done but there was a terrible tension between them, the atmosphere so electric that Maria quite expected to see sparks fly.

'Thank you,' she murmured politely, taking the initiative when she realised that Leo wasn't going to reply. 'I'm glad you could be with us today. If you'd like to go over to the other side of the room there's a drink waiting for you.'

She watched a strange expression cross Sophia's face when Leo calmly allowed his new wife to dismiss the two of them but, although her perfectly painted mouth tightened into a hard straight line, with a room full of other guests waiting to speak to Leo and Maria there was nothing she could do but take her leave of them.

'Leo?' Maria had waited until they were finally alone for a minute before she spoke in an undertone, keeping a smile on her face for the benefit of their guests. 'What's the matter? Didn't they let you know they were coming?'

'I deliberately didn't invite them,' he said through gritted teeth, his eyes as cold and hard as granite.

'But. . .? He's your brother. . .' Maria was puzzled. There had obviously been more than a passing argument between them—something far more serious. But what. . .?

'And she's my ex-wife,' he said in arctic tones.

Now Maria understood the tension between the three of them. This was the woman who'd borne Leo a son and then, even though her medical knowledge had told her that he needed special care, had knowingly neglected him until he was so weakened by the disease he'd inherited that he'd died on his birthday in his father's arms.

'Well.' She threaded her fingers through his and gripped his hand tightly as she spoke, her voice calm and quiet enough just to reach his ears. 'It would give their presence today far more importance than it warrants if we bothered to throw them out.' She tilted her chin to meet the chilly grey of his eyes with the warmth of her own, a fugitive smile lifting the corners of her mouth.

'After all your hard work I'm not going to let anything spoil today so let's just make our way around the room talking to the people you *did* invite.'

He gazed silently into her eyes for long seconds before a smile creased the tiny lines at the corner of his eyes.

'That sounds like an excellent idea.' He leaned forward to deposit a brief kiss on the end of her nose.

'Let's start off as we mean to go on, concentrating on the important things in life—like champagne. . .'

He reached out towards the tray carried by a passing waiter and relieved him of two glasses.

'Leo. . .?' she began doubtfully but he shook his head.

'One glass, sipped slowly, won't do the baby any harm. It might even send the little blighter to sleep so you can enjoy some food without indigestion.'

He chimed their glasses and they drank together, their eyes focused intently on each other almost as though they were making a pact with each other in spite of the circumstances of their marriage.

'Hey, you two,' Peg's voice broke teasingly into the silent communion. 'You ought to be circulating so we all get a chance to speak to you. There'll be plenty of time for gazing soulfully at each other when we're gone.'

'Peg!' Maria muttered, mortified that several of the other guests had overheard and were chuckling at her humourously outspoken comments.

'Sister Mulholland.' Leo bowed gravely in her direction. 'We stand corrected.' He looked across the room and beckoned to his friend. 'I must introduce you to Andreas.'

'Oh, there's no need. . .' Peg began and Maria had to hide a smile when she saw the heightened colour in her friend's cheeks as Leo made the introductions.

His best man was about the same age as Peg and looked devastating in his dark suit and white shirt but the thing which caught Maria's eye was the intensity with which he listened to Peg when she spoke and the unmistakable interest in his eyes as he surreptitiously took in how well she looked in her elegant new outfit.

Later she would have to ask Leo if there was any chance of matchmaking. Whether he thought that *his* friend might be a suitable match for *her* friend.

They continued around the room, spending time with each of their guests, the new ease between herself and Leo allowing her to smile openly.

Unfortunately Maria was also uncomfortably aware that, although they seemed to be taking care not to allow their paths to cross, Theo and Sophia were following them the whole time with their eyes.

Finally Maria couldn't put off a visit to the bathroom any longer.

'I think it must have been the champagne,' she murmured to Leo. 'It's gone straight through me.'

'Not very comfortable in view of the activity of a certain little lodger.' He smiled wryly.

The facilities were quite sumptuous and Maria paused a moment before she rejoined Leo and their guests to take advantage of the well-lit mirror over the basin to tidy her hair and renew her lipstick.

One disadvantage of the fact that she hadn't had a hand in the planning of the event meant that she had no idea how much longer it would be before their guests started to leave.

Leo hadn't said whether they were going to be transferring their belongings straight away or leaving the job until the morning. Now that she came to think of it they hadn't even decided whose home they were going to be living in. All he had told her was that she wasn't on duty this evening.

She took a half-step back from the mirror to take a look at the overall picture she made, pleased to see how much better she was looking these days. Her dark hair was gleaming with good health and her eyes were bright with happiness now that some of her uncertainty had been relieved.

She was just straightening the front edges of her jacket, enjoying the sumptuous feel of the supple ivory silk between her fingers, when the door opened behind her and she glanced up at the reflection.

Her heart began to thump uncomfortably as she saw Sophia walk in, dark eyes settling on Maria as though she'd expected to find her there, her whole bearing full of the tension she was trying to hide.

'So,' she drawled as she leant back against the door. Her pose was apparently nonchalant but Maria recognised that she had positioned herself deliberately, preventing anyone else from joining them. 'Leo finally managed to get someone else to marry him. Oh—' she covered her brightly painted mouth with matching talons in feigned remorse '—I suppose he *has* told you that I was your predecessor.'

'Of course,' Maria said as calmly as though the whole topic was boring. 'He's told me everything.' Without turning, she had managed to fix Sophia's gaze in the mirror and she saw her grow pale.

'Well,' her tone grew venomous, 'with a name like yours and your colouring it's odds-on your family's from the Mediterranean region so I hope you've had all your blood tests done.'

'Of course.' Maria had a feeling that she knew what was coming next and busied herself putting away her lipstick and closing her bag before she turned to face her. 'Didn't you know that Leo and I met as a result of our work with children who have the inherited anaemias?'

'What about you?' Sophia probed, her eyes narrowed into glittering slits. 'Do you carry any of the traits?'

'Beta thalassaemia,' she confirmed quietly. 'I had a brother who died of beta thalassaemia major.'

'Well, you'd better make sure you don't get pregnant or you'll be risking losing a child of your own as well—Leo *has* told you that he's a carrier, hasn't he?'

'Of course,' Maria repeated. 'He told me about his son, too.' She caught hold of the edge of her loose jacket and pulled it aside, curving her hand deliberately over the cleverly concealing folds of her outfit to reveal the growing evidence of the child inside her. 'But obviously some things are worth taking a chance over. . .'

She'd thrown the words at Sophia like a challenge, secure in the knowledge that her new sister-in-law would never hear the true story behind her pregnancy. To her surprise she watched the perfectly made-up face drain of colour, the artful shading over her cheek-bones standing out grotesquely as her dark gaze stared with glassy-eyed horror.

'Oh, God,' she whispered, her eyes like ugly bruises in her white face. 'Oh, my God.' She scrabbled for the handle behind her, apparently unable to drag her eyes away until the last moment as she stumbled her way out of the room, the door sighing softly shut behind her.

CHAPTER SEVEN

'WHAT happened in there?' Leo muttered when she finally rejoined him.

'In where?' Maria stalled for time, still unable to understand why Sophia had reacted the way she had to the revelation that she and Leo were expecting a baby. Although she would have preferred to have been married before she started a family, Maria was well aware that her situation was hardly the sort of occurrence to cause so much shock.

'Maria.' There was a warning in his tone. 'Peg tried to go after Sophia when she followed you but the door was blocked. Then, a couple of minutes later, Sophia came out of there as if she had a devil on her tail. She grabbed Theo and dragged him out of the hotel without so much as waving goodbye.'

'Well, it certainly hasn't been a boring afternoon,' she began brightly, only to subside when Leo glowered at her. 'All right. If you must know, she introduced herself as your ex-wife—just in case you hadn't told me—and warned me not to get pregnant.'

'And?' he prompted, obviously knowing that there was more.

'I showed her my bump and I thought she was going to pass out but before I could say anything she was gone.' A sudden thought struck her. 'Do you think it brought it all back to her? Losing her own child? Was she worried for us?'

'Unlikely,' Leo snorted. 'The only person who matters to Sophia is Sophia.'

'So, we won't be seeing much of them?' In spite of the discomfort of the situation she couldn't help a trace of wistfulness creeping into her voice. Ever since Marco had died she'd had an unsatisfied longing to belong to a family. . .

'They don't spend much time in England. Theo's the chief executive officer of the family holdings in Italy and Greece and the lifestyle over there suits Sophia better.'

Having seen the way the woman dressed, Maria could well believe that her social life was normally somewhat different to this intimate wedding reception.

'In that case I don't understand.' She shook her head. 'I can't see why the two of them even bothered to come, especially as they weren't invited. Then, when she deliberately followed me to speak to me, I thought she was genuinely worried that I might not know that you were carrying beta thalassaemia trait but her reaction to the baby was. . .well, it was weird.' She pulled a face and laughed when he tapped his finger on the end of her screwed-up nose.

'That's not important now.' He smiled down into her dark honey eyes. How could she ever have thought his silvery grey eyes cold? They carried all the heat of molten metal. . .

He flicked a glance at the slim watch circling his wrist.

'It's time to go, Dr da Cruz,' he announced, raising one hand to attract Peg's attention.

'Do we have to go so soon?' She was conscious of a feeling of disappointment. Until that strange episode with Sophia she'd been thoroughly enjoying the unexpected party—the whole unexpectedly magical day.

'If we're going to get to the hotel in time for a meal this evening, we do.'

'Hotel?' The leap of pleasure at the thought that there were still some surprises in store for the day brought the smile back to her face. 'You let me think we were going to be doing removals this evening!'

'Hey!' Peg arrived, closely followed by Andreas, just as Maria thumped Leo's arm in retribution.

'I don't think you're supposed to start beating him before you leave the wedding reception,' the best man's attractively accented voice was accompanied by a wide grin. 'It won't do his macho reputation any good.'

'You Latin men!' Peg exclaimed hotly. 'Surely it's more important to have a good reputation with those who know you than to preserve appearances with people who don't matter!'

'Ah, but who's to know which chance acquaintance would have turned out to be someone important in your life if only you hadn't blotted your copybook with them on first meeting?' Andreas picked up Peg's hand and ostentatiously kissed the back of her fingers. 'It could be those first impressions which make all the difference, couldn't it?'

Maria knew that Leo's friend was only bantering with Peg, the way a man does when he meets a woman who sparks his interest, but she felt her cheeks grow warm as his words struck a personal chord.

Who could tell how the relationship between Leo and herself might have developed if they had been introduced to each other as colleagues on the first day of the conference?

As it was she was afraid that whenever he looked at her he would always remember that when he'd first seen her he had thought she was a prostitute; had believed that she was willing to sleep with him because Andreas had paid for her time. . .

'Maria?' Leo's deep voice broke into her unhappy thoughts. 'Are you feeling all right?'

They had decided not to tell any of her colleagues about her pregnancy until after the wedding so she was grateful for his careful choice of words.

He wrapped one strong arm around her shoulders and she allowed herself to lean against him, drawing comfort from the contact even though she knew it was all for show.

'I'm fine.' She smiled up at him, her eyes travelling over his handsome face in open enjoyment, secure in the knowledge that the guests would see what they expected to see—a new wife in love with her husband.

It was ironic that the only one who wouldn't believe it was Leo. He would be convinced that she was merely playing a part for their audience.

'Andreas?' Leo's call drew his friend's liquid gaze reluctantly from Peg's flustered face. 'Have you ordered the car?'

'It should be waiting on the forecourt already,' he confirmed. 'All you've got to do is make your farewells and you're on your way.'

'Well, then.' Leo put a guiding hand to the small of Maria's back to usher her towards the door.

They passed the scant remains of the sumptuous buffet and Leo reached out for the small package the hotel caterers had left in readiness for him beside the elegant stand which had held their beautiful cake.

'Peg's suggestion,' Leo said as he held it up. 'She said that the bride and groom never have the chance to enjoy the food at their reception so the caterer saved some cake for us.'

'I suppose those are the emergency rations in case we don't reach the hotel in time for a meal tonight!' Maria teased under the cover of the calls of good wishes which surrounded them as they reached the door.

'Oh!' She stopped suddenly and turned to face the happy throng. 'I nearly forgot. . .' She drew back her arm and flung her bouquet over the heads of the assembled group.

One long, dark-suited arm rose out of the reaching forest to pluck it in mid-flight and Maria saw Andreas smile wickedly as he presented his trophy to a furiously blushing Peg before Leo finally managed to escort her out to the waiting car.

'Are we going back to my flat to pick up some things first or will we do that after we've been to the hospital?' Maria had sunk blissfully into the soft upholstery, grateful that at last she could take her weight off her feet. She'd hardly regained her pre-pregnancy weight but her feet were complaining as though she was carrying an elephant around.

'Neither,' Leo murmured as he angled himself towards her, his long legs taking full advantage of the space in the back of the taxi as he leant back into the corner. 'Peg took care of your packing.'

'But. . .'

'Her original idea was to pick up a new toothbrush for each of us from the shop in the hospital foyer,' he continued with a twinkle in his eyes, 'but I pointed out that it was always a good idea to take some sort of robe as well—in case of emergencies.'

For several seconds Maria was speechless, her eyes fixed hungrily on his lean body as her mind was flooded with images of spending the night with him in a hotel bedroom with no more luggage than a new toothbrush. She suddenly realised that he was watching her expression and her cheeks instantly grew warm.

'But we *are* going to go to the hospital before we go on to the hotel, aren't we?' she said confidently, desperate to distract him from his present train of thought. 'I need to check up on one of my special children and the little boy who came in last night with. . .'

'It's all taken care of, Maria,' he broke in, then reached out to capture her hand while she spluttered indignantly, lacing his fingers comfortingly between hers. 'It won't be a problem. Ian was only too happy to oblige and Ross agreed that you needed a couple of days. . .'

'A couple. . .? You spoke to Ross MacFadden without telling me?' She drew in a horrified breath as she visualised the consultant's reaction. She knew only too well that he wasn't noted for his respect and consideration towards the female members of his staff. 'Now there's no way he'll ever write me a decent reference when I want to go for a consultancy.'

'On the contrary,' Leo soothed, gripping her hand tighter when she would have snatched it out of his grasp, 'he had some very complimentary things to say about your dedication to the job.'

'He. . .did?' She subsided incredulously, all the

wind taken out of her sails. 'I've never heard him say anything nice about anyone.'

Leo leant towards her as though he was going to tell her a secret. 'It might have had something to do with my volunteering my services for a presentation at the series of lectures he's giving,' he murmured with a chuckle.

'That's bribery,' Maria objected in mock outrage.

'Who cares if it got us what we wanted?' He brought her hand up to press a kiss on her knuckles and she felt the warmth go right through her.

'Did we?' she whispered, her eyes growing wider as they were caught in the clear silver of his gaze, her brain becoming impossibly scrambled by his nearness.

'Of course we did,' he confirmed as he repeated the kiss on each of her slender knuckles. 'We couldn't invite all those people to our wedding without going on a honeymoon, could we?'

Maria shivered as his meaning dawned on her and leant back into her corner of the seat so that she broke the contact between them.

She had so nearly been tempted into believing that he had arranged for the two of them to have a weekend together because he *wanted* to go away with her. Thank heavens he had reminded her in time that the whole event was just a charade being played out for their friends and colleagues before she had a chance to say something to embarrass both of them.

As the taxi drew up outside the front door of the hotel a little while later Maria thought that she couldn't have imagined a hotel more different from the one in Italy where she and Leo had first encountered each other.

Where the other one had been quite grand and the rooms they'd occupied sumptuous, this one was cosy, with low beamed ceilings and uneven floors covered by antique carpets.

'It's like something out of a story-book,' she exclaimed in a nervous voice once they'd been shown to their room, her gaze fixed firmly out of the window. 'It looks as if it's old enough to be Jacobean at least.'

'Well, I hope the mattress is a little newer than that!' Leo teased, finally drawing her eyes back to the four-poster bed which dominated the room.

She'd been transfixed by her first sight of it, blocking the doorway as her feet refused to take her any further into the room until Leo's presence behind her had forced her to enter.

In a panic she'd made an unnecessarily thorough inspection of the rest of the room and its tiny adjoining bathroom, finally resorting to looking out into the dusk at the nearly invisible view to avoid looking at the bed again.

'Maria. . .'

'Is it getting very late? Surely it's time we went down for our meal?' She found herself gabbling in her nervousness, edging her way around the room to make her escape when Leo started walking towards her.

'Maria.' One lean hand appeared in front of her face, holding the solid wood door closed when she would have pulled it open.

She froze, hardly daring to breathe as she felt the warmth of his body so close behind her.

'Please, Maria, turn around.'

The soft words persuaded her to turn towards him even though she wasn't sure what he wanted.

'What are you afraid of? That the sight of a bed will make me leap on you?' One dark eyebrow was raised quizzically.

'I'm not exactly. . .afraid,' she murmured evasively. She was too nervous to hold his gaze in case her true feelings were as obvious as she feared. Unfortunately when she looked away her eyes encountered the rich splendour of the tapestry curtains draping the bed behind him and she didn't know where to direct her eyes.

'Well, if you aren't afraid what *is* the matter?' His fingers cupped her chin and turned her back to face the quicksilver intensity of his eyes.

'I suppose I'm embarrassed,' she burst out suddenly, knowing that she had to give him an answer even if it wasn't the *whole* answer.

'Embarrassed?' he repeated. 'About what?'

'About the situation. . .you and me. . .everything!'

'Well, that's pretty comprehensive. Could you try to be a little more specific?'

'No. . . Yes. . . Well, *look* at me!' she wailed and pulled a face as she gestured down at herself.

'I've been looking at you ever since I picked you up to take you to the church,' he murmured. His expression softened as his eyes travelled over her from the dark curls framing her delicate face, skimming over the creamy fabric of her outfit and down to the elegant matching shoes on her slender feet. 'Beautiful,' he added in a husky voice.

'But I'm pregnant!' She gestured impatiently towards her elegantly camouflaged waist, all too conscious that the last couple of weeks had at last seen a marked increase in her waistline.

'Beautifully pregnant,' he began soothingly, taking her hand to lead her towards a softly upholstered chair. 'The last few weeks you've really begun to look so much better—much healthier. . .'

'Oh, Leo! You don't understand!' She batted his hand away angrily and stomped across the carpet before she turned back to face him from the safety of the other side of the room.

'I'm over seven months pregnant and I'm on my honeymoon with a man I've never seen.' She threw the words at him like an accusation, then found herself worrying her lower lip between her teeth as she waited for his reply.

'What do you mean?' His forehead was pleated into a frown. 'Is this an example of hormones scrambling your brain during pregnancy?'

'Don't be patronising,' she snapped, planting one fist on each hip belligerently. 'It's obvious what I mean—you just have to look at me.'

His frown grew deeper as he shook his head.

'Oh, for heaven's sake!' She threw her hands up in the air. 'We've made this baby but we've never even seen each other naked.'

The final word seemed to reverberate around the room for hours as she folded her arms defensively across her body.

'That's not quite true.'

His quiet words stopped her breath in her throat and the reminiscent smile which followed them nearly stopped her heart too.

'W-what do you. . .? When have you. . .?' The words wouldn't come.

'When I woke up that morning.' He answered the

question she couldn't frame. 'You were still fast asleep, your hair spread out across the pillow like strands of ebony silk. . .'

His voice had sunk to a husky murmur and she was mesmerised by the intensity of his gaze.

'The sun was slanting through a gap in the curtains and falling across your body, painting it with liquid gold. I'd never seen anything so beautiful before. . .'

'Oh, God.' Maria covered her face with her hands. 'That makes everything worse.'

'Because I saw you and you haven't seen me?' he questioned with a wry smile as he reached for his tie. 'If that's the problem it's easily remedied.'

'No!' She shook her head wildly. 'Because you saw me then when I was. . .was pretty and now I'm all. . . pregnant!' She whirled round and sped towards the seclusion of the compact bathroom but he moved faster, blocking her way effortlessly.

'Maria, Maria,' he crooned as he cupped her shoulders with his palms and massaged the tense muscles at the angle of her neck with sensitive fingertips. 'I know this is very awkward—for both of us. And I apologise for being so slow to understand your concerns.'

She drew in a deep breath and let it out in a heavy sigh as she leant tiredly back against the frame of the door. 'Where do we go from here, then?' she said uncertainly. 'It's still more than two months until the baby's born and we can hardly go round pretending it's not there. . .'

'But I *can* make sure I give you enough space to make you feel comfortable.'

'How?' Her eyes flew to the bed behind him. With only one bed in the room. . .

'Easily.' He smiled reassuringly. 'Until you feel more comfortable with the situation I just have to make sure that you have plenty of time to yourself first thing in the morning and last thing at night.'

'But. . . Wouldn't it be easier if you just asked if they've got another room for you or. . .or a room with twin beds?'

As she watched his smile faded and his eyes emptied of expression.

'I didn't realise you distrusted me so much,' he said coolly. His lips were tight with displeasure and Maria suddenly realised that she had hurt him deeply.

'If that's what you would prefer,' he continued, turning towards the door.

'No.' She grabbed his sleeve as he started to move away. 'I'm sorry. I'm being stupid. . . It must be those mood swings I was warned about. . .' she offered apologetically then stopped, her eyes fixed on his as she mentally crossed her fingers. 'The. . .the bed's plenty big enough for the two of us. It's. . .it's not as if either of us is any great size—yet!'

There was a long silence as his eyes probed hers and she tried to fill them with the apology he would never accept—the apology for hurting his male pride.

'Well,' he said finally, clearing his throat before he continued, 'if you'll give me a minute in the bathroom I'll get out of your way so that you can take your time.' He stepped past her and she noticed with a sinking heart that he made certain that he didn't touch her on his way. 'I can wait for you in the lounge until you're ready to come down for dinner,' he added in a toneless voice.

'Damn. Damn. Damn,' Maria muttered angrily as

soon as she heard the latch of the bathroom door click into place behind him. She had been concentrating so hard on her own embarrassment at the prospect of sharing the room with him that she hadn't realised how insulting the implication of her words would be.

The *last* thing she'd wanted to do was hurt him, especially now that she'd realised just how much she was coming to care for him.

She turned to the small weekend case which had been deposited on the gleaming wood of the linen chest at the foot of the bed and twisted the locks open.

The case was hers—she hadn't even realised it was missing; hadn't even thought to look for it when she didn't know that Leo was arranging for the two of them to go away together. But while she recognised the piece of luggage as the same one that had accompanied her on that fateful trip to Italy she didn't recognise the clothing lying inside it.

'What on earth. . .?' She gingerly lifted out a fragile drift of silky chiffon and it slithered like a midnight blue waterfall to hang in softly gleaming folds from the slender spaghetti straps in her hands. 'Where did *this* come from?'

She caught sight of a flash out of the corner of her eye as a silvery gift tag fluttered to the floor and she bent to retrieve it.

'Happy honeymoon. Enjoy!' she read, followed by Peg's familiar signature.

'Oh, Peg. You idiot.' The fond words were half laugh, half sob as she remembered that even her closest friend at St Augustine's didn't know the full story behind this apparently fairy-tale wedding.

In spite of her preoccupation she heard the sound of

water draining from the basin and she just had time to thrust the incriminating item under the nearest pillow as the bathroom door opened.

'See you later,' Leo confirmed as he made his way towards the door with hardly a glance in her direction. 'Take your time.'

'Take my time?' Maria muttered at the door when he closed it gently behind him, her stomach growling hungrily into the quiet of the room. 'Not likely! I'm starving!'

It was less than five minutes before she was following Leo down to the ground floor, her make-up hastily retouched and her hair released from bondage and given a thorough brushing to lie in a gleaming mantle over the ivory shoulders of her wedding outfit.

She paused as she entered the room, her eyes flicking around the cosy groups of armchairs and settees to find Leo. As her eyes fastened on him in a secluded corner she surprised a startled expression on his face as he watched her walk towards him. Maria felt an answering leap and her hopes rose again that everything would be all right.

'That was quick,' he commented blandly as he stood up and Maria had to stifle a groan of disappointment as he continued to speak as though she was just a chance-met colleague. 'Can I get you something to drink?' he offered politely, 'or would you rather go straight through to the dining-room?'

'Straight through, please,' Maria confirmed calmly and raised her chin a notch even though his cold civility felt like a rebuke. 'If I don't get something to eat soon I'm going to start gnawing on a table-leg.'

The creases beside Leo's eyes deepened briefly as

he gave a short laugh. 'That makes a change. It wasn't long ago you weren't eating enough to keep a sparrow alive.'

'It's amazing the difference it makes to your appetite when you know the food is going to stay with you when you've eaten it,' Maria explained wryly as he held out her seat for her, his manners impeccable in spite of the strained atmosphere between them.

On the surface the meal went well. The food and service were excellent and, providing they spoke of medical matters, the two of them were never at a loss for conversation. But underneath the politeness Maria could feel the tension building.

When she couldn't help yawning for the third time, nearly spilling the cup of tea she'd chosen instead of the coffee she'd rather have had, Leo rose to his feet.

'Time for bed,' he prompted avuncularly as he offered her his hand to help her out of the comfortable armchair she'd taken root in after their meal.

Maria's heart leapt stupidly at his words until she mentally dragged it under control again, reminding herself that there was nothing salacious in his pronouncement.

Even so she couldn't help the wistful daydream that teased her mind as he escorted her into the lift and up to their room.

If, instead of a sham, this had really been their honeymoon would he still be standing there in the ornate glory of the lift with a careful six inches between them? Would he merely take her elbow to guide her along the eccentric steps and turns of the corridor or would he have put his arm around her shoulders?

While her thoughts had been meandering they'd

reached the door of their room and he was opening it, pushing the dark polished wood wide with one hand while he pocketed the key with the other.

'I'm going to have another cup of coffee before I come up so there's no need to hurry with the bathroom.'

He'd turned away as he began speaking and was already part-way along the short corridor before Maria realised that he wasn't coming into their room with her.

She watched his retreating figure with stunned amazement and his long strides had taken him as far as the corner which would take him out of sight before she hastily managed to find her voice.

'Leo,' she called softly, mindful that there might be others already settled for the night in the nearby rooms. He paused momentarily to glance at her over his shoulder.

'Yes?'

'Goodnight,' she whispered into the silence that stretched between them, her heart in her mouth as she waited—hoping to hear him say that he'd be back before she went to sleep.

For a long moment he stood wordlessly, his eyes brooding and shadowed in the subdued light of the corridor.

Finally, 'Goodnight,' he echoed, and disappeared, leaving her to close the door on the last of her fragile hopes.

CHAPTER EIGHT

LEO was as good as his word. He'd said that he was going to organise a job-sharing scheme which St Augustine's would accept and he'd done it. The only trouble was that Maria found it impossible to limit herself to the part-time work she was now expected to do.

'What are *you* still doing here? You should have gone home an hour ago.'

Maria jumped when Peg's voice sounded behind her and she swung round to face her.

'I've just finished a session with Julie Turton's parents and grandparents. I think I finally managed to get through to them that they're actually doing her harm when they give her "special treats" of biscuits and sweets to "make up" for becoming diabetic.'

'Poor kiddie,' Peg murmured as she busied herself pouring boiling water into the tiny teapot she kept ready on a tray in the corner. 'I've lost count of how many times they've had to rush her in with a hyper since she was diagnosed. You'd think no one had explained it all to them the way they ignore all the rules and advice.'

'That's why I had them come in together this afternoon,' Maria said tiredly as she used both hands to brush the straggly wisps of hair away from her face. 'I thought if I went over it again with all of them in the same room they would all know that they were getting the same information and had to obey the same set of rules.'

'But they had you in there for over an hour and a half and you've come out looking like a limp dishrag,' Peg began militantly as she advanced on Maria like an avenging angel with only a steaming cup of tea as a weapon. 'Anyone would think the hospital didn't have any trained counsellors the way you take on the stubborn ones.'

'Don't you start lecturing me again, Peg Mulholland,' she said as she sank gratefully into the chair and, ignoring the saucer, wrapped her hand around the proffered cup. 'I'll be fine as soon as I've had this tea.'

'Providing you don't take your bottom out of that seat for at least the next half-hour when you've finished it,' Peg replied trenchantly, her look as severe as her tone. 'You might have got away with overworking when I didn't know about the baby. . .'

Maria groaned. 'I wish I'd kept my big mouth shut, now. I'd have had several fewer weeks of persecution.'

'That's another thing,' Peg jumped in. 'How on earth did you get to seven months without anyone noticing you were pregnant? In an ordinary office I could understand it but even in a hospital where we're supposed to be trained observers no one had a clue.'

'Partly it was because I lost so much weight in the early stages with morning-, noon- and night-sickness. Then it took me a long time to put it back on. . .'

'But you've got a real football-sized lump there, now.' Peg nodded towards Maria's recently non-existent waist. 'You can hardly say that *that* looks like a hernia!'

'Hardly!' Maria chuckled helplessly, nearly spilling

her tea. 'But being a doctor does help—we get to wear this voluminous white camouflage outfit.' She picked up the edge of her coat to show what she meant and the stethoscope started to slide out of the pocket.

'Oops!' She made a grab for it but missed. 'I can't move quite so fast nor fold up quite so far in the middle these days,' she said ruefully as she accepted the offending article from Peg. 'I'm beginning to feel quite bloated.'

'In comparison with a stick-insect,' Peg retorted rudely, glancing down at her own far more rounded figure. 'You should try battling with my inches. At least yours will all disappear once junior arrives.'

'With any luck.' Maria crossed her fingers then a sly smile crept over her face. 'Anyway, what are you complaining about? I have it on good authority that a certain handsome doctor is rather smitten with you—curves and all. Hospital gossip has it that he's flown over from Italy three times in as many weeks just to see you.'

'Rubbish!' Her friend turned away swiftly but not before Maria had seen the tide of colour staining her cheeks. 'He came over to attend the presentation that Leo did for the lecture series.'

'And the other times?' Maria taunted.

'Oh, hush!' Peg flounced towards the door. 'You sit quietly and finish your tea.'

'Yes, Sister. Of course, Sister,' she mocked with a grin as she toasted the rapidly retreating back with her cup.

She sighed deeply once Peg had gone and let her head drop back to rest against the high back of the chair.

Now that she was alone she could admit just how

tired she really was. She'd thought that job-sharing with Leo would have taken the pressure off her but it almost seemed as if it had made things worse.

Ever since they'd returned from their weekend away he'd been at great pains to treat her like fragile china. More often than not she'd get ready to go into the hospital and find that he'd ordered a taxi to take her to work and when her duty was over and he came to take over for her there would be a taxi waiting to take her home again.

The time they actually spent together was minimal; in the last few weeks it had been barely more than the time it took to hand over responsibility for the patients.

It was the off-duty times that she found most difficult. If they were both home at the same time their conversation seemed to be confined solely to medical topics, almost as though they were afraid to loosen the tight hold they had on the situation.

When each evening had finally dragged until they were both yawning and bed was the only option, Maria found herself clinging desperately to the edge of the mattress in an attempt to stay on her own side of the bed.

She was disgusted to note that Leo didn't seem to find any difficulty in falling asleep, his breathing growing deep and even within minutes of his head touching the pillow.

Night after night Maria watched the numbers on her alarm clock click monotonously around while she remembered the first night they had spent in each other's arms and each time her eyes sheened with tears as she compared it with the nights they'd spent together since.

The first night of their 'honeymoon' had passed

without so much as a memory to hold on to.

After a brief tussle with her self-consciousness she'd finally donned the silky nightdress Peg had given her, grateful for the concealing folds as she slipped nervously between the crisp cotton sheets.

Remembering Leo's pleasure in threading his fingers through her hair, she'd deliberately left it loose, innocently expecting it to invite his attention when he returned to their room.

Unfortunately, before he arrived the events of the day had caught up with her and the next thing she'd known was a knock on the bedroom door as room service delivered her breakfast on a tray the next morning.

The times when she was at home alone weren't any better.

After the frantic activity involved in moving her belongings into his new flat halfway between their two hospitals she found that she couldn't settle to anything and the thought of trying to catch up on her sleep when he wasn't there was laughable.

She'd tried it once, lying down in the centre of the bed early one evening with a light blanket over her legs. Several attempts at courting sleep, following the methods taught at her prenatal relaxation classes, had been no help.

Trying to find a more comfortable position had her rolling over onto her other side but with her first deep breath she drew in the unmistakable mixture of soap and male musk which told her that she was lying on Leo's pillow and all thought of sleep fled.

Finally she had decided that her only alternative, if

she was to retain her sanity, was to keep busy at the hospital.

She sighed heavily as she reached out one hand to deposit the empty cup on the corner of Peg's desk then paused to gather her thoughts.

It had taken some careful arrangement but she was slowly managing to fill the empty hours by scheduling appointments such as the meeting this afternoon with Julie Turton's family. When she had been working a full timetable it would have been impossible to spend such a long time with them but, in spite of the fact that she felt exhausted, she honestly felt that she had achieved something this time.

'What are you still doing here?' a familiar deep voice demanded as Leo entered the room. 'The taxi was supposed to have taken you home a couple of hours ago.'

'That's just what Peg said and in exactly the same tone of voice,' Maria told him, her words covering the leap in her pulse which happened every time she saw him.

'Well, we're both right. You shouldn't be spending so many hours on your feet.'

'I've been sitting down for most of the afternoon,' she said self-righteously.

'In between walking from floor to floor and bed to bed with a couple of forays to interview rooms and intensive care,' he detailed all-too-accurately.

'Peg's a rotten sneak,' she muttered sulkily. 'I'm taking good care of myself. My last check-up was perfect.'

'Apart from a slight rise in blood pressure and too little weight gain.'

Maria blinked in surprise. She hadn't realised that

Leo knew that she'd been for her regular visit to the antenatal clinic, nor that he'd made a point of finding out about the state of her health. The thought that he'd bothered shocked her into silence and made her feel all warm inside.

'Come on, Dr da Cruz. Time to go home.' He walked over to stand in front of her and hold out both hands, towering over her as she sat in the chair.

Tentatively she placed her own in them and saw their pale slenderness disappear in his broader palms as they touched for the first time for so long.

As she'd lain awake in the darkness she'd often wondered if she'd imagined the electricity in the contact between the two of them but she hadn't. Pulling her out of the soft upholstery was a mundane occurrence but it had her pulse racing and her breathing irregular enough to suggest that she'd been using the stairs instead of the lift all day.

'Ready?' he prompted when she didn't move, her feet apparently glued to the floor.

'Oh. Yes. I've got my bag. . .' Her voice trailed away in surprise when he placed a solicitous arm around her waist to usher her towards the nearest bank of lifts. In silence she revelled in the unaccustomed contact, hoping that it might signal a change in the atmosphere between them.

It wasn't until they were waiting for a lift to arrive that she saw a couple of the junior nurses nudging each other and smiling that she wondered at his actions.

Suddenly her heart sank as she realised that the staff grapevine would expect such things from the couple who had married after such a whirlwind romance. Obviously Leo was making certain to provide the show.

With all her pleasure in his display of concern gone she waited stoically until they were out of the building before she turned slightly so that his arm would slip away, her pride forcing her into conversation.

'How was young Steven in intensive care? Any progress?' She was referring to their latest emergency patient. 'Did anyone find out what had happened to him?'

'According to his older brother he'd run away to hide from a group of bullies and made the mistake of trespassing on a building site. Apparently there was an old house in the process of being demolished to make way for a new development and part of a wall collapsed on him.'

'That explains all the cuts and bruises all over him, poor kid.' Maria winced as she remembered the dozens of cuts and grazes and the depth of some of the bruising. 'Why didn't the building company make sure this sort of thing couldn't happen? If it's dangerous surely the site should be made secure from trespassers?'

'It's an ongoing problem, apparently. It doesn't matter how carefully a site is boarded up children and squatters always seem to find a way in.'

'You didn't say whether he'd made any progress yet?'

'Not so far. He's obviously still heavily sedated until we get another scan and find out if his brain is still swelling.'

'So it could be days or even weeks before his poor family know what permanent damage he's suffered. . .'

As ever when they were talking about the patients they had in common there was no lack of conversation between them but by the time Leo was parking the car in his designated space by the flats they'd grown silent, the tension once more like a living presence between them.

Maria had gathered her belongings together and was already swinging her legs out of the car door by the time he reached her.

'Here, let me help.' He held out one hand towards her.

She longed to accept his assistance and just an hour ago she would have done. Not just because it helped her to avoid the struggle of getting to her feet but also because she enjoyed what she had thought were little displays of consideration

Except they weren't, were they? she thought, angry at her gullibility as she disregarded his outstretched hand and scrambled out unaided. It was all display and precious little consideration—for her feelings, at least.

She marched self-righteously up to the door and across the entrance hall towards the flat, totally ignoring his presence beside her.

'I'll unlock the door for you,' he offered as he flicked through the small bunch of keys to select the correct one.

'I'm perfectly capable of unlocking a door,' Maria snapped pettishly as she opened her bag to get her own keys out and promptly dropped the contents all over the floor.

Cross with her own clumsiness, she tried to stoop swiftly to gather everything up again but there was an unexpected argument between her knees and her expanding waistline. For several seconds she flailed her arms wildly, trying to regain her balance before she collapsed in an ungainly heap at his feet.

'Maria! Are you all right?'

He was there instantly, his strong hands lifting her effortlessly to her feet and turning her around as he checked her for any signs of injury. 'Did you hurt yourself?' he demanded, his brows drawn together over his patrician nose as he frowned. 'Let's get you inside quickly and I'll take a proper look at you.'

'It's all right, Leo. You can relax.' Maria forced the words out through the constriction in her throat. 'There's no one here to watch the show.'

'"Show"?' he repeated coolly, taking a step backwards in the face of her refusal to be helped. 'What are you talking about?'

'Oh, come on! We're both reasonably intelligent people.' She finally found her key and twisted it viciously in the lock before she flung the door wide and marched in. 'We both know the *real* reason why we got married and while it makes good PR to act like the caring husband when we're surrounded by our colleagues you hardly need to keep the charade up for *my* benefit.'

She dropped her bag disdainfully on the coffee-table in the middle of the understated elegance of the living-room and the catch burst open, spewing her belongings out all over the floor for the second time.

'Dammit!' She swore through gritted teeth as she stood staring down at the mess, blinking furiously to hold back the threat of tears.

'Maria. . .'

'Don't!' she cut him off, whirling away from his approaching figure to stare out at the fading light, her arms wrapped defensively around her ribs. 'Don't say anything. I'm not in the mood to put up with a lot of. . .'

'Maria. Stop it.' His hands grasped her shoulders and he spun her back to face him, the speed of the movement rocking her back on her heels so that she had to clutch at his arms to steady herself.

'What's going on?' he demanded, his eyes boring deep into hers as she felt the first betraying tear spill onto her cheek. 'What on earth's got into you today?'

'N-nothing.' She sniffed and opened her eyes wide in a futile attempt at stopping any more tears falling. 'It's just. . . You didn't. . .' She gave up the attempt with a shake of her head.

'That's not good enough.' He gave her a little shake. 'You accused me of playing charades and I want to know what brought that on.'

'Well, it's true, isn't it?' She glared defiantly up at him. 'Today, in the hospital, you were playing the caring husband escorting his wife for an audience of nurses.'

'If you want to put it like that, I suppose I was,' he agreed tightly and she watched his lips draw into a narrow disapproving line. 'Of course, it didn't occur to you that I *am* your husband and I might actually *want* to care for you, did it?'

'Why should it?' She tilted her chin up. 'I'm nothing to you, except the woman who was in the wrong place at the wrong time and ended up pregnant with a baby you don't want.'

'That's not true!'

'Ha! Which part?' she challenged. 'Can you deny that you wanted me to get rid of the baby? Can you deny that until Andreas told you I wasn't a prostitute he'd paid for you'd forgotten all about me?'

'Yes.'

The forceful whisper cut through her tirade like a scalpel blade, stunning her into silence.

'Yes,' he repeated, his steely grey eyes intent on her. 'I *do* deny that I'd forgotten about you. You never left my mind.'

'If that's true why did it take you three months to come looking for me?'

'Because I didn't know how to make contact. . .'

'Oh, *please*!' she said in disgust. 'You knew who I was the very next morning at the conference. If I was so memorable you could have walked straight up to me and introduced yourself.'

'So could you,' he retorted. 'This is the nineties. You were just as much at liberty to approach me—after all, you did the night before.'

'But I didn't know who you were. I didn't even know I was in the wrong bed. . .'

'How was I supposed to know that?' he said, his logic infuriatingly correct. 'You appeared in my bed, made earth-shattering love with me and then didn't so much as speak to me the next morning. What was I supposed to think?'

'Oh, God!' Maria covered her face with her hands to hide her embarrassment. 'I never thought about how it must have appeared to you. . .' She sighed. 'So that's why you glared at me in disgust.'

'Glared at you?'

'While you were eating. You were staring at me across the tables and you glared.'

'The only reason I glared was because I had just been told I had to cut my time at the conference short. I'd been planning on finding out about you—where you came from and why you were forced to supplement your income in such a way.'

'Supplement my income. . .!' she gasped, her hands curling into vicious-looking claws. 'You. . .'

'Shh!' He clasped his own hands over hers and brought them up to his chest where he cradled them against his warmth. 'I know it isn't true—in fact I think I knew it long before Andreas told me he'd had nothing to do with your presence in my room.'

'Then, why. . .?'

'I couldn't forget you,' he said sincerely. 'I couldn't forget what you'd done for me that night when I was so depressed and had no one to turn to.'

'But I didn't do anything. I only. . .' She blushed, quite unable to continue, and shuffled uneasily from one foot to the other. Finally she stepped away from him so that he had to release his hold on her hands and perched herself on the edge of the settee, reaching out to switch on a small table lamp in a vain attempt at distracting him.

'Ah, Maria, if you only knew,' he murmured as he joined her and coaxed her into leaning back more comfortably. 'You brought life and light into my soul at a time when I thought there wasn't any left in the world.' He stroked one hand over her dishevelled hair then cradled her hot tear-stained cheek against his shoulder. 'You were sweet and lovely and you seemed to know exactly how I was feeling—how desperate and depressed.'

'Oh, Leo, I was feeling the same way too.' Her expression was wry at the memory of that day and she rubbed her face against the fine fabric of his suit jacket just to enjoy the sensation of being so close to him. 'It was the sort of day that makes you question why you ever became a doctor in the first place and then you were there, as warm and comforting as a log fire in a cold world.'

'You were wrong, you know.' He tilted her face towards his insistently. 'I *do* care about you; I wouldn't want you to get hurt.'

Maria's heart leapt at the sincerity in his tone, her pulse beginning to race. Did he mean that his feelings for her were deepening? Was he, too, starting to fall in love? Was he going to tell her. . .?

'I can't forget that I should bear the major part of the blame for your pregnancy,' he continued, his eyes darkening with self-reproach as his arm tightened around her shoulders. 'I should have remembered to take some sort of precautions for the sake of my *own* safety, never mind yours.'

'Well, if you believed my *profession* made it likely that I could be carrying VD or HIV, or whatever, why didn't you?' Maria demanded shakily, stiffening against him as she realised with a sickening jolt that his only driving force was guilt.

'I'll admit that partly it was the brandy I'd had. I don't drink much, as a rule, and it was potent stuff but it was also because I wanted to believe that what was happening was all just a beautiful illusion—the sort of erotic fantasy that every man dreams about.'

'Do they?' Maria couldn't help the unwilling fascination in her voice. This was a topic she'd never discussed before—barely even thought about in her drive to achieve, to excel.

'What do you think?' His voice had grown husky and a darker hue appeared in the lean planes of his cheeks and he looked away from her curious gaze for a moment.

When he met her eyes again there was a different expression in the depths of his, almost as though he was lost in his memories, and Maria held her breath, a strange electric excitement running through every nerve as she waited for his deep husky voice to continue.

'I turned over in the darkness and found a sleek, naked body in the bed beside me, all soft and warm with a mane of silky hair spread out across the pillow.' He paused for a moment as his eyes travelled over her face, his fingers rising to release her wild curls from their customary bondage.

'It was too dark to see you but my hands transferred a picture directly into my mind as I ran my fingers through this abundance.' He suited his actions to his words, spreading her hair out across her shoulders like a mantle.

Maria shivered, awareness of his touch spreading right through her body.

'Then, when you turned sleepily into my arms and our bodies met for the first time. . .' his words faltered gruffly, as though he was unaccustomed to speaking about his feelings '. . .it was sheer heaven and I never wanted to wake up. . .'

Silence fell in the room but this time there was no rough edge to it, with Maria trying desperately to find something innocuous to talk about. This time she was perfectly content to stay just where she was, surrounded by Leo's strong arm with her head resting on his shoulder. This time she knew that whatever happened between them they had managed to open up lines of communication and would be able to talk about it.

At one point Leo insisted that she stayed put on the settee while he went out to the kitchen and microwaved a potato each to go with the cold meat and salad waiting in the fridge but as soon as their meal had been cleared away he put on some more of the soft piano music that had accompanied their meal and rejoined her on the settee.

She hadn't realised just how long they had been sitting there until her eyes began to grow heavy and she glanced down at her watch.

'It's getting late,' she said regretfully, not wanting this magical interlude to end. 'And you're due in the hospital tomorrow morning.' She angled her head so that she could look up at him without having to lift it from its comfortable position and for the first time was able to examine his face at close quarters.

'You're looking tired,' she said sadly, recognising that the stress of their situation had been taking its toll of him, too, in spite of the fact that he seemed to have been sleeping so well.

'I'm not surprised.' He pulled a wry face. 'I've only just finished my lecture tour; I've got a couple of papers I'm trying to edit ready for publication and, on top of that, I'm job-sharing with my wife and not getting a lot of sleep.'

'*You*'re short of sleep?' Maria demanded in amazement. 'You must be joking! You drop off as soon as your head hits the pillow. I can hear your breathing alter.'

'Ha!' Leo's laugh was dryly ironic. 'I might have fooled *you* into thinking I was sleeping but I can't fool my body or my brain. I'm shattered. . .'

Maria chuckled. 'What a pair of idiots,' she commented as she began the increasingly arduous business of getting out of the soft upholstery. 'I think we both need our heads knocked together.'

'Better than that.' Suddenly Leo's hands were there to pull her to her feet. 'I think we both need a good night's sleep. I don't know about you but I feel as if a great weight's been lifted off me.'

'Yes.' Maria stood for a moment while she explored her feelings. 'I really feel as if I'll be able to sleep tonight.'

As always, Leo ceded the bathroom to Maria first and she made her way towards the bedroom as he carried their empty cups out to the kitchen.

She was too tired and too relaxed to do much more than stand limply under the shower, her hair wound up inside a protective towel so that it didn't get wet. She'd taken to wrapping herself up in Leo's spare towelling robe for the transition to the bedroom, changing into her nightdress while he took his turn in the bathroom so that she was tucked safely out of sight under the covers before he reappeared.

She realised that tonight was different when she walked into the bedroom swathed in his robe to find a midnight-blue slither of silk draped across her pillow.

Her eyes flew over him as he lounged back against the headboard. He seemed perfectly relaxed, his jacket gone and his unbuttoned shirt gaping open casually to reveal his broad, darkly furred chest, his long legs crossed at the ankle as he stretched out lazily on the bedspread.

Finally their eyes met across the width of the room and she knew that he could read the question in her own dark honey depths without a word being spoken.

'I never saw you wear it,' he murmured huskily, one lean hand reaching across to trail sensitive fingertips over the delicate fabric. 'Peg told me she'd packed it for you but. . .' He shrugged.

'Why would Peg tell you about my nightdress?' She felt herself grow pink at the thought of Leo discussing her nightwear with another woman—even her friend, Peg.

'Why wouldn't she when I asked her to get it for you?' he replied simply and she was delighted to see the teasing glint in his eyes directed at her at last.

'What did you do—ask her to choose something she thought I'd like?' Maria was intrigued.

'No.' He paused as though debating whether to say any more then continued, almost bashfully. 'I'd actually seen that one in a window and I thought it would suit you but the shop wasn't open at the time. I just told Peg where it was.'

For a moment Maria was thrilled at the thought that he wanted her to wear the nightdress he'd chosen for her but then she remembered how different her shape was from the first time he'd seen it and hedged shyly.

'As long as you don't expect me to model it for you,' she stipulated. 'I'm not exactly lithe and lissom any more.'

He shook his head as he slid his legs off the bed and straightened up to his full height, walking towards her with a gentle smile on his face. 'But still very beautiful,' he murmured persuasively as he stopped right in front of her.

'I *mean* it,' Maria warned him sternly, a smile trying to lift the corners of her mouth at his blatant attempt at changing her mind. 'I'll wear the nightdress if you want me to but I'm not putting it on until you take yourself off to the bathroom.'

He pulled a face but Maria was sure it was just for show as he muttered, 'Spoilsport,' on his way to the shower.

She finished her own preparations for bed, sliding the deep blue silky fabric over her pale powder-dusted skin before she settled into her own side of the bed. She smiled in lazy amazement at the changes that had occurred in the last few hours, hardly able to believe that she and Leo were the same two people who had driven away from St Augustine's in such an icy atmosphere.

For the first time she actually believed that the two of them might develop a friendship strong enough to sustain them through the tensions of the next few weeks and, who knew, even beyond.

The bathroom door opened and Maria's heart stumbled frantically as Leo stepped into the bedroom with nothing more than a towel wrapped around his hips.

Suddenly she realised that it was the first time since their abortive honeymoon that she'd actually *seen* him in their bedroom. Ever since she'd moved into his flat she'd made certain that the light was turned out by the time he finished in the bathroom and that she was settled onto her side, facing away from the door.

'What big eyes you've got,' Leo teased and Maria flushed as she realised that she was staring at him, her eyes helplessly travelling over him, admiring the lean muscular power of his chest and thighs. Her hands clenched reflexively at the memories of what the dark whorls of body hair felt like to her fingertips.

'D-do you wear p-pyjamas?' she heard herself stammer and wished that she could disappear into thin air when Leo laughed delightedly.

'No, I don't wear p-pyjamas,' he mocked gently, one hand reaching for the tucked edge of the towel.

'Oh!' Maria gasped, turning away rapidly when she realised that he was about to remove his towel, then listening with feverish intensity to the rustling sounds as he lifted the covers on his side of the bed and slid in behind her.

'It's safe to look now,' he taunted her gently when the mattress stopped moving.

'Don't want to,' she said, trying to sound aloof but only managing to sound like a disgruntled child.

'Ah, Maria,' he chuckled and she felt the bed move again as he turned towards her, his voice continuing from right beside her ear. 'Sometimes it's hard to remember that you're a fully trained doctor—you get embarrassed so easily and you rise to the bait so fast when I tease you.'

She could feel the warmth of his breath on her shoulder, the thin spaghetti strap doing little to conceal her shiver of awareness as he stroked the tendrils of curly hair away from her neck.

'Are. . .are you going to turn out the light?' she faltered. 'It. . .it's getting late and. . .and. . .'

There was a long silence behind her before she heard the rustle of bedclothes and the click of the switch that plunged the room into darkness.

'Goodnight.' His words emerged on a tired sigh and Maria was suddenly afraid that her shyness and inexperience had destroyed all the progress they'd made this evening.

'Leo?' she whispered tentatively, her heart feeling as if it would jump out of her throat it was beating so hard.

'Yes?'

The unadorned word was without expression and she could only hope that she had found her courage in time.

'Would you. . .?' She swallowed, her mouth suddenly so dry that she could hardly speak; could hardly force out the words she needed so badly to say. 'Will you. . .hold me?'

Her heart sank when the silence in the room went on and on with no sign of movement and no reply.

Finally she heard the sound of a deep inhalation and his taut murmur, 'Are you sure?'

For a second she was fighting the tears that burned behind her eyes at the aching echo of emptiness in his voice. It was the realisation that he was just as prey to loneliness and uncertainty as she was that drew the word from her.

'Please. . .'

CHAPTER NINE

LEO'S arms were still cradling her possessively against the warmth of his body when she woke up early the next morning and for the first time since that night in Italy she felt absolutely content.

'Good morning, sleepyhead,' a deep voice rumbled up from the depths of the chest she was using as a pillow and she tilted her head to look up at him shyly in the pearly morning light.

'Good morning,' she echoed. 'How did you know I was awake?'

'I thought you might be when you started stroking me.' He glanced down towards his chest and Maria froze when she realised that her fingers had been rhythmically smoothing over the dark pelt between his flat male nipples.

'I'm sorry,' she gasped, snatching her hand away. 'I didn't realise I was. . .'

'Come back here.' He grabbed her hand and replaced it exactly where it had been. 'Don't stop—I was enjoying that.'

'Oh!' She ducked her head as memories assailed her of the way she had explored his body once before and she marvelled at how fearless she had been then and how timorous now. Surely it couldn't all be a result of her pregnancy—the knowledge that although she was still enthralled by the magnificence of his body her own was less attractive to him.

'What's the matter?' He coaxed her chin up with one hand until she had to meet his eyes.

'I'm. . . You're. . . Isn't it time you were getting up?'

'Ah, Maria, you're so sweet and so transparent!' He leant down to plant an unexpected kiss on her parted lips then retreated again until he could watch her face, smiling at her as she felt a blush steal up from her throat.

'Now. Tell me what's worrying you,' he demanded. 'You might as well because I'm not letting you out of this bed until you do.'

'But. . . You're joking!' she laughed. 'You've got to go on duty this morning.'

'Just think how guilty that will make you feel—that you were solely responsible for me not turning up on duty because you wouldn't tell me what's bothering you.'

His nonsense was sufficient to break the tension just enough for her to speak about her fears.

'You look just the way I thought you would,' she burst out, her eyes flashing down to where her pale hand was spread out against the perennial coppery tan of his chest, the dark furring of his silky hair curling up between her fingers. 'Even better than I imagined,' she added candidly.

'Thank you,' he said gravely and she was grateful that he didn't tease her, his eyes holding hers steadily as he waited for her to continue.

'It's just. . .I'm *not*. The way I was, I mean,' she added at last, the words emerging in a jumble as she tried to unravel her thoughts. 'You look so good. . .' she gestured wordlessly towards his sleek, fit body with one hand '. . .and I'm all. . .' she grimaced.

'And you're all. . .what?' he prompted. 'All beautifully lush and ripe with your glorious hair rich and shiny and your skin glowing with health?'

'Hardly,' she objected. 'I'm over seven months pregnant!'

'And you're still the sexiest woman I've ever seen,' he growled as he tipped her away from him to lie on her back. 'Your body has a timeless slender elegance which will look just as good in thirty years as it does now and your pregnancy does nothing to detract from it.'

Maria snorted her disbelief.

'You honestly don't understand, do you?' He sounded amazed. 'You don't realise that the taut curve of your belly over the baby and the extra fullness of your breasts is a blatant advertisement of your fertility and an aphrodisiac for the man responsible for your condition.'

'But they're heavy and cumbersome,' she objected as she tried to pull the sheet up over herself. '*I'm* heavy and cumbersome.'

'Not to me,' he said quietly as he gently released her tight grip on the edge of the sheet and drew it away from her.

She watched in nervous embarrassment as his eyes travelled over her body and saw them linger on the recently acquired bounty of her breasts like a physical caress and she was startled to see her nipples react as though he had actually touched them, tightening so that the silky fabric of her nightdress outlined their proud crests.

'Ah, Maria,' he groaned. 'Your body is just as responsive as I remember.' He stroked the betraying peaks with the tip of one finger and she arched helplessly towards his hand.

'Leo,' she whimpered. 'You can't. . .we can't. . .' She stopped on an indrawn breath as he cupped one breast in his hand and anointed her with his tongue before he blew softly on the clinging fabric. The sudden chill tightened her nipple still further, making her long for his mouth again.

'But you want to,' he murmured persuasively as he trailed his fingers up the slender length of her thigh, gathering the hem of her nightdress as he went. 'You want to see if it feels as good as you remember when I stroke your satiny skin and when you find out that it feels even better than you remember you'll want to find out how much else will be better still.'

'But Leo. You. . . Ahhh. . .'

'You see,' he encouraged as he cupped her intimately and she surrendered, powerless to resist his skilfully arousing fingers and the equally arousing murmur in her ear. 'I told you it would be better than ever. . .'

Maria found herself filled with a new confidence in the following few weeks and she finally recognised in herself the 'glow' of pregnancy she'd scoffed at when she was being so sick.

She'd resigned herself to the fact that she was soon going to have to stop work entirely but, with Leo's full agreement, she'd promised her 'special' patients that she would be calling in to visit them when they came for their regular transfusion sessions or when, God forbid, they had a 'crisis'.

Her heart had lightened when she'd seen how much

more relaxed Leo had become over the traumas of their young charges.

His skills as a physician had never been in doubt but it was his old burden of guilt over his son's death which had caused the destructive scarring on his soul.

Now Maria was looking forward to the birth of their child with a new assurance that, whether the baby had the misfortune to inherit beta thalassaemia disease or the good luck just to carry the trait, she and Leo would be able to cope with it together.

She smiled secretively as her thoughts strayed to the special gentleness he had brought to their lovemaking as her pregnancy grew more advanced, always more concerned with her enjoyment than taking his own pleasure.

'You've got that soppy grin on your face again,' Peg's voice interrupted her thoughts and Maria was fiercely glad that she couldn't *read* them as well.

'You mean the soppy grin like the one you get when you hear that Andreas is on his way to England again?' Maria retorted, not to be outdone.

'Huh!' Peg flounced over to the kettle in the corner. 'With a little more effort you could become really insufferable. When am I going to get rid of you for a while?'

'I'm due in about four weeks now,' Maria confirmed, 'so I could have started my maternity leave a fortnight ago but I've been so well. . .'

'That you decided to stay on and make my life a misery,' Peg completed for her and they both laughed with the ease of long friendship.

'Seriously, though. What have you got for me today, Peg? Any problems crop up in the night?'

Suddenly Peg, too, was all business.

'We've had one little mite transferred to us this morning from intensive care. She was badly savaged by a neighbour's dog.'

'She's still being specialled?'

'Until she settles down with us and you're happy with her obs,' Peg confirmed. 'I've put Dawn with her. She's got the experience and she's calm enough to cope with panicky parents.'

'Any others you want me to take a look at?' Maria slid herself forward in her seat preparatory to heaving herself upright. There was still little obvious evidence that she was so far through the term of the pregnancy and many of the other staff had no idea that there was a baby due at all.

As far as Maria was concerned her little passenger almost seemed to have doubled in size and weight in the last couple of weeks, making her usual energetic suppleness a thing of the past, so she'd be glad when the waiting was finally over. . .

'We've got a new one of your "special" children.' Peg smiled as Maria's attention was caught. 'The family have recently come here from abroad—staying with relatives.'

'What form are we dealing with? How much history have they brought with them?'

'It's another beta thalassaemia and they don't seem to have much information about her treatment. I don't know whether they just didn't bring it with them or what.' Peg put the new file on top of the small pile and handed them to Maria.

'Right, then. Let's start with Rashna Besharati,' she said decisively after she'd read through the sparse information available. 'Are her parents with her?'

'Her mother and an aunt, if you're lucky, because mum is Gujarati and doesn't speak any English and the aunt acts as interpreter for them.'

'In that case, if she isn't here we'll have to get one of the volunteer interpreters up here. Gujarati is Kumar's speciality, isn't it? Can you find out if he's on duty today?'

'Will do,' Peg confirmed as they made their way into the ward.

In the event they found just one visitor beside Rashna's bed and had to wait until Kumar was found to interpret for them.

Maria had to content herself with smiling a lot while she checked the listless little girl over and read through the notes in her file so far.

When Kumar finally arrived there was another wait while he conducted a rapid-fire conversation with the frightened-looking woman who compounded the problems by bursting into tears.

'What on earth's going on, Kumar?' Maria was only just beaten by Peg when she stepped forward to comfort the woman. 'What did you say to her to get her into such a state?'

'It's not me,' he denied with both palms held out towards her. 'She was talking to me about her daughter's illness and she let slip that she and her husband engineered this visit to her sister to try to get help for the girl. Now she's afraid that we'll make them leave without any treatment.'

'Please, tell her that the rights and wrongs of her presence here are nothing to do with me,' Maria directed. 'I'm a doctor and I'm here to try to help Rashna.'

It was obvious that her calm words and reassuring smile had already begun to work their magic even before Kumar had finished translating them and Maria was showered with a torrent of grateful thanks.

'Please make sure she knows that I don't know how much I'll be able to do for Rashna. She's in a pretty bad way.' Maria sat down on the edge of the bed and picked up the little hand not connected to drips and stroked it gently.

The young woman's eyes turned to Maria as Kumar spoke, their liquid darkness filled with sorrow as she spoke again.

'Mrs Besharati asked me to tell you that she has already lost one child this way and just when she has been told that she is carrying another, Rashna has become so much worse.'

'Ask if she's had any tests done to show whether the baby she's carrying has the same illness?'

The ensuing conversation was fast and furious, neither of them allowing the other time to finish a sentence properly before they began speaking again.

Finally Kumar reported back.

'She says she didn't know that such a test could be done. Apparently she lives in a very rural area where medical attention is sparse and they couldn't afford to go to the nearest city for such things.'

'Well, before you go, will you get one of each of the leaflets in Sister's office. You'll find a set in Gujarati published by the Thalassaemia Society in London. In the meantime, her home situation explains why Rashna is in such a bad way. She's very anaemic and jaundiced;

her legs are ulcerated and her spleen is huge.' Maria's hands were moving gently over the apathetic child, pointing out each of the features as she spoke about them.

Kumar was translating her words carefully, holding up a hand at intervals to halt Maria when Mrs Besharati needed clarification.

'Her bone marrow has been hyperactive and this has caused thickening of the cranial bones,' she continued. 'If we were to take X-rays we'd probably find she'd suffered pathologic fractures.' She paused while Kumar translated, watching the sadness deepen on the young mother's face as he catalogued the problems.

Maria began again, knowing that a mother who had already lost one child would understand all too clearly the implications of what she was about to say.

'According to the case history she's had just enough blood transfusions to keep her going but the resulting build-up of iron has been deposited in her heart muscle and that is what's causing her heart to dysfunction.'

Maria watched the mother's narrow shoulders slump even as she tried to smile at her daughter and Maria knew that she was prepared for the worst to happen.

By the time Leo arrived on the ward to take her home all Rashna's test results were back but in spite of the fact that she was hooked up to the complete panoply of what western medicine could do for her condition she hadn't shown any improvement.

'It's not that I don't trust the rest of the staff to look after her,' Maria murmured as she stood holding the rail at the end of Rashna's bed. 'It's just that I hate to go while she's in such a bad way.'

When Leo's hand covered hers in a gesture of

support she was filled with a feeling of warmth.

'We could always treat ourselves to a meal in town,' he suggested. 'Then we could call back in to have a look at her before we go home.'

'You're sure you don't mind?' Maria smiled gratefully up at him, loving him all the more for his understanding nature.

'Of course not. I know you'd only be sitting at home worrying about her.' He accompanied her to collect her few belongings and escorted her out to his car.

'There's a little Italian restaurant not far away,' she suggested. 'It wouldn't take long to walk there.'

'I think you've done quite enough walking for one day, pregnant lady. Remember our agreement? You're only staying on at work as long as your obstetrician is happy with everything. If you go and get yourself over-tired you'll be back home and off your feet so fast. . .'

'All right, all right! I'll get in the car,' Maria submitted hastily, laughing impishly up at him as she settled into the plush leather seat.

In spite of the light-hearted mood at the beginning of the meal the two of them gradually grew more sombre as they discussed Rashna's prospects for recovery until neither of them could eat any more.

The poor waiter was upset by the amount of food they had left on their plates and when they refused even to look at the sweet trolley he was devastated.

'I feel so guilty,' Maria muttered out of the side of her mouth as she and Leo slunk quietly out of the restaurant. 'He looked as if he was going to cry when you wouldn't even have a coffee.'

'We'll have to make sure to starve ourselves for a

week before we go there again so we can do the food justice,' Leo suggested as he unlocked the car doors.

They were both silent on the return journey to the hospital and Maria was very conscious of just how much Rashna's situation must remind Leo of his own son's illness.

'You don't have to come up with me,' she suggested when they arrived in the staff car park. 'I only wanted to look in on her for a minute.'

'So do I,' he said sombrely, 'just in case there's anything I can think of that might help. . .' His voice died away and they both knew what he was thinking about.

'Any change in Rashna's condition, Ian?' Maria demanded hopefully when the first person they saw when they reached the children's ward was the registrar coming out of Sister's office.

He shook his head wordlessly, his grim expression needing no further explanation.

'Damn,' she heard Leo mutter explosively and she surreptitiously reached for his hand and threaded her fingers between his to hold on tight.

'How is her mother coping?' Maria's heart was heavy with sympathy. 'You did know that this is her second child to go this way?'

'Yes. I saw the note on the file,' Ian Stanton confirmed. 'God, I hate this feeling of helplessness. . .'

There was a sudden commotion inside the ward with the shrill sound of a monitor and the swift passage of feet.

'Quick!' Maria whirled towards the door and released the catches to allow them entry.

'It'll be her heart.' Leo's voice was clearly audible

over the swish of curtains and the clang as equipment was swung into position and one part of Maria's brain registered that he sounded very calm—almost too calm.

Mrs Besharati had backed away from her daughter's bedside when the medical staff descended on her and Maria put a consoling arm around her slender shoulders as they watched the frantic activity together for a moment.

She stiffened when she saw her daughter's pale body arch up off the bed as they tried to restart her heart, a gasp of distress leaving her throat at the savage sight.

She grabbed Maria's hand and started speaking rapidly, her eyes full of tears as she shook her head in denial.

'They're trying to make her heart beat again,' Maria said, her words slow and clear as she tried to mime over her own heart what was happening.

When the poor woman only became more agitated Maria wished that there was someone—anyone—who could translate for them to save her having to do so much guessing.

'Mrs Besharati, please. . .' Maria grasped hold of both of her hands and turned her away from the bed where her daughter lay. 'Can you tell me what you want?' She made eye contact with her and slowly began to mime—first, that her daughter's heart started beating again and her eyes opened and then that Rashna's heart stayed silent and her eyes stayed closed.

'Yes?' she questioned at the end of the pantomime and the young woman nodded her understanding before she copied Maria's mime for Rashna's eyes opening and followed it with a shake of her head, then mimed her heart staying silent and nodded her head—while the tears streamed down her cheeks.

'Leo? Ian?' Maria called but the two of them were so intent on what they were doing that they barely heard her. 'Leo,' she repeated louder. 'Please, listen. Mrs Besharati wants you to stop.'

For a moment the two men were so still that the scene around the small child's bed was almost like a posed tableau then, at a nod from Leo, Ian continued the interrupted heart massage.

'Are you certain?' Leo was the first to find his voice. 'How did she tell you that? She doesn't speak any English and you certainly don't know Gujarati.'

'Watch,' Maria said and touched the woman's elbow, gesturing for her to repeat her mime.

There was a simple dignity to the young woman as she stood beside her child's bed with tears streaming down her face and showed them that she didn't want them to fight for her daughter's pitiful life any more.

'That's enough, Ian.' Leo's voice was gravelly as he touched the registrar on the shoulder. Ian had been watching the by-play while he automatically maintained the little child's circulation but at Leo's direction he lifted his hands away and stepped back.

Leo reached across to pull the sheet up to Rashna's chin and Maria saw the slight tremble in his hand when he gently smoothed several straight, dark strands of hair away from her forehead before beckoning the child's mother to make her own farewells.

Maria didn't know what had woken her but it was still dark outside. It wasn't until she went to turn over that she realised that Leo wasn't beside her in the bed.

She listened for a minute but when she couldn't hear any sign of movement in the flat she began to worry.

He'd been very quiet when they'd driven home from the hospital and she'd tried to let him know that she was there for him if he wanted to talk but even when they'd gone to bed he'd been silent, holding her in his arms with a quiet desperation.

Knowing that she wouldn't be able to go back to sleep until she had reassured herself that he was all right, she donned the silky wrap she'd bought to cover her burgeoning shape and padded out towards the kitchen.

The whole flat was in darkness so she had no idea where he might be until she walked into the lounge and felt his presence.

'Leo,' she whispered softly, not wanting to wake him if he'd accidentally fallen asleep in his reclining chair.

A slight flash of movement drew her eyes to the settee and then she saw the darker shape of his head and shoulders outlined against the pale upholstery.

'You should be in bed,' he murmured gruffly into the darkness. 'Did I disturb you?'

'I don't think so. I woke up and you weren't there so I came to see if you were all right.'

She heard his deep sigh in the darkness, her hearing somehow more acute because she couldn't use her eyes.

'I couldn't sleep,' he admitted at last when she had grown accustomed enough to the darkness to see him shrug. 'I was thinking about that little girl this evening.'

'Rashna,' Maria murmured in confirmation of her fears. She had known that Leo must be hurting inside as all the painful memories of his son's sad life were resurrected.

She shivered as her body began to lose the heat from the bedclothes and wrapped her arms around herself.

'You're getting cold,' he commented disapprovingly. 'Go back to bed. I'll be all right.'

'Will you come with me?' she appealed. 'I won't be able to go back to sleep, knowing you're out here and. . .and I need you to warm the bed up again.'

She heard his brief huff of laughter. 'I knew I had my uses,' he murmured as he straightened up and came towards her. 'Do you want me to get you a drink?'

'I'd love one but I'd be dashing backwards and forwards to the bathroom if I have anything now.'

She felt as if the silent battle was half won when she heard him following her into their bedroom and she slid quickly into her side of the bed.

He was slower to get in, sitting silently on the side of the mattress for several minutes before he finally discarded his robe and joined her under the covers.

'Do you want to talk?' Maria said into the darkness when it was obvious that neither of them was ready to go to sleep. 'Perhaps it would help if you tell me what you're thinking . . .'

He was silent for a long time but Maria felt that she knew him well enough now to know that he would only speak if and when he was ready. All she had to do was be patient.

'She's expecting another baby,' he said suddenly, his voice taut with suppressed tension. 'She'd already lost one child and her second one was desperately ill but she's going to have a third. . .'

The mixture of anguish and disbelief in his voice made it necessary for Maria to swallow hard before she could speak.

'Perhaps she and her husband are hoping that they'll be lucky this time—that the percentages will be on their side for a change. Perhaps they think it's worth the risk. . .'

'But what if it's a *third* child with beta thalassaemia? How could they bear to go through it all over again?' he burst out. 'It's the bloody uncertainty of it all. How can they bear the uncertainty. . .?'

For the first time Maria regretted her decision not to have any tests done when it was the right time to find out about their baby. She just hadn't imagined when she'd made the decision according to her own feelings and beliefs that it would have such an effect on Leo.

'I'm sorry, Leo,' she whispered through a throat full of tears as she turned towards him. 'I didn't realise. . .'

CHAPTER TEN

MARIA felt guilty.

The more she thought about it the more she realised that she should at least have considered Leo's point of view when he'd first heard about the baby.

Once he'd told her about the loss of his son to the same set of circumstances as surrounded her own child she should have had the sensitivity to understand that he was going to spend the remaining months of the pregnancy under enormous pressure.

'It's the uncertainty. . .' she repeated, hearing the anguish in his voice when he'd said it.

Oh, it had been easy enough to steel herself against his appeals when he was a stranger but now that she loved him the guilt at her blind obstinacy was taking its toll on her.

'If there was only some way to turn the clock back so I could have the tests,' she murmured into the emptiness of the lounge as she knitted furiously, her needles moving as fast as her thoughts. 'Or if there was some way of finding out now without risking the baby. . .' She sighed, knowing that she could mutter and wish as much as she liked for the rest of the pregnancy and it wouldn't make any difference to the outcome.

The saddest part about the whole situation was that just as she and Leo should have been drawing closer together in preparation for the arrival of the baby they were being pushed further and further apart by his tension and her guilt.

'It was Rashna's death that brought it all to a head,' she said aloud, needing to hear the words that had been circling inside her brain for the last fortnight. 'On the surface it seemed as if everything was all right but underneath. . .'

The telephone shrilled and she saw several stitches slide off the point of the needle as she dropped the knitting on the table beside her seat.

'Dr da Cruz?' Maria frowned as she heard the voice on the other end. It sounded familiar. . . 'This is Kumar at the hospital.'

'Yes, Kumar.' She recognised his voice now. 'What can I do for you?'

'Do you remember telling me to give the Gujarati leaflets about foetal testing to Mrs Besharati?'

Did she remember? Of course she remembered. She'd done little else but think about the whole episode ever since it happened.

'I remember,' she agreed calmly. 'Is there a problem?'

'No problem, except she's desperate for you to be with her when she has the foetal blood sampling done.'

'Me?' Maria was startled. 'But she hardly knows me.'

'She says she trusts you,' he replied. 'You took the trouble to find out what she wanted to say and made the doctors listen.'

'But what about her family? They. . .' For a moment Maria was going to continue her objections but then she remembered that the two of them might share a far deeper kinship than the poor woman did with her sister-in-law. A bond of inheritance.

'When is she booked to have the test? Has she been given a date yet?'

'She's here now,' Kumar said, his tone slightly harrassed. 'She wouldn't let them proceed until I'd spoken to you.'

'Oh, Lord!' Maria glanced down at her watch and calculated travelling times. 'My husband isn't home yet so I'll have to get a taxi. Hopefully I'll be with you in half an hour.'

With Kumar's assurances that he'd let everyone know she was on her way, Maria pressed the button to disconnect the call and pressed another one that Leo had programmed to dial the local taxi company automatically.

She just had time to don a clean maternity smock and comb her hair into some sort of submission before the taxi arrived, only remembering just as she was about to pull the door closed behind her that she hadn't left a note for Leo.

'Gone to St A's,' she scribbled on the message pad beside the phone. 'Obs and Gyn Dept. Foetal blood sampling.'

She dropped the pen, conscious that time was passing but couldn't resist picking it up to add a final message.

'Love you,' she scrawled, knowing that it was the first time she had ever dared to let him know how she really felt about him. For a second her courage nearly failed her and she was tempted to scribble over the words but in the end she let them stand. Perhaps letting him read it first was the coward's way but it was time she told him the truth.

* * *

The obstetrics and gynaecology wing was a little world all of its own—a strange mixture of calm waiting and frantic activity staffed by a special breed of people.

Here everyone was linked by a common purpose—to help women conceive healthy children and bring them safely into the world.

Maria smiled wryly as she sat beside Azra Besharati. No one had batted an eyelash when she'd arrived in the department, thinking that she was just another one of their expectant mums. It was when she donned an over-size gown to accompany the frightened woman that they looked askance at her—until she produced her hospital credentials and explained the special circumstances surrounding her presence.

This time it was one of the midwives who offered to translate for them but it seemed to be enough for Azra that Maria was with her.

By the time the procedure was completed and Azra had been told when to return for the counsellor to discuss the results with her it was several hours since Maria had left her hurried note for Leo.

She knew that it was common for him to arrive home late and had regretted not being able to catch him at the hospital to cadge a lift home but there was always the possibility of a taxi for the return journey if Leo didn't turn up.

In the distance she'd heard the ululating wail of several ambulances and knew that there must have been a nasty accident somewhere in the catchment area of St Augustine's. She spared a thought for the poor souls involved and hoped that she wouldn't be hearing about any of them from Leo after his next spell of duty.

She was just making her way out of the department

on her way to the bank of telephones in the main reception area when she heard the muted buzz of the telephone at the nurses' station.

'Dr da Cruz?' a puzzled voice called after her and she let the door close again as she made her way back towards the young nurse. 'I don't know if I got the message right but there was a man on the other end who told me to tell you not to do anything. Just wait until he arrives. He said he was Dr da Cruz.' She frowned in her confusion until Maria laughed and explained.

'Dr da Cruz married Dr Martinez so now they are Dr da Cruz and Dr da Cruz.'

'Well,' the young woman laughed. 'I only hope you don't both work in the same department or everyone would be confused.'

'We do,' Maria told her, and they laughed together.

'Did my husband give you any idea how long he'd be? Did he say where he was?' She glanced down at her watch, wondering when she would ever get a chance to eat this evening.

'He's down in the accident department,' she volunteered. 'There was a big accident on his way to the hospital. . .'

'Oh, my God,' Maria breathed in horror. Her heart thumped heavily with shock as she remembered the sound of all those sirens. Leo had been on his way to fetch her and he'd been involved in an accident. . .

Suddenly she was running, her feet flying over the smooth expanse of the corridor in spite of her ungainly bulk, the frantic sound of the nurse's voice lost in the urgency to see Leo; to find out how badly he was hurt; to see if there was anything she could do for him; to tell him face to face that she loved him.

The lift seemed to be moving in slow motion, stopping at every floor while people took their time about getting in or getting out until finally she couldn't stand it any more and pushed her way swiftly past a group of chattering youngsters to make for the stairs.

There was a strong sense of déjà vu as she made her way towards the emergency department via the echoing stairwell but never before had she felt such urgency.

She was quite breathless by the time she arrived and had to pause a moment before she could speak.

'The accident victims who came in a little while ago. Where is Dr da Cruz?' she demanded shakily.

'And you are?' the receptionist queried.

'His wife,' she said, feeling a new sense of pride in saying the words aloud. 'Also Dr da Cruz.'

'Oh. Well, in that case I suppose it's all right to let you go through.' She looked dubiously at the pretty smock which only partly camouflaged Maria's swollen body. 'One of the mens' gowns should fit you.'

To be perfectly honest Maria couldn't have cared if she'd been told to dress up as Father Christmas as long as she could see Leo.

As soon as she was through the staff-only doors she grabbed a gown and was forcing her hands into the sleeves as she walked towards the trauma rooms.

'Maria?' Leo's husky voice came from behind her and was full of disbelief. 'What on earth are you doing down here?'

'Leo!' She whirled to face him, her heart in her mouth as she looked for his injuries, but. . . 'You're not hurt!' she exclaimed with delight, her eyes running over his green-clad figure with relief.

'Why should *I* be hurt? I only stopped to help—I was first on the scene and followed the wounded in.'

'But. . .you sent a message up saying you'd been in a big accident on your way to the hospital!'

'Oh, God, sometimes this place is worse than playing Chinese whispers in a maze,' he muttered while he reached up to release the ties on his gown. 'Come on, let's go. They don't need me any more. . .' He stuffed the gown in the laundry bin and sent hers to join it, his voice suddenly clipped. 'I don't think you should be charging around like this after what you've been through this afternoon.'

'Oh, Leo,' she smiled up at him, almost floating with the euphoria of relief. 'I'm all right now that I know you weren't one of the injured.'

'That wasn't what I meant,' he retorted grimly as he gripped her elbow and ushered her along the corridor towards the main entrance. 'I was talking about *your* message.' He stood back to allow her to precede him through the door then continued briskly across the parking area towards his car.

Maria hurried to keep up with his much longer strides, hardly daring to ask him to slow down. He seemed to be so angry. Had it been her admission on the note which had upset him so much? Had she spoiled everything?

'Dammit!' He stopped in his tracks, swinging her to face him. 'What on earth made you do it? It's only two weeks until it's due. Where was the sense in risking everything?'

'I didn't take any risks,' she objected, mystified by his strange mood. 'I phoned for a taxi to bring me here and I've been sitting down for most of the afternoon.'

'That's *not* what I mean and you know it,' he muttered through gritted teeth as he grabbed her elbow again and thrust her towards the car. 'You were so dead set against it so what on earth made you decide to have it done now?'

'Do what?' Maria demanded as he unlocked the doors and glowered at her until she gave in and slid into the seat, grateful for the support when her knees began to quiver with delayed reaction.

'It's my fault, isn't it?' he continued as soon as he joined her in the car. 'It's because I let you know how hard it was living with the uncertainty. That's why you went to have the test done.'

Maria felt her jaw drop open with amazement when she finally realised what he meant.

'No!' She shook her head. 'You've got it all wrong.'

'Oh, you needn't spare my feelings,' he interrupted, obviously not listening to her. 'I've been an idiot and I realise it.'

'Yes, you're an idiot,' she agreed, changing tack in an effort to make him listen to her and it worked, his eyes darting to meet hers when his words stopped.

'You *are* an idiot if you think I'd risk our baby like that.'

'But. . .your message. . .'

'Another version of Chinese whispers, I'm afraid. And this time it's *my* fault.' She explained about the phone call and spending the afternoon keeping Azra Besharati company. 'I never thought you'd read the message and believe I'd gone to have the test done on *our* baby.'

'Oh, God, thank you.' The whispered words were like a prayer as his eyes closed and he dropped his head back wearily against the headrest, seemingly drained by the relief of tension.

'Leo?' she said, tentatively putting her hand on his arm.

'Shh.' He covered it with his own and rolled his head to fix her with a steely, intent gaze. 'No more talking until I get us home. All right?'

She was silent for a moment while her eyes travelled over his face, searching for the hurt and anger which had filled it just a short while ago but they were gone without a trace.

'Yes,' she said through a weak smile of relief. 'Let's go home,' and she settled back into her seat.

The journey was over in no time and they had hardly got as far as the sitting-room before Leo was pulling her into his arms.

'Oh, Maria,' he breathed into her hair as he held her tightly. 'I'm sorry I didn't trust you. I should have known after the fight that you put up before that you'd never do anything to risk the baby.'

Maria closed her eyes to savour the sensation of holding her husband in her arms after the fright this afternoon. She'd been so afraid that just as she found the courage to tell him that she loved him he was being taken away from her.

'I wrote the note in a hurry,' she said, pulling back to look up at him when she finally managed to get her brain working again. 'The taxi was waiting outside to take me to the hospital and I didn't have time to phone you but I didn't want you to arrive home in my absence and not know where I was.'

'And I turned jumping to conclusions into an

Olympic event,' he admitted, guiding her towards the settee.

When he'd drawn her once more into his arms and settled her head on his shoulder he continued, his voice a deep velvety purr beside her ear.

'All I could think about on the way to the hospital was that you'd never have thought of doing it if I'd talked to you—told you what I'd been thinking.'

'But you did. . .' she began, her objection ending when he put one finger to her lips to silence her.

'If I'd told you that I finally understood what you meant about it all being worth the risk. If I'd told you that I trusted you; that I knew that if our baby *was* born with beta thalassaemia disease you would never neglect it the way Sophia did. . . Dammit! I should have told you that I love you!'

'Only if you mean it,' Maria whispered through quivering lips, wondering how much joy she could stand before she simply exploded with it.

'Of course I mean it!' He sounded stung that she could doubt him. 'I think I started to fall in love with you when I turned over in bed one night in a hotel in Italy and found a naked, long-haired nymph beside me who set the world on fire and brought me back to life.'

'Ha!' she scoffed. 'You thought I was some sort of over-sexed courtesan.'

'No.' He shook his head and smiled gently. 'Not once I met you. You were too innocent-looking, too sweet for that.'

'So soft that you thought you could bully me into doing what you wanted?' she reproached him with the memory.

'Thank God you turned out to have a core of steel.'

He tightened his arms around her. 'Otherwise I'd never have had an excuse to get you to marry me.'

'You didn't need an excuse,' she said simply. 'All you had to do was ask. . .' She stopped with a gasp.

'Maria?' He drew back a little to look down at her. 'What's the matter?'

She held her breath for a moment then released it slowly, concentrating on the new sensations inside her body before she glanced at her watch.

'Maria?' he prompted. 'Talk to me. What's the matter?'

'I'm sorry, Leo,' she smiled up at him wryly. 'I know you've been going backwards and forwards all day but would you mind driving the car again?'

'You want to go for a drive?' He was mystified. 'I thought we were going to have a quiet evening at home?'

'So did I,' she agreed, 'but it appears the baby has other ideas.'

'The baby. . .? Oh, my God, the baby! It's early. . .' He leapt off the settee as though he'd been shot from a gun and ran agitated fingers through his hair. 'Where did I put the keys? Have you got your case packed? Can I do anything to help?'

'Yes. You can calm down,' she laughed. 'Your keys are in your right hand trouser pocket where you *always* carry them and my case has been packed for weeks. Now all you have to do is get me on my feet—I feel like a beached whale!' She held both hands out to him so that he could haul her upright.

'Oh, Maria, what did I ever do to deserve such luck?' he breathed as he pulled her up and wrapped his arms around her. 'If you hadn't climbed into my bed that night. . .'

During the long hours that followed they had time to talk.

For the first time Maria felt comfortable asking him about his son. She knew, now, that over the last few months Leo had gradually been coming to terms with the tragedy of his short life and his own part in it.

This time, instead of guilt and anger, she heard joy and love in his voice as he talked about Nico's impish sense of humour and the way he would always greet his father with a hug.

'Did you have any idea that you and Sophia had beta thalassaemia trait?'

'*I* didn't. Not until she tested me after he'd been diagnosed.'

'*She* tested you?' Maria queried in surprise, vaguely remembering that he'd mentioned it before.

'Being a haematologist, she said she would be able to short-circuit the usual rigmarole,' he explained. 'If I remember rightly Theo heard what was going on and that was when she persuaded him to be tested at the same time. . .'

Maria felt a prickle of unease but couldn't put her finger on it immediately and by the time her next contraction had ended she'd forgotten about it, the midwife telling her that she was in transition and it would soon be time to start pushing.

'At least,' she panted a while later as she rested for a few seconds between bouts of mind-boggling effort, 'we know that St Augustine's will be testing this baby as a matter of course.'

'Yes.' He wiped her face gently with a cool damp cloth and then held her hand again, his support unwavering. 'This one will be taken care of from the moment it's born.'

Suddenly things started moving very quickly and it seemed as if it was only minutes before Leo tenderly passed her a tightly wrapped little wrinkled bundle.

'A girl,' Maria breathed, dragging her eyes away from the tiny features to gaze mistily into Leo's tear-filled eyes. 'Oh, Leo, she's perfect. Look. . .' and she offered their baby up to him.

'If she's anything like her mother she's bound to be perfect,' he murmured huskily as he stroked one hand over the tiny head. 'Just as she's bound to be beautiful and kind and caring. . .'

'And if she takes after her father she'll be bossy and self-confident and kind and caring. . .' She reached out one hand to cup his cheek and drew him towards her for the kiss that would complete the circle.

'Oh, Maria, thank you for fighting me,' he said, his voice sounding almost rusty. 'Thank you for sticking to your guns, otherwise this day would never have happened.' He gazed at her with clear grey eyes, their warmth soothing and healing and without a trace of the old hurt and bitterness.

'If it hadn't been for you,' he continued, 'I would never have had the courage to try again, not once I knew that it had been my fault that Nico died.'

'It took two of you with the trait to produce him,' Maria reminded him and she had a momentary flash of the venom in Sophia's face when she'd cornered her at the wedding reception and warned her not to get pregnant.

Maria had been moved into the ward, her bed beside the windows with a view out over a small rose garden when it happened again—as though her subconscious was trying to tell her something.

Suddenly the unease that she'd felt whenever the topic of Sophia came up grew into a nasty suspicion and she carefully composed a question in her mind before she spoke.

'When Sophia ran the tests did Theo test positive?' she asked, keeping her tone casual.

'No.' Leo pulled a face and looked down at the hand he was cradling between his own, one finger tracing the delicate gold band she'd chosen to wear. 'I always thought that was why Sophia married him—because he could give her children without the fear of them inheriting anything more than the trait.' His tone became musing. 'Actually, I was surprised that they didn't start their own family straight away.'

'I'm not,' Maria said candidly as everything suddenly became clear and watched the shock enter his eyes. 'Theo's not happy with her because he doesn't love her. He knows she's only interested in the lifestyle he can give her.'

'How can you possibly know that?' Leo objected. 'You only spoke to them for a minute or two.'

'Call it feminine intuition if you like but I'd like you to do something for me.'

'What?' he blinked at the apparent change of topic.

'Have yourself tested for beta thalassaemia trait,' she challenged.

'Is that a joke?' he demanded with a frown as he straightened up out of the chair beside her bed. 'I told you, I've already been tested. . .' His voice faded away as the implications of her request sank in.

'Oh, my God,' he breathed and sat down again, hard. 'You think she switched the results.'

'It would certainly explain the hold she has over Theo,' Maria suggested. 'She'll never need to lift a finger all the while she's married to wealthy Theo da Cruz and he'll never get rid of her all the time she's threatening to tell his brother that the baby wasn't his.'

'Poor Theo,' he murmured. 'I knew she wasn't happy when I insisted I wasn't going to be the figurehead for the family holdings—that's always been Theo's strength in spite of his apparent laziness. If she set her sights on him as my replacement he probably didn't stand a chance. It was just everybody's bad luck that she got pregnant—with such tragic results for poor Nico caught in the middle.'

'You realise what this means, don't you?' Maria demanded with a wicked grin.

'Uh-oh,' Leo murmured. 'Why do I think I'm going to regret asking?'

'I'll tell you, anyway,' she said sweetly as a bubble of joy began to swell inside her. 'If, as we suspect, your test shows that you *aren't* positive that means that none of our children can suffer from beta thalassaemia disease. The most that can happen is that they inherit the trait.'

'And?' he prompted warily.

'That means there's no reason why we shouldn't have as many children as we want,' she declared triumphantly.

'Oh, God.' Leo sank his head in his hands, his elbows propped on the edge of the mattress. 'It's only minutes since she gave birth to the first baby and she's already planning a houseful!'

'Leo. . .?' Maria touched his head with a tentative hand. 'We don't have to have any more if you don't want to. It's just. . .every time I see you with children it's obvious how much you love them. . .'

When her voice trailed away miserably he lifted his head from his hands and she could see his face.

'You rat!' She tightened her fingers in the thick silk of his hair and tugged. 'I thought you were upset and didn't want any more children and there you are grinning like the Cheshire cat.'

'Ow!' He lifted her hand away and rubbed his scalp. 'Leave me some hair! I'll be pulling my own out soon enough if we end up with a house full of children.'

'A house full?' she questioned with longing in her eyes as new hope blossomed into life.

'Whatever the tests show,' he confirmed. 'As you said, each pregnancy for a couple who both carry the trait has a one-in-four chance of the baby having the disease but you've taught me to realise that it's a three-in-four chance that they won't. And if I'm clear. . .' He shrugged easily.

He captured both of her hands and leant forward to pin them on the pillow, either side of her face.

'I love you, Maria,' he murmured as he hovered protectively over her. 'For now, for always.'

'For now, for always,' she echoed, her heart full to overflowing as she gazed up into eyes that radiated happiness. At last the bitterness and pain had disappeared without a trace and she offered her lips to him to seal their pledge.

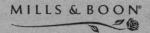